MAKING IT ALL RIGHT

Denise Breeden-Ost

Scripture quotations are from the Revised Standard Version of the Bible, copyright © 1946, 1952, and 1971 National Council of the Churches of Christ in the United States of America. Used by permission. All rights reserved.
Quoted song lyrics are from "Shall We Gather at the River," by Robert Lowry, 1864; "New River Train," traditional, U.S.; "K-K-K-Katy," by Geoffrey O'Hara; and "Stewball," traditional, England.

Cover design by Licia Weber.
Cover photos by Denise Breeden-Ost.
Author photo by Sean Breeden-Ost.

Library of Congress Control Number: 2020915780

ISBN: 978-1-7354885-1-6

Clockflower Press
Bloomington, Indiana
www.clockflowerpress.com
contact@clockflowerpress.com

To my parents,
Glenda and Bill Breeden,
who are still teaching me about love.

PART ONE

1

May

As soon as the dew was off the garden, I took Katy out with me and got started on the beans. It was the middle of August, and hot already at nine—but you can't pick beans wet.

"Hi, Mommy!" Katy bent over and stuck her blond head between me and the bean vines, then lost her balance and sat down on the dirt.

I smiled at her. "Hi, hon. Scootch over, so I can get to my beans."

"Worm," she said, scootching over.

"You found a worm?" I wiped my sweaty face on my sleeve. I had on an old long-sleeved shirt of Hal's, to keep the bean vines from welting up my arms. The thin blue cotton felt like a wool coat in the heat.

Hal would be almost to his lunch whistle by now, at the box plant—Cartersboro was on fast time. I wondered how his week was going. He said the work was noisy and easy, running a nailing machine.

Katy grabbed a handful of my dress and hauled herself to her feet. "*Pick* worm!"

"What? Oh, like tobacco worms?" I'd let Katy help me pick tobacco worms yesterday, and she'd loved it. There'd been too many to finish by hand, though—maybe Hal could dust the tobacco, over the weekend. "You might find bean beetles—they're yellow. Look under the leaves... Don't you want long sleeves, hon, like Mommy?"

"No." Katy's suntanned arms were striped with red welts from the vines, but she shook her head as she peered under the leaves.

I worked my way slowly along the row, dropping handfuls of green beans in the basket by my feet. I was almost halfway done—I could break the beans while Katy was down for her nap, and get them canned before time to start supper. I tried to keep our meals regular during the week, even though it was just Katy and me. Tomorrow was Friday. Hal would be home, and we'd all eat supper together.

I glanced around for Katy, and found her taking beans out of my basket and lining them up on the dirt. "No, hon," I told her, picking them up, "Mommy's beans stay in the basket."

Katy grinned at me. "I pick beans!" She grabbed hold of a hanging bean and yanked.

I stopped her before she could pull the vine up by the roots. "You're not big enough yet," I said, as her lower lip started to push out. "Why don't you look for worms?"

"No worm! Pick *beans!*"

"Well, honey..." If she threw a fit, I'd never get my beans picked. I looked around the garden. Carrots, mustard, peppers, pigweed. "You want to pick pigweed?" She frowned at me, and I tried to sound excited. "You could make a pigweed pie for the pigs! They'll say 'Yum yum, pigweed pie!'"

Katy giggled. "No, pig say *oink oink!*"

"Oh, that's right. *Oink oink!*" My pig-snort wasn't as good as Katy's—she sounded just like a piglet.

Katy bounced on her toes. "Pig pie, pig cake. Mud cake! Birfday cake!"

Mud pies would keep her busy. I filled a tin can with water at the yard pump, got her settled stirring mud and pigweed leaves with a stick, and found my place in the beans again.

Picking beans was always hot work, but it used to be a quiet, steady job. Hardly any job was quiet and steady anymore, unless Katy was asleep. My days' work happened in scraps—in between feeding Katy and cleaning her up, keeping her from pulling the kitchen water bucket over on her head, kissing her scrapes and answering her questions and wiping her nose. Still, I got it all done one way or another. And Katy kept me from getting too lonely.

I'd known I'd miss Hal, when he took the job at the box plant. It was too far to drive every day, so he'd have to board weeknights in Cartersboro. Hal and I had been apart two whole years during the war, though, not even knowing if he'd make it home to marry me. Compared to that, I thought this would be easy. Hal's daddy, Rye, could help me with the farm work during the week. And the pay was good—we'd get ahead on the mortgage, and buy an electric washer and refrigerator. It had seemed worth a little loneliness.

I hadn't counted on the worry, though. The first few months of the job, Hal came home looking so ragged I thought he must be having his war nightmares again. He said he was fine, and I tried to believe him. It did seem to get better. Then Hal had started acting odd. When he got home on Fridays, he'd hug me as hard as ever, but he didn't want to meet my eyes. A couple of times I'd thought he was about to tell me what was wrong—but then he shook his head, and said he had to go check on the cows, and disappeared out the back door.

It had been like that for two months now. By Saturday morning Hal always seemed okay again, and I wondered if I was imagining things. Then he'd leave, Sunday afternoon, and I'd have another five days to worry.

Hal wasn't one to get mixed up with trouble, Communists or anything like that. He didn't gamble or get drunk or fight, and he'd have talked to me before he borrowed money.

Katy oinked behind me, and I turned around. She was over in the carrots, yanking at a green top with both hands. She'd ripped the lacy leaves off half a dozen plants already, leaving the roots tight in the ground.

"No, Katy!" I hollered, and jumped over the bean row. She worked faster when she saw me coming.

I grabbed her hand and pried the carrot tops out of her fingers. "Katy, I *swear!*" I shook the useless leaves at her, then threw them down on the dirt—hard, like I wanted to hurt them.

Then I stopped myself. That was the kind of thing Mom would do. I didn't want to be like that.

I shut my eyes and took a breath. No harm done, really—I could dig those carrots for supper. If Katy could stay out of trouble for a few more minutes…or if I could keep an eye on her, instead of worrying about Hal… I opened my eyes, blowing the breath out.

Katy giggled up at me, and blew too. "Happy birfday to youuu!" she sang.

I sighed. "I'm almost done, Katy. Let's find you some clover to pick."

Anyway, Hal was almost done with Cartersboro. My brother Jamie had gotten him on at the lumberyard in Whelan, and he'd be home for good after Labor Day, in time to cut the tobacco. The wages weren't quite as good, but there'd be no room and board to pay. Our lives could get back to normal, and whatever was bugging Hal now would be water under the bridge.

Which was where I'd ended up, a hundred times this summer. Worrying was as predictable as picking beans—start at the beginning of the row, go till you get to the end. Except worry didn't fill any baskets. I sighed, and straightened up to stretch my back. Katy was stuffing clover blossoms into her tin can. I looked past the zinnias at the end of the garden, up the hill to where the cows stood in the shade of the big oak tree. I couldn't see the tobacco field from here, but I imagined I could smell the long leaves yellowing in the sun. Two more weeks.

Making It All Right

2

Vera

After supper we all take a walk along River Street, hoping for a breeze. Tom's up ahead with Hal, pointing with his cigarette at the blue house on the corner, where the Ohio came up to the second-story windows in '37. Wanda and I follow behind them, with Petey hanging onto my hand. I'm trying not to watch the way Hal's shoulders move in his khaki work shirt. Trying not to watch too obviously, anyway. Hal's half a head shorter than Tom, but I can see the wiry strength of his body from here.

"Well?" Wanda sounds impatient.

"Hm?" I try to remember what we were talking about. Hemlines, I think. "I didn't catch that."

Wanda purses her lips at me. "I asked when you're going to find yourself a husband."

Oh, dear. I give a little laugh, carefully not looking at Hal. "Well, I guess I was hoping a husband would find *me!*"

Hester runs past, red pigtails flying, followed by Freddy making jet-airplane noises. Wanda calls after them. "You two stay away from the water!"

"Yeah!" Petey hollers in his high voice, his hand clutching nervously at mine.

"Don't worry," I tell him. "They know the rules."

Wanda's not done with me. "I'm serious, Vera! You'll end up an old maid at this rate. What happened to that tall fellow you were seeing last winter? He seemed nice."

"Who, Ralph?" I roll my eyes. "He took me out four times, and never once stopped talking about baseball. Looking like Clark Gable only gets you so far."

"Oh, Vera! What are we going to do with you?" Sometimes Wanda sounds more like an elderly aunt than a sister-in-law.

My eyes find Hal again. He tips his hat-brim down against the sun, glances back over his shoulder. My stomach gives a little flutter.

Wanda's settled in to scolding me now, her voice like a mosquito in my ear. I ignore her. It's not as if I don't want to get married. Everybody does. It was practically all we talked about at the ordnance plant, during the war. And since the men came home, it seems like the weddings never stop.

The girls clam up once they're married, though. Ask them about married life and they say, *Can't complain.* Which doesn't mean anything. Nancy giggles and blushes and pretends she's got a secret, but she did that even before she was married. Anyway, I grew up on a farm—I'm not asking how babies are made. Francine gave me a shrewd look once and said, "Don't hold your breath, Vera. The billing beats the show."

And then there was Sybil. She got married in '44, when Bob came home with an artificial foot, but she kept sewing powder bags until they closed the plant on V-J Day. Sybil was different, after the wedding. She moved loose and easy in her skin, and smiled at her sewing machine. Sometimes I'd meet her and Bob in the evenings, walking slow along the riverfront. There was an electricity between the two of them. When they'd take hands, it almost crackled. It hummed in Sybil all day at the plant.

I wanted that. Whatever it was Sybil and Bob had, that none of the other girls seemed to know about. I promised myself that when I got married, it'd be to a man who made me hum and crackle.

Tom and Hal wait for us where the street angles away from the riverbank, and we all pick our way down the weedy slope to walk back by the water. There's a nice breeze off the river. I'm glad when Wanda decides to stroll off with Tom. I bend down to look at a mussel shell Petey's found. I can tell Hal's looking at me. When I straighten up, he's staring out at the river, watching the *Avalon* steaming down toward Cincinnati, but the feeling doesn't go away. My arms prickle with goosebumps.

"Don't you dare!" Hester squeals. Freddy's edging toward his sister with a dripping handful of water-weed.

"Freddy!" I call, in my no-nonsense Aunt Vera voice. Freddy gives me an innocent look, and tosses the slimy mess into the water. Hester squints mean-eyed at him, and moves closer to me and Petey. I pat her shoulder. "He's just bored," I tell her. "He probably won't be so aggravating once school starts."

Hester sighs. "I wish school started *tomorrow.* —Hey Petey, you want to make a picture out of shells?"

I find a driftwood log to sit on and watch them, keeping my eyes away from Hal. Hal's talking to Freddy. After a minute, he trots along the bank to crouch beside me. "Seen any good skipping rocks?" he asks, peering at the ground. I shake my head. He sifts through the gravel at my feet, not touching me. The stubble on his cheek glitters in the evening light.

Sybil and Bob moved to Colorado after the war, for Bob to go to school. They had a baby boy, and then twin girls. I kept on living in my brother's house, sewing wedding dresses now instead of powder bags. I usually had a date for Saturday nights, dancing at the Moonlite or a movie. Handsome men, sweet men, men who made me laugh and stole kisses in the shadows. None of them made me hum or crackle. Maybe a little fizz, now and then. After a couple of years of that, I started to wonder if I'd set my standards too high. My "when I get married" might turn out to be an "if." But I couldn't see spending the rest of my life just fizzing.

And then...Hal. There's no marrying Hal, I knew that from the start. But that night when Wanda sent me out after him with an extra piece of angel-food cake, and he grabbed my shoulders and kissed me—I didn't fizz. I felt like I'd died and turned into hot chocolate. My whole body tried to rush up into my lips, and over into Hal's lips, and then back down, melting between my legs... Then I remembered who we were, and where we were—right there on the back porch, anyone could have walked by. I backed off, as best I could with Hal holding onto me. I looked down at the angel-food cake, all smashed in its plastic wrap, and whispered, "Oh, Hal..."

When I looked up again, he smiled at me with those warm brown eyes. "Shh," he said. "It's all right."

I knew better than that, of course, even then. I wasn't stupid. But when Hal leaned toward me again, I pretended I was.

Maybe I'm still pretending I am.

Hal straightens up, a flat rock cradled in his index finger, and hollers at Freddy. "Beat this, Carrot-top!" He draws back his arm.

I count the skips, and grin at Freddy as he saunters closer. "That's nine. Show him what you're made of, Freddy!"

Freddy tries to look casual, but his jaw's working to hold back a grin of his own. His rock skips sixteen times.

Hal whistles. "Well, I'll be doggone. I think I done picked on the wrong fellow."

Freddy's grin breaks free as he shrugs. "That wasn't so good," he said. "Water's all choppy."

"He's not fooling," I tell Hal.

"He's done twenty-four in a row before!" Hester adds. She never holds a grudge long.

"Two out of three?" Freddy offers, already looking for another rock.

Hal reaches to help me up from my log. The touch of his hand makes my hair stand on end. As he pulls me to my feet, his eyes lock onto mine, and for a wild moment I think he's going to kiss me right here. Then he smiles, and lets go. "Better not," he says. "I'd probably regret it."

It takes me a minute to figure out he's talking to Freddy.

Tom hollers something about ice cream, and the kids rush to catch up with him and Wanda. I follow them back toward River Street, Hal's eyes warming the back of my neck.

3

May

"Looks like you got you some corn," I said, coming in through Grace's kitchen door.

"You think?" Grace hoisted a pan of water onto the stove, with a grunt and a clang. "That brother of yours planted enough to feed the Red Army." Grace and I had been friends since first grade. She'd been married to Jamie for almost six years now, but she still called him "your brother" when she talked to me.

"'Nanas!" Katy said, bouncing on my hip.

I sniffed the air. "You baking a banana cake?"

Grace rolled her eyes. "I must be losing my mind—it's hotter than blue blazes in here. Did you get your beans canned?"

"Fourteen quarts."

"You still leaving the tails on?" Grace asked, getting paring knives out of a drawer.

"Yes, and nobody's been poisoned yet." When I was a kid, I'd thought pinching the tails off green beans must be in the Bible—most of the things Mom slapped me for turned out to be sins. But no, it was just how it was done. I never could stand that reason. Leaving the tails on, I could get my beans done in half the time.

Katy kicked her feet. "Go see Cawol!"

"Okay, hon." I pried her fingers off my collar. "Let's go find your cousins."

"You might as well get started shucking," Grace said. "I'm just waiting on the cake."

Ronny and Carol were out by the garden fence, building a house with cornstalks and junk. When Katy pulled on the door —an old saddle blanket, it looked like—the whole wall fell over. "Don't!" Ronny yelled. "You're wrecking it!"

"Come see the puppies, Katy!" Carol coaxed Katy off towards the woodshed. Ronny rolled his eyes just like his mother, and started propping up the wall.

I dragged two lawn chairs over to the wagonload of corn Jamie had dumped in the shade, and got started shucking. The corn smelled green and sweet, and the locusts in the tulip tree overhead were droning their scratchy song. I yawned. I'd woken up at two-thirty this morning, with a new thought: Maybe Hal was sick. He might've gone to a doctor in Cartersboro, and found out something so bad he didn't want to tell me. Maybe Hal coming home wouldn't make everything all right. Maybe—

"You look about ready for a nap." Grace sat down in the other chair, and handed me a silking brush.

I nodded—I could feel the dark circles under my eyes. "I didn't sleep too good."

"Building a better mousetrap again?"

I shrugged, and pretended to look for a cornworm. If I told Grace the truth, she'd start pestering me to ask Hal what was wrong—or, worse, speculating about all the things it could be.

Grace shook her head. "You ought to save the tinkering for the daytime, May. Get your beauty sleep."

"I know." I gave her half a smile. Grace knew how I was—a problem I couldn't solve was worse than a cockleburr in the bed. I'd lost sleep for a week when I was making that automatic baby-swing for Katy, before Peck Chase helped me get the gearing right. I didn't think Peck could rescue me this time, though.

"Let me know if I need to make more coffee." Grace ripped the shucks down the side of an ear and snapped off the bottom, then added, "Did you hear about the Scudders' cows getting out?"

I hadn't heard. Grace told me. Then she filled me in on her Home Economics Club doings, and the latest from Shiloh Baptist, and the Peters family picnic, raising her voice when the locusts got loud. I added my two cents' worth now and then, but I mostly listened. Grace was a good storyteller. She took my mind off Hal, and kept me awake too.

When the corn was all shucked, we went to work with our silking brushes. I checked every ear twice—it seemed like there was always a strand or two of cornsilk left. "I wonder if you could make some kind of automatic corn-silker," I said, interrupting a story about Grace's brother Deke. "Mount some brushes on a wheel, like a grindstone— What?"

Grace was laughing. "You never did like silking corn! Just a few more—then we can go back in my hot kitchen and can it all."

Grace put the lid back on the blanching kettle, and wiped steam off her glasses. "Your brother's talking about raising more pigs next year."

"Jamie always did like pigs." I cut the kernels off a blanched ear in long yellow slabs. "Remember those spotted ones he raised for 4-H?"

Grace frowned, thinking. "Got Grand Champion one year?"

"Mm-hmm. And my lamb only got red. Jamie lorded it over me for months." I dropped a bare corncob into the slop bucket. "Of course, I was the same way, when I did better." Grandma Stout had told Mom it was no use fussing at us— *Those two are so close in age, they'll be bickering their whole lives.* Mom had pressed her lips tight at that, like Grandma Stout was blaming her.

"Ronny wants to raise a calf, as soon as James thinks he's old enough." Grace looked out the window at the kids. Ronny and Carol were working on their cornstalk house again, while Katy flapped her arms in excitement. "How's Katy treating you these days?"

"Oh, she's pretty good," I said. "She did try to pull up all my carrots yesterday."

Grace snorted. "The little devil! At least she's still cute—wait till she's old enough to smart off at you!" She took off her glasses and wiped at them again, then laid them on the counter. "These things are so steamed up and sticky, I'm just as blind with them on."

"My *face* is steamed up and sticky," I said. "Do you have something to keep the sweat out of my eyes?"

Grace found a rag in her corner cabinet, and watched me tie it around my head. "There. Now you look like Lana Turner."

I laughed. "I guess you *are* blind!"

Around four o'clock, I left Grace finishing up and headed home to make supper. Katy bounced on the truck seat, chattering about the puppies and the corn house, then suddenly put her head down in my lap and went to sleep. She'd missed her nap.

Jamie and I used to walk over to Hal's house when we were kids, cutting across the Frys' pasture and jumping the creek. Hal and I lived in that house now, but it was miles farther by road—out along one winding ridge, down into the valley and up another. Hot wind gusted around my face, carrying whiffs of manure and drying hay. I reached to tuck a loose strand of hair back, and found Grace's "Lana Turner" rag still tied around my head. I smiled, my face sticky with corn juice. Canning was more fun with company.

Out of habit I glanced left at the top of Ort Hill, catching a glimpse of our place on the next ridge. The house's white siding stood out against the dark summer green of the mulberry tree and the faded blue sky.

Hal would be home in a couple of hours. I'd lean into his hug, breathe his familiar smell. He'd kiss me. And look away.

I drove on down into the valley, my smile gone. Hal didn't seem sick. But neither had Daddy, until his first stroke. Last night I'd kept thinking of Daddy just lying there, week after week, while all his farmer muscle wasted away. And me trying to run the farm with Sissy, and Jamie and Hal both off in France, and Mom getting meaner and meaner... But seeing Daddy like that was the worst. I didn't know if I could stand that again.

I dodged a pothole in the road, and gave my shoulders a shake. Of course I could stand it—I'd stand whatever I had to stand. But more than likely, Hal was as healthy as ever, and I was losing sleep over nothing.

I shifted down and turned onto Salt Branch Road. Hal would be on his way home soon, tired and hungry. Time to quit fretting about the future, and start thinking about supper.

4

Hal

Halfway home. The wind in my face smells like river. Mud, water, fish. Whiff of diesel from a tug. Another hour, we'll turn off the river road, up the long switchback hill out of Vevay. Then it'll start smelling like home.

Walt turns his head to spit out the window. Nice thing about Walt is, he doesn't talk just to talk. Just chaws his tobacco and keeps the Packard on the road.

Sometimes I wish I had a plug of tobacco to worry at. Never could stand the stuff. But it might take my mind off things.

I don't know how this all happened. I guess I always figured you could only be in love with one person at a time. And I loved May. I still love May. I love both of them so much it makes my head spin. All week in Cartersboro with Vera, I'm in love and happy, and all weekend at home with May, I'm in love and happy. I'd feel like the luckiest man alive, if it weren't for the going back and forth. Fridays and Sundays about kill me.

Vera doesn't know I gave my notice at the factory. I don't know how I'm going to tell her. I can't stand to leave Vera. Can't stand leaving her, and can't stand her being left. I never wanted to hurt anybody.

I look out the side window so Walt won't see me tearing up. A couple of kids are out playing with their dog. The little one looks like Katy.

More than once I've been that close to telling May. Seems like May always knows what to do. But I couldn't stand to hurt her, either.

Mostly I've tried not to think about it. Like the war. What happened in France, you left in France. Vera's in Cartersboro, and May's at home. I try to keep it that way in my head.

Fridays and Sundays, that's harder than it sounds.

5

Vera

I never meant for things to get out of hand.

I liked Hal fine, when Tom started bringing him home for supper last winter. Hal was handsome, and quiet, and funny, and he appreciated my cooking. But he was married. I didn't even flirt with him. If our hands touched, passing the butter, and made me a little breathless, I'd get busy cutting up Petey's meat or remember something in the kitchen. It was thrilling, and maddening, and I knew it wasn't going anywhere.

And then Hal kissed me on the porch. After that, my stomach went all to butterflies every time he walked into the room. At night I cried in frustration. Of all the men in the world, why did I have to fall for a married one? And happily married, at that. When Hal talked about May and little Katy, his eyes were soft with love. I could see he was a good father, a good husband. Why wasn't he *my* husband?

Weeks went by, spring heading toward summer. Hal didn't kiss me again. I knew he shouldn't. I wished he would. I told myself to stop it, but I couldn't. At least wishing wouldn't hurt anything.

Except my peace of mind. I snapped at Petey for tracking mud, and sewed a left sleeve into a right armscye, and felt like screaming when Wanda told me all about Betty's niece's diph-theria for the third time. I couldn't wait for Hal to show up at supper, and when he did I could hardly eat, and when he went back to his boardinghouse afterwards I was miserable.

The weather turned hot all at once, the first week of June. Usually in the summer Tom and Wanda and I would sit out on the front porch late, waiting for the bedrooms to cool off. But this year I could hardly stand their company—Tom smoking or dozing, Wanda pestering him to talk. I was used to being bored, but now I felt like I might die of boredom. The night Wanda started trying to enlist me in her Now-Thomas-don't-you-think-we-need-a-television-set campaign, I gave up and went inside, shutting my bedroom door behind me despite the heat.

I was too edgy to sew. I tried to finish a letter to Sybil, but it was hopeless—I kept mentioning Hal, and his name glowed on the page like a neon sign. I threw the letter away, turned out the light, and pulled my chair close to the window.

There was the slightest breath of a breeze. I leaned toward the coolness, shutting my eyes. After a while I heard the sleigh bells on the screen door jingle, as Tom and Wanda came in to bed. Hester had started sleepwalking when she was four, and Wanda made Tom nail bells on all the doors—I couldn't step out for a little fresh air anymore, without Wanda thinking Hester was headed for the river.

The breeze died away, came back, died away. Hal had been tired and jumpy at supper, with dark circles under his eyes. He looked that way a lot—I wondered if he was one of the ones that hadn't quite gotten over the war. When I'd stood up to get our dessert, his eyes had followed me, savoring my face like a cool breeze. He'd stared so long I got worried someone would notice, and fled into the kitchen.

Remembering, my face felt like a steam iron. I pressed it against the rusty windowscreen, thinking of Hal's top shirt buttons open in the heat, the scent of his sweat I'd caught as he said goodbye after supper.

The screen shifted in its frame, and I sat up. Better not fall out the window. Though it must be cooler outside...and the screen was just the pop-in kind. No bells on the windows, either. I slipped my feet back into my shoes.

The ground was farther down than I thought. Look before you leap, Mama always said, but I never was good at that. I crash-landed in the bushes, scrambled to my feet, and looked up at the window while I picked twigs out of my hair. There was no way I could climb back in. I sighed. I'd have to use the door, and jingle the sleigh bells, and listen to Wanda's hysterics.

No hurry, though. It was cool out here. A few early lightning bugs blinked at the edge of the yard. And there were stars, half hidden by the dark canopy of the elm tree. I'd missed the stars since coming to Cartersboro. Back home on the farm I'd seen them every clear night, on my way to the privy.

I tiptoed across the yard like a kid playing hide-and-seek, and stepped into the street. The sky sparkled like a black skirt full of sequins. My skin tingled. I wanted to do something wild —fling my clothes off and dance, run down to the river and skip rocks in the starlight. I raised my hands a little from my sides, like a bird thinking about flying, and the air cooled the sweat under my arms.

Something moved in the dark under the elm. A chill ran all over me, but before I could take a breath I heard his whisper. "It's okay, Vera. It's me."

"Hal?" My heart went crazy in my chest. I put my hands over it.

"It's okay," he said again, stepping away from the tree trunk. Maybe I looked scared, standing there clutching my chest.

I wasn't scared. Now that Hal was here, I felt like I'd known he was here all along. As if that was why I'd climbed out the window. I took a step toward him. "Hi."

"You okay?" he asked. He must've heard me tumble into the bushes.

"Yes, I'm fine." I didn't really want to explain about the sleigh bells.

"I'm just out for a walk." Hal's shoes creaked as he shifted his weight. "Couldn't sleep."

"Me neither," I whispered.

"Want to come along?" His voice shook a little.

And then we were walking, like a held breath let out. The night big and dark and strange around us, the sidewalk hard and familiar under my shoes. I matched Hal's stride, or he matched mine, and we swung along in step.

You don't have to talk, when you're walking. I stopped trying to think what to say, and just looked around. Stars, tall shadowy trees, here and there a light behind curtains. Crickets. A faint shout from somewhere downtown. We walked in and out of smells—honeysuckle, river mud, fresh paint on somebody's fence.

I reached out and took Hal's hand—then realized what I'd done, and started to pull away. Hal held on. My heart felt like it might knock itself to pieces. My hand was so happy, holding his. My legs were happy, and my breath was happy, and my brain kept forgetting whatever it was trying to say. I let Hal lead me, keeping pace with him, feeling when he was going to turn a corner. It was nice, not deciding. Just following along, smiling in the dark.

After a while, I noticed Hal hesitating a little at the corners, like he wondered if *I* was going to turn. I almost giggled—for heaven's sake, let's not get lost. I got my bearings, and turned onto Vine Street. Hal turned with me.

As we angled back toward Tom and Wanda's neighborhood, I quit feeling so happy. I wanted…what did I want? I wanted Hal. My hand was sweating in his. The breeze stirred my dress, breathing honeysuckle on my thighs. Every time we crossed a street or turned a corner, Hal didn't stop and kiss me.

And then we were on Howe Street, and there was the big elm in Tom and Wanda's yard. We walked slower, and stopped. "Better get some sleep," Hal whispered.

"Yes." I didn't let go of his hand. He didn't let go of mine.

We stood there a minute, like we were both waiting at the corner to see if the other one was going to turn. Then Hal pulled on my hand, or I pulled on his, and we turned at the same time, and we were kissing again. All the wanting in me let loose at once. My hands clutched at his sweat-damp shirt. His fingers curled tight in my hair.

When I pulled back—to take a breath, or maybe to think— Hal followed me with his lips, and I let him. His arms wrapped me close, my thighs trembled against his, our lips melted into each other again, soft on soft...

After a long time, Hal stepped away. Cool air flowed in between our bodies. I felt like I might be glowing in the dark. It was too dark to see, but I gazed up at him. This time I didn't say "Oh, Hal." And if I had, I'd have meant something different.

Hal cleared his throat softly. "Um...you need help getting back inside?"

I stifled a laugh. I'd forgotten all about my crash landing. "Yes, I guess so," I whispered.

"You ought to have you a fruit crate to climb up on," Hal whispered back, leading the way alongside the house.

"I'll get one tomorrow." I stepped into Hal's stirruped hands, and he lifted me fast and easy. I pulled myself over the sill and landed in a heap on the rug. When I knelt to look back out the window, Hal was looking up at me, his face a smudge of white. I wanted to lean down and kiss him, but I was afraid I'd fall on him instead.

"Sleep tight," he whispered.

I grinned. "Don't let the bedbugs bite."

Then he was gone. I sat on the rug, still feeling his hands around my foot, his face pressing into my skirt as I'd swayed against him. All that walking in the cool of the night, and I was warmer than I'd been before. "Sleep tight," I whispered to myself, still smiling. I felt like I might never sleep again.

6

May

I was putting supper on the table when Walt's car pulled into the driveway. "Daddy's home!" I called to Katy.

"Daddy-Daddy-Daddy!" Katy came running, and crashed full tilt into Hal's legs as he came in through the screen porch.

Hal picked Katy up and swung her around, singing "K-K-K-Katy, beautiful Katy!" like he always did. Then he shut his eyes and squeezed her to his chest, hanging on like she was keeping him afloat. I saw him swallow hard, and my own throat hurt. Katy started to squirm, and he put her down to hug me. I'd thought I was ready for the way his eyes dodged away from mine, but I wasn't.

It was hard to swallow my supper, and harder to say ordinary things about tobacco worms or the garden, but I managed. And then there were evening chores to do, and Katy to wash and put to bed. Just two more weeks...

But when I came downstairs and found Hal sitting at the table, staring at the ice melting in his tea, I blurted it out before I had time to think. "What's wrong, Hal? You've got to tell me."

Hal looked around, like I might be talking to somebody else. Then he sighed, and ran his hands through his hair. I pulled out my chair and sat down, waiting. He cleared his throat. Finally he said, "Well, May, I guess... The thing is...I'm in love with another woman."

My mouth fell open. After a minute I heard myself say, "Well, I'll be damned."

Hal got up suddenly. He paced over to the door and leaned his head against the frame. I just stared, the way Jamie's dumb dog Whitey used to do after it ran into a tree.

After a minute, Hal turned back toward me, rubbing his face with one hand. "God, May, I'm sorry." His voice cracked. "I never would've thought I'd get into something like this."

I didn't know what to say to that. There were tears on my face. I knew I looked terrible when I cried, all red and blotchy, but I couldn't move to reach for the dishtowel. He was going to leave me. Hal.

Hal was crying too. He didn't look terrible. He looked like a sad little boy in a picture, big brown eyes swimming and eyebrows puckered.

A wave of heat rushed up my neck, and all at once I was mad. I slapped the table with both hands, hard. The sting in my palms made me madder. I shoved back my chair and stood up, yanking at the ties on my apron. "I should *hope* you're sorry!" I hissed at Hal, trying to keep my voice down. I pulled the apron over my head and threw it on the table. "You're a married man! What're you *thinking?* What about Katy?"

Hal shook his head. "I know," he whispered. "I know." He pulled a red hanky out of his hip pocket and blew his nose, still wagging his head back and forth. He looked like one of those awful figurines, Winston Churchill or a basset hound. I wanted to smack him.

I clenched my fists and turned my back. My ears were roaring like a chimney fire. The curtains on the kitchen window moved a little, in a breeze I couldn't feel. My blurry face stared back at me from the windowpane above the screen. There was Hal's reflection too, small in the corner of the glass, folding up his hanky. Shaking his head. I gritted my teeth.

Get ahold of yourself, Maydie.

I almost jumped, the voice came so clear and sudden in my mind. Daddy's voice, as stern and loving as when he was alive. *Get ahold of yourself.*

My heart pounded against my ribs. I pressed a hand over it. I couldn't get ahold of myself. I could hardly think past the roaring in my ears.

"May?" Hal said. I looked at his reflection, feeling my shoulders hunch up. He sighed. I wanted to walk away, but I was already up against the counter. I shifted my feet. The floor was sticky under my left shoe, where Katy had dribbled molasses this morning.

I never could stand a dirty floor. I ought to just mop it right now. I'd already swept, before I put Katy to bed—before I asked Hal what was going on, and he... I turned around, and pushed past Hal onto the back porch.

Hal watched me cranking the handle of the porch pump. "What're you doing?" he asked. I grabbed the mop and carried my bucket of water into the kitchen. Hal started dragging chairs out of the way, but I shouldered him aside and did it myself, then wrung out the mop and started scrubbing.

I'd thought I could count on Hal. I'd thought he loved me.

The wet mop turned the painted floorboards shiny brown. I bent down to pick loose a dried piece of corn under Katy's high chair, wiping my nose on the shoulder of my dress. I shoved the mop towards Hal's feet. He backed out onto the porch, and I mopped the place where he'd stood, my mouth hard against my teeth.

When the kitchen was done, I started on the living room, spoiling my mop water with dust from under the braided rug. Sweat ran down my legs as I pumped another bucketful, not looking at Hal. I kept going, on into our bedroom, mopping around the carved legs of the bed and dressers. Hal was leaving me. I tried to make myself believe it. He'd leave me here alone with Katy...

No. Hal might not love *me* anymore, but he'd never leave the farm. He grew up here. He'd make me leave, and bring this

other woman—I plunged the mop hard into the bucket, slosh-
ing water on the floor.

My back ached as I climbed the stairs. It seemed like a year
since I was canning corn with Grace. Driving home, telling
myself Hal and I would figure it out… I wanted to spit. Or cry.

Katy grunted in her sleep when I turned on her bedroom
light. Her floor wasn't dirty. I mopped it anyway, then leaned
on the side rail of her crib and looked down at her. Her closed
eyes scurried back and forth like squirrels on a tree branch. My
fingers ached on the mop handle. What on earth was I going to
do? Take Katy to live with Mom? I shut my eyes, and swallowed at the sourness in my throat. Maybe I was wrong, and
Hal would go live in Cartersboro, and we'd still have a home.

I left the spare bedroom alone, and carried my mop and
bucket back downstairs. The living room floor was still wet, so I
went out the front door.

There wasn't any moon. The katydids and crickets filled up
the dark with their noise. I sat on the porch swing, tucking my
feet up and pressing my face against my knees, smelling my
own sweat. I thought of Katy growing up without her daddy—
what would I have done without my Daddy? When the tears
tried to start up again, I bit my knuckles. *Get ahold of yourself.*
Crying wouldn't help me or Katy either one. I had to figure
out what to do. And first I needed to know what Hal was going
to do.

After awhile I heard scrapes and thumps from inside the
house—Hal putting the kitchen chairs back. The living room
floor was probably dry enough to walk across now. I made
myself unfold my legs and stand up. I dumped the dirty mop
water into the hollyhocks, moving stiff as an old woman. Then
I headed back in to the kitchen.

Hal had poured us both fresh glasses of ice tea. There were
two clean saucers and two clean forks next to the napkin holder
—we'd been going to have cake, maybe play some cards.
Instead, I'd had to ask what was going on. I should have stuck
to my plan and waited, instead of switching horses midstream.
But then what? Would Hal have just left, and not even told me?

I bit my lip hard, and sat down. The important thing was to find out what was next.

Hal took a breath, but I spoke first—I couldn't stand for him to start apologizing again. "So, what are you going to do?"

Hal slid his glass a couple of inches to the right, then moved it back to the left. "I don't know, May," he said. "It makes me about sick to think—"

I frowned. "Just tell me, Hal. Are you leaving me, or are you wanting me to go?"

Hal scrunched up his face like I'd said something terrible. "Now, May, I…" He trailed off.

I waited. Then I said it for him, pushing the words out through a tight throat. "It's not any use pretending, if you don't love me anymore. I just need to know, so I can…" So I could what? Pack my suitcase? Or Hal's? Hal's was still packed, full of the week's dirty clothes to be washed tomorrow.

Hal was staring at me. "Don't *love* you?" he said. His voice was almost a whisper, rough with feeling. "May, I—God, May, I love you more than *anything!*"

"You—" I started, but suddenly I couldn't breathe. Hal wasn't leaving me? Had I gotten it all wrong? I felt my face turn red, but hope was pounding in my chest. If he still loved me… And I could see he did. His heart was in his eyes.

If he loved me, though, why— I hadn't heard that part wrong. But I could forgive him, if it meant having everything back to normal. If Hal would just come on home after Labor Day, and be Katy's daddy, and love me. Surely I could. *Forgive seventy times seven,* I heard in my head, and frowned. I didn't need Mom's advice. But if Hal really meant it… "So, you're leaving…this other woman?" I asked.

Hal put his head in his hands, almost knocking over his ice tea. "God, May, I don't know," he mumbled. "I love *her,* too."

"You love her too," I repeated dully. That didn't make any sense.

"I love her like anything," Hal said, looking up at me through his fingers. "With all my heart. And I love you with all my heart, and I love Katy, and—" He broke off in a half-sob, and wiped at his eyes.

I felt a sudden ache in my belly, deeper than I'd thought my belly went. My mouth moved, but I couldn't think of anything to say.

Hal was shaking his head again. "I don't know what I'm going to do, May," he said. "I can't stand to hurt you, and I can't stand to hurt *her...*"

I watched his head going back and forth, trying to understand what he was saying. He couldn't decide? He loved us both, and he couldn't make up his mind? His eyes pleaded with me, as if I had the answer. As if I could tell him to stay with me or—"What's her *name*, for Pete's sake?" I asked, not really meaning to.

"What?" Hal looked startled, then almost relieved. "Oh—um, Vera. Her name's Vera."

There'd been a Vera that played ball with us when we were kids. One of Grace's cousins. Everybody said she looked like Greta Garbo. I'd seen a photograph of Greta Garbo, but Mom wouldn't let me go to the picture shows. She said Hollywood was Satan's playground, full of vice and wickedness.

Hal was looking at me, his forehead wrinkled up again. He wasn't avoiding my eyes anymore. That was something. Maybe. My head felt like it was full of river mud. I glanced at the clock, but I couldn't tell what time it was. "All right, Hal," I said. I stood up. "I just..." No. If I kept talking, I'd start crying again, or yelling. "I'm going to bed."

Hal stayed at the table while I filled my washbasin and carried it off to the bedroom. I washed up quick—I didn't feel like being naked when Hal came in. I was pulling my nightgown on when I heard his chair scrape back, and then the squeak and splash of the porch pump. Hal kept an old tin dishpan on the screen porch, so he could wash out there in the summertime.

I lay down with my back to the room, tucking my arms in close despite the heat. *Vera. Her name's Vera,* Hal said again in my head. I could hear it in his voice, see it in his eyes: Hal loved her, this Vera. Really loved her.

Like he loved me? That was in his voice and his eyes, too. *I love you more than anything...I love her with all my heart...* How could that be?

I sniffled, and moved my teary face to a dry spot on the pillowcase. Hal would be in to bed soon. Surely, after all this, he'd be satisfied to go to sleep. I couldn't imagine anything more than that, not after he'd... Had he? He loved her, he was in love with her. But he hadn't said...

I squeezed my eyes tight shut, trying not to picture Hal in bed with Greta Garbo. Or with anybody. Instead I found myself remembering the flood of '37, when Daddy drove us all in to Vevay to see the river. The brown water looked as cold as death, and wider than the world. Daddy and Jamie ended up going out in a rowboat, helping get people off rooftops. Mom prayed beside me in the truck, fingers knotted on top of her pregnant belly. I watched things float by—half a haystack with a rooster on top, a woman hanging onto a dead cow. What a thing to have your arms around, I thought. But you could see she wasn't about to let go.

7

Vera

"Now, don't you sign up for that dividend scheme in the paper!" Wanda's voice carries in from the porch like a fiddle playing off-key. "Betty says it'll leave your widow owing money to the government!"

Tom sighs. "For pity's sake, Wanda, that's the silliest thing I ever heard."

I sigh too, and lean over my sewing table, basting white cotton underlining to pink satin. It's hot in my room, but I'm making good time on the bridesmaids' dresses for Flora Riddle's wedding. I get a lot of sewing done on the weekends, trying to distract myself from missing Hal. It's only Friday evening, and already I'm missing Hal.

After that first nighttime walk in June, Hal would whistle under my window every night he was in town. We'd head down along the river and out to the middle of the bridge, or up the hill past the broom factory. When we were away from houses, we talked. Mostly I talked. I told him about growing up outside High Brooks, how Mama and Tom and I managed after Pop left us. When I talked about our old house standing empty now, falling to ruin, Hal put his arm around me, and even my sadness felt sweet.

I was so happy, walking in the dark with Hal. Of course I was crazy with wanting, too—kissing him goodnight was like standing at the edge of a cliff, with every heartbeat telling me to *jump, jump, jump*. But I knew better. I thought I knew better.

Then one night we walked along Spring Street, and Hal turned up the front walk of Mrs. Moore's boarding house, and I didn't hesitate, just went along as if it was any corner in town. The screen door wasn't latched, and nobody was in the parlor. I followed Hal up the dim stairs toward his room. My heart was racing, but my feet were steady on the wooden steps.

I felt like I ought to look different, after that night. And the next night, and the next... Like everybody would know. But life just went on. I broke up Freddy and Hester's fights, and wiped Petey's nose, and helped Wanda repaint the kitchen. I met Sue and Francine for malts on Saturdays, went to church on Sundays. I smiled at Hal across the supper table. June went by, and July. Nobody noticed a thing.

Now it's August. We walk the same way every night, over to Spring Street and up those stairs to Hal's door. Hal's bed. I know I ought to be ashamed. I don't know why I'm not. Maybe I'm too happy. I feel all glad inside my skin, the way Sybil looked after she got married. I wish I could talk to Sybil. I don't think Sue or Francine would understand. Sue's too busy taking care of her mother for dating—and to hear Francine tell it, marriage is more morning sickness and dirty socks than romance.

But Sybil knows, I bet. I want to ask her, Do your breasts... *reach?* Mine always just sat there in my brassiere, before. Men liked them, but having them was never that exciting. Now I'm afraid Tom and Wanda will notice mine at supper, turning toward Hal like flowers following the sun. I hunch my shoulders, and try to think of something else. But in Hal's room at night, my brassiere in a pile with the rest of my clothes, I stand up straight and let my breasts reach for Hal's hands, and I smile into his smiling eyes...

I wouldn't say that to Sybil, of course, any more than I'd tell Sue and Francine. I know better than that. Love happens in pairs: Sybil and Bob, Tom and Wanda, Francine and Marvin, Flora Riddle and her chubby fiancé. One plus one equals two. That's how it's done. Nobody wants hear about my two plus two equals three.

Of course, two-plus-two-equals-three does happen. If you believe the movies, it happens all the time. But this isn't like that. Hal's not just fooling around with me. And I'm not trying to steal Hal from May. As if I could. The love in Hal's eyes when he looks at me, in his hand holding mine before I leave him at night—Hal loves May like that too, only that love is older and deeper, full of memories and work and family. It's in his voice when he talks about May, even if he's just telling Wanda she's doing fine. I wouldn't try to break that love. That'd be breaking Hal. It'd be wrong.

It's wrong now. Even if May never finds out, it's wrong. I've thought about calling the whole thing off. But that wouldn't undo what's done. And the thing is, it doesn't *feel* wrong.

I unroll another length of pink satin and smooth it out. On the porch, Wanda sighs loudly and says, "I don't know if I'll have the girls over for bridge next week."

"Why?" Tom doesn't sound very interested. "Don't you like them anymore?"

"Of course not! I mean, yes!" Wanda's foot taps the porch boards impatiently. "Last week Mabel sat on a slingshot Freddy left in the couch!"

Tom chuckles. "Sounds dangerous."

"And Hester sneaks around like some kind of spy—she scared Joanne half to death!"

I hear a match scrape along the side of Tom's chair, and catch a whiff of smoke. Most of the men smoke, since the war. Tom still looks funny to me with a cigarette in his mouth, like a boy playing gangsters. "Well," he says, "I guess we could get rid of the kids."

"Oh, Thomas, that's not the *point!*" Wanda says. I wonder what her point is. It sounds like she's got one, but she's going to wear Tom out with complaining before she gets to it.

Wanda wasn't always like this. She seemed happier during the war, when we were staggering our shifts at the ordnance plant so we could watch the babies. Wanda loved mothering babies. When the doctor said she couldn't have any more after Petey, she cried for a week. Now I think she's bored. Bored with the kids, who aren't babies anymore. Bored with the house, bored with me. And Tom's bored with her. That's a terrible thing to think. But Tom never looks at Wanda the way Hal looks at me. I wonder if he ever did.

Sometimes I miss those days too. Not the war, of course. But I get lonely, sewing by myself day after day. At the plant, all of us girls were in it together, cursing that awful silk burlap, trading gossip at lunch break. And it was important work. Bridesmaids' dresses are only important to brides.

Flora's picked a nice shade of pink, though. And the texture's delicious, slick as a buttered pan. I lay out the underlining for a bodice piece and start cutting the satin to match. All those bridesmaids, silky and slippery-smooth on the outside— but against their skin, just plain white cotton. It seems like a waste.

I ought to make a wedding dress wrong-side-out. Ordinary on the outside, but it'd be secretly sliding over your hips, stroking your legs, caressing your neck... Getting married might be a whole new experience.

Every night with Hal, it's new again. New, and familiar, and new. Hal's body, lean and wiry. Sawdust from the box plant on his neck, in the curly hair of his chest. His work-sweat smell, like a horse just in from the field. My mouth following the curve of his collarbone, my knees weak as his hand snakes between my legs. His cotton shorts tenting up toward me. My mouth tingling with curiosity—I slide down to kiss him there, pushing his shorts aside. Skin even softer than lips, soft as rose petals, soft over hardness. Hal's fingers curl in my hair. I lick the soft skin like an ice cream cone, and feel a shiver run through him. It's like a hot popsicle, like grapes rolled on my tongue, like a mouthful of melon. Hal's hands easing me away, lifting me—I rise up on tiptoe, and it slides between my legs all wet, and I'm wet too, wet as a hot bath, quivering at the touch of him. We stand like that, him moving back and forth, kissing like we'll kiss forever. I'm coming apart, unraveling at all my seams. Hal lowers me to the bed, slides into me, and I do come apart, falling backwards into the dark. Turquoise spins behind my eyelids. "Shh," Hal says. I put the back of my hand in my mouth. Hal moving, in and out, here and gone. His eyes— delighted, like he's only just discovered me. My throat wanting to shout something loud. His face tight and fierce, then soft and open as a baby's.

He lies down onto me, kisses my cheeks and forehead, rolls to my side. I stroke his damp hair. Our sweaty skin touching— arm, thigh, belly—feels like the same skin, no line between us. I lie perfectly still, happiness in my chest like a sky full of stars.

Hal always offers to walk me home, but I won't let him. He lies naked in the bed, watching me pull on my clothes, smiling like there's nobody in the world he'd rather be with. He reaches for my hand. I bend down to kiss him, then tiptoe out and down the stairs, past closed doors and Mrs. Moore snoring like a sawmill in the back bedroom. I ease the screen door shut behind me, not wanting to go.

But once I'm walking, out alone under the dark trees and the stars, I'm all right. Better than all right. I'm a jug filled to the rim, walking slow so I won't spill. I'm part of the air, like smoke or rain. The dogs don't bark at me.

"Guess I'll hit the sack." Tom's voice from the porch startles me, and I blush as if he and Wanda can hear my thoughts—as if they can see me sitting here, with a scrap of pink satin pressed to my lips. The bells jingle on the door, and Tom's footsteps climb the stairs.

Wanda's still on the porch, tapping her fingernails on the arm of her chair. I can feel her frustration from here. I lay down my shears—best turn out my light, or she'll come in and pick at me just to let off steam.

Still, I wish Wanda could have what I have. Even with the lonely weekends. Even knowing it's wrong. Everybody ought to have love.

8

Hal

At first it was almost a relief, telling May the truth last night. Now I wish I'd kept my mouth shut. Or lied. I never was any good at lying.

May'll hardly look at me today, like my face hurts her eyes. She made my breakfast, didn't eat hers. May's always favored her daddy, but today it's her mom she reminds me of. Shoulders pulled in like she's cold. It's almost ninety degrees out.

I want to tell her, I don't know how I got so confused. I never could think straight if I didn't sleep good. At home, anymore, I just wrap my arms around May, bury my face in her hair and sleep like a baby—but over in Cartersboro last winter, it was just me and my nightmares. After a while, everything was numb and grey. Except Vera's smile, sparkling like sunshine after a storm...

But if it'd just been wanting Vera—well, you learn to handle that. That first time I kissed her, I wised up about five minutes later, told myself I'd better cut it out. And I did. I never expected her to fall out a window at me. I never expected to fall in love with her.

Maybe I'd have been okay even then. Except Vera loved *me*. She wanted me. I wanted to give her what she wanted… And I felt like I was a million miles from home.

I want to tell May, I just got all mixed up. By the time I thought about what I was doing, I couldn't see any way to back out of it without hurting somebody.

I can't believe May thought I didn't love her anymore. God. I want to tell her I love her again. But I look at her face, and I can't even open my mouth. I've broken May's heart.

Come tomorrow night, I'll be breaking Vera's heart too. It's the only way, I see that now.

I feel like a worm.

9

Vera

Sue and Francine are already at a corner table when I jingle in through the door at Hook's. I wave at them while Joey makes my egg malt. Sue's wearing the new dress she's been working on. Francine sits sideways to the spindly table, making room for her belly. She's due by Halloween. I wonder if she'll still come on Saturdays, after the baby, or if it'll just be Sue and me then.

Back during the war, there'd be a dozen of us girls at Hook's every weekend, making a ruckus—Velma and DeeDee squabbling, Francine teasing Sybil about Bob, Sue asking if anybody wanted to split a sundae. Most of the factory girls went back to their hometowns, once Uncle Sam didn't need them anymore. The ones that stayed are mostly married now. Francine's the only one who still has time for a malt with Sue and me. Sometimes I think Francine would just as soon forget she's married.

"Howdy, stranger," Francine says, as I pull up a chair and set my malt on the table. "We thought maybe you'd forgotten us."

"Not likely! My fitting took longer than I thought." I smile at Sue. "Your dress looks great!"

"You think?" Sue turns pink, matching the watermelon print of the dress.

"Anything would look great on Sue," Francine says. Sue flaps a hand at her, turning even pinker.

I spoon a bite of whipped cream off the top of my malt. It tastes like a vanilla cloud. "So, what'd I miss?"

"Let's see…" Francine stirs her pineapple phosphate with the straw. "Sue's mother can't sleep in her new nightgown. Marvin spent half his paycheck at the tavern last night. Oh, and it's hotter than the hinges of Hades. Am I forgetting anything?"

"I think that's as far as we got," Sue says. "What's your news, Vera?"

"Not much." Not much, if you don't count Hal's warm eyes, and Hal's strong shoulders… "Except, just between you and me, Flora Riddle's mother is a pain in the neck."

Sue laughs. "What *is* it about brides' mothers?" Sue's married off four brothers—she ought to know.

Francine starts to say something, then takes a drink of phosphate instead. Her mother hasn't spoken to her since she got pregnant and had to marry Marvin.

"I'm with you on the weather," I say, unwrapping my straw. "It's too hot to eat—I think I'll just live on egg malts." I take a big slurp of my malt—and almost gag.

"What in the world, Vera—" Sue looks alarmed. Francine's staring at me.

"Ugh!" I grab a napkin and scrub at my mouth. "*Yuck!* This malt's *awful!*"

Francine shakes her head. "I never could stand egg malts."

"Vera *likes* them," Sue points out.

"I do," I agree. "But this tastes like a mouthful of nickels. I don't know what's…" I reach for the straw.

"Good grief, don't taste it *again!*" Francine pulls my glass away.

"Here, try this." Sue slides her Coke over to me, then dips the spoon into my malt and licks it cautiously. "Tastes okay to me. We can trade if you want."

"Thanks." I take a swig of Coke and swish it like mouthwash. "Must be something wrong with my taste buds. Maybe the pickled beets we had for lunch."

Francine laughs. "Taste buds are weird. When I had morning sickness, I could've sworn somebody was putting tuna fish in my coffee!"

"Eww." Sue makes a face, and takes a drink of my malt.

Suddenly sweat's running down my sides. *No*, I think. *It can't be that.* I take another drink and wipe my face with a napkin, trying to look like I'm just too warm.

"Nothing like puking before breakfast," Francine's saying. "I used to sit on the bathroom floor and *curse* that Lysol! It was supposed to work."

Lysol? The Coke in my mouth suddenly tastes like housecleaning. I try not to make a face—and not to think of the oatmeal I couldn't finish this morning. Or how when I was cutting up a chicken the other day, the crunch of my knife through gristle almost made me throw up.

"Are you all right, Vera?" Sue asks, interrupting Francine. "You look a little pale."

I nod, and swallow hard. "I'll be okay. Maybe I'm coming down with something—Petey threw up last night." Which isn't true at all. I never lie to Sue and Francine. I've never even kept a secret from them, until Hal.

"Could be the heat, too," Sue says.

Francine's frowning a little. I can almost see the gears in her head starting to turn.

"So Marvin had a good time last night, did he?" I ask desperately.

Francine lets out a gusty sigh and rolls her eyes. "Oh, Lord. I swear, that man…"

Sue gives me a concerned look as Francine starts in on her favorite subject. I wink at her, and try to smile, but my face feels numb. I can't follow what Francine's saying—I watch Sue, and try to chuckle at the right times. Meanwhile I'm telling myself not to jump to conclusions. Hal's always used his "pros," after those first couple of times. And my so-called monthlies never were that monthly anyway. How long has it been? I try to count backwards in my head, but it makes me dizzy. When Francine waves her straw to make a point, dribbling pineapple phosphate across the table, I jump up. "I'll get us some more napkins."

"It's fine——" Sue starts, but I'm already halfway to the counter.

I ask Joey for a banana split while I'm at it. I don't want a banana split, but we can share it, and it takes a while to make. I lean on the counter and stare at the little light bulbs above the mirror of the backbar, trying to calm down. Behind me, Sue laughs, and Francine says, "I know——I couldn't believe it!"

What if it is true? What would they think? Sue and I stuck by Francine, even when her own family didn't. We went with her and Marvin to the J.P., and bought them an automatic toaster. But then, they were getting married. Hal may be worth ten of Marvin, but he still can't marry me.

And what about my family? Tom and Wanda wouldn't throw me out, would they? Tom would probably be too busy beating the stuffing out of Hal.

"Here you are, Miss Stinson." I jump a little, but Joey's just trying to hand me my banana split. I give him a nervous smile and dig through my purse for a quarter.

Francine ate most of the banana split, while Sue told us about Darla Connor's disastrous wedding cake. Usually I'd think of a story to tell too, but today it was all I could do to sit still. I fiddled with my spoon, and went to the counter for more napkins we didn't need. It was a relief when Sue had to get back home to her mother, and we all said goodbye.

I didn't go home, though. I couldn't stand to face Tom and Wanda and the kids, with my head spinning like this. Instead I came down here to the river, my favorite spot to be alone. I poke at the sandy mud with a piece of driftwood, trying not to cry. It isn't true. Anyway, I don't know it's true. It might not be.

What if it is?

It wouldn't be the first time it ever happened. There was Ellen Trueblood, at the plant. She disappeared back to the farm—some story about her mother being sick, but word got around. And that girl welder with the green eyes, who hid it for seven months before they fired her. She went back home too, somewhere in Ohio.

I can't go back home. There isn't any home. Not since the day Mama had me read her that letter. Pop, wherever he was, had run up a bunch of debts, and they were going to take the farm. I couldn't believe it. All the years Mama and I had worked—Tom too, before he went off with the WPA—paying the mortgage when we didn't have money for flour...

But Mama just nodded, and kept pouring kerosene into a lamp. "Well, I guess that's that," she said. I stared at her with my mouth open, while she told me that Mr. Townsend at the dry-goods store had been asking her to marry him for years, and she reckoned it was time she said yes.

I couldn't even take that in. "But Mama," I said, "The farm —it ought to be yours now! We could get a lawyer, or—"

I quit talking when I saw Mama wasn't listening. Her mind was made up. She got a sheet of old newspaper and cleaned the lamp chimney, her wedding ring clinking against the glass. She'd never taken that ring off, in eleven years without Pop. There was a hard knot of callus under it. Her palms were striped with callus, too, like a man's. Like mine.

Mama always said we were lucky. "Be thankful we've got food on the table and a roof to keep the rain off it," she'd tell me. I knew she was right. We could have ended up out on the road, like the Ratliffs and the Wards. Our cow had thrown twin calves the year Pop left, and our spring kept running when the well went dry. That was luck, and I was thankful. But I was proud, too. It was hard work that took our luck and made a life out of it. By the time Tom left, I'd been strong enough to take over the plowing, and at sixteen I could sew anything Mama could. We traded sewing for what we couldn't grow, and we always sang while we worked. I loved the life we'd made. I hadn't ever thought Mama might want something different.

Mama wasn't in love with Mr. Townsend. Maybe he was in love with her. When we went to visit, he'd take her coat and hold her chair, for all she was almost as tall as him. I could just remember the way Pop used to come in from the field and grab Mama in a big hug. "Oh *Lordy*, what a pretty gal I got!" he'd holler, and Mama would laugh.

But that was before times got so bad, and Pop got so quiet, and one day Tom and I came home from school and Pop was gone.

Mr. Townsend had a one-bedroom apartment above his store. There wasn't room for me. Mama wrote to Tom, and it turned out that Wanda was feeling low in her second pregnancy, and they could use an extra pair of hands. So after the wedding I got on the train to Cartersboro and waved goodbye to Mr. Townsend and Mama, and to High Brooks, and to home.

The State of Illinois sold the farm. I walked out there once, when I was back visiting Mama in High Brooks. I found the house standing empty, with its gutters full of dead weeds. Inside, the parlor floor was rotted through, and white fungus grew up the walls.

So I can't go back home. And I can't get married. And I don't have any other ideas. Except hoping it isn't true. But it's just like when I read that letter—there's a sick, scared feeling in the back of my throat, saying it is.

10

May

Saturday was awful.

I'd thought maybe Hal would tell me in the morning what he'd decided to do. But he was quiet, sneaking glances at me like a kid in trouble. I told myself to be patient. Hal never was one to make up his mind fast. He could spend ten minutes deciding between chocolate and vanilla ice cream—if we were in a hurry, sometimes I'd have to tell him what to get. I pictured him frowning at a soda-fountain blackboard, and gritted my teeth. It wouldn't help to get all mad again.

Meanwhile there were the chickens to feed, and Hal's clothes to wash, and the yard to mow. My arms and legs felt stiff and heavy, and I had to stop myself from snapping at Katy.

Hal was out working most of the day. Every time he came in, my stomach twisted up with dread. He'd open his mouth, and I'd brace myself to hear that he was leaving me, or throwing me out, or getting rid of this Vera—and he'd say he'd got all the tobacco dusted, or could I pick up some roofing nails when I went to Peck's. Then he'd give me a sort of hangdog look, like there was something he was hoping I'd say. I didn't say anything.

After lunch I put Katy in the truck and went off to Whelan to run errands, leaving quick before Hal could think of a reason to come along. I needed a break from my stomachache.

"Well, if it ain't Miz Tinker Bell!" Peck Chase's big voice boomed and squeaked in the dusty dimness of the hardware store. He limped out from behind the counter and thumped me on the back. "And here's Little Bit!" Katy hid her face against my shoulder, and I gave her a squeeze. It always took her a minute to warm up to Peck.

"Hi, Peck," I said. "How've you been?"

"Oh, can't complain." Peck straightened a stack of matchboxes, and went back to his stool behind the counter. "What you after today?"

I glanced at my list. "Roofing nails, a couple of light bulbs, sandpaper..." My own voice sounded too normal, as if this business with Hal should have changed it.

"You know where to find them." Peck waved a hand at the shelves, and grinned. "And then I want to hear what you're working on."

I felt a smile tug at my mouth. Peck never let me go without a report on my latest project. He'd been an engineer in the first war, and he'd been giving me spare parts and tinkering advice since I was six. I put Katy down and went to weigh out half a pound of nails, breathing in the store's familiar smells—dust and machine oil, old cardboard and new hickory handles. When I was little, I'd thought you could fix anything in the world with the stuff in Peck's store.

When I brought my things back to the counter, Peck was kneeling beside Katy, showing her a big brass hinge. "See," he said, "Your frame-side plate's got three knuckles, and over here you've got two..." Katy bounced on her toes excitedly as the hinge squeaked open and shut. Peck handed it to her, and got to his feet with a grunt. "So what you got going, Tinker Bell?" he asked me.

"Not much," I said. "Made us a new milking stool last week —the old one was cracked."

"Mm-hmm," Peck said. "What's new about it?"

I gave him a sidelong look. "It's just a stool. Legs, a seat." Peck pretended to glare at me over his half-moon glasses, until I grinned and added, "It does hold the bucket so Bess can't kick it over."

Peck nodded in satisfaction, and handed me the yellow pencil from behind his ear. "How'd you manage that?"

"Well…" I flipped over a sheet of sandpaper, and drew my stool—curved to match the bucket, with a piece of stiff wire finishing out the circle. "Your bucket sits down through this wire, and rests on a little, what'd you call it—bracket? Ledge?"

"We call that a 'doohickey,'" Peck said, peering at my drawing. "How'd you fasten your wire?"

Katy was pulling at my skirt. I picked her up and propped her on my hip, dodging the hinge she was still flapping around. "Ran it in a groove around the back, to a couple of wood screws."

"How's it work?"

"Good—now." I made a face. "I had to keep re-doing the angle. Thing kept tipping over on me."

"That ol' gravity'll get you every time." Peck winked at me. "That's forty-six cents. Now, *I* heard there's a fellow making a gadget you clamp onto a cow's back, keeps her from kicking."

"Hmm. I wonder how that works." I shifted my grip on Katy, and found a dollar in my purse. "It won't matter once Hal's back, anyway—Bess never kicks for him."

Peck chuckled as he counted out my change. "More than one way to skin a cat."

I tried to smile at him, but now I was thinking of Hal again. I sighed. "Well, I'd better get on down the road."

When I started to take the hinge from Katy, Peck said, "Ah, she can keep that old thing."

"Are you sure?" It looked new to me.

"Course I'm sure! Give her something to think about. You can see she's a tinkerer, like her mommy." Peck nodded at Katy, who was poking her fingers through the hinge's screw holes.

"Well, thanks," I said. "You take care, Peck."

"You too, Miz Bell."

After supper, Hal played with Katy while I washed the dishes. "Trotty-horse, trotty-horse, goin' to the *mill!* Not got there yet, he's a-trottin' there *still!*" he sang, bouncing her on his knees as she giggled. I scrubbed at a burnt spot on the meatloaf pan. Katy always cheered Hal up—but he still hadn't told me what he was going to do.

"Trotty-horse, trotty-horse," Hal started again, this time in a Little Orphan Annie voice. He didn't sound like a man trying to make up his mind whether to leave his family.

Suddenly my stomach gave another hard twist. What if Hal wasn't even trying to decide? What if he was just putting it off, like he'd put off telling me about it? What if he went off to Cartersboro tomorrow evening and left me hanging, not even knowing if he'd be back on Friday? I stared at my hands, limp in the greasy dishwater. *I don't know what I'm going to do,* he'd said. *I can't stand to hurt you, I can't stand to hurt her...* Didn't he see that not knowing hurt even more?

Before I took Katy up to bed, I told Hal I was having my woman's time. I'd never lied to him before. But I felt like I might scream if he tried to sweet-talk me with his "make hay while the sun shines" line. When I came back downstairs, he glanced up from the Western he was reading with a halfway kind of smile. I looked at him a minute, then filled my wash-basin and went off to bed.

It was too early to go to sleep. I stared into the darkness. I realized I was chewing on my knuckles, and made myself stop. This waiting was making me a nervous wreck. But I wasn't going to beg Hal to make up his mind. To pick his vanilla or his chocolate... I felt my hands clenching into fists. *It's not fair,* I used to whine when I was a kid. And Mom would snap back, *Well* life's *not fair, Missy, so you'd best get used to it.*

After an hour or so Hal came in to bed, smelling like Lava soap. I listened to his breathing as he fell asleep.

What if I just made up *my* mind? Told Hal what to do? *You have to leave her, Hal.* My lips moved, trying out the words. *Prom-*

ise me you'll never speak to her again. If he promised, could I trust him? He'd promised when we got married, and look how that turned out. I squeezed my eyes tight shut. *Promise you'll quit loving her.* Could he do that? I knew Hal's love. It was like a baby's laugh, like springtime—bright and warm, with nothing held back. And when we were first in love, it was like the first springtime in the world, with all the birds singing like they'd just invented singing. I felt tears trickling into my hair.

Hal's body gave off heat like an oven. I edged away from him and kicked the sheet off. The bugs outside were still making a racket, *chirp chirp, katydid katydidn't katydid...* I thought of spending the rest of my life wondering if Hal still loved Vera. Wondering if he was thinking of her. Wondering if he really had to stay overnight when he took the tobacco to Madison, or... My face felt tight. What kind of person would I turn into, thinking like that, year after year?

And then, of course, Hal might say no. Maybe he loved Vera more than he loved me. *I love you with all my heart...love her with all my heart...* If I backed him into a corner, I might just make him leave me. Or, more likely, he'd say he had to think about it, and I'd be right back where I was now.

I could leave him. The idea hurt my chest, but I made myself think it through. I'd have to go somewhere. Not to Aunt Ciceline's big house in Frankfort, with Mom and Sissy. I missed Sissy—but I didn't need Mom's mean eyes judging me, and I wasn't letting her near Katy. It'd have to be Jamie and Grace. I could sleep on their couch for a while, until... Until what? I couldn't type, and my sewing wasn't anything special. I didn't have the schooling to be a teacher or a nurse. All I knew how to do was be a housewife, a farmwife. A wife. I squeezed my eyes tight shut, but tears kept leaking out anyway. Maybe Hal couldn't stop loving Vera—but I didn't think I could stop loving Hal, either. I didn't want to leave him. I didn't want him to leave me.

There had to be some other way. Something I wasn't thinking of—some way to keep Hal, for me and for Katy. A way I could make happen, instead of waiting and waiting for Hal to decide. I pulled the sheet up and dried my face with it. If I could just think straight...

I didn't think straight, though. My thoughts went in circles for hours, like cows following their own muddy tracks around a pond. Hal loved Vera. Where did they meet, anyway? Hal and I grew up together. Hal loved me. Hal didn't know what to do. Katy, asleep in her crib upstairs...*trotty-horse, trotty-horse*...Hal was a good daddy. I loved Hal. Did Vera love Hal? Hal loved Vera. I shook my head against the pillow, like Hal shaking his head in the kitchen Friday night. Back and forth—stay or go, me or Vera, Vera or me...

I woke up with a gasp, and fought down the yell in my throat. Mom's face red with rage, screaming at me, her hand swinging for my cheek— Only a dream. I hadn't seen Mom since she moved away, just after I married Hal.

I was panting, my own face hot. Hal's arm lay heavy as a sandbag across my stomach. I lifted it off me and turned on my side, looking past Hal to the window. The sky was just turning pale. I heard King Tut's long, screeching crow from the chickenhouse, and almost laughed when I recognized Mom's voice from my dream. He'd probably been crowing for hours—he wasn't much use as an alarm clock.

Then I remembered everything. How could I have forgotten it, even for a moment? Hal. Vera. Sweat prickled on my arms and back, and my mouth felt like old paper. I took a deep breath, trying to pull myself together.

And the idea came. Like a latch dropping into place—click. I frowned. Had I thought of that last night, or did I just come up with it? Or dream it? It didn't matter, of course—it was crazy. But suddenly my heart was hammering in my chest. *Was it crazy? Get ahold of yourself, May.* I chewed on my lip and tried to think it through calmly, like it was just a scheme to stop Bess from spilling the milk, or a faster way to shell peas.

It made sense.

It didn't count on Hal picking me over Vera.

It meant I'd still have a husband, and Katy'd have a daddy.

It was crazy.

Some people might think it was crazy to shell peas with a clothes-wringer, too, but it worked.

King Tut crowed again. Best get up, anyway. I rolled out of bed and eased open my dresser drawer. My reflection was dim in the mirror. Tall and shouldery, like Daddy—not really what you wanted in a girl. I pulled on my underthings and yesterday's dress, then went to work on my hair, dragging the brush through the tangles. For a moment I saw Mom's face again, her fine blond hair braided and pinned so tight it pulled at her skin when she scowled. *Just a dream.* I couldn't even remember what she was yelling about. Mom was always yelling. Always so sure she knew what was right and what was wrong.

I had Daddy's hair, too, brown and wild. I twisted it into a soft bun, levering bobby pins in along my scalp. As the dream faded, my idea got clearer in my mind. *Was* it crazy?

What was crazy was waiting for Hal to decide who he loved more. What was crazy was letting this wreck our whole lives, just because that's how things had always been done.

Maybe I ought to think about it some more. This wasn't shelling peas, after all. I might come up with a better idea.

My reflection looked back at me, its face still shadowed. I wouldn't come up with a better idea. This was going to be the best I could do. I took a deep breath, shut my dresser drawer with a thump, and switched on the light.

11

Hal

"Morning, Hal."

I squint at the light. May's up and dressed. I smile at her. "Morning."

She doesn't smile back. Oh, hell. Another day of knowing how bad I screwed up.

I sit up, rubbing my face. "How'd you sleep?"

May shrugs, stands there tapping the hairbrush on her leg. Stupid question. Better shut my mouth and put my pants on.

May waits until I'm almost dressed. Then she says, "Well, I figured out what we need to do."

"Hm?" I'm fiddling with my suspenders.

"You'll just have to bring her here to live."

Huh? I stare at her.

"Vera." May sounds impatient. "She can come live with us. We've got a spare bedroom."

Spare bedroom? I need some coffee.

"Oh, for Pete's sake, Hal, it's not that hard to understand." May drops the hairbrush on the dresser. "I've got chores to do." And she's gone. After a minute I hear the porch pump squeaking.

I must not have heard her right. Except I'm pretty sure I did. I get my suspenders straightened out, head for the kitchen.

May's dipping water into the percolator. She doesn't look like she's off her rocker.

"Sorry, hon," I tell her. "You're going to have to explain that again."

May keeps moving—lighting a burner, measuring coffee. "You love Vera?"

"Yes. I mean… yes, I do."

"And you don't know what to do." May snaps the lid down on the percolator. "So I'm telling you. Bring her here to live. I'll air out the spare bedroom." She picks up her egg basket.

"You want Vera to live here?"

"I think it's the best we can do."

"Well, honey—" She can't mean that. But May never says anything she doesn't mean. "We can't just—"

"Why not?" She's got that look, like she's already thought of everything I might come up with.

I try anyway. "Because…people *don't*."

May starts for the door. "People don't do a lot of things, Hal."

People don't fall in love with another woman. She doesn't say it, but I hear it just fine. My face turns red. "Well, but… even if—"

May cuts in before I figure out what I'm trying to say. "There's no point talking it to death, Hal. You bring Vera on home with you after Labor Day, and we'll make the best of it." She gives me a hard look, then goes off to the chickenhouse.

I get the cows in their stanchions and wipe their udders down, pull up the stool beside Bess. My head's spinning. What about —well, marriage, and right and wrong, and what'll people think? Not that I've ever cared much what anybody thinks, except May.

May thinks I'm an idiot. She's got a point, too. I'm one to be talking, about right and wrong. I lean my forehead against Bess's rough coat, and shut my eyes.

May's smarter than me, I don't mind admitting it. Look at this milking stool she made—Bess can be as spoiled-rotten as she likes, that bucket's not going anywhere. There's not a woman in a million would come up with that. Or a man, either.

Howie Trulow used to talk about a fellow he knew that had three wives. Mormon—they're not supposed to do that anymore, but I guess this fellow did. Unless Howie was making it up. Howie always had a good imagination.

But there's a difference between something that's fun to think about, and something you'd *do*.

But May's telling me this is what she *wants* to do. And she's fed up with my dithering. That look she gave me...like a minefield. All grass and birds singing, but you put a foot wrong, there'll be hell to pay.

Anyway, it doesn't matter what I think. I'd drink turpentine if it'd make things right with May.

Bess stamps her hoof—she's done, and here I'm still trying to milk her. I strip her udder down, give her an extra pat on her way out the door.

12

May

The chickens were off the roost and waiting for me. They charged out into the chickenyard when I opened their sliding door, and clucked over their feed like it was something new. I stood watching them a minute, trying to shake off my irritation. I'd been ready to scream by the time Hal quit dithering and arguing. Wasn't it enough to come up with a plan, without having to explain it twenty times?

Watching my chickens always settled me down, though. King Tut crowed and flapped his speckled wings, raising a cloud of dust. I picked a caterpillar off the fence and tossed it to him. He called a hen over to eat it—he was a good rooster, even if he couldn't tell time.

Back in the kitchen, I put Hal's shaving water on to heat and started breakfast. My hands shook a little as I measured the flour for biscuits. Maybe I was still upset—but at least I wasn't still wondering whether I'd have a husband, come Friday. And maybe it was just that I'd hardly eaten yesterday. The smell of sausage browning made my stomach growl.

Hal brought in the milk cans. He shaved at the little mirror on the porch while I fried his eggs, then came to the table and took the plate I handed him. He didn't say anything. Maybe he was done arguing.

I split a biscuit open and spooned blackberry jam into it. Hal reached for the jam, then saw the peach preserves and hesitated.

"That's the last of the peach," I said. "Go ahead and finish it off."

He gave me a cautious smile, and picked up the jar. "You're the boss."

I was hungry, and the food was good. I glanced at the clock as I chewed—I'd have time to pick and can another mess of beans, before I got started making Sunday dinner.

Hal cleared his throat, and I looked up. He was poking at the end of a sausage with his fork. "Just—you're sure, May?" he asked. "About Vera, and all? Because—well, you know I love you. And I'm—"

I waved my hand to cut him off. *I love you, and I love her.* I didn't need to hear that again. "I'm sure, Hal." Why wouldn't I be sure? "Unless—she's not some kind of a...harlot, is she?" I blurted out, then blushed. That was a word Mom would use. Did use, when she'd told me I couldn't marry Hal before he shipped out. *There's no telling what that boy'll get up to, off in foreign parts with a harlot on every street corner.*

"What? Oh—no!" Hal laughed a little. "Vera's real nice. You'll like her. She sews."

Sews. What did that have to do with anything? I wasn't inviting her to a quilting bee. Though who knew what it would sound like, by the time Hal got done explaining it to her. I put down my fork. "You make sure and tell her it's to *live* here," I told him. "Not like a houseguest, or— She'll just be part of the family."

Hal nodded slowly, then sighed. "All right," he said. "I'll ask her."

"Good." I took a drink of coffee. Maybe now I could think about dinner, and beans, and the rest of what I'd need to do this week—pick peaches, make crabapple jelly, air out the spare room...

"You want me to call you on the telephone?" Hal asked, mopping up the last of his egg with a bite of biscuit. "Let you know what she says?"

I shook my head automatically. "It's long distance. You can tell me on Friday," I said.

But my throat had gone sour. *What she says… Ask her…* My plan hadn't settled things at all. Now, instead of waiting for Hal to make up his mind, I'd be waiting for Vera to make up *her* mind. I didn't even know Vera. And if she said no, I'd be right back where I started, with Hal trying to decide which one of us he loved more.

"All right, then." Hal said, and sat back with his coffee. I swallowed hard. I couldn't take it all back now—*Oh, never mind, I forgot we'd have to ask Vera…* What else did I expect?

Katy hollered, upstairs. After a minute I heard her bumping down the steps on her bottom. I looked down at what was left of my breakfast. Purple-red jam, smeared into orange egg yolk and beige gravy. It looked like some kind of disaster.

I wasn't hungry anymore, but I picked up my fork.

13

Hal

Sunday dinner with the family, like always. Ma and Rye, James and Grace and their kids. Roast chicken, mashed potatoes, fresh-picked corn, bean salad, deviled eggs, biscuits, tomatoes. Food's never this good in Cartersboro.

May had me so discombobulated this morning, it didn't dawn on me till halfway through breakfast what this means. I won't have to leave Vera. Here I've been gearing myself up to tell Vera it's over, and kicking myself for hurting May—and now May's got the whole thing figured out.

I ought to be jumping for joy. But it kind of feels like in France, when I'd dream I was home in my own bed, Ma calling me to breakfast—I keep thinking I'm going to wake up any minute, back to the smell of sour boots and smoke, Johnson in the next foxhole crying in his sleep.

Johnson didn't make it home. Him, or Hop Chase—Peck's boy. Or those fellows from up in Norton, that all joined up together...

"Hal!" Ma's voice pokes like a pin, and I jump. "You see a bug or something?"

I sigh. Must've been staring into space. "No, Ma. Just thinking."

Ma raises her eyebrow at me. "Well, pass me the tomatoes while you're thinking. I've asked you twice."

"Sorry." No point dwelling on what's over and done with, anyway. Enjoy what's in front of me. May helping Katy with her potatoes, Ronny and Carol making faces at each other, Grace passing me the coleslaw.

Rye's talking, of course—telling James how May can pitch a haybale like a man. He's been saying that all summer, but you'd never know it from James's face. James must be about the best-natured fellow in the world.

Ma smiles at me. "Be good to have you back home, Hal. Save May doing the man's work on top of her own."

I fork another piece of chicken onto my plate. "Now, Ma, I'm not over to Cartersboro playing hopscotch."

"Didn't say you were." Ma keeps hiking her eyebrow up like that, she's liable to get a cramp.

May gets up to pour more ice tea. My eyes follow her—the curve of her hip under her dress, the way she holds her mouth when she's filling a glass. May's something to look at. You wouldn't say pretty, exactly… Beautiful, is what she is. Soft and strong both. Strong enough to damn near throw me, when she gets excited in bed.

I've hardly touched May all weekend. She's got her woman's curse and all. I wish I could sleep at home tonight, just to hold her. I don't fancy getting up at two tomorrow morning, though —it's a drive, and Cartersboro's on fast time.

Not much longer. This week, and half of the next, and I'll be back where I belong. Home with May. And, if Vera's up for it, home with Vera too.

14

Vera

FOR RENT: Modern sleeping room for business man, above Drug Store. Phone 3213 or see Mr. Ross, Hook's Drug Co.

FOR RENT: Sleeping rooms for girls and ladies. Apply in person, after 7 p.m. or on Sunday. 404 E. Lincoln Street.

No, I don't think Tom will throw me out. But I ought to have a plan, just in case.

FOR RENT: Single or double rooms, close to railyard. 13 Elm St. Phone 2938.

I know that house—dingy windows, cigarette butts around the front steps. I yawn, and turn the folded classifieds over, keeping them hidden inside my *Better Homes and Gardens*.

"Damn, it's hot!" Tom slouches down farther in his chair and props his feet on the coffee table.

Wanda frowns at him over her *Ladies' Home Journal.* "Language, Thomas! And use the ottoman, that's what it's for."

It's not a bad idea anyway, getting out of Wanda's house. I can afford it—I pay room and board here, since Hester started school. And a place with no sleigh bells on the doors would be convenient, at night.

ROOMS FOR RENT: Modern home, breakfast avail. Quiet. Mrs. Moore, 845 W. Adams. Phone 2126.

Hmm, I could rent the room next to Hal's—talk about convenience!

Be serious, Vera. That'd be too obvious. Besides, I can only hide the truth from Hal for so long. After that, maybe he'll feel different about our nights. And then there'll be a baby. I guess. Honestly, it feels more like a stomach flu. I threw up this morning.

I thought about telling Hal. Smiled, picturing the pride and excitement on his face.

Except it wouldn't be pride and excitement, would it. So I'm not telling him until I have to. I want to enjoy the time we have left, before my belly ruins everything.

Tom's right, it is hot, and the house smells like tuna casserole. I feel like I'm wrapped in a sweaty sock. I close the *Better Homes and Gardens* over the classifieds, and fan myself with it.

"Don't bend that magazine, Vera," Wanda says. "I have to give it back to Betty."

I sigh, and drop the magazine in my lap. I ought to go take a look at that place on Lincoln, but it's too hot to walk anywhere. Maybe I should take a nap. I'm always tired lately.

I can hear Hester and Petey arguing in the front yard. Tom stares at the ceiling, tapping his shoes together on the ottoman. A fly lands on my hand, then buzzes away. Flies can taste with their feet, according to Freddy. My fingertips stroke the arm of my chair, imagining the taste of wood. Imagining the taste of Hal's skin. It's Sunday—Hal gets back to town tonight. Not in time for supper, but he'll be under my window later. Skin ready for the tasting…

"This says there are more than ten million teenagers in the United States now," Wanda says, rattling her magazine.

"I believe it," Tom says, yawning. "Fellow they're hiring for Hal's job looks about fourteen."

Suddenly I'm wide awake. "What?"

"I'd be surprised if he's shaving yet," Tom says. "I don't know what they're thinking."

"No, I mean—is Hal changing jobs, or…?" I try not to grip the arms of my chair.

Tom grunts. "I didn't tell you? Hal gave notice—he's done, day after Labor Day. Found work closer to home. I don't blame him, it's a drive and a half."

I don't hear whatever he says after that. I mumble something about the kids, and go outside. Sit on the porch steps, trying not to throw up. Or cry. Whatever that feeling is, pushing up in my throat like a fist.

After a while, I go in and help Wanda put supper on the table. I feel like a paper doll—stand here, say this. Eat, wash the dishes, listen to *Jack Benny*, put the kids to bed. Inside my head it's like a radio, tuned to nothing and turned up loud.

Finally I say goodnight, shut my bedroom door, and cry until my eyes hurt. *Sleeping rooms for girls and ladies*—what a joke. I'm not some plucky career girl in a movie, ready to conquer the world. I'm just Vera Stinson, and I'm in love with Hal, and Hal's going to leave me.

Why didn't he tell me? Probably the same reason I won't tell him I'm pregnant.

If I am pregnant.

I am.

He would have told me, before he left. He will tell me.

But now I know. What am I supposed I do, beg him to stay? I know better than that. Even if he knew I was…

No. I won't try to take him away from May. I won't.

There's Hal's whistle. I stare stupidly at the window.

I'll have to pretend I don't know. I want these last few days. I want to store up every bit of love I can get, while I can get it.

Hal whistles again——two soft notes, high then low, like a bird calling my name. I scrub my face with a corner of the bedsheet, take a deep breath, and go to pry out the screen.

15

Vera

Hal kissed me, like always, as soon as I'd picked my way out of the bushes. Except it wasn't like always. His mouth felt nervous on mine, and his hands cradled my back like he was afraid I'd break. He must be thinking about leaving. I hoped he couldn't taste the tears on my face. Maybe my eyes wouldn't be so red by the time we got to Mrs. Moore's.

But we didn't go to Mrs. Moore's. Hal turned us left, toward the river. His hand was damp and cold in mine, and when I looked at him under a streetlamp, he was staring straight ahead, working his mouth like he was chewing a twig. Or trying to find words. He was going to tell me. I couldn't think of any way to stop him.

We stepped off the street, onto the rough grass and dirt of the riverbank. No moon tonight, just hazy stars, the last streetlamp casting long shadows across the grass. Hal led me to the bench by the big sycamore, and sat down beside me. The late-summer noise of bugs and frogs spread out over the wide darkness of the water.

I waited, holding Hal's hand, staring into the dark until my eyes could tell the blackness of the water from the blackness of the shore. The Ohio felt big, and old, and slow. Hal and I seemed small and young beside it. Somehow that eased my mind a little. I wasn't in any hurry to hear what Hal was going to say. I breathed in the riverbank smell—dead fish and mud. A cricket started chirping under the bench.

"Vera," Hal finally whispered.

"Mmm?" I kept my eyes on the river. A boat was coming around the upstream bend, just a shadow with a lantern on the bow. Probably back from checking trotlines.

"I—that is, May—" Hal said. "I told May about you. About us."

It was like a shock from an electric fence. I held myself still while my body went hot, then cold. Then I asked, "Well?" My voice felt strangled.

Hal sighed. "I never meant to hurt May."

I made a sound that might have been a laugh or a sob, and stood up. I walked around to the lamp-lit side of the sycamore, and stood picking at the tree's grey bark. Flakes broke off, showing the whiteness underneath, like a moon. A whippoor-will started calling, down past the boat ramp.

Hal got up and came to stand beside me. "Vera," he said, raising his voice over the whippoorwill's racket. "May wanted me to ask you something."

I bet she did, I thought. Did he think I wanted to hear this? Bad enough he was leaving. I was breathing fast, almost crying again. I blinked hard, and picked off another piece of bark, letting more moon shine out.

Hal tried to go on. "She...May...me and..." When I shifted my feet restlessly, he spoke all in a rush. "We want you to come live with us. I mean, be part of our family."

"What?" I stood stock-still for a second. I looked up at Hal, but his face was a ghostly blur. "Oh, good grief," I said, "I can't even *see* you." I grabbed his hand and pulled him toward the street.

It was eight uphill blocks to Mrs. Moore's, and we walked them fast. Neither of us spoke a word, but Hal's words rattled around inside my head until they were as meaningless as the whippoorwill's call. *Live with us, told May, family, whip-poor-WILL, whip-poor-WILL...*

I was panting when we got to Hal's room. I felt my way to the lamp on the bedside table and switched it on, squinting in the sudden light. The room looked like it always did. Iron bedstead, blue cotton blanket tucked in Army-tight. Dresser, chair, table. Tomorrow's shirt hanging on the back of the door. And Hal, with his hand still on the doorknob. Looking like Hal. Hal's brown eyes, Hal's dark curls and strong shoulders, Hal's soft lips. Hal's face, looking glad and hopeful and scared all at once, like he'd just asked me to marry him.

I wiped at the sweat on my forehead, and asked, "Now what were you saying?"

Hal's eyebrows crooked up, like two caterpillars peering at each other. "May and I want you to come live with us," he said quietly.

So I hadn't heard him wrong. But it still didn't make any sense. I frowned at him for a minute, then asked, "For how long?"

"Well, for good." His voice trembled.

"Hal...That's—" It was nonsense, was what it was. He might as well say *May and I want you to fly to the moon.* Or *whip-poorwill, whippoorwill.*

"I know," he said. "But Vera, honey..." The hope in his eyes won out over the scared, and he took a step toward me. "I don't want to leave you. I love you with all my heart."

The words sounded odd—like he'd said them before, except he hadn't. Not to me. I shivered, and paced from the bed to the table and back. I didn't want him to leave me either. But... "How soon do I need to make up my mind?"

Hal frowned a little, like that wasn't the question he was expecting. "Well, I...before I go home Friday? May'll want to get things ready... And I'll be going home for good, a week from Tuesday. I got on at the lumberyard in Whelan."

I felt dazed. "All right," I said. Hal opened his mouth, and I added quickly, "I'll think about it." His shoulders went down a little, but he nodded.

I could see Hal was disappointed when I said I wanted to go home. I was disappointed too. But I felt like I couldn't catch up with myself—as if part of me was still waiting for Hal to say he was leaving. I needed to think, even more than I needed Hal's arms around me.

Once I was out in the night, though, I didn't think. I just walked. My feet carried me home, but when I looked up at my window I couldn't bear the thought of being inside. I stepped back into the street and went on walking.

Walking alone, past midnight—Wanda would have a heart attack, if she knew. Of course, I'd walked home from Hal's dozens of nights now. But coming home from Hal's was just a walk from here to there, Adams to Vine to Howe. The night felt bigger without a destination.

I circled the neighborhood over and over, waking up dogs and tripping on curbs in the dark. After a while I started to go over what Hal had said. It seemed to need a lot of going over.

Finally, coming along the riverbank again, I realized I was stumbling with tiredness. I dragged myself over to the big sycamore, and flopped down on the bench.

I've been sitting here awhile—long enough for my feet to quit throbbing. Long enough to think about the axe murderers Wanda worries about, and to decide that there probably isn't one in those bushes.

A tugboat chugs slowly upstream, pushing a barge. Its red lights and yellow windows make wet, wobbly stripes in the river.

I keep thinking of Sybil. How happy she was when she married Bob. I picture the two of them walking together—is there a riverfront in Denver?—both pushing strollers, the little boy walking in between. That's all I want. Love, happiness, a family.

Come live with us... Part of our family... I guess Hal did ask me to marry him. Sort of. And it's a little late to get picky about morals. But it's easier to picture Sybil and Bob walking with kids I've never met in a town I've never seen, than to imagine myself in Hal and May's family. A farmhouse, white or grey, chickens out back, a garden. Me in the kitchen, making breakfast. Hal coming in and kissing me—that is what he meant, isn't it? What else could he mean? May...

I can't picture May at all. She could be seven feet tall with blue hair, for all I know. Why on earth would she come up with this? She can't mean it. But if she didn't mean it, then why would Hal ask me?

The whippoorwill isn't singing anymore, and the bugs and frogs have mostly gone to sleep. I can hear the little ripples at the water's edge, like fingers playing with bathwater. I catch my head nodding, and rub my eyes, making the lights across the river blur and streak. I don't want to go home to bed, with everything upside-down and backwards like this. But I've got enough worries, without a policeman finding me asleep on a park bench.

16

May

Iva always kept Katy for me on wash day. I'd get twice as much done without a child underfoot, and they both loved their "Mammaw Mondays." Usually I stayed for a cup of coffee when I walked Katy over in the morning, but today I kept feeling like I'd forgotten something at home—left a burner on, maybe—so I hurried back.

I got home hot and breathless, but everything was as it should be. I shook my head, and dipped a drink from the water bucket. I was on edge, that was all. I wouldn't find out what Vera said until Friday—if I kept fretting like this all week, I'd wear myself to a frazzle.

The thing to do was get to work. I gathered the clothes and sheets from our bedroom into a pile, then went upstairs and got Katy's things. I hesitated by the cedar chest in the upstairs hallway. Should I go ahead and wash the spare-room sheets? It'd be a waste of time, if Vera didn't end up coming. But it might rain next Monday... I realized I was clutching Katy's laundry tight against my belly. *For Pete's sake, May. It's just sheets.*

I opened the cedar chest and knelt down to dig through the layers of quilts. The sheets were on the very bottom, creased hard from being folded so long. They weren't too musty, but the sweet, dry smell of red cedar was overpowering. I liked my sheets to smell like sunshine—even with Hal gone, I washed and ironed them every week.

Suddenly I was breathing hard, my hands clenched on the smooth cotton. It wasn't just sheets. All this year I'd been sleeping lonely, counting the days till Hal would come home. Meanwhile Hal couldn't wait for me a few more—weeks? Months? When did it start? What was he *thinking?* I flung the folded sheets back into the chest and slammed the lid.

Out in the washhouse, I sorted the wash into piles, my hands moving fast and jerky. I didn't want to be crying. I didn't want to be mad. *Work, May.* I blew my nose on a dirty undershirt. *Just work.* I hauled the big kettle of hot water from the porch stove. Soap flakes from the blue box, cold water from the yard pump. I shoved the white things down into the soap suds, and watched the agitator turn and back. A pillowcase full of air kept bobbing to the top, but I jabbed at it with the laundry paddle until it stayed under. There was plenty of extra room in the machine—I'd washed all of Hal's white T-shirts on Saturday, so he'd have them for work. I blew out a loud breath, and stomped off to get the spare sheets.

Then five more trips to the pump, filling the rinse tubs. The weight of the buckets pulled through my shoulders, pressed my bare feet hard to the ground. I could feel myself calming down as I pumped and carried and poured, slopping cold well water on my dress. It was a relief. I'd never been that mad at Hal before. I hadn't thought I could get that mad at anybody but Mom.

I thought about Mom as I fed the warm, soapy sheets through the wringer. I wasn't mad at her when I was little. Just scared. Seemed like I got in trouble every day, but I never got used to it—I'd be bawling before her willow switch touched me. I swore before I was ten that I'd never switch my own kids, or slap them around. I didn't want my children scared of me.

Things changed the year I turned thirteen—the year Sissy was born, and Mom got born-again. We'd always been Christians, of course, but Mom came home from that revival a whole different kind of Christian. According to the preacher at Mount Zion, anybody that wasn't saved-and-sanctified Holiness might as well be a Devil-worshipping heathen. I hated that church. After a while, Daddy said I could stay home on Sundays, with him and Jamie.

From then on, I didn't even have to misbehave. Mom woke up in the morning already mad at me. It wasn't fair. Pretty soon I quit bawling and started fighting—arguing, smarting off, yelling. Jamie said that only made things worse. Easy for him to talk—he wasn't stuck in the house with Mom all day.

By the summer I was sixteen, it seemed like Mom and I fought all the time. We'd simmer down when Daddy was around, but as soon as he was gone it'd all boil over, me screaming at Mom, her slapping me again and again. She had to reach up to slap me now—I was a head taller, and could have knocked her down, but I didn't dare. I turned my cheeks' burning into rage, yelling things that hurt my throat.

Then one day Daddy came in early for dinner, and we didn't hear him. When he coughed to get our attention, we both swung around and stood staring at him, breathing hard. Mom's face was red, and one of her blond braids had come down. Daddy looked at us. He looked at Sissy, crying under the kitchen table. Then, with a nod at Mom, he took my arm and marched me out of the house.

We walked, fast. Daddy let go of my arm once he saw I was coming along. I wanted to explain, but it was all I could do to keep up with his long legs. I half-ran beside him, out Shaw Ridge Road to Barkworks, almost to Covert Road. Then back, past the house, to the woodlot where he'd been working. He sat down on a log. I sat too, trying not to pant too loud. My bare feet throbbed from the gravel.

Daddy spit a stream of brown tobacco juice on the ground, and kicked sawdust over it with the toe of his boot. Then he shook his head. "I sure hated to see that, Maydie."

I hadn't thought my cheeks could get any hotter. I'd been calling Mom a red-faced sow, a mean old witch... Daddy had heard all that. He'd seen her slapping me. I scowled so I wouldn't cry. "I'm sorry, Daddy," I said, "But I can't help it, she makes me so mad!"

"Mmm," Daddy said. "You mad now?"

I thought about it. I was breathing hard, but that was from walking. "Not like I was. But——"

"Hard to run two miles and stay mad at the same time?" Daddy smiled, and I relaxed a little. Maybe he wasn't too disappointed.

Then he pointed his finger at me, with his thumb cocked up like a pretend pistol. "Pay attention now, Maydie," he said. "Here's what you're going to do. From now on, your mother tells you to do something, I want you to do it. If you get mad, take a walk—or split you some firewood, or shovel manure. Whatever you need to do, till you get ahold of yourself. We ain't going to have any more of this screaming and meanness."

I felt my shoulders slump. He thought Mom and I argued about *chores?* Well, sometimes we did, but… "She says I've got the Devil in me! She tells me I'm going to Hell! All the time!" My voice squeaked, and I swallowed down tears.

Daddy nodded, and spit again. He watched a little woodpecker hop up the side of a sassafrass. Then he said, "Well, Maydie. I wouldn't worry about that. People say a lot of things. You make your own peace with the Lord, you'll do all right."

He still didn't understand. I kicked at a stick on the ground, scaring the woodpecker away. "But she's after me and *after* me about it, Daddy! And it's not just saying things——" I stopped. He'd seen Mom slapping me. I was embarrassed to say how she'd cornered me last week and switched me like a little kid. He must've seen the welts on my legs. Maybe he thought I deserved them. I twisted my hands in my apron.

Daddy sat quiet, long enough for the woodpecker to come back. I listened to it tapping at the dry bark. Finally he said, "Your mother's had a hard row to hoe, Maydie, and she ain't strong. If her faith helps her get through, it ain't your place or mine to judge."

I interrupted him. "She makes it her place to judge *me!*"

Daddy let out a tired sigh. "Well, I don't know what to tell you. I imagine she just wants to keep you out of trouble. Try and see it her way."

I picked a burr off my skirt, and didn't answer. I didn't want to see it Mom's way. I wanted Daddy to see it my way.

But when Daddy put his long arm around me, I leaned against him. It was better to just feel the damp cotton of his work shirt on my cheek, breathe in the sweat-and-cows smell of him, than to argue. I wondered if Mom really was trying to keep me out of trouble. She slapped me for smarting off, mostly. This morning she'd been after me about chewing gum, which her preacher said was a sin, and I'd said I didn't think Jesus went around looking in people's mouths for gum. She'd slapped me hard and fast, like she could smack the words away before God heard them. Like she was scared.

After a while, Daddy squeezed my shoulder. "It'll be all right, Maydie. Just try keeping your mouth on a short lead. You can't find anything nice to say, say 'Yes Ma'am.' Okay?"

I sighed. "Okay."

And I did. I said "Yes, Ma'am," over and over, day after day. When I got too mad, I took it out on a pile of firewood. Jamie liked that—he'd never much cared for splitting wood. And it did help. Mom still preached and glared, but she didn't hit me as much. After a while, she quit hitting me at all. Sissy didn't hide under the table anymore. She went to church with Mom, and didn't cause trouble. I made cornshuck dolls for her, and taught her to read before she started school, and I never hit her once.

I wrung the whites out of the second rinsetub into the laundry basket, and carried them out to the clothesline. I hadn't ever hit Katy, either, more than a swat on the behind to get her attention. I thought of her chattering to me on the way to Iva's this morning, and smiled a little. Katy wasn't scared of me.

I untwisted the thick white ropes of the sheets and hung them to dry. The cool, wet cotton slapped gently at my face and arms. I'd had a letter from Sissy, at the end of last week.

I'd meant to answer it Saturday, but I'd forgotten. A lot had happened... I sighed, and shook out an undershirt. I didn't feel mad anymore. Daddy's advice was still good.

17

May

Dear Sissy,

I wondered if Sissy minded me still calling her that. By the time I was twelve, I'd hated for anybody to call me Maydie. Of course Jamie wouldn't stop, so I'd made sure never to call him James, either. But with a name like Providence, Sissy might not feel the same way.

I hadn't seen Sissy since she was nine. I felt bad about it, but visiting her would've meant visiting Mom. Three years ago Sissy was still a cute little girl, with blond pigtails and a smile like a sunny day. She wore long skirts, long sleeves, and stockings, even in the summertime. Mom had tried to make me do the same, until Grandma Stout heard us arguing about it. "Oh, Pearl, for land's sakes," she'd said, "May's just picking tomatoes —it's not as if she's out flinging herself at the neighbor boy!" Mom had pressed her mouth tight shut at that, and didn't mention it again.

I sighed and looked at my letter. "Dear Sissy" wasn't much of a start. It'd be nice to get this finished up while Katy was at Iva's. I took Sissy's last letter out of my stationery box and read it over. She'd been helping in Sunday School. They'd put up peaches. Aunt Ciceline got a brand new Bendix washing machine with no wringer, that used all new water every load— Mom said it was wasteful, but Sissy liked it. Mort Ackerman, the preacher's youngest boy, bought her a dish of ice cream at the church picnic. Mom had a sick headache Sunday evening, and Aunt Ciceline said she had her braids pinned too tight.

The last line was always the same. "Give my love to Hal and little Katy. Mom and I pray for you all every night." I rolled my eyes, and picked up my pen.

> Sorry my letter's so late. Our weekend got busy. How is everything? We're fine here.
> It sounds like you're ahead of me on peaches. I'm going to pick at Mr. Ferry's tomorrow. Altha Combs will come over to help me can them Thurs.—it wouldn't seem right to do peaches without her. You remember Altha, Grandma Stout's cousin? The one with the orange-slice candies?

That's probably what Sissy would remember. I remembered Altha's stories. Mom said her talk was gossip and irreverent babble, but I thought she was better than the radio.

I could feel Mom reading over my shoulder as I wrote, watching for a bad influence. I wondered if she knew that Sissy was sweet on the preacher's boy. Best not mention it.

> Katy's doing fine, talking more every day. She learned "bean" this week, and "worm" when she helped me pick tobacco worms—she loved that! Hal's due home for good on the 7th. (That's 9 days—not that I'm counting!) Bess is pining for him. She never gives as much milk for me.
> I got the crabapples picked and jelly made today, after the wash. I might get the fall garden thinned and weeded too, while Iva has Katy. (Iva makes supper for us on wash days, too—I feel

*like I'm on vacation!) I've got turnips, carrots, collard greens, and
cabbage up and looking good.*

What else could I say? I couldn't tell Sissy about Hal and
Vera, and it was hard to remember what had happened before
all that. I wrote a few lines about Jamie's family, and copied
down the recipe for Grace's banana cake. Sissy always loved to
bake.

When I was done, I read my letter over for anything that
might upset Mom. It was fine. More than fine—it sounded
normal. You'd never guess that everything was up in the air, or
that I'd been in a rage at Hal this morning. "Keep it short,
keep it cheerful!"—like the posters said during the war.

I'd been good at making things sound normal back then,
too, in my letters to Jamie and Hal. At first it wasn't hard.
When Jamie enlisted, I'd taken over his farm work and left
Sissy to help in the house. It was like getting out of a prison.
Daddy was strong and quiet, and never lost his temper when I
made a mistake. I missed Hal and Jamie, and I worried about
them, but I was happier than I'd ever been.

When Grandma Stout took sick, that second summer of the
war, Daddy got even quieter. I hadn't thought much about
Grandma Stout being his mother, before that. Weeks after she
died, I looked up from hoeing cabbages and saw tears running
down Daddy's face. When he saw me looking, he said, "We just
keep on, Maydie. It'll get better, by and by."

That was the last thing Daddy ever said to me. He had his
first stroke that afternoon, another the next morning. He spent
the last few months of his life helpless in bed, with Mom tending him and praying over him day and night. It took the Army
forever to send Jamie home on compassionate leave—we never
found out why. Meanwhile, Sissy and I managed the house and
the garden, tended the stock and dug the potatoes and canned
the winter's food. The neighbors helped us get the corn in. I
worked until I was falling down with tiredness, but it didn't
make anything right. Jamie stayed gone, Hal stayed gone,
Daddy stayed almost gone. And there was Mom. After Daddy's

strokes, I never did anything right in Mom's eyes again. I didn't want it to hurt, but it did.

One cold night I gave up on "short and cheerful." I sat up late writing to Jamie, and poured my heart out. I had to tell somebody. Sissy was still a kid, and Grace never did understand about Mom and me. Neither did Hal. Jamie knew Mom. *She won't even let me speak to Daddy now*, I wrote.

> *She says my soul's black with sin and I'll keep him from coming to Jesus. She needs me to lift him, but she says if I don't mind her she'll hire a boy from church. She sets Sissy to pray over him, the few hours she sleeps. I sneak in then and talk to him. Sissy's scared to death Mom'll find out. I don't know what to do, Jamie. She hates me. I feel like I'm liable to kill her.*

I paused, then carefully erased "kill her," and put "go crazy" instead.

When I was done, I sat looking at my letter. Six V-Mail sheets of tiny pencilled misery, spread out across the kitchen table in the lamplight.

Jamie's letters home were addressed to all of us. He talked about lousy food, pretty sunsets, a dog that looked just like his old Whitey. Once he said he'd just gotten a dozen of our letters, all at once. *I don't know why the mail couldn't find us*, he wrote. *—The Germans knew right where we were!*

I thought about the newsreel I'd seen after Christmas, when I went in town shopping. Guns and smoke and fire. Tired, grimy faces under helmets, dead soldiers crumpled in the snow. I thought of Mom's hard eyes and mean mouth, Daddy's big hands lying idle. I measured that against the Germans knowing right where Jamie was. Then I gathered up my pages and put them in the stove.

Monday supper always felt like a luxury, eating food I didn't have to cook. Iva smiled as she passed me the ham. "Nothing like wash day to make a woman eat like a man."

I took a slice with my fork, and passed the plate to Rye. "Oh, it's not bad," I said. "Three people's wash—with the electric washer, it's hardly even work."

Rye pursed his lips at me. "That electric-washer get your electric good and clean?"

"Mm-hm." I nodded, keeping a straight face. "Nothing like clean electric. Hard to iron, though."

Iva snorted at us. "You two are about as bad... Anyway, May, I bet you did more than the wash, and you probably didn't eat any dinner."

"I had a tomato sandwich at noon," I protested.

"Hm," Iva said. "I don't call that dinner."

Katy stuffed a handful of mashed potato in her mouth. "Here, hon, use your spoon," I told her. "You're hungry too—did you work hard today?"

"Oh, we had a big time," Iva said. "Tell Mommy what we did!"

Katy swallowed the potato, and bounced in her seat. "I eat worm!" She giggled.

Iva laughed. "Oh, Katy, you devil. You didn't eat any worms."

"I eated worm, *and* bugs. And...a *car!*" Katy grinned. "Num-num!"

"Yum-yum," I agreed, cutting up a slice of tomato on her plate.

"You want some sugar on that tomato, Mixie Mouse?" Rye asked Katy.

I answered for her. "No thanks, PopPop."

Rye took a bite of his tomato. Sugar crunched in his teeth. "My granddaddy swore tomatoes were poison unless you put sugar on them."

"We know." Iva gave him a dry look. "I guess that's why we're all dead in our graves."

Rye winked at her. "I didn't say he was right."

With Katy settled, I started in on my own plate. Iva's food was always good. Rye managed to eat his share while he told us some scheme he'd heard about with aluminum poultry houses.

I half-listened. I was thinking how lucky I'd been, marrying into Hal's family. Rye had the same kind twinkle in his eyes that Daddy had. And Iva reminded me more of Grandma Stout than of Mom. Grandma Stout was older, of course, and taller too, but they were both on the heavy side—and both of them had a way of taking charge. Iva smiled more.

She was smiling now, as we finished up our meal. "Katy helped me make a lemon cake, too," she said. "Should we have it now, or later?"

"Ooh, I don't have room yet," I said. "And Katy's still working on her green beans."

Rye leaned back in his chair and patted his flat stomach. "I'll have some now," he said, "And then I'll have some later, to keep you gals company."

"You might think you will!" Iva raised an eyebrow at him. "I didn't see *you* doing any wash today."

"I raked the hay, and split a cord of firewood," Rye said, looking injured.

"Hm," Iva said. "Well, all right. I don't know where you put it all, though." She cut a thin wedge from the cake on the counter, and passed it to Rye. I could smell the lemon. "You can have a bigger one when we all have some."

Rye grinned at her. "Yes, *Ma'am!*"

18

Vera

The house is quiet. Tom at work, Wanda at her Ladies of the Beautiful Ohio meeting, the kids outside. The electric fan roars softly, stirring the thick air. Out in the hydrangeas, a cardinal chirps the same note over and over.

The train for Flora's dress spills off my lap onto the living-room floor, where I've spread a sheet to keep the white satin clean. I've got about a mile of rolled hems to do. Tedious, but it's a nice change from hunching over my machine. I can sit back in the rocker, and listen to the quiet.

I roll the satin under my left thumb and slipstitch my way along, thinking. I've been thinking ever since Sunday night. Yesterday I was thinking so hard, I put Wanda's *Ladies' Home Journal* in the dishtowel drawer, and almost started a fire broiling bacon-and-cheese sandwiches.

How am I supposed to make a decision like this? I've never decided anything in my life. That's not true—I decide how much to charge for a dress, and whether I need a new iron, and how many yards of fabric to buy. But that's just arithmetic. The only time I ever decided anything big was when I started my sewing business after the war. That was obvious—all the factories wanted men, and I couldn't type.

How does anybody make up their mind? About marriage, say—some fellow asks you, and you have to say yes or no. It seems like that ought to be just as obvious. Anybody could see Sybil and Bob belonged together. It was obvious for Francine, too, when she turned up pregnant.

And there's that. Should I tell Hal, now? I can't even decide that much.

I don't know about the other girls—Nancy, or Deedee, or Velma. They just turned up engaged one day, and we all started talking about the wedding.

Sue and Francine and I still talk about weddings. Somebody's always getting married. A few weeks ago Francine was telling us how Patty Newlin spent her whole ceremony falling out of her strapless gown—she demonstrated with her hands, in case we didn't understand which part was falling out.

Sue glanced around. "For heaven's sake, stop it!" she whispered through her giggles.

"It's okay," I told her, poking a straw into my double-chocolate malt. "I'm a seamstress—they'll think we're discussing a fitting problem."

Francine shook her head. "The preacher was about to faint! I would've caught him, too—he's a doll."

Sue looked scandalized. "Francine! He's a preacher!"

"Nothing wrong with a handsome preacher," Francine said. "Gives the congregation something to look at."

"This is the one that did Nancy's wedding?" I asked. When Francine nodded, I made a face. "He prays like he's reading a bus schedule."

Sue raised her eyebrows. "You like them to jump around and yell?"

"No," I said, "But—"

"You ought to hear my grandma's preacher, down south!" Francine waved her spoon at us. "He'll go along praying, reeeeal quiet and slow…and then—*JE-sus!*"—she shouted it and slapped the table, forgetting the spoon in her hand. "The whole congregation jumps just like that, too—especially the ones that were asleep! Sorry." She handed Sue a napkin.

Sue dabbed at the root beer on her sleeve. "What were you saying, Vera? About praying?"

I shrugged. "Oh, I guess I got spoiled, back home. Our preacher didn't make a big scene or anything, but when he prayed, you'd swear God was right there in the room, hanging on every word." I smiled, remembering Pastor Locke's gentle voice. He always asked God to take care of people by name.

Sue nodded thoughtfully, but Francine's eyes were bugging out. "Jeepers creepers, Vera, you're going to drag *God* to your wedding?"

Sue giggled. "Oh my—I wonder what he'll wear?"

"Probably not a strapless gown," I said, and Francine laughed so hard she had to run to the bathroom.

I trim another section of edge smooth, and pull the white satin taut. Three-quarters of a mile to go. I guess it doesn't matter what kind of preacher I want, now. A wedding isn't exactly in the cards, whatever I decide.

Hal and I belong together, as sure as Sybil and Bob do. And then I've got Francine's reason too. If it were that simple, I'd have said yes before the words were out of Hal's mouth.

But it's not that simple. And for all my thinking, I still don't have the slightest idea what I'm going to do.

19

Hal

God, just looking at Vera gives me goose-bumps. Sitting there in my straight-back chair, one brown curl sticking out above her ear. I love when a woman's hair is a little mussed up. I kneel down behind her, kiss the back of her neck. Reach around to feel her nipples standing up hard through her clothes.

She pulls away like she's got something on her mind. "What kind of person is May?"

"Mmmm..." I scoot around in front of her, start on her dress buttons. Trace the edge of her brassiere, watch her skin flush pink. Her nipples aren't the only thing standing up. I lean in against her stockinged legs.

Vera tucks her legs under the chair. "*Hal.* If I'm going to... I need to know some things." Her mouth looks soft, but her eyes are all business.

I sigh. Rest my forehead on her lap a minute, trying to shift gears. I haven't asked her if she's made up her mind. Figured she'd let me know. But I guess she needs to talk about it some.

I get up. Sit on the bed, pat the blanket beside me. "Bed's softer." She comes over, sits. I put my arm around her. "All right, shoot."

"May," she says. "Tell me about her."

"Hmm…" I shut my eyes, let myself see May. Wiping Katy's face, stirring something in a bowl. Her mouth open wide when I'm loving her, like she's fixing to sing. *May's beautiful.* I can't say that. *Kissing her feels like coming home. She smells like this one cedar tree always smells when it rains…*

Vera picks up my hand, taps a finger across the calluses on my palm. Goose-bumps. I clear my throat. "Well, I don't know," I say. "Brown hair, brown eyes. Bigger than you—not fat, just built big…"

She sighs. "No—I mean, okay, but…what does she *think* about?"

"Well, I…" Yesterday evening when it was time for me to go, May asked if I was ready, and I said just about. She said she had me a supper packed. Stood there looking at me, twisting a dishtowel in her hands. I didn't know what she was thinking about. Still don't.

"Sorry." Vera laughs a little, bumps me with her shoulder. "Silly question."

Still, I want to do better by May than that. I squeeze Vera's hand. "One thing is, you can count on May. May doesn't let you down."

Vera peers up into my eyes like she can see May there. Her breath brushes my cheek. "How'd you meet her?"

"Um, well, we grew up together," I say. "Same school. You know, it's awful hard to think, with this pretty girl snuggled up against me…"

Vera giggles, swings her legs across my lap. Her skirt rucks up to the tops of her stockings, and she leaves it there.

This time when I kiss her, she doesn't act like there's anything else on her mind.

20

Vera

"Higher!" Petey yells. "As high as Freddy!" I give his swing a big push, and his giggle rises almost to a shriek.

Freddy's swinging standing up. He waves at Petey, showing off, and grabs the chain again quick. Hester ignores both of them, pumping her own swing like it's serious business. She does most things that way.

My dress is damp with sweat, despite the shade of the park's big hickories. I ought to be home finishing Flora's train, with a cold glass of lemonade and the fan on high, but Petey begged me to come to the park. He says Hester won't push his swing anymore, now that he's four. Besides, Wanda has a headache, and she's been crabby all day.

"Stick your feet out in front, Petey," I tell him. "And now tuck them under——" He tries, but his timing's all wrong. I laugh. Then my eyes tear up suddenly. If I go with Hal, who'll push Petey's swing?

"Watch this!" Freddy's sitting on his swing now, with the chains all twisted up. He picks up his feet, and spins into a blur of red hair and green shirt. I can't remember when I last saw Freddy use a swing the right way. I shake my head as I get out my hanky. I'm being silly. Petey's got a big brother and a big sister. Hester will have him pumping his own swing by the end of the year—and then Freddy'll teach him how to jump off it and break his arm.

Anyway, I still don't know if I'm leaving at all. I keep noticing *what* I'll be leaving. Wanda's crabbiness, yes, but there are the kids, too. I made those suspender-shorts Petey's wearing—for Freddy, when *he* was four. Hester knows all my bedtime stories by heart. And then of course there's Tom. And Sue, and Francine.

I thought it might help to know more about May, so I could picture myself living in her house, and hold that up beside my life here. But Hal wasn't much help.

I can't even imagine what May must be like, to come up with an idea like this. I kind of want to meet her. That's hardly a reason, though.

Maybe I'm doing this all wrong. I keep trying to add up the two choices and see which one is more, but that's not what I need to know. I need to know what I want.

Now Freddy's standing by his swing, twisting it up with his hands and arguing with Hester. "*Bruce-Gentry-Daredevil-of-the-Skies* is *not* dumb!" he yells, as her swing flies past. "You haven't even seen it!"

"Did too—I went with Rita." Hester tosses her head to get the hair out of her eyes. "It didn't make any sense."

Freddy throws the swing hard away from him. "*You* don't make any sense, *Pester!*" The swing comes back faster than he expected, bucking and spinning. He ducks, and Hester laughs. I give Petey another push.

What do I want? I want Hal, mainly. And I want a home. Not Wanda's home, and not some run-down boardinghouse full of drunks. I don't want to be the talk of the town, with a big belly and no husband. But I don't want to leave these kids, either. And I don't want to end up in some kind of awful scene with May. But I don't want to be lonely...

That's all about what I *don't* want.

Hester's humming something under her breath, in rhythm with her swinging. When I was a kid and couldn't decide something, I used to do eeny-meeny-miney-mo.

I mouth the words, giving Petey a push with every line. When he swings away, that's "Go," and when he comes back it's "Stay." The last word falls on "Stay."

And it's just like when I was a kid—as soon as the rhyme tells me what to do, I know what I really want.

21

May

I thought I'd worked off my mad on Monday, but it kept coming back. I'd find myself glaring at nothing, or on the verge of tears over some ordinary stubbornness of Katy's. I worked harder as the week went on, feeling desperate—if this crazy plan of mine was going to have any chance at all, I had to get ahold of myself, and *keep* ahold. Tuesday afternoon, after the ironing, I made bread-and-butter pickles. Wednesday I picked and canned another batch of beans and fourteen quarts of tomatoes, made a yellow cake, and washed the kitchen windows.

It was hard to keep my mind on mustard seed or canning lids or flyspecks, knowing that over in Cartersboro, Vera was deciding whether to come home with Hal. Deciding what my family would look like, a week from now. Vera probably thought I was out of my mind. My face went hot with embarrassment, then with anger. Who was Vera to judge me?

And then I'd stop myself—back up from that thought like it was a rotten floorboard, go another way. Check on my canning kettle, feed the pigs, do the evening milking. An hour later I'd think something else—like where was Hal going to sleep, if Vera did come—and have to back up again.

Katy played under the kitchen table, and got fussy when she was tired, and tried to "help" with the chores. When I had the patience to let her, she did help, in her way—she made me smile, the way she concentrated on breaking a bean or folding a handkerchief.

By Wednesday evening, I felt like I was getting myself together. It was like pushing dirty laundry down in the washer—things always floated back up, but if you kept at it, they'd stay under eventually.

Thursday morning I put Katy in the truck still half-asleep, and went to pick up Altha Combs. Altha was waiting in her porch rocker, with her black pocketbook in her lap and an old white-oak basket by her feet. She always met me outside, these days. Her house was a mess—she couldn't keep up with it since her arthritis got bad, and she wouldn't let anybody help her. Mice had gotten into the clutter she'd always had—worn-out shoes, saved newspapers going back to the thirties—and laid their pissy smell over the stale odor of the little dogs she used to keep. I'd wanted a house dog like Altha's, when I was a kid, but Mom said it was filthy to have a dog in the house.

"Morning!" Altha called, in her creaky, cheerful voice. "Let's get cracking—ripe peaches won't wait!" She waved away my offer of help on the steps, handing me her basket so she could get both hands on the railing.

I swung the basket away as Katy leaned from my hip to grab at it. "Woops, Katy, you don't need that!"

Altha made wide eyes at Katy as she eased her way off the last step. "Oh, mercy me!" she exclaimed. "That's Katy? Why, I thought Katy was a baby! This is a great *big* girl!" Katy buried her grin in my shoulder, watching sidelong as Altha snapped open her pocketbook and peered inside. "Let's see, seems like I had something in here for a big girl… Here!" She pulled out a wax-paper package of bright orange-slice candies. I smiled. Some things never changed.

I helped Altha into the truck—she was as bony and light as a sparrow—and we drove towards home, with Katy chewing a mouthful of sticky orange candy like a wad of tobacco.

Altha rolled up her window partway as I speeded up on Chambers Pike. "I sure do appreciate you letting me do peaches with you," she called, over the rush of the wind. "Reminds me of old times."

I nodded. "I was just writing to Sissy the other day, that it wouldn't feel right to put up peaches without you."

Altha laughed. "How old's Sissy getting to be?"

"Twelve, going on thirteen," I said.

"My lands!" Altha said. "Time just flies by! Seems like yesterday she was Katy's size."

Altha could probably say the same about me. She'd known me all my life. I'd helped her and Grandma Stout with peaches every summer, once I was big enough. During the Depression, Mr. Ferry let his neighbors pick the peaches he couldn't sell, and Grandma Stout and Altha worked together to put up peach halves, peach butter, dried peaches, peach preserves… No matter how hard times got, we always had peaches to eat.

Back home, Altha unpacked her basket on the porch table. She always brought her cherry rolling pin, and her own paring knife, its black blade worn to a crescent. She tied on her apron, and settled into the rocker I'd carried out for her. "I don't know what I brought that knife for," she said. "I can't hardly take hold of a knife anymore." She rubbed one crooked hand with the other. "This old arthritis is just terrible, May. I've still got most of my mind, and my heart keeps thumping away like I was your age—but here I sit, with hands that won't grab and knees that won't push. Can't even cut up a peach!"

I checked the water I'd left heating. "I don't know how you manage. Did you ever try that cayenne-pepper salve Peck was talking up?"

"Well, now, I did, and it worked a sight better than aspirin—but you go to rub your eyes, you'll be sorry!" Altha grinned. "It does help me sleep. I just wish I could be more of a help to you."

"You keep half an eye on Katy, that'll be plenty of help," I said, tying on my own apron. "And you can wipe jars, and test the preserves. I'll keep you busy."

"I can pack, too, when you're ready," Altha said. She winked at Katy, who was still clinging shyly to my skirt. "And save me out some nice halves for pies."

"Mmm!" I said. Altha's famous peach pie had perfect peach halves laid into a creamy custard, cut-side up so their red middles showed like flowers. Grandma Stout had tried and failed to imitate that pie. Altha wouldn't give her the recipe. She called it a family secret, and when Grandma Stout pointed out that she *was* family—they were cousins, twice removed—Altha said the secret was on her father's side. It was the only time I ever heard them argue.

Altha leaned back and started her chair rocking. Her wispy white hair was braided and pinned up like always. Under her apron, she had on the same faded flour-sack dress she'd worn in '44, the last time she did peaches with Grandma Stout. Her feet left the floor every time the chair rocked back, and her toe reached for the floorboards at just the right moment on the way down. She'd rocked Daddy in that chair when he was a baby, back in Kentucky. "Altha was born to comfort babies," Grandma Stout had told me once. "It's a shame she never had any of her own."

"Dreaming?" Altha asked me.

"I guess. Better get to work." I got busy, putting jars in to scald and bringing things out from the kitchen, while Altha chatted with Katy.

When I scooped my first half-dozen blanched peaches out of the hot water into the cold, and set the dishpan on the table to peel them, Altha gave a little nod. I knew that nod—it meant we were all settled in now, and Altha Combs was ready to talk.

"Well, May," she began, "I guess you heard about Roger Sims."

"Didn't he pass away?" I asked, slipping the rosy skin off a golden peach.

Altha nodded. "Three weeks back." She didn't mind that I'd heard the news already—she knew what Roger Sims had died *of.* She knew how long Lizzie Harp was in labor with her twins, too, and what her mother-in-law said about it. I felt my shoulders relax a little as Altha warmed up. I'd been a little worried she'd start asking questions—Altha had a nose for secrets. But now she'd hit her stride. Her familiar voice blended with the soft rattle of simmering water and the buzz-tap of yellowjackets against the porch screen. Now and then she stopped to chat with Katy, who was sticky with peach juice and orange candy.

By the time we started packing the peach halves, Altha was past the ordinary news and well into the juicy stuff. She listened in on every call that came over the party line, and traded gossip with friends all over—if somebody was up to no good anywhere in Knobs County, Altha was the first to know. As her gnarled fingers settled peach halves pretty-side-out in the jars, she told me whose husbands had run off, and why they'd fired that schoolteacher over to Marlin, and whose wife had been seen in Madison wearing red lipstick and shoes to match.

Katy trotted back and forth between the porch and the yard, grabbing handfuls of the peach trimmings I was saving for preserves. She didn't seem to be paying any attention. Probably just as well, though Altha's gossip today wasn't any racier than what I used to hear her tell, when I was Katy's age.

Today, though, Altha's talk was getting to me. I kept thinking, surely people had enough trouble, without other people holding it up to gloat over. I tried not to listen, but that was impossible—Altha told stories like nobody else.

Now she was talking about how fast Rachel Perry got engaged to Walt Adams after Jim Perry flipped his tractor. "Jim wasn't even cold in the ground!" she chuckled, then turned serious. "Served him right, too. Jim Perry was mean as a snake —no woman ever ended up in the hospital that much by accident. It's no wonder, either, his daddy was just as bad... Rachel should've known better than to marry him in the first place. Folks tried to tell her." Altha paused, pursing her lips. "I wouldn't be surprised, though, if that baby she's carrying turns up with red hair." Walt was the redhead—all the Perrys were dark.

I watched my knife circling a peeled peach, my thumbs easing open the fruit, juice dribbling into the white enamel pan. Hal was a good husband. That was why I was trying to keep him. But what would Altha say, if she knew my plans? *Should've known better. Serves her right, too...* My stomach gurgled around the peaches I'd been nibbling on.

"Did you hear about that Bryson over by Rayburn?" Altha said. She was back in her rocker now, jabbing the floor with her toe to keep it moving. "They say he came home from work one day, and his wife and three kids were just *gone!* No note or anything. They searched the whole place, stuck a pole down the cistern. Not a sign of them. Food still on the table, clothes in the closets. I guess he went crazy. They had to put him in that place down to Madison."

"My, that's terrible," I said, shaking my head. Altha nodded in agreement, and leaned up to steal a scrap of peach from my preserves bowl.

"Now, *Macon* Bryson," she said, licking her fingers, "Howard's boy—you knew he was in jail?"

I'd never thought about it before, but Altha never told stories about happy people with decent lives. Evidently, to make a good story somebody had to be miserable. Or do something unheard-of. I went into the kitchen for more jars, and stood for a minute in the breeze from the fan. Surely Altha wouldn't just toss *my* troubles onto her gossip fire and fan the flames. Would she? Of course, if Vera came, people would have to know. Even if we kept it quiet, she was bound to turn up pregnant eventually...

I felt my breath coming fast, and shook my head sharply. That was one of those rotten floorboards. I picked up my crate of jars, then set it back down. It was getting hot out—time for that cake I'd saved in the refrigerator. Cold yellow cake was almost as good as ice cream, on a hot day.

When I got back to the porch, Altha was telling Katy about a little girl who didn't listen to her mother. I handed them each a bowl of cake with sugared peaches on top, and leaned against a porch post to eat mine. The first batch of canned peaches sat steaming on the table like jars of sunshine, and the canner lid rattled in the sudden quiet. Not even Altha Combs could gossip through a mouthful of cake.

22

Hal

Vera said yes. Last night. I still can't hardly believe it. I wanted to whoop and holler. Almost called May on the telephone, first thing this morning—but Ricky from downstairs was hanging around in the hall by the phone, and Lord knows who'd be listening in on the party line at home. Anyway, May hates for me to make a long-distance call. Best tell her on Friday.

I settled down some anyway, over breakfast. Good news or not, we're not out of the woods yet. For one thing, Vera's still got to get out of town with me. She doesn't want a big scene. Neither do I—Tom'd break my neck in seven places, if he thought I was up to anything with his sister. So we made a plan —I'm going to mention to Tom that May's wanting to rent out a room, and then this weekend Vera can "hear" of a seamstress business in Whelan for sale on short notice, and it'll all just happen to work out. Hopefully.

And then it just has to work out at home. I sure hope May and Vera get along.

"Hal! You asleep over there?" Charlie's hollering at me across the noise—he's out of box-ends. I slap a fresh batch of slats and cleats on my nailing machine, tap the foot pedal—*Ka-CHUCK*. Turn the box-end around, *Ka-CHUCK* again, pass it

on for Charlie and Lawrence to *Ka-CHUCK* the sides and
bottoms on. Four hundred boxes an hour, four thousand a day
—*Ka-CHUCK. Ka-CHUCK. Ka-CHUCK. Ka-CHUCK. Ka-
CHUCK.*

Course, you can't hardly hear our nailing machines over the
rest of it. Saws screaming, matcher-planers grinding away,
conveyor rollers whirring. Wood hitting metal, metal hitting
metal, guys hollering, blower roaring its head off. It's a wonder
I can hear myself think.

Not that you need to think, to go *Ka-CHUCK* all day long.
One of these days, they'll make a machine that can load its
own slats and adjust its own nail feed, we'll all be out of a job.

Except I'll be long gone by then. Gone back home. There's
not a machine in the world could do my work on the farm. You
want to do any good, farming, you've got to think. You've got
to know your equipment, your ground, your animals—where
Bess likes to hide her calves, which field dries out first, a million
little things.

There's a bang like a shell going off. I flinch, but I keep
working. Happens all the time. I hadn't been here two days,
before a truck hit the loading dock and I hit the deck. Charlie
laughed at me—"They about get you, soldier?"—but I just
peeled myself off the floor and got back to work. Nothing else
to do. I wasn't the only one, and it got easier after awhile.

Except for the nightmares. Those stayed bad. Until Vera
started coming home with me—well, "home" to Mrs. Moore's.
There's something about being held at night—even though I
felt bad about it, even though she had to leave before
morning... I don't think I would have made it this long, without Vera.

And now she's said yes. Five more days of this racket—then
I'll take Vera home with me for real. God, I hope everything
works out all right.

I imagine it will, though. It's May's idea—and like I told
Vera, you can always count on May.

23

Vera

Lunch today was a disaster—and not just because of Wanda's leftover meatloaf, which was dry enough the first time around.

The kids were off playing with Betty's kids, so it was just Wanda and me at the table. My eyes ached—I've been sewing practically every minute since I made up my mind, hurrying to get Flora Riddle's whole wedding ready before I leave town next Tuesday. Wanda was going on about Mabel Hamilton's redecorating. I tried to say "Mm-hm" often enough, while I moistened the meatloaf with coleslaw and thought about seam allowances.

Then, with just a few bites left to go, Wanda got quiet. She put down her fork, and looked at me with that little crease between her eyebrows. Uh-oh. I chewed faster, but the meatloaf in my mouth seemed to be growing—I tried not to gag.

"Vera," Wanda said, "When's the last time you had a date?"

"Um, I don't know," I said with my mouth full. I washed the meatloaf down with a gulp of milk. "I've been so busy with these dratted alterations…"

Wanda wasn't distracted, by my manners or my language either one. "It's been *months!*"

It was true. Ever since Ralph and his runs-batted-in. My nights were a little full, these days. I shrugged. "Sometimes a girl needs a break."

Wanda pinched up her mouth like a teacher. "Have you thought about what we talked about?"

"What we talked about *when?*" Wanda was always talking about something. Just in the last twenty minutes she'd talked about Mabel Hamilton's lamps, and Mabel Hamilton's living room carpet, and Mabel Hamilton's television set, and... I tried to take a deep breath. I didn't have time to get bogged down in bickering.

"The other evening," Wanda said, as if it were obvious. "About you getting married."

Married? I rolled my eyes despite myself. "For heaven's sake, Wanda—I haven't had a date lately, so you think I need a *wedding?* What, are they selling fiancés down at the mercantile?"

Wanda's eyes widened at my tone. "*Vera!*"

"Maybe there's a sale on!" I went on, in a fake-excited voice. I was being awful, but I couldn't stop. "If I hurry, you think I can get a good deal?"

"There's no need to be that way, Vera," Wanda said. "I'm only concerned about you. You need a family of your own. You'll end up in trouble, just dating and running around."

"Good grief, Wanda," I said, "Do you want me to go out or stay at home? I'm losing track." I had a sudden impulse to tell her the truth. It'd serve her right. I stuffed a chunk of meatloaf into my mouth.

Wanda sighed reproachfully. "You know what I mean, Vera, even if you're going to be ugly about it. —And don't think I haven't noticed you flirting with Hal Dixon."

I almost choked on the meatloaf.

"I'm sure you think it's all in fun," Wanda went on. "But you're playing a dangerous game, Vera. Men can't help themselves—things get out of hand before you know it." She took a bite of coleslaw, and chewed self-righteously.

I stared at her. I knew I ought to argue, to deny it, but all I could think was, *there goes our plan.* It wasn't much of a plan to begin with, and it'd never fly if Wanda was suspicious. I'd thought Hal and I were being careful enough.

"I'm telling you, Vera," Wanda said sternly, "It's time you settled down. You need a home of your own, not somebody else's spare room. It's time you found a man who'll say 'I do' and put a ring on your finger. You can't sit the rest of your life in our spare room, sewing other women's wedding dresses."

I frowned. Something about what Wanda was saying... *Our spare room.* She'd said it twice, and with a little extra weight to the words. I took a drink of milk, ignoring Wanda's expectant glare. What was it? *Our spare room...* Then the light dawned. Mabel Hamilton's redecorating. Carpet and new furniture and a television set in the living room—and a new "den," with the old furniture and the radio and all the kids' games. The kids could eat cookies and listen to *The Shadow* in the den while Mabel had company in the living room, and nobody ever sat on a slingshot.

And Mabel's new den was Mabel's old spare bedroom. That was what this was all about. My face was hot, but I kept my voice steady as I asked, "You wanting my room back, Wanda?"

Wanda jumped like I'd shouted "Boo" at her. "Wanting your —Vera! I don't know what's gotten into you today!" She shook her head, but her cheeks were pink. "I'm just trying to... It's time you grew up, Vera, and found someone to take care of you."

Oh, for pity's sake. "I can take care of myself, Wanda!" I snapped, and got up to scrape the rest of my lunch into the garbage. "You want you a den like Mabel Hamilton's, just say the word and I'll find me a room to rent. I make enough to pay my way, if you hadn't noticed—I'm not in there sewing other women's wedding dresses for kicks!"

I reached for Wanda's plate, but she grabbed hold of it. We both tugged at it for a second, before I realized how silly we must look, and let go. Wanda got up without looking at me and took the plate to the sink. She set it carefully on top of mine, then turned to face me. Tears were smearing her makeup. "Vera Stinson," she said, her voice high and tight, "You know very well I wouldn't turn you out on your own. Haven't we been good to you, these past eight years?"

I didn't answer. It was mean—but she'd started it. And I hate when people start crying in the middle of an argument.

Wanda's sad mouth hardened a little. "You think you're so smart, Vera," she went on, faster and louder. "You don't have any idea what you're throwing away, with your I-can-take-care-of-myself. The day Thomas put this ring on my finger was the happiest day of my life. I just want you to be happy, and all you can think is I want my spare room back!"

Wanda stopped for breath, still holding up her left hand with the ring on it. Then she turned back to the sink and snatched up the dishrag. "I'll do the dishes. You can get on with your sewing."

I let her have the last word, and shut myself back in my bedroom. I'd lost my taste for the fight anyway.

I'm doing my best not to take out my feelings on these dratted alterations. Flora's gained an inch in the bust since the first fitting, and if I'm not mistaken, her belly isn't far behind. Thank goodness her dress has an Empire waistline—I don't have time to make a maternity gown out of it.

Wanda's putting away the dishes in the kitchen, slamming the cabinet doors. She was lying, for all her tears. She does want my room. I can see the new den now—the radio where my wardrobe is, the couch against the wall, a shelf full of board games instead of my sewing machine. Wanda will be as thrilled to see me go as I will be to leave.

But not thrilled enough to swallow some story about Sue's cousin hearing of a great opportunity in Whelan, and—what luck!—Hal and May having a room to rent. Not now. If Hal and I had been a little more careful... I could kick myself.

24

Vera

I took care not to catch Hal's eye during supper. I hoped Wanda would think I was taking her advice. It didn't matter—my skin could feel Hal from across the table, like a heat lamp. Lately I wanted him more every day, even being pregnant. *Because* I was pregnant? I'd never heard of that. There must be lots of things I hadn't heard of. At least I wasn't vomiting all the time, like Francine had. As long as I thought about something else when I was cutting up a chicken, and stayed away from egg malts and fried onions...

After supper I sewed the covered buttons down the back of Flora's dress, then helped Petey play Crazy Eights with the older kids while I tried to think of a new plan for getting away. I couldn't just go for a walk and not come back—if I vanished the same day Hal left, Wanda would put two and two together, and Tom would be coming after Hal with a baseball bat. Besides, there were my things. Nobody goes out for a walk carrying a steamer trunk and a sewing machine. I had to *move out.* And it had to be next Tuesday. And I'd need someplace to go where Hal could meet me, and some way to get there. And it all had to seem...likely. Every plan I came up with sounded like something out of *Bruce Gentry, Daredevil of the Skies*—in other words, dumb.

Maybe Hal would have an idea. I hoped so, because as the evening wore on, I found I couldn't think of anything *but* Hal. The hairs on my arms kept rising up, like tiny compass needles pointing toward Mrs. Moore's boardinghouse. By the time the kids went to bed, I was having trouble telling hearts from spades.

Now the house is quiet. The night's cooling off a little, but I keep getting hotter. I feel like I've been waiting for Hal forever. I want to hang out the window and yowl like a cat in heat. When he finally whistles outside, I can't pry the screen open fast enough.

He kisses me in the yard, one callused finger stroking the side of my neck. I kiss him back, deeper and deeper. I want to kiss all the way into him, spill over and fill him up like a pitcher... He chuckles, and whispers, "Let's get out of the yard, okay?"

My legs are too warm and rubbery to walk straight. I lean on his arm, staggering like a drunk. Halfway to his boarding-house, I stop him in the shadows, pull his face down to kiss him some more. His hands grab fistfuls of my dress. I wish he'd just rip it open, split it down the back seam and let some of this heat out. But then I'd have to mend it—I grin against the sandpapery stubble of his lips. We keep kissing as we walk on, until I trip over my feet and have to quit.

Once we're safe in his room, everything swirls together and I can't tell before from after. Hal's teeth smooth as a row of buttons, the bitter taste inside his ear, my dress falling to the floor in the dark. His lips feeling their way down my neck, making my legs tremble against his thighs. On my knees on the bed, pushing back into Hal behind me, feeling like an animal. Twisting around so my hands can feel his skin, wrapping my legs and arms around him, wishing for more legs and arms. The darkness of the room, the heat of Hal's body and mine, the stars shining behind my closed eyelids...

I start laughing. "Shh," Hal whispers, raising up on his elbows—but I can't stop. I pull the pillow over my face, and the laugh comes rolling up out of my belly, a big round laugh like a fat woman standing with her legs apart, hands on her hips. Hal kisses my hands on the pillow, and I laugh harder, and Hal moans, and I hold him close.

We lie tangled together, all mixed up, like one animal. One happy animal, with two happy heartbeats.

The half moon in the window wakes me up. Still nighttime. I've always been careful not to fall asleep at Hal's. But I'm not worried. The laugh still glows in my belly, like a little sun under my hands. Hal's body is draped along my side, slick with sweat. I turn my head to nuzzle his face.

"Have a nice nap?" he murmurs into my hair.

"Mm-hmm." I could lie here forever. The warmth in my belly spreads out like a sunrise, shining its way up slowly through my chest and throat. When it pours into my mouth, I smile. I open my lips and let it out. "Hal," I say, "I want to get married." It comes out soft and clear, and I know it's true. Maybe the truest thing I've ever said.

"Mmm, me too," Hal whispers, giving me a squeeze.

My smile falters, and I can hear my heart beating. Hal thinks I'm just being sweet. I'm supposed to laugh now, let it be a joke. But it's not. I lie there, tasting the shape of the truth in my mouth. Then I say it again. "I want to get married."

Hal raises his head. "What do you mean, hon?"

My heart stutters suddenly. Do I have it all wrong? I shiver, and Hal tucks the sheet around my shoulders. "That's what you meant, wasn't it?" I say. "You and May? You said it was for good, right?" I turn to look at Hal, but there's only the dark shape of his head against the window.

"Oh," he says, "Of course. I mean—yes, that's what we meant." He laughs nervously. "For a minute there, I thought you'd…" He trails off.

It would be easy to let it go. But if I can't tell the truth to Hal, who can I tell it to? And it's true. I draw a deep, quiet breath, and say it again. "So I want to get married."

Hal sits up, the sheet slithering off his body. I keep talking, struggling to find words. "I don't mean leaving May. And I know we...we can't do it under the law, but... that's what I want."

Hal strokes my leg through the sheet, then gives it a pat. "Well, hon," he says, "Sometimes you've just got to take what you can get."

I stop breathing. The warmth in my belly turns cold. *Take what you can get?* That's all he has to say? I squeeze my eyes shut.

Hal pats my leg again. "You all right, hon?"

Suddenly I'm crying, ragged breaths gasping between my teeth. *Quiet, quiet,* I warn myself, but then I wonder why it matters.

"Vera," Hal whispers, as I sit up on the edge of the bed.

I pull away from his hand on my shoulder, and twist around to face him. My belly is warm again—no, hot—hot and fierce as a desert sun. "I want to get married!" I hiss at Hal though my tears. "If I'm going to go home with you, and leave the kids, and—" I stifle a sob. "And you love me, and it's for good... I want you to marry me, and I want to marry you. In the sight of God."

Hal lets out a gust of a sigh, and flops back down on the bed. "Well, Vera—"

"And don't tell me I have to take what I can get!" My voice squeaks with the strain of keeping quiet. "I *know* that!"

Hal just lies there, while the heat pounds in my face. After a minute I get up and feel around for my clothes. When I'm dressed, I find the lamp and turn it on. Hal puts his arm across his eyes. I look at him lying there. Maybe I should just go.

Then he sits up, pulling the sheet around him, and rubs at the stubble on his chin. "So," he says slowly, his forehead wrinkling, "You want to have some kind of a wedding...but it doesn't have to be legal?"

I nod. "Just in the sight of God," I say again, and wonder why. I can hear Francine laughing in the malt shop—*You're going to drag* God *to your wedding?* Normally I don't think about religion one way or the other, from one Sunday to the next—and here I am I'm talking about God to a naked man. I'm ruining everything, and I don't even know why it's important.

But it is important. I bite my lip, and wait.

Hal runs a hand through his hair. "Well... You mean a preacher and all, or can we just...make do?"

He's serious. I get out my handkerchief to blow my nose, and sit down in the chair. "I guess we'd have to make do," I say. Hal stirs, but I hold up my hand. "But not just you and me in your room. *Somebody* has to pronounce us man and wife." I sound like a kid playing pretend. I shut my eyes and put a hand on my belly, trying to feel that warmth again. What do I really mean? What does it take to be married, if it's not the law?

"So—" Hal says.

I open my eyes. "Somebody has to pray," I say. "We have to say our vows, and there has to be some kind of a preacher, and he has to pray." Like Pastor Locke used to, asking God to take care of us by name.

Hal sucks at his lip a minute. Then he says, "Well, how about I talk it over with May. I imagine we can work something out."

"Okay." I feel a little deflated. Hal's looking at me, his brown eyes soft. "I guess I'd better go home," I say.

Hal gets up and pulls on his pants, then walks me downstairs. We kiss at the door, our lips gentle this time, careful with each other.

I'm halfway home before I realize I didn't tell Hal about our cover story being kaput. And it's Thursday night—I won't see him again until Sunday. I stop and look back up the street, then sigh and go on. I can't do any more tonight.

25

Hal

Home again. After Katy's in bed, May cuts us both a piece of oatmeal cake and we play a few rounds of Gin Rummy. She beats me five hands out of six. I keep getting distracted by the way her mouth points here and there when she's looking at her cards. She was upset last weekend, of course, and then she had her curse... I'm hoping she'll let me make it up to her tonight.

Maybe she's still upset, though. I don't want to come off like I don't care. She looks cool as a cucumber—laying down the last hand, adding up the points. I make a face at the score, go out on the porch to wash up.

Telling May that Vera said yes wasn't quite how I thought it'd be. Vera kind of took the wind out of my sails last night, with her whole wedding thing—not that I'd mind marrying her, but what would May think? And then when I got home, I had to give May the news by fits and starts, in between Katy yelling "Chick-chick-chick!" or telling something about "Wonny and Cawol."

Damn, that water's cold. Feels good, after the first shock—but hoo-ee. I'm getting spoiled, having hot water on tap all summer.

May didn't act that surprised, about the getting-married business. Not like I was. Maybe you have to be a woman. She got a little worried when I said "In the sight of God." Wanted to know if Vera was Holiness or something. May's mom is Holiness, and they don't get along. I told her no. I don't know what Vera is, but if she was Holiness I'd have heard about it by now. Once we'd gotten that straight, May was fine. When I said Vera wanted some kind of a preacher to pray, she just nodded—like maybe she's got a preacher in the kitchen drawer. I wouldn't be surprised. May doesn't do things by halves.

Anyway, it's all settled, and she seems okay. And I don't want to make a big deal out of tonight. Just be like always. Pajamas on, dump the washwater, back to the kitchen. May's turned away from me, putting a glass in the cabinet, but I smile anyway. "Well," I say, "You reckon we ought to make hay while—" I see her shoulders draw up. "Never mind," I say, quick. Pick up my Western. "It's all right." Head off to bed, try to read about Boone Caudill and his woman troubles.

I wish I hadn't brought it up, now. Except I wouldn't want May to think I'm not interested anymore. I hope she believes me, that it's all right. It's not as if I can't wait. I love her—that's what matters. I just want her to be happy, and Vera to be happy.

I wish it wasn't so complicated.

26

May

Hal went off with Jamie right after breakfast on Saturday, going up to Dearborn County to look at some hogs. I fed Katy and strained the milk, then went upstairs to clean the spare bedroom.

I had to shove the door hard with my hip to unstick it from its frame. Hot, stuffy air rolled out, like I'd opened an oven. I hadn't been in here since I'd put the winter coats away this spring.

Katy ran in past me to look out the window. I nudged her aside and raised the sash. The fresh air would clear out the musty smell before long—I just needed to dust and sweep, and make the bed.

"This used to be Daddy's room," I told Katy. "When Daddy was little."

Katy laughed. "No, Mommy! Daddy big!"

I smiled at her. "He used to be little, like you." She laughed again, like I'd told a great joke.

This had been Hal's room most of his life, in fact—right up until he married me. Then we'd rented a place in Whelan for a few months, until Rye and Iva bought the little house up the road and sold us the farm. When we'd first moved in, I'd felt like I was using Iva's kitchen, sleeping in her and Rye's bed-room—but after three years now, it felt like home.

Katy looked in all the vanity drawers, finding an old comb and a couple of matchbooks, while I dusted cobwebs down from the corners of the ceiling. The coats in the wardrobe could go in our bedroom closet, downstairs. Maybe I'd put the Log Cabin quilt on the bed—no, that was a double. I ran my dustrag over the bedframe. What single size quilts did I have?

Two people in a single bed would be tight. Maybe Hal ought to sleep downstairs, and—what, Vera and me take turns? Suddenly I felt dizzy. I sat down on the bed, shut my eyes, and tried to picture the quilts in the cedar chest. There was Grandma Stout's Bear Paw quilt—but that was all blue and white, not very feminine... My stomach rolled, and I swallowed hard. Iva's crazy quilt—no, that was a double too. The Rising Sun was a single, and the Monkey Wrench. One of those.

"Mommy?" Katy pulled at my arm.

I opened my eyes and stood up, handing her a rag. "Here, hon. You can help me dust."

I finished dusting the bedframe, and told myself Vera would be fine in here. A woman wants her own bedroom, with her clothes and all. I should clear out those extra kitchen chairs, if she was bringing a sewing machine—and there was an enamel pan in the milkhouse that would do her for a washbasin. What else did she need?

A wedding, evidently. I snorted softly to myself. Hal had been nervous as a cat, trying to explain that. As if I'd balk, after coming this far. *In for a penny, in for a pound*, Daddy used to say—and a homemade wedding wasn't any nuttier than the rest of it. I didn't see the point, but if that was what it took to straighten this out, that was what we'd do.

"Drive, drive, drive," Katy sang, running her finger along the stripes of the mattress ticking. "Drive a car, Mommy!"

"You go ahead," I told her. "Mommy needs to sweep."

Finding a preacher, now... *that* might be a trick. The pastor over at Shiloh Baptist was all right, but I couldn't see him signing on to this. Mom's old preacher, Brother Willis, would fall down in a fit. Not that I'd ask him. Brother Willis had a handshake like a sour dishrag, and he didn't show his teeth when he smiled.

Katy ran across the hall to her room, talking to herself. She'd been fussy last night—probably teething again. In between getting up with her, I'd lain awake thinking. Now that this thing with Vera was really going to happen, I had to wonder what Grace would say. And Jamie. And Iva and Rye. It didn't take much wondering. They'd hit the ceiling, every one. I'd imagined explaining it fifty different ways, but in the end I just had to hope they'd get used to the idea, in time. You work things out, when you're family. Like Grace's brother and his wife, raising the baby after Grace's little sister got herself pregnant. That seemed like a catastrophe at first, but now little Peggy was starting second grade, and the family had almost forgotten she wasn't Deke and Lucy's girl. Families made room, made do, stuck by each other—even when things got messy.

This ain't the same, Missy, and you know it. Even just in my head, Mom's voice made me flinch. I could see her face, mouth hard with judgment. I knew what she'd say. Words like *wickedness* and *lust* and *sin. Shameless. Putting that hussy in your spare bedroom, not ten feet from your baby girl's crib… You wait, Missy, you'll see where your stubbornness gets you…*

I took a step backwards, feeling cornered. Mom wasn't even here. She didn't know anything about it. I was just trying to keep my family together—why did it have to be *wrong?* Why did *everything* have to be—

I dropped the dustpan with a clang, scattering dirt across the floor. "That's enough!" I said, in a rough whisper. More than enough. I'd had enough of being judged by the time I turned fourteen. I glared at the dustpan on the floor as if it was the one judging me. This was my house, and my family, and anybody that didn't like it could go to blazes.

"Mommy, help!" Katy whined from her room. I found her trying to raise the rail on her crib, heaven knew why. When I yanked it up, she gave me a sulky look. I could see the tiredness under her eyes—she'd be ready for her nap early today.

I was tired too. I sighed. No need to get myself in a lather. Hal's news had stirred me up again, but I just needed to calm down, and decide what to do, and do it. Starting with sweeping up the mess I'd made. My house or not, it wouldn't look like much if I went around throwing dirt on the floor.

I made up the bed with clean sheets and the Monkey Wrench quilt, and shut the vanity drawers Katy had left open. Grace and Jamie, Iva and Rye—this was none of their business. We could just tell them Vera was staying here, and let them wonder. I caught my own skeptical look in the vanity mirror. Grace, at least, wouldn't stop at wondering. But I didn't have to tell Grace every little thing. Keeping quiet would buy us some time, to settle in and get on with our lives.

And this "wedding" business—I could be the preacher myself. No need to drag anybody else into it, with their Bible verses and judgments. Lord knows, I'd heard enough praying to do it in my sleep.

I put the extra chairs in Katy's room, gave the spare bed-room—Vera's room—a last once-over, and gathered up the winter coats to take downstairs.

The coats barely fit in our bedroom closet, with Hal's shirts and my dresses. I scooted hangers along the closet rod and shoved at the mothball-scented wool. Upstairs, Katy was hollering "Woo-woooo!"—playing train with the chairs. If she stayed busy, maybe I could get Hal's wash done before lunch. She was awfully tired, though. I sighed. If this round of teething was like the last one, I'd be up and down the stairs at night for weeks. Going past Vera's room, where—

I shook my head sharply, backing up from that thought.

Of course, Vera might wake up before I did, when Katy cried, and go—

I stood with my hand on the closet doorknob and my heart pounding in my ears, picturing a half-asleep Katy cradled in another woman's arms. Then I shut the door.

Hal's wash could wait till the afternoon. I had furniture to move.

27

Vera

"Here you go, buddy." I spooned sugar onto Petey's shredded wheat, then poured milk into both our bowls. Petey grinned at me with sleep in his eyes. I smiled back, trying to ignore the smell of Wanda's Saturday-morning omelet. Breakfast was my queasiest time, and my nerves weren't helping. Yesterday—in between two fittings, three meals, and helping Wanda measure for curtains—I'd finally come up with a new plan. Now I had to try and pull it off.

I choked down a few mouthfuls of cereal, then cleared my throat. "I've got some news!"

Wanda looked up from stirring her coffee, with a little frown that said the news couldn't be good. Tom reached past Freddy for the ketchup.

"Sue Perry has a cousin in Cincinnati," I said. That much was true. "She says a dress factory's opening there, and they need lots of seamstresses."

"So?" Tom asked, smacking the bottom of the ketchup bottle.

I took a deep breath and explained. How, with my experience, I'd be a shoo-in for a job. How the cousin, "Jeanne," had

113

a bedroom for rent, and Sue said I'd love Cincinnati. "So I thought I'd give it a try," I finished.

Tom passed the ketchup to Wanda. "Cincinnati's a big place."

"I know." I tried to sound confident, but not too confident. "Jeanne says she'll look out for me, though. They're in a nice neighborhood."

Tom took a bite of ketchup-smeared yellow omelet, and I swallowed hard. "Well," he said, "We'll see."

I nodded. "The thing is, I've found out at the last minute. They're only hiring next Wednesday, to fill all the shifts. Jeanne said to get a good job, I ought to be there early, so I'll have to get up there Tuesday and spend the night. I'll barely have time to pack!" I did my best at a laugh.

"Now, hold your horses, Vee," Tom said through a mouthful of toast. He leaned back in his chair, giving me a big-brother look. "They just say that so more gals'll show up, and they can hire them cheaper. There'll still be jobs next week—and next month, and next year."

I smiled at him—but Hester spoke up before I could. "You can't move away, Aunt Vera! You're part of our family!" She looked dead serious, even with a milk mustache.

Freddy rolled his eyes. "Maybe she's tired of being part of our family."

"No, I'm not," I said firmly. "I just think it's time I tried something new."

"You kids eat your breakfast," Wanda said, but her eyes were on Tom, and her frown was thoughtful now.

"You don't need to be going off on your own," Tom told me. "Us Stinsons stick together."

"Is Aunt Vera going away?" Petey asked, looking anxiously at his sister. Hester just scowled at me. I patted Petey's shoulder.

"Nobody's going anywhere," Tom said, looking exasperated. "Anyway, I can't drive you to Cincinnati in the middle of the work week, and we've got the Labor Day picnic on Monday."

"I thought I'd take the train." Cincinnati was almost on Hal's way home—he could pick me up at the train station there.

"Now there's an idea!" Wanda finally spoke up. She looked excited, as if she were the one trying something new.

Tom set his cup down hard on the table. "Good grief, Wanda, I'm not putting my little sister on a train to Cincinnati, without more to go on than somebody's-cousin-says-there-might-be-a-job!"

I bit my lip. I hadn't expected Tom to balk this hard. I felt like pointing out Tom's "little sister" was a grown woman, and had to remind myself that I didn't want a scene.

Wanda poured Tom more coffee, nodding. "Well, Thomas," she offered, "Maybe *I* could drive her up. I could skip my Ladies meeting."

Tom snorted. "You're not taking my car on the highway. With your lead foot? I'd as soon let Freddy drive her."

Freddy made a muffled choking sound, and Wanda flushed a little.

"I was thinking—" I started, not sure what I was going to say. Then Freddy's laughter burst out through his nose, along with a lot of milk.

"Dammit, Freddy!" Tom pushed back his chair, wiping at his shirt front. He shot me a resentful look as I grabbed napkins to mop the table. "You tell this Jane you'll get back with her in a couple weeks," he said. "There's no need to go off half-cocked."

Petey burst into tears.

That was that. I knew if I kept trying, Tom would just get mad. He doesn't pay much attention to me most days, but he's been set on keeping me safe ever since Pop left, when he was eleven and I was six. I guess my plan didn't sound safe enough.

Tom doesn't know it's too late, to keep me safe. God, he'd skin Hal alive. I remember how he used to fight, in school—and it's not that long since he came home with busted knuckles from some scrap after work.

I can hear the kids outside. Hester begging Freddy to walk her and Petey to the park. I wish I could go with them. If I'm leaving, I need to make up with Petey and Hester first. But if I'm leaving, I have to finish this hem, and the other hems, and the buttons, and... *If* I'm leaving.

I should have stuck to our first plan. I was wrong, thinking Wanda would throw a wrench in—she was practically jumping out of her seat, she's so eager to have me gone.

No, that's mean. Wanda wouldn't send me to live in Hal's house if she thought there was any danger. And if she'd even hinted at that, Tom would've nixed the whole thing. *And* skinned Hal alive. Big brothers are a pain in the neck.

Does May have a big brother? I've been so wrapped up in Hal, and worry, and plans, and hems—I've never even asked about Hal and May's family. May could have three brothers and a dozen mean aunts, all set to rake Hal and me over the coals.

But Hal says you can count on May. And I have to count on Hal. Whatever it is, we'll handle it together, and it'll blow over, given time.

I run out of thread, make a knot, and cut a new length. Then I sit staring at the needle in my hand. It doesn't matter about May's brother, or whoever, if I can't even get there. Should I try the seamstress-shop-in-Whelan story now? And hope Wanda doesn't say anything, and Tom doesn't think it's odd that I've stumbled on another "last-minute opportunity"? That's worse than a long shot. Wanda would spill the beans, and Tom would go nuts, and the kids would have to see it all... I can't face that. The thought makes me sick.

Which means it's back to looking for a boardinghouse, and waiting for everybody to find out I'm pregnant. Imagining the whole other life I might have had, and didn't. And losing Hal. Losing Hal, because I didn't try. Does that mean I don't love him? Don't love him enough? No, I do. I can tell I do, by the ache in my chest, right above the knot in my belly.

28

May

I'd thought I could have things put back together before Hal got back. But a stuck bolt on the bedframe slowed me down, and there were cobwebs and dust behind everything. Katy didn't stay busy, either. Once the excitement of furniture-moving wore off, she'd clung and whined and cried for an hour before falling asleep on her bedroom rug.

When Jamie's car pulled into the driveway, I was halfway down the stairs with the vanity mirror, and I blushed as if I'd been caught at something. I hurried the rest of the way down and looked around the bedroom. Grandma Stout's "Gleaners" picture on top of a stack of vanity drawers, bedsprings propped against the wall, the empty dresser looking like a bombed-out building. There was nothing I could do to make it less of a mess.

"May?" Hal's voice came from the kitchen. "Where are you?"

"In here," I answered, softer. Best let Katy get her nap out, even if it was early. I leaned the mirror on the bedframe and glanced in it, wiping a hunk of cobweb off my hair.

"Lord have mercy, May, it looks like a tornado hit in here!" Jamie grinned at me from the bedroom doorway, while Hal stared at the mess like a cow spooked by a new gate.

"That would explain it," I said. "You want to help move a dresser while you're here?"

"Funny thing," Jamie said, "I was just saying to Hal, 'I feel like moving a dresser—I wonder if May's got one we could move.'"

I rolled my eyes at him, and pointed. "That one goes in the spare bedroom." I didn't look at Hal.

"You're the boss." Jamie grabbed one end of the dresser. "C'mon, Hal." He kept talking as they eased it out through the door and up the stairs. "This is nothing. When Grace was expecting Carol, I wore out three wardrobes carrying them back and forth."

I had to smile. Jamie never was one to ask nosy questions. I found my screwdriver behind the lamp, and started putting the mirror back on the vanity.

"Can you wait to eat?" I asked Hal, when they came back downstairs. It was time for lunch, but I'd just as soon get this done before Katy woke up. Hal nodded.

"Not me," Jamie said. "I'm so hungry, my stomach thinks my throat's cut."

"Well, I won't make you move the bedsprings too, then," I said.

"You sure?" he asked. I waved my screwdriver at him, and he left.

Hal stood in the doorway, fidgeting, while I slid the drawers back into the vanity. When I looked up, he smiled nervously. "Can I help?"

"Mmm, I think I've got it now," I said. I picked up a rag to dust where the dresser had been. Hal was quiet. I wanted to tell him to go on and let me work. Instead, I said, "Katy's been so restless at night. I got tired of running up and down the stairs."

"Oh," Hal said, nodding slowly. He looked at the single bedframe where our bed had been, then at the double bedsprings and mattress still leaning against a wall. "Well, all right then."

I got my dresses out of the closet and started out of the room, but Hal was in my way. I sighed. "I guess if you want to help..." I handed the dresses to him. "You can take these upstairs. Hang on, I'll give you some more." I went back for his shirts, and draped them over the dresses in his arms. His smile looked relieved.

I ended up being glad of Hal's help. The bedsprings weren't that heavy, but it was a trick to get them around the corners. We worked without saying much, backing and turning together like a pair of old workhorses. As we wrestled the double mattress onto the bed in the spare bedroom—our room, now—I caught a whiff of his smell, clean sweat and Lava soap. His arm brushed mine, the curly hairs tickling my skin. I wasn't sure I wanted the tremble that ran through my belly. I looked away, and went to get the sheets.

After lunch, Hal carried water for me to do his week's wash—just being nice, he knew I could carry it myself—and went to patch the barn roof. I did two small loads, whites and darks. Hal's hammering echoed off the house and washhouse when I went out to the clothesline, sounding like three hammers.

I hung work pants on the line by their cuffs, shaking the legs open and sliding my hands into the pockets to straighten them out. Last night, when Hal had said that about "making hay..." I hadn't meant to put him off. I'd almost turned around and told him it was okay. But then he said, "That's all right." And in my head I heard, *That's all right, there's always Vera.*

I'd always been willing to "make hay" with Hal on his weekends home, if it wasn't my woman's time. Sometimes I was tired, but it was generally worth my while. And I knew Hal had been waiting all week.

Except he hadn't been waiting all week, had he? And so last night I'd let him go, and then stood there scrubbing at a stain on the countertop, trying not to think about Hal with Vera.

What did he do, anyway, climb in through her window? Every night, or what?

I'd stayed in the kitchen long after the bedroom light went out. Then I'd washed up on the porch instead of in the bedroom, hurrying in the dark as if somebody might see me. When I got in bed, I was careful not to touch Hal.

Now I left the empty laundry basket under the clothesline, and took a shovel and bucket to the garden to dig potatoes. I might as well start supper while Katy was still out—sleeping through lunch, she was bound to wake up cranky.

That's all right, there's always Vera. Hal hadn't said that. But it was true. I could just cook Hal's meals and do his wash, talk with him about Katy and the farm, leave the rest to Vera. Maybe he wouldn't even mind.

Nonsense. I turned up a chunk of dry garden dirt, and bent down to pick the new red potatoes out of it. I was Hal's wife, not his pal or his cook. It was awkward, was all. I moved on to the next potato plant and pushed the shovel into the dirt. Tonight, when Hal asked, I'd be ready. I'd smile at my husband, and go up with him to our new bedroom, and be his wife.

But Hal didn't ask. We'd had our supper and put Katy to bed, played a couple of hands of cards. Hal went out to wash up. When he came in, he gave me sort of a half-smile and went off through the living room. I heard him climbing the stairs, then the creak of the bedsprings.

I sat at the table, picking at a thread on my sleeve. What was I supposed to do now? The thread pulled out, leaving the whole sleeve-end unhemmed. I sighed. I'd have to mend that before I did the wash on Monday.

I heard another creak, and imagined Hal propping up in the bed, opening his Western at the scrap of brown paper he marked his place with. The bedroom seemed a long way off. Maybe Hal wasn't interested. He'd always been interested before. But I'd always been willing, before. *There's always Vera.*

I didn't even know how to start something with Hal. He was the one who started things. And it wasn't as if I was all fired up or anything. Just willing.

The thread I was fiddling with had twisted itself into a knot. I picked at it. My fingernails ached from gripping the mattresses when we moved them, and my shoulders were tired. I wanted to go to bed. I didn't know what I wanted to happen once I got there.

Well. I got up and dropped the knotted thread in the wastebasket. I might as well wash up. And no need to do it on the porch, either.

Hal glanced up when I carried the washbasin into the bedroom, then went back to his book. I set the basin on the dresser, and turned my back on him to get undressed.

The cold water felt good on my sweaty face, and raised goosebumps as I soaped under my arms. I couldn't see Hal's face in the mirror, only his hands holding up the book. He hadn't turned a page since I came in. I imagined his eyes on me as I washed, moving down my spine, brushing the backs of my legs. I scrubbed at a streak of dirt on my ankle, wishing he'd say something.

When I pulled my nightgown on over my head and turned around, Hal didn't look up. Maybe he really was reading. I pulled back the sheet and lay down, not quite touching him.

Hal kept his book open for a few more minutes, then closed it and turned out the light. I felt the bed shift as he settled in.

I stretched, scooting over a little so my shoulder touched Hal's, as if by accident. He was warm. I listened to the katydids scratching away outside. The ceiling in here was lower than the one downstairs, and it sloped down at the corners. Even in the dark, it made the room feel small and secret, like a tent or a cave.

My mouth was dry, and my heart wouldn't settle down. Hal didn't move. I wondered if he was mad. If he'd just say something... Maybe he thought I was asleep already. I cleared my throat. "Does it feel familiar, sleeping in here?"

"Mm-hmm," Hal said. After a pause, he chuckled. "Not so much sleeping, toward the end there. More pining for a gal I knew, name of May Stout."

I gave a little snort, but I felt my cheeks turn warm.

Hal took my hand. "I used to lie awake half the night, thinking how bad I wanted to kiss you."

Good grief. I'd lain awake too, back then—but I'd spent half my nights worrying that Hal didn't like me, and the other half worrying that Mom would make him quit coming to see me.

Hal turned towards me in the dark. "I'd think about your eyes," he said. "The way you'd give me that stern look whenever I flirted with you... Made it mighty hard to get to sleep."

"Should've tried warm milk," I said. Nerves made my voice shaky, but Hal laughed. He scooted closer, sliding his knee across my thighs. I pushed away a thought of Vera. When Hal lifted his head, I took a thin breath and turned to meet his kiss.

The first time Hal kissed me was on the path by the creek, in the middle of winter—his lips warm on my cold cheek, then my mouth. I could feel his relief when I didn't pull away. Like now. My heart sped up, and now it wasn't just nerves.

Hal kissed his way along my jawline to my neck, ran his hand over the thin cloth of my summer gown. "I used to picture your breasts, too," he whispered.

I snorted into his hair. "You did not. I bet you didn't even know what a naked woman looked like."

He chuckled again. "I had a good imagination."

I laughed. Not at what Hal said, but at the familiar soft heat rising in my body, crowding out my thoughts. It was all right. I shut my eyes, and pulled him closer.

29

Vera

I could kiss Wanda.

Tom drove us to church this morning—Wanda said we'd all be a sweaty mess if we walked seven blocks in this heat. She sat between Tom and me in the front seat, and fussed at the kids in the back for the first three blocks. Then she smiled suddenly at Tom. "I've just had a thought, Thomas," she said. "Doesn't Hal live up by Cincinnati?"

Tom nodded. "Thereabouts. This side of the river."

"Well," Wanda said, "Why doesn't Vera catch a ride with him—wasn't he leaving on Tuesday?"

"What?" Tom squinted at Wanda. "Catch a ride where? Oh, that Cincinnati business? Wanda—"

"You know Hal will get her there safe," Wanda said, straightening Tom's collar, "And he can look the place over. I'm sure it's fine."

Tom craned his neck to back into a parking space. "Good grief, Wanda, I don't see why you have to bring this up right —"

"I knew it would work out," Wanda said. "This way, Vera can get one of the good jobs. There's nothing to worry about, Thomas. She just wants to stretch her wings."

And then we had to hurry into the church—which was why Wanda brought it up right then, of course. I didn't hear a word of the sermon. I've hardly heard a word all day. Who would have thought it? Wanda! There's no arguing with her once she's set on something. Tom might grumble a little more, but come Tuesday evening I'll be loading my things into Hal's truck and waving goodbye.

And Wanda will get her new den. I can forgive her that, I guess. It's not as if I'd be in any jeopardy, riding to Cincinnati with Hal in broad daylight. And I won't have to worry about her making trouble, when I write from Hal and May's—by then she'll have all the new furniture arranged.

30

May

Hal was in a good mood Sunday morning. He said he wanted to take Katy and me to the French Riviera for Labor Day. It wasn't Labor Day yet, and the picnic table at the Vevay ferry-boat landing was hardly the Riviera, but he sweet-talked me into it. Everybody'd be coming over for dinner in the afternoon, so I threw together a picnic breakfast and made us a thermos of coffee, and we went.

Katy loved it. She ran around collecting pinecones while Hal and I ate our hard-boiled eggs and bread with jelly. When she spotted the ferry coming across the river, she was beside herself, pointing and bouncing on her toes. "Mommy, look! A boat! A car! Cars on a boat!"

"It's a ferryboat," I told her. She'd seen it before, but she must not remember. "It's giving the cars a ride." Katy quivered with excitement as the boat came closer, its side-wheel churn-ing the water.

"You want to go see?" Hal finished his coffee, and took Katy to watch the ferry unload. I packed up our things, tossing the eggshells into the weeds.

When I joined them by the water, Katy was wide-eyed. "Mommy, come!" she said. "Ride a boat!" Hal had paid our fare to ride over and back on foot, just for fun. He grinned at Katy, then at me, and let Katy tug him down the ramp onto the ferry. I followed them and stood by the side rail, watching them explore as we chugged out across the current.

A farmer Rye's age got out of his pickup truck and leaned on the rail beside me. "That your little girl?" he asked. When I nodded, he said, "She sure favors her daddy."

I nodded again. "He was towheaded when he was little, too." Katy just looked like Katy to me, and Hal looked like Hal —but other people always saw the resemblance.

Katy leaned out from Hal's arms, trying to see the side-wheel. The man laughed. "Reminds me how exciting it all used to be," he said. "Riding across every day, you forget how big the river is." He spit a stream of brown tobacco juice into the brown water.

I thought about how big the river was, all the way from Pennsylvania to the Gulf of Mexico. Imagining the dark weight of all that water pouring downstream under the boat, I felt a little seasick. I pulled my eyes away from the river and watched Hal. He was raising and lowering his arm, showing Katy how the front ramp worked. A frown puckered Katy's forehead, and for a second I did see Hal in her face.

Hal laughed at whatever Katy was saying, his dark curls catching the light. What would he look like, if I hadn't known him most of my life? Handsome—blue work shirt against tanned skin, arm strong around Katy where he'd set her on the railing.

Hal glanced back and winked at me. I blushed, and pretended to be watching a barge.

Sunday dinner was as noisy as always. Everybody complimented my fried chicken, and Grace's vinegar slaw, and Iva's rolls. Rye told a story about the time his dog, Ol' Blue, treed a bobcat, and Jamie talked about the pigs he was thinking of buying. Grace kept her kids in line, and I tried to stop Katy from banging her spoon on her highchair tray.

Hal was his usual quiet self. I was glad—I'd forgotten to tell him what I'd decided, about keeping this Vera business to ourselves. I'd thought I might mention Vera in a casual way to Iva and Grace, before the meal—but I hadn't been able to think how to put it. *Oh, by the way, we're going to have a...* what? Visitor? Woman? New family member? Nothing sounded right, and I gave up. They could meet her themselves, next Sunday at dinner.

"Next Sunday," Grace said. I gave her a startled look, but she was answering something Iva had said. "May's been waiting on us all year."

"What's that?" I asked.

"We'll have Sunday dinners at our place, for a while," she said. "Hal won't be leaving on Sunday evening anymore, and it's time you had a break."

"Oh, it's not any trouble," I said, starting the potatoes around for seconds. "You and Iva always help out."

"Well, and now you can help out," Iva said—then, to Jamie, "Better pass to the left, James, or we'll have a mess."

"Sorry." Jamie handed the chicken platter across Ronny to me, and took the corn from Rye.

"I guess we could've had you today," Grace said. "I didn't think of it being Labor Day tomorrow."

Hal looked up from salting his tomatoes. "No, I'm working."

"Why on earth?" Grace asked, surprised.

"Oh, I told them at Whelan I could start the week of Labor Day, but the box plant thought I was working *through* the week of Labor Day," Hal said. "I ended up splitting the difference."

"More beets, please!" Carol yelled.

"Hush, Carol!" Grace said. "You had beets."

"They run that plant on holidays?" Rye asked Hal.

"They're putting in some equipment while they're shut down," Hal said. "Needed an extra man. I'll get time-and-a-half."

"So you'll be home when?" Iva asked Hal.

"Tuesday evening," Hal said.

"Ronny got *more* beets!" Carol was whining.

"Ronny ate his beans," Grace told her. "I swear, child, if Ronny had a cow-pat on his plate, you'd want one too."

Iva raised an eyebrow at Hal. "All that driving, just to work two days?"

Hal shrugged. "Just trying to keep everybody happy."

"Here, Cawol!" Katy leaned sideways in her highchair, holding out a handful of half-chewed beets. When Carol ignored her, she waved her pink-purple fist at Iva. "Here, Mammaw!"

Iva smiled at her from the far end of the table. "Why don't you save those for me, Pumpkin," she said. "Put them on your plate."

Katy put the beets down and patted them. "Mammaw beets!"

Carol was looking from Katy to Iva. "Mammaw Dixon," she said after a minute, "Are you *my* Mammaw?"

"No," Ronny said scornfully, before Iva could answer. "Mammaw and Pappaw Dixon are Uncle *Hal's* mommy and daddy. Not Daddy's!"

Carol frowned. "Then who's Daddy's mommy?"

Ronny looked confused, and Jamie stepped in. "My mommy's Grandma Stout. You remember, in Frankfort?"

It took me a second to realize that "Grandma Stout" was Mom. Mom was Katy's grandma too, of course, but Katy had never met her. Jamie took his family to visit Mom now and then. He'd always gotten along with her better than I did.

"Mary Lee has Sunday dinner at her *own* Mammaw's house, every week," Carol said. "One Mammaw, and then the other Mammaw."

"She probably does," Grace said, scraping together the rest of Carol's green beans with her own fork. "All us Peterses won't fit in Ma-Peters's house. Or anybody else's."

"And there ain't enough Stouts or Dixons either one to fill a dinner table, this side of the river," Rye added. "We've all got to throw in together." He made a well in his mashed potatoes with the back of the gravy spoon, and poured it full of gravy.

When Carol opened her mouth to ask another question, Grace put a forkful of beans in it. Carol made a face, but she chewed.

"Don't worry about it, sweetie," Iva told her. "I'll be your Mammaw anytime you want. No such thing as too many grandkids."

Jamie reached for the rolls basket, took a roll for himself, and tossed one across the table to Hal. Then he pretended he was going to throw the butter dish.

Grace looked exasperated. "James…"

Jamie grinned at her, and passed the butter like a normal person. "You get all your furniture moved?" he asked Hal.

"You're moving furniture?" Grace asked, surprised.

I nodded, feeling my face turn red. "Felt like a change."

"Well, and—" Hal started.

"And we needed to make some room," I went on quickly, before Hal could give away the whole thing. What had I decided we'd tell them? "We've got somebody coming to…stay. A friend of Hal's sister."

Jamie gave Hal a funny look. "You don't have a sister."

"Or a brother, either," Rye added, reaching for the slaw.

"No," I said impatiently. "Hal has a friend in Cartersboro, and this Vera is his sister. She'll be living with us."

"Hired girl?" Rye asked.

"No," I answered, feeling out of my depth. "I mean, she'll be helping out and all, but… She just…needed a place to stay, and we've got room… You'll need to set an extra place next Sunday," I added, to Grace.

Grace rubbed her chin. "Is she in—" Then she glanced at the kids, and said, "Well, she's welcome. —Use your fork, Carol, not your fingers."

Hal pursed his lips thoughtfully, then gave a little nod and passed the pepper to Rye. Iva was looking at me with her head cocked, like a robin listening for worms. I avoided her eye, and got up to pour more ice tea.

* * *

Katy hung onto my skirt and whined while Iva and Grace and I cleaned up the kitchen. Sunday dinner was right at her nap-time. Carol tried to cheer her up, making faces and getting underfoot. Between them, they were enough of a nuisance that nobody got around to asking any awkward questions.

Katy cried when everybody left, but fell asleep after a few minutes. I carried her up to her crib, then sat down at the kitchen table with my sewing basket. Hal leaned on the counter, eating a leftover biscuit with jelly.

"I don't see how you can eat anything," I said, threading a needle.

"Hollow leg," Hal mumbled, with his mouth full. He watched me sew for a minute, then said, "So you figure we'll just tell folks Vera's staying with us?"

I nodded. "For now. Let us get settled in, before…" I let it trail off, and frowned at the yellow dress I was mending.

Hal went to the refrigerator and got out the ice tea. "Makes sense," he said.

It didn't make sense, of course. It was a mess. Iva knew something was up. And Grace thought Vera was pregnant out of wedlock—she'd never leave it alone. If I'd planned it better, figured out exactly what to say…

Hal drank his tea, then said something about the cows and went out through the porch. I cut my thread and turned the dress right-side-out. The sleeve I'd hemmed wouldn't lie straight. "Oh for Pete's sake," I muttered, tugging at it. I should have ironed it first. I wasn't about to go back and do it over, though. That dress was on its last legs anyway—I'd be lucky if it survived the summer.

31

Hal

Sunday night at Mrs. Moore's. Late—Vera's gone home. I ought to be sleeping, but I've been thinking instead. Thinking about Vera, and May. And then thinking about that one whore.

Anyplace you've got soldiers, of course, you'll have whores. Most of them weren't really whores, just regular women. I went with a few. But then I got to thinking, what if the war didn't go our way, and you had tanks and soldiers all over home—no crops, no jobs—and May was the one standing in a doorway, trying to feed her family... After that, I stayed away from whores. If I got too riled up, I'd "wash a load by hand."

But then I got a three-day pass to Paris, with Howie and Gus Trulow. Paris was something else. Women hollering "Hey, Bay-bee!" out of windows. One girl showed us her tits right there in the street. We stopped in an alley and shared a reefer Gus had. Gus always had something. I took a drag or three, being socia-ble—I'd tried it before, never saw what all the fuss was about.

We ended up in this real fancy brothel place, drinking beer and watching the show. After awhile, I noticed I couldn't quit grinning. Maybe there was something to this reefer stuff after all.

Then this black-haired woman wanted to dance. I was a little light-headed, but I tried. Her dress was soft as butter. It was red, but I wasn't really looking at it—just loving running my hands over that soft, slick stuff.

The two of us wound up by ourselves, in this room that was all red. Walls, sheets, everything. Both of us naked. I couldn't quit looking at her. Not standing back and looking—I was a couple inches away, staring at her skin, smelling the sweat underneath her perfume. She was soft and round, not skinny like the women in the street. I looked at her ears, the freckles on her shoulders, her breasts rising up like hills. I felt like I could look at her the rest of my life.

Then she started talking. In French of course. But I swear, I understood every word. She told me what to do. How to touch her. Those other whores had given me what I wanted, but this one—*she* wanted things. I'd never thought of doing some of that. She was all polite, *"S'il te plait"* and *"Cherie."* But when I did what she said, she went wild. Growling, moaning, little yelps. And not just to rile me up more, get me to pay extra. It was all about *her.* Funny thing, though, it did rile me up.

She tasted like purslane, with salt on it. I remember thinking that. And all of a sudden I was at home, hoeing the beans in Ma's garden and chewing a mouthful of purslane. And damned if I didn't start crying—crying like a baby, right there in that bed with the red sheets.

The whore pulled me up close and held me, stroked my hair. I cried. Told her about Ma and home, and how I was engaged to May and so what was I doing in bed with a whore. I told her I didn't want to do wrong by May. I tried to explain how I was doing stuff every day I'd have sworn was wrong, I mean shooting some German kid in the face, blowing people's legs off, but wasn't it right to fight for your country—and if that was right, then how could a beautiful sweet woman like *her* be wrong…

She listened to me awhile, whispering things in French. Then she kissed me to shut me up, and rolled me onto my back, and gave me the time of my life.

Sometimes I think maybe I just dreamed the whole thing. Maybe it was the reefer. But now and then I'll find myself staring at the muscle of May's arm, or studying on Vera's belly button, like I could keep looking for the rest of my life…

I don't remember the end of that night. I didn't have any money left the next morning. I hope I gave it all to that whore. I hope I remembered to thank her.

32

Vera

And so I packed my things, and went to the Labor Day picnic, and climbed out my window to meet Hal one last time, and helped get the kids off for the first day of school. And today after work, Tom and Hal loaded all my earthly possessions into Hal's truck, and I said goodbye.

Hester had resigned herself to my going once it was decided, but Petey hadn't. When I'd gone to pack my pincushion, I'd found all the pins pushed down tight. He knows I hate that. I knelt down on the sidewalk and hugged him and Hester together. He wouldn't hug me back, but he leaned on me, and I kissed the top of his head.

Tom squeezed me so hard I grunted, and told me to be good. "Give us a holler if it doesn't work out," he added, looking off down the street.

"Oh, Thomas, she'll be fine," Wanda said. "Now, Vera, you watch out for those big-city men—and let us know when you get engaged!" She gave me a quick hug and a smile. She'd been smiling all day, and she'd baked Hal a blackberry chiffon cake to take home.

Freddy stood well back from all the hugging. When Tom shook Hal's hand, I offered Freddy mine. He shook it awkwardly. "You behave, now," I told him.

Then I climbed in the truck beside Hal, and we drove away, and I cried. Hal patted my knee and didn't say anything. Now we're past Charlestown, and the wind has dried the last of my tears. When I blow my nose, Hal smiles at me. "They'll be all right," he calls across the wind. I nod, and smile back. They will.

It's too windy to talk much. I watch the woods and fields speeding past, green and bronze and yellow, and read signs. Burma-Shave rhymes, an ad for a Cincinnati bank. My Cincinnati story was a good one. For a minute I imagine myself living in the city—riding streetcars, running a sewing machine in a long row of sewing machines, eating lunch with the other factory girls. Not a bad life. Except I wouldn't have Hal. And I'm expecting a baby.

Pine Lodge Motor Court—Cabins Modern All Comforts. Suddenly I want to stop. Spend the night somewhere. Slow down. I'm not ready to meet May. What will I say to her? What on earth will she say to me? Am I sure this is what I want?

Hal glances at me, then takes my hand. I start to pull away, out of habit. But there's no-one here to see—just the two of us, and people alongside the road minding their own business. And besides, there's no more need to hide. The wind rushes through the cab, tugging at the scarf over my hair. I imagine it blowing away all the months of sneaking around, all the making up stories and climbing out windows and worrying. I squeeze Hal's hand, then move the cakebox to the floorboard and scoot over next to him.

We come down onto a river road, steep green hills on our left and the wide Ohio on our right. A string of barges is headed downstream, heaped with sand. I could lean in close to Hal now, and ask him about May—is she really going to be our wedding preacher? Or I could ask him about their family, get some idea what I'm in for. But I don't. It's too windy, and it's too late. I should have asked him Sunday night, or last night. But we were busy. And I didn't need any more to think about.

So I just sit here, rushing toward a new life at seventy miles an hour, with Hal's fingers tracing a pleat of my skirt up and down my thigh.

Hal turns and aims his voice at my ear. "Not that much further. Half an hour, forty-five minutes, we'll be home."

We'll be home. I lean my head on Hal's shoulder, and close my eyes.

PART TWO

33

May

I was picking corn for supper when Hal got home. Katy saw the truck in the driveway when we came out of the corn patch, and ran toward the house, hollering her "Daddy-Daddy-Daddy!" I followed at a walk, my apron-load of corn bumping my thighs. In the back of the truck, a few crates and boxes were tucked between a black traveling trunk and a sewing-machine cabinet. An electric fan turned slowly in the breeze.

When I came into the kitchen, Katy was in Hal's arms, peering shyly under his chin at Vera.

Vera was untying a blue-green scarf from her hair. She folded it into a neat triangle, and gave me a nervous-looking smile. "Hi," she said.

"Hi," I answered automatically. Vera didn't look like Greta Garbo. Her chin was a little pointy, her hazel eyes close-set.

Hal shifted Katy to one arm and handed Vera a glass of ice tea. "Well, May," he said, "This is Vera. Vera, May."

Vera said something, but I couldn't make it out. My ears were roaring. "Pleased to meet you," I said. My voice sounded muffled. I gave my head a little shake.

I heard Hal's voice again, distant and tinny. He raised the tea pitcher towards me, and I nodded. My knees wobbled suddenly. I pulled out a chair and sat down, still clutching my apron full of corn. Hal handed me a glass, and I took a long drink. The cold of it felt like an icicle in my chest. I sat up a little straighter.

Hal was talking. "...that curve outside of..." I heard, and "...two wagons..." Something about the trip. I shut my eyes, and took another drink of tea. The noise in my ears was fading.

Then Vera's voice, saying, "Would you like me to shuck the corn?"

"Oh, no," I answered, and stood up. I was still light-headed, but my legs held. "I'll get it."

"We might ought to unload the truck first," Hal suggested. "It'll be dark before long."

It took us three trips to carry everything in. Then we were all standing in the downstairs bedroom, with the trunk and the sewing machine and the stacked crates. It felt crowded. I started to go out—but Katy had hold of my skirt, and she was busy staring at Vera.

Vera sat down on the bed. "What do you have there, Katy?"

Katy opened her free hand to show a tangle of brown cornsilk.

"Oh, cornsilks!" Vera said. "Those smell so good."

Katy brought her hand to her face and sniffed, then smiled.

"You have a pretty smile," Vera told her.

Katy fingered her teeth thoughtfully, getting the cornsilks wet with slobber. Then she walked over to Vera, dragging me with her, and held out the cornsilks.

"Mmm," Vera said, sniffing them. "Smells like summertime."

"I help Mommy get corn," Katy said.

"Did you?"

Hal chimed in from the doorway. "Katy's a big girl—aren't you, Katy?"

Katy nodded. "I a *big* girl," she told Vera.

I felt silly, standing over the two of them. I stared at the pattern of the quilt, pink and yellow on white. The late sunlight made the colors glow. My eyes followed the squares and triangles to where they curved up over the single pillow.

"Can I help you with supper?" Vera asked, looking up at me.

"The chicken needs to bake a little longer," I said. "We've got time for your wedding."

"Now?" Vera looked startled.

Hal squinted at me. "Right away?"

When else? "I don't know why not."

"Well," Hal said, "I was going to get a ring. And Vera might want to unpack…" He looked at Vera. Vera looked at me.

"Usually you have the wedding before you move in," I said. Then I realized how awful that sounded, and added, "Anyway, that's how *we* did it." That was even worse. I shut my mouth tight. What was wrong with me? This whole thing was my idea.

Vera looked back at Hal, her eyes a little wide. "We could do the ring later," she said. "I don't mind." Hal scratched his ear and frowned.

I took a deep breath, and said carefully, "It's too hot in here to unpack now, anyway. We can go out in the yard, where there's a breeze. It won't take long."

Hal shrugged, then grinned at me. "You're the preacher."

Vera still looked like a startled deer, but she stood up, and brushed at her dress. "Better get to it, then," she said, "Before it's too dark out to read the Bible."

The Bible? My stomach did a somersault. "Well," I stammered, "I hadn't thought…I mean, I don't know if we have a Bible in the house…right now…" We didn't. Mom had taken hers to Frankfort.

"I've got a New Testament." Vera stepped over Katy, who was peering under the bed, and rummaged in a crate. "My friend Sue gave it to me—her mother didn't like the new translation… Here."

It was thinner than Mom's Bible, and the black leather cover was shiny and new. "What do you want me to read?" I asked.

"Oh, just the Corinthians thing," she said. "I always liked that."

I gave her a blank look. I'd never paid any attention to what chapter-and-verse Mom was quoting at me—other than John 3:16, which she didn't even bother to quote after a while. *John three-sixteen,* she'd say, shaking her head at me. *John three-sixteen!*

"It's marked." Vera pointed to a black ribbon dangling from between the gold-edged pages. "Chapter thirteen."

"Oh." I couldn't think what else to say.

Hal stirred in the doorway. "Well, then," he said.

I tucked the Bible under my arm. "Come on, Katy, we're going outside."

"I'll just fix my hair," Vera said. "You-all go ahead."

"I a big girl," Katy said, as the three of us headed for the back yard. "Mommy a big girl. Chotchy a big girl." She'd taken to calling her rag doll "Chotchy" lately, for some reason. "Daddy..." Katy looked doubtfully at Hal.

"Daddy's a man," I reminded her.

"Daddy a big man," she agreed, picking her way down the porch steps. "Chotchy a big *boy.*" She twisted to look back at the house. I could see her wondering what to call Vera.

"Tell you what," I told Katy. "Why don't you and Daddy pick some flowers."

Katy grabbed Hal's hand. "Pick flowers! *Big* flowers!" She waved her free arm in a circle.

Hal chuckled. "That big, huh?"

I watched them heading for the garden, and sighed. I wasn't starting off on the best foot. I'd almost fainted, there in the kitchen. And I couldn't believe those catty remarks I'd made— like Grace in a nasty mood. You'd think I didn't want this to work. I heard the screen door open and shut behind me, and squared my shoulders. This was my plan. My plan, to keep my family together. Time to pull myself together and see it through—pretend wedding and all.

Hal and Vera faced each other, with the blooming rose-of-sharon behind them. Katy sat on the grass, tearing up marigolds into Hal's hat like Hal had shown her.

"Okay," I said, "I guess we'll do the Bible reading first." *Get it out of the way*, I thought, but didn't say. I opened the Bible, tipping the thin pages toward the evening light. Chapter thirteen...there. "'If I speak in the tongues of men and of angels, but have not love, I am a noisy gong or a clanging cymbal.'" Mom used to call me some kind of cymbal. *You think you're so smart, Missy, you're just sounding brass and tinkling cymbals!* I tried to swallow, but my mouth was too dry. I read on, slogging my way through the words like they were shirts to be ironed. The whole thing was about love. "'Love is patient and kind...'" Had Mom ever *read* this? "'Love bears all things, believes all things, hopes all things, endures all things...'"

I finished the reading, and shut the book with a thump. Katy flung a handful of flower petals at Vera's skirt. My heart was pounding for no reason, and I felt like I might cry. I clenched my teeth. *Get ahold of yourself, Maydie.*

Hal and Vera were both looking at me expectantly, like I was a real preacher instead of a rattled housewife in a work dress. "Okay," I said, "Then you say your vows." I dug in my apron pocket for the old envelope I'd written them out on, as best I could remember. "Who wants to go first?"

"Hal, I think," Vera said, smiling nervously.

"All right—Hal," I said. "Do you take Vera to be your wife, to have and to hold..." I'd left out the part about it being lawful. Halfway through, I realized I'd forgotten something else —"cleave only to" something... Cleave? I imagined an ax splitting a log, and blinked. I must have that wrong. I read the rest of it, ending with, "Um...As long as you both shall live?"

"I do," Hal said, and winked at me.

I turned to Vera and read it all again. She gazed up teary-eyed at Hal and repeated, "I do."

"Okay," I said, "So, I now pronounce you—"

"Wait!" Vera said, and I jumped. "The prayer?"

"Oh, that's right." I hoped the sunset light hid my blush. How could I forget? I hadn't even written anything down. "Well..." I looked out towards the garden, at the row of zinnias blazing orange and pink and red in the sunset, and tried to think when I'd prayed last. Sometime before Daddy died... A drop of sweat ran down my arm. I could hear Mom's praying in my mind, sing-song and tearful. *Root out the sin in our hearts, dear Lord Jesus, put Satan behindst us and make us fit for Thy holy will...*

Vera and Hal were waiting. Why had I ever said I'd do this? Any of it?

"Look, Mommy!" Katy grinned up at me, pulling Hal's hat down over her ears.

"We're almost done, Katy," I said.

"Almost done," she said cheerfully, and tried to throw a marigold petal at me. It stuck to her sweaty hand.

Hal shifted his feet in the grass. I'd better get this over with. "Let's all bow our heads," I said, and shut my eyes. *You make your own peace with God,* Daddy had told me. I had as much right to pray as anybody—and I didn't have to do it like Mom. "Dear God," I said, then cleared my throat and started again. "Dear God...uh...please bless this wedding."

I opened my eyes. Hal and Vera were holding hands. Their eyes were shut. At least now nobody was staring at me. I looked at Hal's bowed head, his dark curls glossy with Brylcreem. "Please bless Hal, God. Help him, um...be a good husband. Bless Vera, and help her be a good...wife." Vera's head gave a tiny nod. Katy lay down across my feet with Hal's hat over her face.

Was that enough to say? What if God was actually listening to my hemming-and-hawing—would he know I wanted this to work? The Bible felt sweaty in my hand. A bumblebee crawled out of a rose-of-sharon blossom behind Vera's head, and flew away.

"Dear God," I said again. My voice shook a little. "I know this isn't the usual way. I hope you see I'm...we're doing the best we can. Hal—" I stopped, looking down at Hal's hands holding Vera's. Then I squeezed my eyes shut and said what I knew was true, all in a rush. "Hal and Vera love each other, and me and Hal love each other, and I hope you can see your way to bless that, and give us...give us the grace to see it through. Help us be patient and kind." Now I was blinking back tears. *Get ahold of yourself.* I wiped my eyes, and shrugged. "Amen."

Hal and Vera raised their heads. "Amen," Hal said.

"Amen," Vera whispered, wiping her cheeks.

I sighed. "And, I guess…I pronounce you man and wife." I handed the Bible back to Vera. I felt like I'd just walked a hundred miles. At least it was done.

Almost done. "Can I kiss the bride?" Hal asked, with a crooked smile.

Dear God, I said again in my head. "Yes," I said out loud. I looked down at Katy. She had marigold petals in her hair.

Hal took my hand, and I looked up again.

"Thank you," Vera said quietly, and smiled. It was a real smile this time, not a nervous one, and it lit up her whole face. I felt my own face stir a little, like it wished it could smile back.

"Let's go have our supper," I said. I dropped Hal's hand to pick Katy up, and headed for the house, leaving the two of them to follow us in.

34

Vera

My bedroom looks more like home when I've hung up Mama's sampler—*Surely goodness and mercy shall follow me all the days of my life, and I will dwell in the house of the LORD for ever,* with yellow roses and violets. Mama made it for me when she married Mr. Townsend. I told her she was supposed to be getting wedding presents, not giving them, but she said she wanted me to have something from her in my new home.

The closet has winter coats stored in it, but there's enough room for my things. My Sunday dresses seem out of place, with their full skirts and bright colors. The floral-print dress May was wearing today looked fairly new, but it was feed-sack fabric—I noticed an old stitching line on the sleeve—and made to a pattern Mama and I were using ten years ago. Even my everyday clothes look a little citified. But they'll do. I made them to last.

I can't quit yawning. It's dark out, and it's been a long day. Everything after five o'clock would've been a long day by itself —saying goodbye, the ride here, meeting May, the wedding... When I found myself standing in the yard with Hal, in front of a "preacher" in a shirtwaist dress, I felt a little silly. I tried to remember how clear and true it had felt, when I told Hal I wanted a wedding. This was real. It was for good.

I tried not to mind as May stumbled through things. She did as well as some real preachers I've seen. I concentrated on the words—*the greatest of these is Love…As long as you both shall live*—and looked at Hal.

Then May prayed. And in the middle of her prayer, it was like the sun came out. Like May had been halfway somewhere-else before, and suddenly she was all there. Not just May, either —we were all right there. Hal and me, Katy with her flowers, the sky and the white farmhouse and the locusts singing in the trees. And God, I guess. Anyway, I had that feeling I always had when Pastor Locke prayed. Like somebody was listening. Like we were in the house of the LORD, and goodness and mercy would follow us all the days of our lives.

I'm tearing up about it again now. May's hard to read—she seemed almost grumpy before the wedding, and afterwards she was busy with supper and distracted by Katy—but right then, in that prayer, I knew I was welcome here.

I'm putting my underthings in the vanity drawers when Katy trots in, giggling and looking over her shoulder. May follows her, and scoops her up as she tries to hide behind the sewing machine. "All right, Katy, I caught you. Time for bed."

"No! What's that?" Katy leans sideways in May's arms, trying to see into my trunk. There are sleepy wrinkles under her eyes.

"I'll show you tomorrow," I tell her. "Night-night."

"Say night-night, Katy," May says.

Katy frowns at me. "Her—her—" She pats May's shoulder, trying to find words.

"Vera." May sounds tired and patient. "Say night-night to Vera."

"Vewa go night-night?" Katy asks. "At my house?"

"Yes, I'll be right here," I say. "See you in the morning."

May turns to leave, but Katy grabs at the doorframe, stammering urgently, "What—what—"

May sighs, and stops. I smile at her. I know that sigh—when Freddy was little, he could never get to sleep until all his questions were answered. "What—" Katy says, rubbing her eyes. "Where Vewa sleep?"

"Right here," May says. I nod, patting the quilt beside me.

"I sleep *upstairs*. With Mommy and Daddy." Katy's voice is firm, but she looks at May to be sure.

May's eyes move from Katy to my hand on the quilt, and back to Katy. "Yes," she says, "Mommy'll be right across the hall."

"Right across a hall," Katy repeats, then slumps against May's shoulder and sticks her fingers in her mouth. May sighs again, and carries her out.

Katy's words ring in my ears as I fold a camisole and lay it in the drawer. *Upstairs, with Mommy and Daddy.* I make a face at myself in the vanity mirror. All my dreams of sleeping the whole night with Hal, waking up beside him in the morning—I never gave much thought to Hal sleeping with May. I mean, of course he will, sometimes. But this is our wedding night. Sort of.

The trunk is empty. I stare into it a moment, biting my lip. How will we decide who gets Hal, which night? That sounds like two sisters bickering over a rag doll—I don't want it to be like that. I don't know how I want it to be.

I shut the lid of the trunk, wondering how many more things I haven't thought of.

35

May

Once Katy was settled, I went back down to the kitchen. I could hear Vera in her bedroom, still unpacking. I was glad—I didn't feel up for any more conversation. I just wanted to go to bed.

I went out to the porch to pump my bathwater. The pump handle squeaked as I cranked. SQUEAK, a-squeak, SQUEAK, a-squeak... It sounded like that Bible reading—*BEARS all things, BELIEVES all things, HOPES all things, ENDURES all things.* Better put some grease on it tomorrow.

Hal came in from doing chores and followed me back into the kitchen. He looked a little surprised to see me with my bathwater so early, but he just smiled and sat down to take off his boots. I set the washbasin on the table, and stared at the reflection of the overhead light in the water. It was Hal and Vera's wedding night. On our wedding night, I was so nervous I cried. And so happy I cried.

Hal turned a boot in his hand, flexing the toe where it was starting to crack. "Going to need new boots before winter."

I nodded. "Those have lasted you pretty well."

"Mm-hm." He leaned over and set the boots behind the door.

Neither of us said anything for a minute. I stirred the cold water in the washbasin with my fingers, while the silence pounded like a heartbeat between us. My throat felt hot and tight. I swallowed, pushing the feeling down.

Hal started, "May, if you—" I shook my head without looking up, and he stopped.

Then I dried my hand on my skirt, and picked up the wash-basin. "Goodnight, Hal," I said. "See you in the morning."

I was halfway across the living room before Hal said good-night. Upstairs, I put Hal's pajamas and his pillow out on the cedar chest in the hall. When he came up to get them, I pre-tended I was asleep.

I knew it was the rat dream as soon as I saw the feed bin. My stomach went cold. *Wake up,* I told myself. *Run!*—but the dream held me tight. Chickens scattered, wings flapping, as the bin's snug-fitted boards came closer. Choking with fear, I reached for the heavy, sloping lid.

I woke with a gasp, jerking my hand back so hard I smacked my knuckles on the headboard. The window was wrong...and where was Sissy? Then I came back to myself—my grown-up self—and blew out a long sigh. It was just the rat dream. I hadn't had it in years.

Before it was a dream, it had been a real rat—in the chick-enhouse feed bin, when I was a kid. I'd screamed and slammed the lid when I saw it, scaring the chickens half to death. Daddy and Jamie came running, and I sobbed out an explanation. But when Daddy lifted the feed-bin lid, there was no rat. Jamie started laughing. I tried to hit him, but Daddy caught my arm, and sent Jamie off to finish up the milking.

"It *was* in there," I insisted, crying. "It was a great big rat—"

"I ain't doubting you, Maydie," Daddy said.

"Well, where'd it *go?*" I stared at the yellow cracked corn, half expecting the rat to come burrowing out.

Daddy let the lid fall shut. "Think, Maydie. Was it there yesterday?"

"No." I shivered.

"So how'd it get in?"

My eyes widened in outrage. "*Jamie* put it—"

"No," Daddy chuckled. "Jamie ain't smart enough to catch a rat. That rat got in there all by himself."

I thought. "There's a hole?"

"That's my girl." Daddy patted my shoulder. "Ol' Ratty's made him a back door, and when you come screaming at him, he skedaddled. Don't you worry, Maydie—we'll fix Ratty's wagon."

After breakfast, Daddy helped me find the hole, and we nailed a flattened tin can over it, like a patch on a pair of work pants. I never saw that rat again.

I didn't dream about it right away—not until I was sixteen or seventeen. In the dreams, I'd lift the lid and see the rat, but I was too scared to scream. All I could think was, Daddy was wrong. We hadn't shut the rat out, with our tin-can patch. We'd shut it *in*, and it had been in there all along. All those times I'd fed the chickens, it had been right there under the cracked corn, with its twisty body and its teeth like yellow nails—

Then I'd wake up, choking back a scream so I wouldn't wake Sissy. I'd pull her warm little body close for comfort, and lie awake until the fear died away.

I wished I had Sissy to snuggle with now. Or Hal. I used to hold Hal and stroke his head, when he'd wake up with those nightmares after the war.

But Hal was downstairs. With Vera.

My nightgown was damp with sweat, and I was wide awake. Maybe I should go down to the kitchen, find something useful to do. But I'd have to go past the downstairs bedroom—Vera's room. Vera and Hal's room, tonight. I might wake them up. Or they might be awake already.

I lay still and listened to the katydids in the mulberry tree outside. Not that I could've listened to anything else, through their racket. *KatyDID katydidn't, katyDID katydidn't... Love BEARS all things, ENDURES all things...* For Pete's sake. I turned onto my side, and wrapped my pillow around my head.

36

Vera

I woke up to a rooster crowing. He'd crowed several times already, but now it was getting light. Hal grunted as I got out of bed. I went out to pee, holding my breath to fight down queasiness—the outhouse was clean, but it smelled like what it was. On my way back in, I stopped under the rose arbor, which smelled like heaven. Bats were swooping over the yard in the twilight. I stood watching them, stretching out the cramps of eight hours in a single bed with Hal, until the mosquitoes drove me back inside.

The kitchen water bucket was empty, so I filled it at the porch pump and hoisted it back to the counter. Someone had fitted a convenient spigot halfway up the side of the bucket, so you could wash your hands over a dishpan. I used the dipper to fill the percolator, and went looking for coffee.

"What do you need?"

I jumped. May was behind me, barefoot and carrying her washbasin. Hal followed her in, straightening his suspenders.

"Coffee?" I said, shutting a cabinet door. I felt like I'd been caught snooping.

"There in the green jar. Two scoops, for a full pot." May was already dressed, with her hair pinned up. I straightened the belt on my housecoat.

Hal winked at me, and went to comb his hair at the mirror on the screen porch. I'd been so glad when he came into the bedroom last night, carrying his pillow. After the long, strange day, I'd just needed to lie down in his arms and let him love me. And he had.

I put the coffee on, then went to get dressed. When I got back to the kitchen, Hal was gone—milking, I guessed—and May was tending a skillet at the stove. I smelled sausage and onions, and felt queasy again.

"How do you like your eggs?" she asked.

I swallowed. "I'll probably just have toast and coffee."

May started whisking flour into a bowl of milk. Her eyes looked tired. "There'll be biscuits in a minute," she said, "If you'd rather have those."

"Biscuits sound good. Can I help with anything?"

She dumped the milk into her skillet, and nodded at the fridge. "You can get out the jelly. Ought to be a peach and a grape in there. Top shelf."

Breakfast was ready by the time Hal came back from the barn—biscuits and gravy, with three eggs over easy for Hal and two for May. My two biscuits looked lonely on the plate.

"You riding with Jamie this morning?" May asked, pouring Hal's coffee.

Hal nodded. "He said he'd be by at seven."

"And then tomorrow you'll drive?"

"No, Jamie and Don Parish already had a carpool going. Don's tomorrow, I'll drive Friday." Hal ate half his biscuits and gravy in three bites, then said to me, "I'll have to wait and get you a ring then. Jewelry store's too far to walk on my lunch break."

I nodded, nibbling at a biscuit and wondering who Jamie was. The taste of homemade grape jelly almost gave me an appetite.

"Grace called on the phone," May told Hal. "Ronny was throwing up half the night, so she's not coming to help me with beans today." She reached for the peach jelly. "I hope Jamie doesn't take it. Rye's got the Mack boys and Leroy lined up for you Saturday, but he was counting on Jamie too."

Hal nodded. "We'll just have to manage with what we've got."

I had half a dozen questions, but I picked one. "What's happening Saturday?"

"Cutting tobacco," Hal said through a mouthful of biscuit. "Whoops, there's my train," he added, as a car horn sounded outside. He got up, took a last drink of coffee, and leaned down to kiss May goodbye. I blinked—I'd never seen Hal kiss anyone else before. Then he was bending to kiss me too. His lips tasted like coffee. "Bye," he said, and went out, grabbing the lunch box May had set by the door.

May stared after him, working her mouth thoughtfully. When she saw me watching her, she picked up her fork again.

I finished my second biscuit, and carried my plate and Hal's to the sink—no, to the counter with the dishpans. "Where do you keep the dish soap?"

"Underneath. The blue box." May pointed with her fork, and scraped up the last of her gravy. When I reached for a hot-water faucet that wasn't there, she added, "Kettle's on the stove." I blushed—I'd heated dishwater on the stove my whole childhood, but I was used to town life after eight years.

Wednesday afternoon

Dear Tom ~~& Wanda~~ & Wanda,

I know you're waiting to hear that I'm safe and sound in Cincinnati. Well, I am safe and sound, ~~but not in Cincinnati.~~ but it turned out that ~~Jeanne~~ Sue was wrong about the factory. ~~They're She thought~~ It's a long story, but ~~the upshot of it all was that~~ I decided ~~since I was already packed~~ I'd best go on ~~home with Hal~~ to Hal and May's place. ~~They asked~~ I'm going to stay here ~~awhile~~ awhile. ~~To be honest,~~ ~~Actually,~~ ~~I'm~~ May can use the help, and they have an extra room. So ~~Wanda can~~ don't keep my room for me.

~~I I'm~~ I hope you are all well. You can write to me here. Give the kids my love.

Love,
Vera

So much for not making up stories anymore. But I'll have enough to manage, with whatever the family here thinks about all this. May didn't say. I didn't ask.

I copy the letter over without the crossing-outs and put it in an envelope, then wonder what name to put with my return address. "Vera Stinson" feels like a worse lie than anything in the letter. But if I write "Vera Dixon," I might as well drop an atomic bomb while I'm at it. Finally I just write "V." Tom calls me that half the time anyway.

May and Katy are both napping, but I couldn't rest until I got my letter done. May said she didn't sleep well last night. Maybe that was why she was so quiet this morning, while we were picking and breaking beans. Or maybe she's upset—but she didn't seem upset, just not very sociable. I wish I knew what she's thinking, about me being here. She answered my questions about the family absent-mindedly, until I gave up and sang songs with Katy instead.

I did learn a few things, though. I run through the family members in my head, trying to keep them straight—Iva and Rye, Jamie and Grace, Ronny and Carol. It's funny, to think of Hal as part of a whole family tree. In Cartersboro, he was just Hal. Here he's a husband, and a father, and a son, and a brother-in-law, and an uncle.

Hal's different here, too. I can tell this is where he belongs. There's an easiness about his shoulders and mouth that wasn't there in Cartersboro. When he brought in the milk this morning, he was whistling "Pop Goes the Weasel." It's good to see him happy in the daytime. It's good to see him at all—I could look at him all day. Too bad he had to go to work.

37

May

"Whew!" Vera said, coming in from the garden. "It's broiling out there!" She came past me to get a drink of water, trailing a whiff of sweat and tomato vines.

"How many more did you get?" I asked her, scrubbing at a Ball jar with the bottlebrush.

"About half-again what you had."

"Good. We'll get two canners full."

"You want me to wash some jars?"

"No, I'm about done. You could start the water heating, on the porch stove." I wished I could think of something to say to Vera, besides giving orders. She'd only been here two days—but I couldn't sit around making small talk. There was too much to do.

The porch pump squeaked as Vera filled the canner. I'd forgotten to grease it yesterday. I counted the clean jars one more time—seven with wire bails and seven screw-tops, three of them wide-mouth—and started sorting through the box of lids.

"Up!" Katy grabbed my legs. "Mommy, pick me up!"

"Not now, hon." Was that three wide-mouth, or three regular?

"*Up!*" Katy jumped up and down, her head bumping the bottom of the box.

"Why don't you go find your doll?" I said, counting the screw-top jars again.

Katy scowled up at me. "Chotchy is *old!*"

"Really?"

"Him threw up."

"Oh, my." I counted out zinc lids and glass lids, then got out the new jar rubbers. Katy ran off into the living room, yelling Chotchy's name.

"Is there a knife you like for tomatoes?" Vera asked, rummaging in the utensil drawer.

"Just a paring knife," I said. "No, the other one. —Oh, for Pete's sake! I've lost count again."

"Sorry." Vera made a sympathetic face. "I always have to write numbers down, or say them out loud. Or both."

I shook my head. "I don't know what's the matter with me today." I counted out eleven regular rubbers and three widemouth, and dropped them into the dishwater. I never was any good at talking to strangers. I was used to working alone—or with Grace, who would do all the talking if I didn't feel like it. Vera kept asking questions, and trying to catch my eye. She was just being friendly, I told myself. Anyway, there was no help for it.

It wasn't much cooler on the screen porch, but there was a breeze now and then to carry off the steam. Vera blanched tomatoes while I filled jars. Katy lay on the floor, pushing the screen door open with her feet and letting it bang shut.

"How many quarts do you usually put up?" Vera asked, plopping a peeled red tomato into the bowl.

"Depends," I said. We might need a few more, with another person. I wiped the shoulder of a full jar, stretched a rubber onto it, and screwed down the lid. "There's still a lot of green ones out there."

"Do you ever make green tomato relish?"

I shrugged. "Usually just cucumber. Grace makes piccalilli, and we trade."

"My sister-in-law made mock mincemeat out of green tomatoes once, but I didn't much care for it."

"Doesn't sound very good." I put my last jar in the canner, and started coring more tomatoes. Katy had stopped kicking the door. She stared at her feet on the screen, looking half-asleep in the heat.

"My Mama makes the best mince pies," Vera said, wiping her forehead with the back of her wrist. "And her pie crust... Mmm! Mine's never that good."

I cut the core out of a yellow pineapple tomato that must've weighed two pounds—it would almost fill a quart by itself. "Seems like store-bought lard doesn't have as much taste as it used to."

"You know, I think you're right." Vera dipped tomatoes out of the blanching pan into the cold water. "And it's not as soft."

"I think they're doing something to it," I said. "It makes a good pie crust, but I miss the taste." The canner lid rattled, and I turned the heat down. Grandma Stout taught me to make pie crust—and fried apple pies, with dried apples. Maybe I ought to dry some apples this year.

"Mama even sold her pies at Christmastime, for a while," Vera said. "Before the Crash."

I wondered how her family had gotten through the Depression. Probably just worked hard and hoped, like everybody else. I worked in silence awhile. Katy rolled a green tomato around on the floor, making train noises.

When my timer went off, I took the lid off the canner, and waved my dishtowel at the cloud of steam that billowed out. "One of these days I'm going to can tomatoes in the winter-time," I said, "When it's nice and cool."

Vera laughed. "Now, there's an idea!" She watched as I took jars out and snapped down wire bails. "Have you tried the new two-piece lids?"

"No. I've seen advertisements for them. Can you use the same jars? —Just a minute, hon." Katy was pulling on my skirt.

"Just the screw-cap ones." Vera started spooning salt into the next batch of jars.

"I've got about every kind of jar there is," I said. "Some of Mom's, and Grandma Stout's, and Iva gave me half of hers when Hal and I got married."

Hal's name felt awkward in my mouth. I'd been chatting away with Vera like I'd known her for years—even enjoying myself. I picked Katy up and wiped a tomato seed off her cheek.

Vera finished filling a jar and snapped the bail down halfway, then held out her hands to Katy. "Want me to hold you, while Mommy puts the jars in?"

Katy thought a moment. Then she scrambled into Vera's arms, and turned back to me. "Do mommy-bird!"

I glanced at Vera. "Oh, Katy, I don't—"

"Mommy-bird! Mommy-bird!" Katy begged, bouncing on Vera's hip.

I shrugged, a little embarrassed, and raised the wire jar-lifter high above the table. "Here comes the big mommy bird," I told Katy, "And here's a yummy worm...*Chomp!*" I grabbed a jar of tomatoes.

"Fly away, mommy bird! Feed babies!" Katy yelled, as I swooped the jar up and into the canner.

"Thank you Mommy!" Vera said, in a baby-bird voice.

Katy giggled. "'Nother worm!"

I did the other two jars Vera had ready, then started scooping tomatoes into the next one. Katy squirmed down from Vera's arms. "Mommy, come! Get Chotchy."

"I've got to do these jars," I said. "You can go get Chotchy."

Katy hesitated, then grabbed Vera's hand. "Come! Chotchy threw up."

"Is she sick?" Vera asked, following Katy around the table.

"No," Katy scoffed. "Her is a *boy!*"

"Oh, he is?" Vera nodded thoughtfully. "Well, we better see how he's doing."

"Chotchy is *old,*" Katy said firmly, as they went off through the kitchen.

Katy was getting used to Vera fast, too. *That's good,* I reminded myself. *She's part of the family now.* I pushed another tomato down in the jar, red juice rising almost to the rim.

38

Hal

I bought May's wedding ring from the Sears catalog—but a wedding ring's a wedding ring, right? How many kinds can there be?

Turns out Evans Jewelry's got more kinds than you can shake a stick at. I'm hunting through the only tray of plain gold bands in the place, looking for one like May's, while Mr. Evans talks a mile a minute about your topaz and your emeralds and your filigree work. He must think I'm Mr. Rockefeller.

Just a gold band, with scallops along the edges... There's not one. I look again, starting to sweat. Nope. Now what?

"Who's the lucky gal?" Mr. Evans asks, with a wink. He doesn't know me from Adam—which is good, or he'd know I was already married.

"It's a secret." I pick out the two rings closest to what I want, hold them up on the tips of my pointer fingers. One's plain, the other's got a design. I sigh. I sure don't want to give Vera a nicer ring than May's, or one that's not as nice either. I don't even know what makes a ring nice.

May would buy the cheaper one. She's not one to spend extra for fancy. But the cheaper one looks fancier, to me, with that crisscross on it. Maybe fancier than May's. Why couldn't there be one that's just the same?

"You know, a lot of fellows'll pay over time," Mr. Evans is saying. "Something like this, now—that'll show her how you feel." He holds out a ring with enough diamonds on it to blind a fellow. That's not even fancy, it's just god-awful. I wouldn't buy that if I had a million dollars.

If I had a million dollars, I'd get Vera that one there, with the white gold all carved to catch the light. It's simple, but it sparkles. Like Vera's smile, lighting up a whole room. I'd get May a new one, too. She wouldn't see why. But I bet she'd like that one, with the forget-me-nots all around it. Pretty and sturdy both.

Hell, if I bought May and Vera ten rings apiece, it wouldn't show them how I feel. And I've still got to pick one. I don't want to hurt anybody's feelings. My lunch hour's about over. Eeny-meeny-miney-mo... I put the smooth ring back in the tray, and set the crisscross one on the counter. "Tell you what," I say, "How about I give you cash on the barrelhead for this one, and you keep the rest."

Mr. Evans chuckles, as he measures the string I brought and boxes up the right size ring. "You knew what you wanted when you walked in the door, didn't you?"

"Mmm." I open my wallet and count out the bills. It's ten till one—I've got time to stop by the candy store next door and get Katy a sack of peanut brittle. I hope they've only got one kind.

39

Vera

Six-thirty on a Saturday morning. In Cartersboro, Tom and Wanda would still be in bed. Here, only Katy was asleep. After chores and a big breakfast, Hal was off getting ready for his tobacco-cutting crew, and May was out in the garden. I nibbled at a piece of toast while I sliced apples for pie. When I took a drink of coffee, my new wedding band clinked against the cup.

After the apples, I started on the butter, cranking the handle of May's tabletop churn. I had to look away from the paddles whirling in the jar of white cream—my nerves this morning weren't helping my stomach. Hal's mother was due to show up any minute now, to help cook dinner for the crew.

I hadn't asked Hal how his family took the news about me. I couldn't imagine they'd been pleased—but there were a lot of ways to not be pleased. I wished I knew which one to expect from Iva. She'd had a week to get used to the idea, but it was bound to be awkward at best.

May came in from the screen porch with a dishpan full of potatoes, and unloaded more vegetables out of her apron—onions, carrots, a cabbage the size of my head, all shiny-wet from the pump in the yard. May was being quiet again this morning. Maybe she was nervous too.

The handle of the churn was getting hard to crank. I looked at the jar again, and found it full of yellow butter. "That was quick!" I said, surprised.

May nodded. "The gearing makes it spin fast."

"Huh." I looked at the mechanism on top of the churn, but it didn't mean anything to me. "Sure nicer than the wooden kind."

May nodded again, and scooped flour into a mixing bowl. "There's a jar in the refrigerator for the buttermilk."

I was putting the jar back when a woman's voice called out "Morning!" from the porch. May jumped, and dropped a butter knife.

"You must be Vera," the woman said, coming into the kitchen. "I'm Iva, Hal's mother." She stuck out her hand, and I wiped mine on my apron before I shook it.

"Pleased to meet you," I said. Iva was short, and plump— solid plump, not soft plump. Behind her wire-rimmed spectacles, her eyes looked me over like they were measuring me for a dress. The wedding band on my finger felt three inches wide.

"I see May's got you using one of her contraptions." Iva unloaded the dishpan she was carrying—two jars of pickled beets, half a loaf of bread, and a blue apron that matched her checkered feed-sack dress. "You should see the gadget she's got for applesauce. Our May's always trying something new."

"Oh, Iva," May said, getting out a rolling pin. "Daddy bought that churn before Sissy was born. The new ones are all electric."

Iva snorted as she tied on her apron. "Electric churns, electric sweepers…pretty soon they'll be trying to sell us electric toothbrushes. —Why, look, it's my best girl!" She picked up Katy, who had toddled in rubbing her eyes, and kissed her loudly on top of the head.

"We won't have Grace today," May told Iva, fishing Katy's boiled egg out of the water bucket. "Carol and Jamie took Ronny's stomach bug, and Grace thought she'd better not break quarantine."

"Good of her," Iva said, settling Katy into her high chair. "Some things are best not shared."

May peeled Katy's egg, and mashed it in a bowl. I tried to breathe through my mouth—I never cared for the smell of boiled eggs in the morning.

Iva took a package of ground meat out of the fridge. "You want me to make the meatloaf?"

"Of course," May said. "It'll have to wait and bake after the pies. —Iva's meatloaf's better than mine," she added, to me.

"Oh, I don't know." Iva got a mixing bowl from a cabinet. "I did bring my own bread, in case you didn't have any stale enough."

May draped a circle of dough into a pie pan, and gave Iva a sidelong look. "Grace puts crackers in her meatloaf."

Iva raised an eyebrow, and snorted again. "You can tell, too."

I stood on tiptoe to reach the cabbage grater. This was going better than I'd expected. Iva didn't seem upset at all.

Katy was in a good mood too, poking at her egg and chattering to Iva. She had hysterics for a minute when a ladybug crawled across her high chair tray, but calmed right down after May picked it up and tossed it out the back door.

"Pretty scary bug, I guess," I said, as May went back to her pie crust.

May nodded. "She'll pick tobacco worms with her bare hands, but hardshell bugs just give her fits."

I chuckled. "Petey used to be afraid of butterflies. With Hester, it's volcanoes… How many carrots do you want in the coleslaw?"

"Two's plenty. Just for color." May scooped sugar over the apples I'd sliced.

"Peel me one for the meatloaf, if you would," Iva added. "Those your kids?"

When I realized she was talking to me, sweat broke out on my arms. "Hester and Petey? Oh—no—I mean, they're my brother's kids, there's Freddy too, he's older…"

"Kids get funny ideas sometimes," Iva said, shaking pepper over the meat.

"When you're done with the meatloaf, you can see if the beans are dry enough to pick," May told her. "The sun's just getting on them."

I finished the coleslaw in a daze, trying to take this in. I'd just married Iva's already-married son, and she was asking me about my kids? Cool as a cucumber about it too—*that* was impossible. May didn't seem to notice anything odd.

When Iva finally went out to the the garden, I turned to May and asked, "Doesn't she know—"

But before I could finish, there was a crash. Katy's high chair was on its back on the floor, with Katy underneath it. May rushed to pick her up, and Katy clung to her, screaming. Seeing the worry in May's face, I stepped around her and gently felt the goose-egg rising up under Katy's fine, blond hair. No blood. "She's okay," I mouthed at May through Katy's wails.

May rocked Katy, while I got the pies in the oven and started peeling potatoes. As Katy's crying settled into sniffles, I could hear May murmuring, "It's okay, you're okay, hon, it's okay…"

I sighed. "My. You think she was trying to climb out of the highchair?"

"I guess," May said, looking tired. "I should have kept a closer eye."

I shook my head. "They always get ideas right when your back's turned. Hester took her walker down a flight of concrete steps once, when I went to answer the phone."

"Oh, my!" May said. "Was she all right?"

"A broken tooth and a black eye," I said. "Could've been worse." Wanda hadn't thought so, though. What a scene that had been.

"Kids bounce, I guess." May gave Katy a squeeze. "Ready to go play, hon?"

"No. Mommy!" Katy buried her face in May's shoulder.

May looked at the clock. "I'll hold you a little bit more," she told Katy, "And then Mommy needs to cut up the chicken. You can show Mammaw the pirate hat Vera made you."

Mammaw. Iva. I took a breath—but Iva was already coming back in, with a mess of green beans. "My goodness, child," she said, at the sight of Katy's tear-streaked face. "What on earth happened to you?"

"I falled down!" Katy slid off of May's lap and ran to Iva, while I swallowed my question again.

40

Hal

I get to the end of a row of tobacco and straighten up, stretching my back. My watch says it's lunchtime, and my stomach agrees.

"Feeding time, boys!" Rye hollers behind me, just before I was going to holler it. I roll my eyes, and lay down my tobacco knife. Rye's got in the habit of running things, with me off in Cartersboro.

We all head for the house. Rye's telling the Mack boys how he's heard out East they cut their tobacco one leaf at a time, starting at the bottom. Lame-brainedest thing I ever heard. Leroy looks doubtful, but Henry and Joe are eating it up. Henry thinks Rye walks on water anyway. I used to think so too. Spent a few years mad as a hornet, when I figured out Rye doesn't know half as much as he thinks he does. After awhile I learned to just let him talk.

We take turns washing our hands, sticking our heads under the yard pump. The cold water feels good. And the women have got us quite a spread, in the kitchen. Nothing like cutting tobacco to give you an appetite. Katy sits on my lap and chatters at me. I listen to her instead of Rye. I don't know how he can talk so much and eat so much at the same time.

Pie and ice cream, then back out to the field. Rye cocks the sassafras twig in his mouth, nods at the sun. "We might get done today," he said. "Going to take us till dark, though. I hope you brought enough cash with you, Henry."

Henry's jug-handle ears turn red. "Uh...cash for what, sir?"

Rye looks surprised. "Didn't Joe tell you? You owe me thirty cents an hour, for learning to cut on my tobacco crop!"

"Well, sir...I..." Henry looks at his brother.

Rye laughs, and slaps him on the back. "Naw, son, I'm just funning with you. You do a man's work, you get a man's pay, same as Joe." Henry blushes even harder, and grins.

His tobacco crop? I pick up my knife, jerk it through a tobacco stalk. We split this crop fifty-fifty, and I own the land now.

"Better slow down, son," Rye hollers from the next row. "Don't want to run a spike through your hand."

I was younger than Henry when I did that. I puff out my cheeks and reach for another stalk. Rye can't help being Rye.

41

Vera

"Get you a plate, Vera," May said, putting the kettle on to heat. "We'll clean up after we eat."

Iva opened the breadbox. "I saved us back some biscuits."

"Good thing," I said. "I forgot how a crew can eat. Hard to believe it was only five of them."

"More ice cream!" Katy demanded. She was still sitting on Hal's chair.

"How much did she have already?" May asked Iva and me. We both shrugged, and she sighed. "Oh, I guess it won't hurt her." She dipped Katy a bowlful from the ice-cream freezer on the porch.

We ate quietly, resting our ears from the noise of the men. All the food was delicious. After eight years of Wanda's dry meatloaf, Iva's was heavenly. Iva brushed off my compliments, but she looked pleased.

Then I turned to ask for the butter and found May staring at me, with a forkful of green beans halfway to her mouth. Iva was busy dishing herself more coleslaw, and didn't notice. I gave May a questioning look. Her eyes went from me to Iva, and back to me. She'd just realized what I'd been trying to ask her, when Katy fell.

"You want this last dab of slaw?" Iva asked.

"What?" May said. "Oh—no, you all finish it."

When Katy dropped her spoon and Iva bent down to pick it up, I mouthed "She doesn't know?" at May. May gave her head a tiny shake. She looked surprised, or upset—or both. Had she thought I knew that? May-thought-I-knew-Iva-didn't-know... It sounded like Abbott and Costello, except not funny. My face felt hot. Had Hal told me about some cover story, and I'd forgotten? No, I would've remembered that—I'd been so tired of lying...

I hoped I hadn't said anything too disastrous. Surely if I had, Iva wouldn't be smiling and offering me more meatloaf.

"Did they say how far along they were?" May asked, scraping a plate into the slop bucket.

Iva reached across the table for a stray fork. "Rye thought they might get it done, despite James's epizootick."

I laughed. When Iva cocked her head at me, I said, "I haven't heard that word in I-don't-know-how-long!"

Iva chuckled. "Where are your people from?"

Oops. Why had I opened my mouth? Now she was paying attention to me. I tried to keep smiling. "Southern Kentucky, on my mother's side—they were the ones who said 'epizootick.'"

"You don't sound much like Kentucky," Iva said.

I put a jar of beets in the fridge. "Mama does. I grew up in Illinois, and my teacher got on me about it." I hoped I wasn't ruining whatever story Hal and May had told.

"Miss Clara was fierce about that too," May said, taking serving spoons out of dishes. "She said she wasn't going to have us sounding like a bunch of hillbillies."

Iva snorted. "Nothing wrong with sounding like country people, if that's what you are. —Well, looky there!" Katy was asleep under the table, with dried ice cream on her face.

"Good," May said. "If we hurry up, we can get a nap too." She carried Katy off to her crib. Iva poured hot water into the dishpans, and the two of us started on the dishes.

"Have you always lived around here?" I asked Iva. Maybe I could head off any more awkward questions.

Iva shook her head, drying a glass. "My people were share-croppers, in Kentucky. All the ground down there was wore out, though—wouldn't hardly grow weeds. Me and Rye decided to try our luck in Indiana."

I looked out the window, at the rolling fields and wooded low spots baking in the sun. "This is a pretty place, with the hills and all."

"Yes." Iva straightened the row of glasses in the cabinet. "Still looks mighty flat to me."

I nodded as I scrubbed a plate. "Mama said where she grew up, they had to cut steps in the ground to get down to the spring."

"Oh, yes!" Iva laughed. "We had a couple places like that. And then it'd rain on that red clay, and you'd wind up sliding the whole way down on your behind!"

I grinned at the picture. "Mama always said we didn't know what work was, doing our chores on level ground."

When May came back, Iva made room for her at the rinse pan between us. "Just in time," she said. "Vera was about to get ahead of me."

May handed her a plate to dry. "I sure appreciate your help, Iva," she said.

Iva waved the thanks away with her dishtowel. "If there was any sense to the world, women'd all be born triplets."

"Hm," May said. "Wash, rinse, and dry?"

Iva nodded, then pursed her lips thoughtfully. "Of course, you'd have to all three marry the same man, for it to do you any good."

I kept my eyes on the dishwater, so I wouldn't look at May and start giggling. This was crazy. Even so, I realized in sur-prise, I was enjoying myself. The day had felt familiar and easy —like working with Mama.

"What was it Leroy was talking about?" May asked Iva. "Somebody getting married?"

"His cousin Sadie," Iva said, drying a bowl. "You hadn't heard?"

May frowned. "Sadie Hanlon? Wasn't she seeing one of the Edgerton boys?"

"Dobie, the youngest." Iva shook her head. "And now she's pregnant. Dropped out of school, of course."

"That's too bad. Sadie was always smart, wasn't she?"

Iva pressed her lips together. "Smart about *some* things."

"And they're getting married?" May asked.

"Got married," Iva said. "Last Friday. I imagine Newt offered Dobie a shotgun escort."

"Well, at least the baby'll have a daddy," May said, rinsing a canning jar.

"Such as he is." Iva made a sour face, then added, "Course, Sadie's mother was the same way. She thought she was smart too, until she had to try to convince everybody that July minus April comes to nine months."

I swallowed hard. The pie and ice cream in my stomach seemed to be fighting with the meatloaf. I handed May a serving dish, and said, "Seems like people ought to forgive and forget, after a while."

There was a little silence. May glanced at me, then looked back down at the rinsewater. Iva rubbed a green glass relish plate dry with her dishtowel, and kept rubbing it while she gave me a long look. "Well," she finally said, "'Ought to' and 'is' aren't spelled the same. And Sadie *ought to* have known better than to wind up that way to begin with."

I bit my lip, wishing I'd kept my mouth shut.

May handed Iva the gravy boat. "And then some folks," she said, "Wouldn't have anything to say at all, if they couldn't talk mean about other people." Iva raised one eyebrow at her, and she added quickly, "Not you, Iva. But you know how some people are."

Iva let her eyebrow down. "That's true." She put the relish plate in the cabinet, and wiped the gravy boat dry. "Where do you keep this?"

"Up high," May said. "Let me get it."

I felt Iva looking at me as May put the gravy boat away, but I kept my eyes on the platter I was washing. "Anyway," Iva said, "I hope it turns out as well as it can. I always did like Sadie."

I volunteered to take the slop bucket out to the pigpen. Now I'm lingering, watching the pigs and trying to catch my breath.

There was gossip in Cartersboro too, of course. But I'd forgotten what it's like in the country, or even a little town like High Brooks. In Cartersboro, people were always coming and going—with the factories and the river, and then the war, and then the GI Bill. Old gossip moved on, and new gossip took its place. Things blew over.

In the country, people don't just talk about the trouble their neighbor got into last week. They talk about the trouble she got into three years ago, and the trouble she's bound to get into next. They talk about her mother, and her uncle that never was quite right, and what the schoolteacher said about her brother back in the third grade. If they have time, they'll talk about her grandpa's chicken-killing dog.

It'd be funny, if I didn't know better.

I knew what we're doing would upset people. I guess I thought it would blow over, fade away when a new story came upriver on the boat. But there's no riverboat here—just farm fields and kitchens, and the same people telling the same stories about each other, year after year. Short of a war or a drought or an earthquake, May and Hal and I are going to be big news for a long time.

And what does Iva think I'm doing here? I wish she'd go home, so I can ask May. I'm so frazzled I want to sit down and cry.

No, what I really want is to go back in the house, and not have anything to hide. Or anything to not hide. Just talk and laugh and work with May and Iva. They already feel more like family than Wanda ever did.

Mama would say, *you can't have everything, Vera.* But I can't help it. I want everything.

42

May

I glanced out the window as I swept in front of the stove. Vera sure was taking her time with the slop bucket. I couldn't blame her—she must be rattled.

"Where does this go?" Iva asked, pulling the extra chair back from the table.

"Katy's room," I said.

Iva nodded, then pointed near my feet. "You missed something."

I flicked the stray bit of cabbage out from under the stove with my broom, as Iva went off through the living room with the chair. Had Hal not told Vera what we'd said about her? He'd been supposed to fill her in. What a mess. What a mess it could have been, anyway. Vera had done all right...

I turned my broom around to sweep from the left, so the straws wouldn't wear all one way. Mom's brooms were always bent hard in a right-hand curve. Of course, Mom swept the floor like she was killing snakes. Sweeping never felt like a fight, to me. I liked the way the broomstraws whispered on the boards.

"What do you want me to do next?" Vera asked, coming in from the porch.

"You can mop," I told her.

She already knew where the mop and bucket were. SQUEAK a-squeak, SQUEAK a-squeak, went the pump.

"Start over by the stove," I said, when she carried the bucket in, "So Iva won't have to cross your wet floor. She's upstairs."

"Okay." Vera smiled at me over her shoulder as she wrung out the mop. Then she glanced towards the living room, and her smile vanished. I followed her eyes as she straightened up.

Iva stood in the living-room doorway. Frowning. Something was wrong. My first thought was Katy—but before I could ask, Iva said quietly, "Made some changes, haven't you?"

Oh—the bedroom furniture. But why was she upset about it? This was our house now. Anyway, it wasn't news—we'd talked about it at dinner last week. "Just making room for Vera," I said.

Iva raised an eyebrow at me, her grey eyes like steel. I tried not to look ashamed.

Vera's mop was dripping on the floor. Iva's gaze followed the sound, then moved to Vera's face. Vera looked back at her uncertainly. Drip. Drip. Drip. Suddenly Vera's eyes went wide. She drew a quick breath, then pressed her lips together carefully. Drip. Drip.

"Well," Iva said, letting her eyebrow fall back into place. Her mouth made a disappointed line. "I don't guess it's any of my business." She reached back to untie her apron, then frowned —she wasn't wearing an apron anymore. "What, did I…" she muttered, and turned around to retrace her steps.

Vera was looking white around the mouth. "Sit down," I told her. She pulled out a chair and sat, hard.

When Iva came back, she didn't meet my eyes. She folded the apron in her hands, smoothed it several times, then laid it in the dishpan with her other things.

"Iva…" I said, but I couldn't think how to go on.

Iva settled the dishpan on her hip. "You think Grace'll still want us for dinner tomorrow?" she asked, in a flat, tired voice.

"Uh…" I struggled to shift gears. Grace had said the kids were better already, so Jamie should be fine tomorrow. "I guess she'll let us know if not."

Iva nodded. Then she looked up at me suddenly, and her eyes weren't hard anymore—they were worried. "You take care, May."

"You too," I said.

I followed her onto the porch, and watched her cross the yard to the road. She wasn't walking like herself—the set of her shoulders was all wrong.

"Oh, my," Vera said in a wobbly voice, as I came back into the kitchen. "Oh…my stars…and garters!"

I gave her an impatient look. Iva was a force to be reckoned with, but there was no need to get dramatic. "Heaven knows what that was all about," I said.

"Oh—" Vera said again. "Well, it…" She paused, looking like she was picking her words. "Your bedroom door's open?"

"Yes." What, did she think Iva was shocked to see Hal's pajamas on the floor? I'd been in a hurry this morning. "But I —"

"Mine is too," Vera said. "And…um…Hal's clothes and things are all in your room, right?"

I nodded. What was she driving at?

"Well," Vera said, staring at her fingernails, "Hal's shirt and socks from yesterday are hanging over the footboard of my bed. And there are two pillows. On the bed."

She looked up at me, chewing at her lip, while I tried to get my tired mind to work. I wished she'd just spit it out. Vera's room—two pillows, Hal's dirty clothes. My room—one pillow, Hal's dresser… Hal's pajamas… "Oh," I said, as my stomach dropped through the floor. "Oh."

I heard a whimpering sound. Vera was biting her lips tight, like she was holding something in. Then it broke out—a giggle, high and silly. I stared at her. She covered her mouth with both hands, then hid her face in her apron, her whole body shaking with laughter.

What was wrong with her? There was nothing funny about it. Maybe she was hysterical. Maybe I ought to slap her. I tapped my foot against the leg of the table, waiting for her to get over it. I was seeing Iva in my mind—not the Iva who'd been glaring around my kitchen like the Day of Judgement, but the Iva who'd taken off her apron without noticing, and left it upstairs. Iva was never absentminded. Then I knew what it was I'd seen, as she walked away—Iva had looked old. Old, and worried, and helpless.

Nonsense. Iva wasn't fifty yet, and she could keep up with me any day. But the picture in my mind didn't change. I shot an irritated look at Vera, who was winding down. If she was laughing at Iva, I might slap her anyway.

Vera wiped her eyes, looking sheepish. "Sorry," she said. "I just..." She took a long breath, then asked, "So Iva doesn't know what I'm doing here?"

"Hm? Oh." I let out an exasperated sigh. "Didn't Hal tell you?"

"Tell me what?" Vera got up to finish her mopping.

I started moving chairs out of her way. "Well, we thought... We wanted a chance to settle in, before people got all..." There wasn't any way to say it that didn't sound bad. I patted the back of a chair. "We decided not to tell anybody. Not right away."

Vera scrubbed at a smear of dried ice cream with the mop. "You must have told them something. Iva knew my name."

I shrugged, though she wasn't looking at me. "We said you were the sister of a friend of Hal's, and you were coming to stay."

"Oh." Vera dunked the mop in the bucket and wrung it out. She mopped in front of the refrigerator and across to the living-room door without saying a word. I couldn't tell what she was thinking. I stepped out onto the porch, and she worked her way towards me. Finally she said, "Iva doesn't miss much."

"No." I couldn't add anything to that.

Vera gave the mop a last rinse. "Well," she said, hanging it on its nail, "Is that all there is to do?"

"Yes," I said. Then I shook my head. "No."

She gave me a questioning look. When I didn't say any more, she went and dumped her mop water in the yard. A blue jay in the rose-of-sharon shrieked at her, then flew away.

I looked at the kitchen stool by the porch table. If I sat down again, I didn't think I'd have it in me to get up. Feeding a crew always wore me out, as if the noise and size and smell of the men was work in itself. Vera put the mop bucket upside-down in its corner, and I said, "Somebody's got to go talk to Iva. Heaven knows what she's thinking."

Vera sat down on the stool, swinging one foot. "What'll you tell her?"

I sighed. I could hardly expect *Vera* to talk to Iva, but... "By all rights, Hal ought to do it. She's his mother."

Vera raised her eyebrows, and said drily, "Hal's not all that good at explaining things."

I almost laughed—it came out as a snort. "Oh, I'll go," I said. I took off my apron, then hesitated. "Katy'll probably wake up."

Vera nodded. "I'll listen for her."

Sitting there with her heels up on the rungs of the stool, playing with her apron string, Vera looked like a girl. But she'd been taking care of kids since before Katy was born. "Katy's only ever been left with family," I said. Of course, Vera was family now. At least, that was the idea.

"We'll do okay." Vera smiled at me, and yawned.

"Maybe you can get a nap in, before she wakes up," I said. I left my apron on the porch table and went out, catching the screen door so it wouldn't bang.

43

May

I walked slowly up the gravel road towards Rye and Iva's house. The sun was hot on the top of my head—I'd forgotten my hat.

What'll you tell her? Vera had asked, and I hadn't answered. I didn't know.

I'm sorry, Iva. I'm sorry. That was all I wanted to say, thinking how Iva had looked at me. I kicked a round rock. It smacked a hedge-apple tree, scaring up a couple of cardinals. I hadn't meant to upset Iva. I just didn't want to get everybody all in a state...

Through a gap in the fencerow I caught a glimpse of the men working in the back field. They looked small, among the yellow-green tobacco plants and the loaded sticks propped slantwise. I picked Hal out by his dark hair, Rye by his shirt— he never stripped down like the younger men.

One of the cardinals landed in the sumac next to me and chirped, loud and harsh. I sighed, and started walking again. It was just fifteen minutes' walk to Rye and Iva's, but at this rate it'd take me half an hour.

I'm sorry, Iva. I owed Iva more than an apology. What could I say to ease her mind? *Vera had some of Hal's things in her room, to mend, and...* My face went red, even imagining the lie. Iva would see right through it, and worry even more. I'd have to tell her the truth—and then try to convince her that we weren't all out of our minds. I kicked another rock into the weeds. I couldn't even convince Iva to try using the Victorio strainer for her applesauce—I'd tried, just last week.

I crested the hill and came in sight of Rye and Iva's house, its kelly-green trim glowing like a beacon against the white siding. Iva had picked out that color, when they bought the place. It had made my eyes ache—but I'd kept my mouth shut, and helped her with the painting. Hal had been plowing the back field that day, and the air smelled like spring earth and wet paint. Iva had told me stories while we worked, about their family back in Kentucky.

That was three years ago now. It was funny, but I didn't mind that color so much anymore. Maybe the house clashed with the grass, but it was Rye and Iva's house, now. Part of the family.

Maybe I didn't have to convince Iva of anything. Maybe I could just tell her.

In any case, I was here now. I followed the stepping stones across the yard, and knocked on the kelly-green doorframe.

"Come on in," Iva called from the darkness behind the screen.

She was at the kitchen table, cutting up apples into her biggest kettle. Maybe I'd imagined her looking old—here I felt like napping all afternoon, and she was starting another batch of applesauce.

"Want some help?" I offered, reaching for the knife drawer.

Iva twisted her knife to crack an apple in half. "Did you come to chop apples?" When I shook my head, she pointed her chin at an empty chair. "Best save your strength for what you come for."

I sat down, taking an apple from the bucket on the table. It was pale yellow, freckled with grey flyspeck. I rolled it back and forth in my hands. Iva went on working.

"Well, Iva," I finally said. "Maybe I ought to just tell you the whole story." Iva nodded, and cut out a wormy spot.

She kept her eyes on her work as I talked. When I told how I'd asked Hal to bring Vera home, her knife paused halfway through an apple for two heartbeats—then she finished the cut, and halved the two pieces into the kettle without looking up. I went on, while her face got more and more grim.

"And, well, we wanted some time to settle in," I finished. "So we thought we wouldn't tell everybody right away..." My throat felt hoarse, though the tale hadn't taken long to tell.

Iva cut up the last three apples, and laid her paring knife carefully on the table. Then she said, "Am I 'everybody'?"

I looked down at the apple in my hands. "No, Iva. And I'm sorry. We didn't mean to hurt your feelings."

Iva waved that idea away, and hefted the full kettle onto the stove. She started wiping the table, her dishrag rubbing hard at the white formica. "Let me see if I've got this straight," she said. "Hal went and broke the rules, so now you-all figure you'll go ahead and break *all* the rules, while you're at it?"

"No!" I answered. I realized I was clutching the apple to my chest, and put it back in my lap. "I mean, it's just this one thing. Just to keep the family together. We're still the same people we were before."

Iva raised an eyebrow at that. "You didn't marry by threes, before."

I felt a little aggravated. "Well, what was I supposed to do?"

Iva folded her arms, the wet dishrag wadded in one hand, and looked at me like I was being slow. "You were supposed to tell him to leave her. If a sheep strays, you go after it and bring it back—you don't go straying too."

Nobody around here kept sheep. I hoped Iva wasn't going to start quoting the Bible at me. *Love bears all things, believes all things...* I squeezed the apple, feeling the tiny give of its hard flesh under my thumbs. "Well, Iva. I don't know what to say that'll convince you. Hal's a good man, and a good daddy. I didn't want to lose him." I saw Iva draw a breath, and hurried on. "I know, you didn't say that—but he might've... He loves

Vera." My thumbnail broke through the skin of the apple. Iva's eyebrow was up above her spectacles again. "He does," I insisted. And who was I to say that was wrong? Mom thought it was wrong to chew gum. "Anyway, Iva, I'm not trying to convince you. I just…I wanted to tell you the truth."

Iva sighed. Then she got out a long wooden spoon to stir the apples, jabbing it down between the raw chunks. I could smell the fruit at the bottom starting to cook.

When she spoke into the steam rising from the kettle, her voice was softer. "I know I was too easy on Hal, bringing him up. Course, an only child's apt to be spoiled anyway. But I was about run off my feet when he was little, taking care of Poke— Orion's granddaddy, you wouldn't remember him. He got awful senile at the end. And then Rosie Morris and her babies moved in with us, after her man died. We called her a hired girl, but she wasn't good for much. Course, we couldn't pay her, either—Orion had all he could do to make the mortgage, with prices like they were." Iva put the lid back on the kettle, and gave a little laugh. "A few years there, it seemed like all I did was wash. It was diapers and soiled sheets, from one end of the day to the other… We didn't go hungry like some, thank heavens. But I kind of let Hal run wild." She paused, tapping the spoon handle on the table, her mouth crooked into a wry smile. "He'd get into the awfullest messes! His heart was always in the right place—he just didn't *think.*" Iva's smile faded as she turned back to me. "I probably should've been harder on him. And now here *you* are, still letting him get away with—"

I shifted in my chair, and Iva stopped. "Well," she said, "That's how it looks from here. Anyway, I didn't mean to go on and on. Done's done. I just wish somebody'd put their foot down with him." She pulled a step-stool over by the Hoosier cabinet, and got her cone-shaped colander down from the top.

If Iva hadn't managed to put her foot down with Hal in all his childhood, I didn't see how I was supposed to do it now. I didn't say that, though. I was hoping she'd "go on and on" some more. I'd never suspected Iva of having any regrets. But she just dusted off the colander and its wooden masher, and set them on the table.

"Well, Iva," I finally said, "Maybe Hal is spoiled, I don't know. But he works hard, and he loves me and Katy." Saying that made my throat tighten up, and I swallowed. "You brought up a good man, Iva. He's worth…bending the rules for."

Iva's eyebrow twitched. "So it's my fault, in the end?" She said it lightly, but then her face turned serious again. "I just don't want you all to get hurt, May. You start making your own rules, people get upset."

"I know." I tried to look like I knew what I was doing.

Iva sighed. "You still wanting to keep it quiet?"

I stared at her, feeling my face go hot with shame. Of course —I should have known. Our secret wasn't out. If we asked her to, Iva would take it with her to her grave. And we'd treated her like…like everybody. "I guess so," I said. "Just for now."

Iva nodded, and stirred the apples again. "What about Orion?"

Rye would hit the ceiling. But now that I was thinking, I knew he wouldn't tell anybody else, any more than Iva would. I nodded. "You can tell him."

My shoulders felt heavy. I wanted to shut my eyes and not think about anything. But I should get back and see how Vera and Katy were doing. At the thought of Katy, I felt home pulling at me like a short lead. I stood up, setting the apple on the table. "I ought to get home."

Iva put down her spoon, and came over to put her hands on my shoulders. "I'm not saying it's all right," she said, looking up at me. "But I'm glad you told me."

I nodded, clenching my teeth so I wouldn't cry.

"Now you get on back to your kid," Iva said. "I've got to do up these apples." She kissed my cheek, and gave me a little push towards the door.

I went out into the sunshine, blinking the tears out of my eyes.

44

Hal

Funny—back when I'd imagine being at home with May and Vera, I never pictured both of them mad at me.

They let me finish my supper, and then they started in on me. Taking turns. I had time for two pieces of apple pie while I listened.

I guess I forgot to tell Vera what May told everybody, about her coming. Considering all the messages I was running back and forth, it's a wonder I didn't forget my own name. It sounded like Vera did all right with Ma anyway. But I guess she didn't like it much. Vera kept putting her hands on her hips when she was telling me off, even though she was sitting down. Kind of cute.

I said I was sorry. I figured that'd be all—and a good thing too, I was worn out. And then May drops her bombshell. Says Ma found my pajamas and things all here-there-and-yonder and got in a state, and so May went and told her everything. Says we should've done that to begin with. And then, about the time I get my jaw scraped up off the table, she says Ma's going to tell Rye. I about choked. I think I said something like "You gals sure know how to fix things up." Both of them looked at me like I wasn't worth a hill of beans. I looked right back. What was May thinking? *Rye?* Just what I need.

And then Vera got sort of weepy and disappointed-looking, and said, "I thought I could tell the truth now, Hal." I braced myself for another thunderbolt, and told her she could tell me anything. But she just said, "The truth is that I love you." I was relieved. I said I loved her too. I would've put my arms around her—but my arms aren't big enough for her and May both, and I didn't want to get in any worse trouble.

Things settled down after that. I had another piece of meat-loaf to round off my pie. May asked Vera about still keeping it quiet—other than Ma and Rye—and Vera said she guessed it'd be easier to tell more later, than to tell less. She got that right. I told her what my granddad used to say, "Better to keep your mouth shut and be thought a fool, than open it and remove all doubt." It was good to see her smile.

Whew. Not the way I like to wind up a long day. I guess all's well that ends well. Except for Rye—and I'm not going to think about Rye. I leave May and Vera finishing up in the kitchen, and go looking for my pillow and pajamas. They were on Vera's bed last night, May's the night before. I figure I'll go where I'm put. Kind of like peach pie or apple pie for dessert —either way, a fellow'd be a fool to complain.

45

May

The cab of the truck was crowded on Sunday, with Katy in my lap and the potato salad in Vera's. Katy giggled as Hal flew over the hills, but by the time we turned onto Shaw Ridge Road, Vera was looking green. "I'll be all right," she said, when I mentioned it. "Just a little carsick."

"You don't like our tickle-bumps?" Hal said, grinning at her.

"Tickle-bump!" Katy cheered into the wind.

"You can take it slower going home," I told Hal, as we pulled into Jamie and Grace's driveway. Vera gave me a faint smile.

I wondered how Grace would take to Vera. Jamie liked everybody, but Grace was harder to please, and she made up her mind fast. I'd kept sneaking glances at Vera on the way over, trying to see her the way Grace would. I remembered thinking she wasn't that pretty, when I first saw her, but I couldn't tell now. I'd barely known Vera five days, and already she just looked like Vera to me.

Katy ran off to join Ronny and Carol, who were playing with the puppies. Hal and Vera and I went up the steps to Grace's kitchen together. "We're here!" Hal called.

Iva turned around with a handful of forks. "Well, I'll be," she said. "You *are* here!"

"Yep, it's you, all right," Grace added over her shoulder. Hal sighed.

"You can put the salad there by the bread," Grace told me, bending down to take a ham out of the oven. "And don't get too settled, Hal—James wants you to have a look at Bossy."

Hal put his hat back on. He reached a finger towards the frosted cake on the counter, but Grace flipped his hand with her dishtowel. He yelped, and ducked out the door.

"Bossy kept backing out of the stanchion this morning," Grace said, poking a fork into the ham. "Probably just being ornery... I hope this is worth eating."

"It always is," Iva said, setting out the salt and pepper.

Vera stirred behind me. "Oh," I said. "Grace, this is Vera. Vera, Grace."

Grace gave Vera a friendly nod, and stuck a second fork into the ham to lift it onto a platter. "Nice to have you. Don't worry, I never hit company with a dishtowel."

Vera smiled. Her color was coming back. "Good to know. Anything I can do?"

"Why don't you go see what the men want to drink," Grace said. "Milk, tea, or water. If Rye can't make up his mind, tell him he's getting Hawaiian punch with the kids."

Iva chuckled. "That'll put the fear into him."

I watched out the window as Vera headed for the barn, stopping by the woodshed to talk to the kids. Any minute now, Grace would get rid of Iva, too, so she could grill me about Vera in private. I sighed quietly, and put on my apron. "What should I do?"

"Not a thing!" Grace frowned at me. "You put your feet up, May Dixon. You've been doing for us for a year, it's about time we got to do for you."

I flapped a hand at her. "You-all always bring stuff."

"And you brought potato salad. Sit!"

I sat. Vera had made the potato salad, but I thought better of mentioning her name. "You-all over your bug?"

"Yes, everybody's fine now." Grace checked a pan on the stovetop.

"And you never took it?"

"I never take anything."

It was true, Grace was never sick. I fanned myself with a *Farm Journal*. "I'll be glad to see the end of this heat."

"Heavens, yes," Iva agreed, sticking a serving spoon into the Jell-o. "It's too hot to sleep at night."

"Oh, Iva," Grace broke in, "Could you get me a jar of piccalilli out of the cellar?" Iva glanced at me as she went out. I didn't need the warning—I'd known Grace since she was six.

As the cellar door creaked open outside, Grace turned to me, grinning like a schoolgirl. "Now, May, what about this—"

"Aunt May! Aunt May!" The screen door banged behind Ronny and Carol.

"What in the—" Grace started.

"Get Buster!" Ronny hollered, jumping up and down.

I covered my ears. "Buster?"

"The best puppy!" he yelled. "Come see!"

Carol shoved past his bobbing elbow. "Shut up, Ronny! The all-black one's cuter!"

"Don't say 'shut up,' Carol," Grace said. "And nobody said —"

"*Mommy!*" Katy yelled from outside, trying to pull the door open. "Mommy, *come!*"

I gave Grace a shrug, and followed Ronny and Carol outside.

The puppies' legs were still so short that their bellies dragged the ground. As I knelt down, Ronny picked up a black-and-white one. "See, Aunt May?" he said, as it squirmed and grunted. "Buster's the biggest."

"No, Ronny!" Carol was near tears in frustration. She dumped a black puppy onto my lap. "This one! It's got a star on its head!"

"Now, hold on," I said, as Ronny looked belligerent. "Let's not fight. They're *all* cute."

Carol frowned uncertainly. "You want *all* of them?"

The black pup fell off my lap, and I rubbed its ears. "Who said anything about *wanting* one?"

Carol opened her mouth, then looked stumped.

"That lady," Ronny said. "The one that..."

Katy finally got a word in edgewise. "Vewa!"

"Vera?" Now I was stumped.

"Yeah," Carol rushed in, "That lady, she said you wanted some puppies, and—"

"Shut up, Carol," Ronny said. "She said *a* puppy."

"*My* puppy," Katy added, patting a brown one so hard it fell over.

I set the pup on its feet again. One of its ears was flopped up on top of its head, and I smoothed it down, trying to make sense of the arguing. "All right," I finally broke in. "I want you to tell me *exactly* what Vera said."

Carol looked at Ronny. Ronny twisted his mouth to one side. "Well... First she said, 'those are some cute puppies.' And Carol said—"

"'You can have one!'" Carol put in.

"Yeah, and then *she* said 'well, you'll have to run that possi... prosti...*prosposition* by your Aunt May... But I bet if she saw them right now, she'd fall head-over-heels in love!'" Ronny beamed at me. He was sure of that last part, anyway.

"Mmm." I nodded slowly. "Well, they're as cute as can be. I'm sure glad you came to fetch me." That was the truth— they'd gotten me away from Grace.

"Get this one!" Carol said, grabbing the black pup again.

I fended her off, and stood up. "I'll think about it." Carol and Ronny both looked crushed. "And dinner's about ready, so —"

"Come eat, puppy!" Katy called happily, hefting the brown pup upside-down in her arms. It yelped, and I helped her turn it upright. Its ear was all squirrelly again. "Puppies eat dinner with their mommy," I said. "Where do the puppies live?"

"In a box!" Katy shouted, and stomped eagerly off towards the woodshed, the pup's hind legs dangling to her knees.

"Let's put them all back where they go," I told Ronny and Carol. "See, there's Mammaw Dixon ringing the dinner bell."

Vera caught up with us as we headed for the house. Carol grabbed her hand and announced breathlessly, "Aunt May said she might get the black one!"

"She did not!" Ronny objected.

"Let's not start that again," I cut in. I set Katy down beside Carol. "You two take Katy on in and help her get washed up. Go on—I want to talk to Vera."

"Did I make a mess of things?" Vera said, looking worriedly after them.

"No..." I shrugged. "Not too much, anyway. And you saved me from the third-degree."

"That was the idea," she said.

I gave her a startled look, but she was watching Carol help Katy up the steps. Last night I would have sworn Vera wanted to tell everybody the whole story—and here she was thinking up schemes to help keep the secret. Thinking fast, too.

"The kids think we're getting a puppy now, though," I observed.

"Katy too?" Vera sounded regretful. "I tried to talk over her head."

I thought of Ronny struggling with *proposition.* "Her cousins must've explained it to her. She'll be okay."

As I reached for the kitchen door, a big hand came over my shoulder to pin it shut. "Whoa, now," Jamie boomed in my ear, "Nobody goes through that door until May says hello to her favorite brother!"

I turned and rolled my eyes at him. "You mean my *only* brother."

"That too." Jamie kissed my cheek, then smiled past me at Vera, who smiled back. "We already welcomed Vera to the loony bin, so I guess we can all go in."

"You sure we don't need the password?" Hal asked, giving Jamie a friendly shove.

Jamie's answer made Hal and Vera both laugh, but I missed it—I was watching Rye. His eyes were on Vera, and his mouth looked like the sassafrass twig he was chewing had turned to wormwood on him.

Jamie opened the door. "Ladies first!" I tore my eyes away from Rye, and led the way inside.

46

Vera

I followed May into the kitchen. Iva was setting glasses on the table, and I gave her the men's drink orders—two teas and a water.

Grace tucked a curl of ash-blond hair behind her ear, and smiled at me. "Vera, I've got you here by Ronny. And Hal, you're next to James, so he won't need to throw anything. — You kids quiet down!" She was wearing a striped feed-sack apron, over a peach day dress with the new fuller skirt.

Rye sat down between Hal and me, not looking at either of us. He'd been full of stories yesterday, joking around with the tobacco crew, but now he just put his sassafrass twig in his shirt pocket and glowered at his plate. He'd avoided my eyes at the barn, too.

James whistled as he sat down. "Boy oh boy," he said, "If this tastes as good as it smells, I might not be able to stand it."

It did smell good—smoky ham, yeasty rolls, a vinegar tang from the relish dish, onions... The fresh air had cured my carsickness, and my stomach was growling.

Carol was chewing on the end of her pigtail. I smiled at her, through a pang of missing Hester. Alone in my new bedroom Friday night, I'd cried with homesickness for the kids.

Grace put the butter dish on the table. "Hair out of your mouth, Carol. Rye, would you ask the—No, hang on…" She found a spoon for the potato salad, then sat down.

Iva unfolded her napkin. "James, why don't you ask the blessing."

James's prayer was short and sweet. We passed the dishes around, and I helped Ronny fill his plate. He had Grace's blond hair, with Jamie's cowlick on top.

It was another big meal—I'd seen more food in two days than Wanda and I put on the table in two weeks—and all good. It was years since I tasted fresh horticulture beans. They were creamy, and delicious with the ham.

"Would you like more ham, Vera?" Grace asked. When I said no thanks, she added, "Are you getting settled in?"

I nodded, swallowing a bite of tomato. "Yes, I'm feeling pretty much at home."

James winked at me. "Not too quiet, after big city life?"

"It's nice," I said. "Not so quiet when—what's that rooster's name?"

Hal chuckled. "Ol' King Tut thinks sunrise is at three. And four, and five…"

"Sounds like it's time for Chicken à la King-Tut," James said. Ronny laughed.

"You planning on staying a while?" Grace asked me, reaching for the salt.

May shifted in her seat. I gave her a little smile as I said, "If they don't throw me out."

Carol suddenly stood up on her chair, craning to see Ronny's plate. "I didn't get any Chicken à la King!"

"Sit down, Carol," Grace said.

"Nobody's got Chicken à la King, dummy," Ronny said, rolling his eyes.

Carol turned red, and stomped on the chair seat. "Mommy! Ronny called me a dummy!"

Grace looked exasperated. "Sit *down!* There's not any chicken. Ronny, be nice."

Carol sat down, sulking. Grace rolled her eyes at me. "I swear, these two and their bickering... Do you have any kids?"

"Not yet." I was glad of the table between us, even though I'm still just thick in the middle, not round. "Your kids were mighty polite when I got here," I added. "They made me feel right at home."

"You stick around, you won't be thinking 'polite,'" Grace said, but I could tell she was pleased.

"Aw, Grace." James poked a gob of butter into a roll. "That's just kids. You remember how we all were."

"I remember how *you* were," Grace retorted. "Nobody's wondering where these two got it."

James put on a hurt face. "Me? —Don't you listen to her, Vera." He pointed his fork, with a piece of ham on the end of it, at May. "*This* is the one you want to watch out for!"

May shot him a skeptical look, and put a spoonful of potato salad on Katy's plate.

Jamie pointed the ham at me. "May took a wrench to my bike once—made it so the handlebars spun clear around, halfway up Ort Hill. I about got killed!"

May snorted. "You did not. You fell over, was all."

"'All,' except pulverizing my—" James glanced at Iva. "Anyway, I *could've* been killed."

"If I'd wanted to kill you, I'd have pulled the shoes out of your brake hub." May took a drink of ice tea. "Anyway, that's what you got, for hiding my corn doll."

"I didn't hide it! I just put it where it belonged!" James protested, looking innocent. May glared at him. I could tell they were both enjoying the argument.

"Where'd he hide it?" Hal asked. May just gave an exasperated sigh.

James finally ate the bite of ham he'd been waving around. He grinned at Hal while he chewed it, then swallowed and said, "Cornfield." Hal hooted with laughter.

"You were awful," May said to James.

"Was not," James said. "Anyway, a ten-year-old oughtn't to be playing with dolls."

I laughed in surprise. "You could sabotage a bike when you were ten?"

May shrugged. "Just loosened a bolt. I fixed it later."

"May's got an eye for machines," Hal said. "Helps me work on the tractor." I could hear his smile, but I couldn't see him past Rye. Rye was chewing fast, with his mouth shut tight. He might as well have been deaf.

"Anyway," James told me, "May ever gets mad, you check your bike before you go to pull a hill." May stuck out her tongue at him.

"Mommy!" Carol yelled. "Aunt May stuck out her tongue! Aunt May stuck—"

"Hush!" Grace said, pointing a warning finger at Carol. "I saw her."

May looked apologetically at Grace. "It's hard to behave when you have to eat dinner with your little brother."

"Don't tell *me*," Grace said dryly. "I eat dinner with your little brother every day." She sighed, and turned back to me. "Do you—"

"Looks like we do need that other quart of peaches," Iva said, handing Grace the empty dish. When Grace stood up, she got up too, and asked, "Anybody want more to drink?"

Grace looked thoughtful when they both sat back down. Her eyes paused on my wedding ring as I reached for my roll. She waited until Iva was taking a drink of milk, then asked me, "Is your husband in the Service?"

Iva made a choking sound and set her glass down abruptly. I smiled at Grace. "Army, during the war. Hal, would you pass me the corn?"

"Me too," Ronny piped up.

"What's he do now?" Grace asked.

I dished out corn for myself, then Ronny. "He's a farmer," I said. "Works away, too, of course, but farming's what he loves." I could feel Rye's silence getting bigger beside me.

Grace drew breath for another question. May said suddenly, "So! Do you think we ought to get a puppy?"

"Yeah!" Ronny and Carol answered together, then chanted, "Yeah, yeah, yeah!" while Katy laughed and banged her spoon on her tray.

"Well," Hal said, when they paused for breath, "That'd depend on the puppy."

"Get the black-and-white one!" Ronny bounced in his chair, and I put a hand on his shoulder.

"No, the——" Carol started, but Grace broke in.

"You two hush! Aunt May doesn't need your advice!"

I winked at Carol. "When I was a kid, we had a batch of baby chicks that thought a puppy was their mommy!"

"Did he eat them?" Ronny asked, looking worried.

"Nope—never so much as growled. They'd sit on his head, eat his food..."

Rye chuckled. "Now, I had a coon hound that——" He stopped, glanced at me, and looked back down at his plate. "Ah, you-all don't want to hear about that."

"What?" James said incredulously. "Not want to hear about Ol' Blue?" He turned to me, shaking his head. "Why, Ol' Blue could climb a tree faster than a scared cat! Ol' Blue could find a lost child in a blizzard before its nose got cold! You ain't *seen* a dog, if you ain't seen Ol' Blue!" He grinned at Rye. Rye took a bite of meatloaf without looking up. James cocked his head, his grin fading.

"Vera," Iva said. I turned to face her, feeling a little frazzled. "What do you put in your potato salad? It's delicious!"

"Um..." I said. "Well, the main thing is, you dump most of a jar of relish over the potatoes while they're still hot." I poked at my potato salad with my fork. "And then mustard, paprika, salt and pepper... I put some onion. Mayonnaise, after it's cooled down."

"I'll have to try that," Iva said. "Sweet relish?"

"Whatever I have. This was May's relish—she ought to get the credit." I smiled at May, but she was helping Katy with her Jell-o.

Iva nodded, then turned to Hal. "Did you-all figure out what Bossy's trouble was?"

Hal nodded. "Piece of tin flashing in the sun."

James grinned. "You should've seen Hal sticking his head in the stanchion. I was tempted to close it up on him—could've charged folks a nickel to come see."

Hal grunted. "See if I help you out next time."

"Well, I didn't *do* it," James said. He added, to me, "I call Hal before I call the vet. I had a calf acting crazy this spring, and Hal found a warble on her back I hadn't even noticed."

"Oh," I said, hoping he wouldn't go into any more detail. I'd seen Mama squeeze a warble out of a kitten once. I put down my fork, quicker than I meant to.

Grace gave me a thoughtful look, but she left me alone for the rest of the meal. I was glad—I had enough to do, keeping my stomach where it belonged.

May made Hal drive slower on the way back, and she shooed me off to my room for a nap as soon as we got home.

It does feel like home. I felt myself relax, and my stomach start to settle, when I walked in the door. It's too hot to sleep, so I'm just lying in the breeze from the fan. Thinking about James's grin, and the way May came alive, scrapping with him. Rye, chewing away with his shoulders hunched. Grace's curiosity written all over her face, and Iva changing the subject.

I'd thought I was done with lying. But I have to admit, part of me is relieved. Rye's bad enough—it'd be impossible to get to know people if *everybody* was in a tizzy. Seems like Iva's made some kind of peace with it, but I have a feeling she's more an exception than a rule.

Anyway, it's just temporary. If nothing else, the news will be out when my belly starts to show.

And I guess I didn't *lie*, exactly. Probably just as well. Grace is a lot smarter than Wanda. And less boring, too.

That's what it is—why, despite being queasy and hot and missing the kids, despite Grace's questions and Rye's silence, I'm lying here smiling. For the first time in years, I'm not bored.

I picture little May in pigtails, taking a wrench to James's bike, and laugh out loud.

47

Vera

I parked the wheelbarrow, loaded with Katy and our baskets, under the apple trees. May propped the ladder against the first tree and started to climb.

"Mommy!" Katy flung herself halfway out of the wheelbarrow, and I barely caught her as the whole thing tipped over. She pushed me away and ran to May, yelling, "*Down,* Mommy!"

"How can I pick the apples if I stay down?" May asked from halfway up the ladder.

"*Vewa* up!" Katy looked back uncertainly to where I was picking her breakfast out of the grass. "Mommy stay down!" she repeated firmly, but I saw her lip quiver.

"I don't mind," I said, brushing grass seeds off of a triangle of toast. Katy had wanted "toast, like Vewa!" with her egg this morning.

"Are you sure?" May asked. She climbed down and took Katy's bowl from me. "She's not really this spoiled—only before breakfast."

"It's hard to be brave on an empty stomach," I said, winking at Katy. "You were forgetting your basket, anyway."

"No, this tree's about done," May said, "And Iva's got all she wants. We can shake the branches, and pick the apples up off the ground."

"Won't they bruise?" I asked.

"Well, we're making applesauce." May's voice was dry. I looked to see if she was teasing me, but she was fixing a barrette in Katy's hair.

I kicked off my shoes. "Nice ladder," I said, starting to climb. I'd noticed it looked odd, when May was carrying it. Now I could see how its pointed top fit into a fork in the branches, making the whole thing steadier.

May came over to stand below me. "The one I saw a picture of was bent wood, but I couldn't manage that."

I stopped climbing to look down at her. "You *made* it?"

May shrugged. "Just bolted on a piece of an old hay rake," she said, as if she made ladders every day. "I had to wrap all those rags on it to keep it from rubbing the bark." I shook my head, impressed.

When I stepped off onto the first branch, it was like being a girl again. The thick green leaves hid the world—May and Katy were almost invisible, a few feet below me. I found a handhold and walked out until the branch quivered under my weight. "Ready?" I called down.

"Go ahead."

"Don't let me clobber you." I got a good grip on the overhead branch, then bounced, pushing with my bare feet. The leaves around me shook like a windy day, and apples thudded and smacked into the grass. Katy squealed with laughter.

When I stopped shaking, May said, "Okay, Katy, let's pick them up!"

I stepped sideways, onto another branch. "These seem early," I called to May. "What are they?"

Her voice drifted up through the leaves. "Apples, mostly."

This time I was sure she was teasing. I chuckled as I shook down another hailstorm of fruit. "No, what *kind?*"

"Transparents. Rye planted them."

"Pretty." The apples were big, with pale golden skin that almost glowed.

"I want ice cream!" Katy announced.

"How about your egg?" May offered. "Or your toast, remember? Like Vera's?"

Katy made grumpy noises as I shook down more apples.

"Look at the cow-bee, hon!" May said. "See where he's been eating the apple?"

"Bee?" Katy sounded nervous. I didn't blame her—cow-bees are big.

"He won't hurt you—just don't touch," May told her. "I think he's asleep!"

I smiled to myself as they whispered together. Katy wasn't spoiled. I liked May's way with her. She didn't fuss all the time, or get mad at Katy's baby ways. May didn't smile often, but when she did, it was usually at Katy. I worked my way out along another branch, trying to think of the word for how she was. Kind, that was it. May was kind to Katy. I'd never thought of that word for a mother before. Of course, the mother I'd watched most was Wanda, who didn't much care for kids once they could walk and talk and use slingshots.

"Wake up, bee!" Katy yelled, loud enough to rouse every bee in the county. I laughed, and climbed up to another branch.

48

Vera

Back at the house, May started washing jars, and I went out to get the mail. There was a letter from Cartersboro, but it was from Wanda, not Tom. I stuffed it in my dresser drawer for later, and went out to the screen porch to peel apples. Katy was out in the yard, spinning the wheel of the upside-down wheelbarrow. I kept half an eye on her as I turned the yellow apples against my knife.

May set a crate of wet jars on the table with a jingle of glass. "Oh, don't peel them," she said.

"Really?" I blinked at her. Applesauce with peelings didn't sound very good. But then, I'd never canned applesauce— Mama and I had always dried our apples, and Wanda just made pie filling and jelly.

May nodded, lining the jars up in rows. "The strainer takes the peelings out."

That must be the "gadget" Iva had mentioned. "So, just core them?" I asked, cutting the half-peeled apple in quarters.

"It does that too. Just cut them like that."

"Good heavens." I dropped the pieces in with the ones I'd peeled and cored. Apple seeds rattled on the bottom of the pan. "That just doesn't seem right... Is it like a colander for persimmons?"

"More or less. That's what Iva uses for her applesauce." May put the jar rubbers to simmer, then picked up a peeling from the table. It spiraled down from her hand to the floor, a whole apple's worth in one long piece. "You're a good peeler, aren't you?"

I made a face. "Plenty of practice." Mama and I had picked up bushels of "drops" every year, from the orchard outside High Brooks.

Just quartering the apples, May and I filled the first pan and started on the second in no time. When Katy got tired of the wheelbarrow, May gave her one of my apple peelings to play with. She marched around the porch with one end of it in her mouth, twisting around to see it trailing behind her. I laughed when she bumped into my legs.

While I stirred the apples on the stove, May put together her strainer. It had an orange twisty part, and a perforated tube, and all manner of chutes and funnels—by the time she was done, it looked more like a fancy sausage grinder than a colander. "Don't tell me you made *that* yourself," I said.

"No, this is boughten." May tightened down a wing nut. "Grace and Jamie went in on it with Altha Combs, for a wedding present."

Katy was fascinated with the strainer. When the apples were cooked soft, I held her up so she could watch May scoop them into the funnel on top.

"Look!" Katy gasped, bouncing on my hip. As May turned the crank, juice and applesauce oozed down the chute into a cake pan.

"Wow!" I was tempted to bounce too. "And look over here!" The peelings and seeds were coming out the end, squeezed almost dry.

May kept cranking as Katy and I marveled. "It'll do tomato juice and pumpkin, too," she said, with a note of pride in her voice. "If I could get it to shell horticulture beans and dress chickens, I'd be all set."

I grinned. "Or out of a job!"

I put Katy down when she got tired of watching. She went back to the yard, hanging onto the screen door for balance on the steps. May handed me the tin cup she was scooping with. "I'll get the cinnamon and sugar," she said. "Make sure you dump the cake pan before it runs over. And watch your shoes —it drips."

I scooped hot, sweet-smelling apples into the funnel, working the chunks down into the machine with the wooden pusher. The crank-handle creaked softly as I turned it. Now and then a dribble of grease-streaked juice fell to the floor at my feet.

"Oh, don't!" May grabbed my wrist, and I jumped. "If it sucks the pusher down, you'll get a face-full when you pull it out. Just do like this."

I raised my eyebrows, as May nudged the steaming apples down the funnel. "I never knew applesauce could be dangerous."

"We could get you some goggles," May offered, waving away a fly.

I glanced sideways at her. "Maybe a welder's helmet?" Her mouth twitched, and I added, "You need some signs, like at a factory. *Safety equipment must be worn in this department at all times.*"

The twitch turned into a chuckle, and I smiled. May scraped down the strainer's chute and emptied the cake pan into the kettle for me, then went to stir the second pan of apples. I could feel her watching as I scooped and cranked and nudged. After a minute, she asked, "Did you work in a factory?"

I nodded. "I sewed powder bags at the Cartersboro ordnance plant, during the war." I stopped to empty the cake pan. "Did you do any war work?"

"No." May wiped a drip of applesauce off the table. "I was wild to go, but they needed me on the farm."

I watched her straighten the row of empty jars. *Farm work is war work,* I thought—a slogan from some poster—but I didn't say it. There was pain in the set of May's mouth. "Did you—" I began.

She interrupted me. "Where'd Katy get to?"

"Under the lilac bush." Katy was invisible in the greenery, but I could hear her voice now and then.

"Good. Oh, shoot, look—" May crossed the porch to pull the screen door shut. "It's been open all that time. It sticks like that when Katy hangs on it."

"I thought there were a lot of flies in here." I shooed several away from the pulp in the scrap bowl.

May sighed. "I'll get us a flystrip."

She hung the flystrip above the table, and moved my kettle of applesauce to the stove. "We'll have to watch this—applesauce burns easy."

"I burned tomato sauce once," I said ruefully. "Cooked it down all day, and then let it scorch in the last hour. Ruined the whole batch."

May nodded, but she didn't seem to be listening. She adjusted a burner, and glanced out at Katy's hiding place. Her easy mood was gone—it felt like she'd walked away and shut a door behind her. I stifled a sigh, and scooped more apples.

Katy came back in after a while. The apple peel was wrapped around her neck now, and a fly was following her. She poked at the juice puddle on the floor for a minute, then went to wipe her sticky hands on May's skirt. "Mommy, up!"

"In a little bit, hon," May told her, measuring sugar. Katy lay down on the floor, chewing on the end of her apple peel.

"When this gets good and hot, we can start filling our jars." May took the saucepan of jar-rubbers off the back burner, turned, and almost stepped on Katy. The hot pan swooped through the air as she staggered and caught herself awkwardly against the table. "Katy, I *swear!*" she said sharply, then sighed.

My eyes followed the pan as she set it down. She hadn't spilled a drop. "You OK?" I asked.

"Yes." She looked down at Katy. "Are you all right, hon?"

"What's that?" Katy asked, pointing.

"What? Is my—" May reached to straighten her hair. But it wasn't hair that was dangling past her ear—it was the flystrip from above the table.

"Oh, for Pete's sake!" she said, pulling at it.

"Wait," I said, "Let me—"

The thumbtack at one end of the flystrip dangled by May's ear like a little red earring, and the yellow cardboard tube at the other was stuck above her temple. In between was a yard of gummy, yellowish tape, which May's tugging had only wrapped tighter around her bun.

Katy was on her feet, craning to see. "Mommy, *up!*"

May started to wipe her gluey hand on her apron, then thought better of it. "Hang on, hon. Mommy's put her head in the flystrip."

"Fly? See fly!" Katy demanded.

I peeled at the tape gingerly. The glue was almost liquid in the heat, and smelled worse than turpentine. It trailed long threads as it came free, and left thick smears in May's brown hair. I tried not to look too dismayed—May was watching me out of the corner of her eye. The cardboard tube let go last, swinging dangerously close to my dress.

"See fly! Fly on Mommy?" Katy's voice was getting more urgent. She pulled at May's skirt.

I stepped back, holding the flystrip at arm's length. A couple of flies were still stuck to May's bun. One was waving its legs. I looked away and swallowed. "Um, you want me to..." I said, but I wasn't sure what to offer. "There's glue all over."

May shook her head at the whole mess. "I'll just tie a rag over it for now, and we can finish what we're doing."

"See fly, Mommy! See fly! Mommy, *up!*" Katy was almost climbing May's dress.

"There aren't any flies, Katy," May said. "Vera took the flies out."

"Well..." I started, then bit my tongue.

May looked at me. "What?"

I scrunched up my nose apologetically. "There's still a couple, in the back."

"Oh, for..." May sighed impatiently, then noticed the flystrip still dangling from my hand like a gooey yellow apple peeling. "I'll get you a newspaper to wrap that in. —Yes, Katy, Vera can show you the flies in a minute." She went into the kitchen, calling over her shoulder, "And then we need to get on and fill our jars."

49

May

I was going to use kerosene on my hair, but Vera convinced me to try soap first, with the hot water left over from our canning. The heat just made everything stickier, and shampoo didn't help. When I tried a cold rinse, the glue hardened up like old pine sap. I sighed, and dumped the washbasin off the back steps.

"No good, huh?" Vera asked sympathetically when I came back into the kitchen. "I was thinking, alcohol works for gummy stuff. Do you have any whiskey?"

I gave her a look. "Not a whole washbasin's worth."

She grinned. "I could sponge it on."

I got the Jack Daniels from the medicine cabinet, and sat in a kitchen chair so Vera could slosh it on my head. The sour fumes burned my eyes.

"It's sort of melting it," Vera said, "But—woops! That was a bit much." Whiskey dribbled down my neck as she worked at my hair with a comb. I squinted as it pulled—and pulled... "No," she said finally, "It's not coming out." She took a deep breath, and let it out slowly. "Maybe...liniment or something?"

I stifled a sigh as Vera rummaged in the medicine cabinet. I wasn't really in the mood to be a science experiment.

"Absorbine Junior," Vera said, peering at a brown bottle. "'Wormwood, Thymol, Menthol, and Acetone. Treats sore muscles, bites of nonpoisonous insects, and simple ringworm.' It doesn't say anything about flypaper, but…" She gave me a questioning look. I shrugged.

More cold liquid trickled across my scalp, with a reek that made me gasp.

"Are you okay?" Vera asked.

"Yes," I wheezed. "At least nobody drinks *this* stuff."

"It's about the same," Vera said. Her voice sounded strained too. She tugged with the comb. "I don't think it's going to—"

The comb clattered to the floor. Instead of picking it up, Vera bolted out through the porch. I jumped up and followed her as the screen door banged. "What's—" I started, but she'd disappeared around the corner of the house. I heard heaving and coughing. Vera was throwing up.

I went back in the kitchen and picked up the comb, listening to see if the door had woken Katy from her nap. All quiet upstairs. I dipped Vera a glass of water, and sat down at the table. Another cough came from outside the window.

Maybe Vera had picked up Jamie's stomach bug. I thought of her pale, sick face in the truck on Sunday. And the breakfasts she picked at. And how sleepy she got in the afternoons. I felt like I might throw up myself.

Vera's face was white when she finally came in. She sat down and sipped at the water, not looking at me.

"So," I said, "You're pregnant?"

"I guess so," she said.

"You guess so," I repeated. I felt like my insides were falling down a hole. *It was bound to happen sooner or later,* I told myself. *It doesn't change anything.*

Vera picked up the comb and ran her thumbnail over its teeth, making a chirping sound. "I was going to tell you…"

I shook my head. I thought of Hal shaking his head, back and forth like a toy Bassett hound. *I don't know what I'm going to do, May.* No wonder he hadn't been able to make up his mind.

Chirp, chirp, chirp, chirp... Vera's comb sounded like a pond-full of frogs. *Chirp, chirp, chirp—* Suddenly it fell silent, and she looked up to meet my eyes. "Hal doesn't know," she said.

"He—" I frowned. "You didn't tell him?"

"It didn't seem..." Vera bit her lip, and looked down at the comb. "I didn't tell him."

Was that true? I thought of how Hal had been when I was expecting Katy—so excited and worried about the baby, he'd almost forgotten to flirt with me. And I'd seen the way Hal kissed Vera goodbye this morning. A cramp ran through my stomach, making me grunt. No, Hal didn't know.

Another jab of pain. Was I getting sick? That flystrip had arsenic in it, didn't it? *Nonsense, May.* I made myself take a deep breath, and the cramping settled into a tight ache. Vera was watching me. I tried to think of something to say. "When are you due?"

"I don't know—in the spring. March?" she asked, as if I would know.

I nodded, as if I did know. "Katy was born in February. You'll be needing a coat, and things..." My mouth seemed to be talking all by itself.

"I can make that," Vera said.

Her color was getting better. She looked at me like she wanted something, but I couldn't think what. I wanted to go to bed and curl up around my aching belly. I glanced at the clock above the stove. "Oh, my," I said. "I need to pick beans for supper." I got up, making myself stand straight.

Vera stood up too. "What can I do?"

She wasn't showing at all yet. Of course, I didn't know how she'd looked before. I pulled my gaze away from her belly. "You could put the chicken in the oven. And listen for Katy— I'm surprised she's still out."

"What about your hair?" she asked.

My hair. I put up a hand and felt a gummy patch above my ear. *To hell with my hair,* I thought. "I don't know," I said. "I guess I'll rinse the liniment out, anyway." Maybe after supper I'd try kerosene.

* * *

Hal took a bite of chicken, and peered at me curiously. "Rosie the Riveter?"

What? I glanced across the table at Vera, who pointed at her head. "Oh, that," I said. I'd pinned my gummy hair up as best I could and tied an old red bandanna over it. I thought of telling Hal it was the latest fashion, but I was tired. "I put my head in a flystrip."

Hal stifled a smile. "Flystrip, huh?" He peered at me. "I don't see any flies."

"On back! On back!" Katy exclaimed. She waved her spoon, sending a green bean flying. "Daddy see fly! Mommy, *off!*" She leaned sideways in her high chair and made a grab for my scarf.

I caught her plate as it skidded, and set her up straight. "Katy! Settle down—you're liable to tip your chair over! Mommy washed the flies out. No more flies."

"No more flies." Katy made a sad face.

"How'd you get it washed out?" Hal asked.

When I just sighed, Vera answered him. "We tried soap and water, and whiskey, and Absorbine Junior. Nothing worked."

"I wondered what the smell was." Hal lost his battle with the smile. "Kinda like a tavern with rheumatism."

I tried not to scowl at him. He was just being silly, and we hadn't seen each other all day.

"Kerosene might work," he suggested.

I shrugged. It probably wouldn't. And I was sick of nasty smells, even if I wasn't the one heaving in the rose arbor. "I imagine I'll just cut it off."

"Cut it off?" Hal repeated. He and Vera both looked startled.

I nodded, and took a small bite of lima beans. My stomach was still achy.

"But your hair's so long," Vera said. "Surely we could—"

"No use crying over spilt milk," I said. "Can you cut hair?"

Vera nodded reluctantly. "Not anything fancy."

"You can do it tonight, if you're not too beat. Get rid of some of the smell, at least." I saw Hal reaching for the butter, and handed it to him. "How was work?" I asked him.

Hal split open his second baked potato and buttered it. "Oh, it was all right," he said. "Mostly moving stuff around."

"We got twenty-one quarts of applesauce today," Vera told him.

I wondered how much more we ought to put up. Vera's appetite wouldn't stay small for long. And babies liked applesauce... My stomach gave another cramp at the thought.

50

May

The cool steel of Vera's sewing scissors touched the back of my neck, raising goose-bumps on my arms. "Are you sure?" Vera asked.

"Yes," I said, a little sharply. How many times did I have to say it? Hal acted even more nervous about it than Vera—he was hiding in her room, reading his Western.

"All right, here we go," Vera said.

The scissors made a sound like a knife on a whetstone. One stroke, two, three—my head felt suddenly light.

"There you go." Vera dropped a brown ponytail into my lap. It was almost as long as my arm, had a gummy streak along one side, and smelled faintly of Jack Daniels and Absorbine Junior.

"What am I supposed to do with this?" I asked.

"Just keep it out of the way." Vera sounded preoccupied. She ran her fingers through what was left of my hair, fluffing at it. "Now let's get your head wet."

I dunked my head in the washbasin on the kitchen table, then sat back down, dripping. Vera got to work combing and cutting.

I lay the ponytail on my lap. The hair was frizzy in the muggy night air, catching on my fingers as I tried to smooth it out. *Like something off a wild animal,* Mom used to say as she yanked the brush through the knots. If I reached up to stop the pulling, she'd smack my knuckles with the brush. My hair had been soft and blond like Mom's when I was little—it got wild about the time Sissy was born, and Mom acted like I'd changed it just to spite her.

I fought with my hair too, when I got older. But Grandma Stout could always tame it. She'd take the brush from me and gather up my rough brown curls with gentle hands. Sometimes she went on brushing long after the tangles were out, like she was polishing something precious. My hair was just like her sister's, she said—it was our Welsh blood, which came from royalty. If Mom sniffed at that, Grandma Stout would say, "A woman's hair is her glory." Mom hated for other people to quote the Bible at her.

After Grandma Stout died, I didn't brush my hair for months—just pinned the bedraggled braids back up every morning and tied a scarf over the whole mess. Mom didn't like it, but I ignored her. With Grandma Stout gone, and Jamie and Hal off fighting the war, it was all I could do to keep saying "Yes, ma'am" to Mom.

I almost ran away, that summer. I was all ready to cut off my matted hair and hitchhike to Cartersboro, to work in a war plant. I'd begged Mom to let me go—first in '41, when the recruiters for the ordnance plant came to town, and again after Jamie enlisted. I knew I could do factory work, maybe even be a welder or an engineer. I could be helping Jamie and Hal win the war. But Mom said factory towns were chock-full of sin, and she'd be switched before she'd send me off to one, with my wicked ways. I didn't know what wicked ways she meant, and I was afraid to ask. I just lay awake at night, planning my escape. In the morning I'd see Daddy's grieving face again, and I'd put it off another day.

And then Daddy had his strokes. Sitting by his bed that first week, while he slept and woke and slept, I finally picked up the hairbrush. It took me three days to work the tangles out. I dropped handfuls of dry, dead hair out the bedroom window, letting the wind carry them off across the fields. I looked at Daddy's strong right arm, lying useless on top of the sheet, and I knew there wouldn't be any running away for me.

"Okay," Vera said. "You're done."

"Done?" I repeated, blinking up at her. I hadn't realized my eyes were shut. I might've been falling asleep.

"Mm-hm." Vera tipped her head critically. "I can give you a permanent wave later, if you want. But you've got plenty of curl."

I wondered whether Vera had a permanent wave. I imagined her with a red scarf over her short brown curls, going to work in the factory, making—what was it she said, powder bags? Was that some kind of ammunition?

Vera moved a little, and I realized I was staring at her. "Thanks," I said.

She smiled. "Better wash it, or you'll itch all night."

I sighed. "How many times can a person wash their hair in one day?"

Vera rubbed her chin. "We could go for a record."

I let out a breath that was halfway between a laugh and another sigh. Then I rolled the ponytail into a ball, and went to get the shampoo.

51

Hal

At lunchtime I join the other men in the B shed, pull up a crate and unpack my lunchbox. Chicken salad today—May's chicken salad, plenty of pepper.

"Just so you know, boys," Shorty says, lighting up a cigarette, "If Ray shows up today, I'm liable to have urgent business elsewhere."

"Me too," Harvey chimes in.

The other fellows nod and chuckle—even James, who gets along with everybody. Ray's the office manager. He usually eats in the building, but he came out here yesterday. Guess he wanted to talk. Anyway that's what he did. All about how great it was during the war, with all the girl workers at the lumberyard—*wearing those coveralls, bending over and squatting down—mm-hmm, they did a right good job...* Grinning like a possum eating shit.

I've got nothing against looking at women—I was looking at May so hard this morning, I buttoned my shirt wrong twice—but I didn't care for Ray's smirk. Especially considering what we were all doing, while he was back here looking. "You boys really missed something," he kept saying. What a jackass.

"How come Ray was home during the war anyway?" I ask, starting on the second half of my sandwich.

"He's got a heart condition," James says.

"Wish he'd get a *mouth* condition," Shorty adds.

Bucky cackles and slaps his knee, and I notice his shoes are on the wrong feet. Bill told me once that Bucky's got a Silver Star—more guts than brains, I guess. I don't know what the Navy was thinking, to take him. Like sending a kid to war.

"Ray spent the whole war playing grab-ass," James tells me. "He pretty much left the married ones alone, I guess—"

"Good thing, too," Bill says. "If he'd laid a hand on Reva, I'd pound that son-of-a-bitch into the ground."

"—But they say the single girls had twice the work, doing their job and watching out for Ray too."

I shake my head, spit into the weeds. Looking's one thing, but grabbing's another. And if a girl's not in favor of the grabbing, well—that's not a jackass, that's a sleazebag.

The guys all start in telling me about Ray, what their sisters and wives say about him. Pretty funny stuff. Those girls have gotten their revenge in the end—nothing makes a fellow look the fool like being laughed at by a bunch of women.

When the feed-mill whistle blows again, it's back to stacking two-by-eights, with Bucky's help and hindrance. Moving stuff from here to there, like I told May. Doesn't pay as good as the box plant, but I'm mostly outside—and going home every night would be worth it at half the pay.

I remember May wanted to go out for war work, but her mom wouldn't let her. Just as well, I guess. May doesn't even like me to wink at her in front of Ma and Rye—I'd hate to imagine her working under somebody like Ray. Just thinking about it, I want to go in the office and pop him one. Then I chuckle at myself. May probably would've hit Ray with a two-by-four, saved me the trouble.

May looks damn good with short hair. I mean, she looked good before, but the curls make her face...softer, or something. When I tried flirting with her this morning, she said she didn't have time for any foolishness, in that brisk voice that makes me want to follow her around. I hope she'll have time tonight. If we're still taking turns, she's the one I'll be with...

I better quit thinking about May, and pay attention to what I'm doing. Bucky about took my head off with that last board.

52

May

Katy and I made relish Wednesday morning, while Vera sewed in her room. Katy hadn't slept well—she had a dozen new chigger bites—and she'd cried when she saw my short hair, but the food-chopper cheered her up. She cranked the handle while I fed in the vegetables, singing "Grind, grind, grind!" She couldn't resist a machine. Maybe she would be a tinkerer, like Peck said.

After lunch I helped Vera mark the hem on her new green dress, then fixed the screen door so it wouldn't stick open. Both jobs took twice as long as they should have, with Katy climbing on me and grabbing for things and getting mad. I didn't know whether to be sorry or exasperated when she pinched her fingers in the door and burst into tears. I wrapped a cold washrag around her hand and carried her to the living-room rocker. She cried in my arms for awhile, then started chewing on the washrag. "There," I said. "That's better." I stroked her hair, careful of the chigger bites on her scalp.

Vera came out of her bedroom and sat in the chair by the window, with the green dress in her lap. She gave Katy a sympathetic look. "Probably all she needed in the first place was a good cry."

I nodded. "Some days it's the only way she can settle down."

"Freddy and Petey were both like that." Vera smiled at the needle she was threading. "Hester would just hide under a blanket until she fell asleep."

I rocked. Vera's needle glinted in the sunlight as she sewed. I wondered if it was hard for her to leave those kids. I'd cried buckets when Mom took Sissy off to Frankfort—but pretty soon I'd had Katy on the way, to take my mind off it.

Vera would have her own baby, in the spring. My stomach felt uneasy at that thought, but not like yesterday. Maybe I was getting used to the idea.

"Do you miss living in town?" I asked.

"Not really," Vera said, straightening a twist in her thread. "It's different… There was always somewhere to go, in Cartersboro—movies, the malt shop. Picnics, in the summer." She started sewing again. "At first I didn't think a person could ever get bored there. Or lonely, either."

Katy hummed, sucking at the washrag, and I patted her back. Vera turned the dress in her lap. "One thing, though," she said slowly, as if she were talking to herself, "When you're lonely in town, with all those people around…It's a whole lot lonelier lonely."

Katy twitched suddenly, her arms flying up and flopping back down. Vera smiled, and didn't say any more. Katy didn't usually need quiet to fall asleep—those chiggers must be maddening. I rocked and patted her, feeling her head getting heavier on my arm.

I'd never lived in a town, except those few months in Whelan when we were first married. Whelan was nowhere near as big as Cartersboro, but I'd hated having houses all around, people everywhere I looked. It was hard to imagine anybody being lonely, all packed together like that.

I knew what lonely was like, though. All this last year, waking up without Hal. Talking to Rye about hay, or Grace about kids, chatting endlessly with Katy, when the one I wanted to talk to was Hal. Reminding myself he'd be home on the weekend. The weekend seeming so far away.

Vera's hands were still now, and her eyes were half-closed. She was dozing off too. I brushed at a fly on my cheek, and realized it was just a curl. I'd been doing that all morning.

What if it had been me, lonely in Cartersboro? And Hal had come along? Handsome Hal, with his warm smile. Hal, with his admiring eyes. Hal, somebody else's husband. Would I have smiled back? Let him kiss me? Sneaked off to be with him?

Katy frowned and mumbled something. I rocked a little harder, feeling my heartbeat in my temples. I knew the answer, as sure as I knew my name. I might have smiled at Hal. Maybe I'd have fallen in love with him, and cried myself to sleep over it. But I wouldn't have done what Vera did.

The sureness felt heavy, weighting me down like Katy's sweaty body in my lap. I thought of Mom, so sure she knew who the sinners were. Hollering about my wickedness, while she slapped me so hard my ears rang.

Vera's head wobbled a little, and her mouth fell open. Her face looked older, without its cheerful alertness. I wondered why she'd done what she did. I knew I wouldn't ask. As for what Hal did... No. Better not to stir all that up again. Better to keep my mind on making this whole thing work.

I stood up, shifting Katy's limp weight to my shoulder, and went to put her in her crib.

The telephone rang as I came back downstairs, startling Vera awake. It was our ring—two longs and a short—and I hurried to answer it before it woke Katy too.

"Hi, May, it's me." Grace always sounded rushed on the telephone. "Did you hear about Wilma Blackford's mother?"

"No, what?"

"She died last night. Picking corn, and had a heart attack."

"Oh, my," I said. "That's terrible." Wilma's mother couldn't be much older than Iva.

"Yes, it is," Grace agreed. "I'm going to have James drop them off a meatloaf on his way to work. Wilma's got three kids now, I think—and you knew Paul lost a leg, in the war?"

I nodded, though of course she couldn't see me. "I'll send something with Hal, too."

"The visitation's Friday evening," Grace said. "I thought we could drive over together."

I nodded again, slowly, then said, "All right."

"I'll pick you up at seven. Bye."

I hung up the receiver and stood in the living-room doorway, watching Vera thread her needle again. Vera, the sister of a friend of Hal's. Vera, that Grace was dying to know all about.

I sighed. Grace hadn't made Wilma's mother pass away. But I had a feeling I'd just been set up.

53

Vera

Oh, my. Gracious. I don't know what to do with myself. I'm so hot and bothered I'm pacing the bedroom floor, and the electric fan isn't helping a bit. I don't need a fan—I need Hal. And I don't have Hal, because he's with May tonight. I guess it's fair, to take turns. But I thought I was done being lonely.

No, not lonely. Loneliness is cold and empty, not hot and bothered. Think about something else...

We played rummy this evening, once Katy was in bed. The first time I picked up most of the discard pile, May gave me a doubtful look. "You sure you want to do that?" she asked. Hal chuckled—he knows how I play. I won that hand, and then May won one, and I won two more.

Then I started noticing Hal. I love the way his hair tries to curl into his ears. He pursed his lips, studying his hand, and I thought about how soft those lips were. How warm. I was starting to feel soft and warm myself. I tried to pay attention to the game. There was no point in getting all worked up—Hal's pajamas and pillow were on May's bed tonight, not on mine.

I drew a three I didn't need instead of the eight I'd meant to pick up, and discarded a king that played right into Hal's hand.

Maybe May and I ought to play poker for Hal. She'd win anyway, if I was this scatterbrained.

"Your turn, hon," Hal said. I drew and discarded, barely looking. I didn't give a hoot about the game any more. I just wanted to throw down my cards and climb into Hal's lap.

Was that what May would've done, before I came? May's tall —if she sat on Hal's lap, he'd have to look up to kiss her. I pictured her fingers stroking the dark clipped hair at the nape of his neck. She'd kiss the sun-wrinkled skin beside his eyes. I could imagine the peach-fuzz hair there on my own lips. And the warmth of lips on my own face...

"Now, don't be getting carried away," Hal said. I blushed like a furnace—but he was talking to May, who'd just laid down three aces.

I won that hand by blind luck. May shook her head at me as she put the cards away. "Here I was worrying about you," she said, "When I should have been watching out for myself."

"I haven't beat Vera yet," Hal said. "Good thing it's not poker."

May yawned. "Past my bedtime."

"Mine too," Hal said, giving her a look. A shiver ran across my belly, low down.

I went to the outhouse before bed, and stopped to smell the rose arbor on my way back. The kitchen window was lit up in the darkness like a movie screen. There was May, drying a glass. Hal behind her, his hands on her waist. He bent to kiss her neck, and my heart skipped a beat. I could feel Hal's hands, Hal's kiss. And I could feel May's hipbones in my own palms. The smell of the roses mixed with the taste of May's skin.

A mosquito whined alongside my head. I smacked at it, and looked away from the window. What was I, a Peeping Tom?

When I came back in, Hal was standing beside May as she hung up her dishtowel. I got my washbasin and pumped it full. The tin pan Hal washed in was sitting on the porch table. I imagined his skin rising in goosebumps from the cold water— then tried to stop imagining it as I went back through the kitchen. "I guess I'll go to bed," I said. My voice sounded hoarse in my ears.

"Goodnight," May said.

Hal gave me a kiss. A nice kiss, but not the kind I was wanting. "'Night, hon," he said.

"'Night." I wanted to dive into him. Instead I gave him a shaky smile, and wobbled away to my room.

Thinking of something else isn't working. I should just get ready for bed.

I peel off my clothes and wash all over twice, trying to cool myself down. Without my girdle, my waist is as straight and thick as a tree trunk. I spent yesterday morning altering a couple of dresses, and finishing the green sailor dress I started back in June. I added several inches of growing room to the waistline of that one—it's still not a maternity dress, but it'll last me a while, I hope.

Now that May knows I'm pregnant, I guess I ought to tell Hal. I thought of it last night, when I joined him in bed. But then I felt almost shy. Like it was women's business. And maybe he'd worry about loving with me, if he knew—I'd worried about it, early on. And then Hal started kissing me, and slid his hand down across my straight waist, and I lost my train of thought.

I pull on my nightgown and lie down on top of the quilt, still too restless to sleep. The floorboards overhead creak, May checking on Katy one last time. Her steps cross the hall back to her room. I imagine her lying down beside Hal in the dark, her nightgown shining like moonlight. I think of Hal running his hand up under the white cotton, over her hip and waist to her breast. He cups the soft weight of it. The nipple rises up to meet his touch, and May draws in a breath.

You'd think picturing Hal with someone else would make me jealous, but it's making me melt like butter. I try thinking of something else again. New bedroom curtains—maybe a pinstripe…

May's leg drapes over Hal's, and I feel the fine hair on his thigh brush my skin. Hal's fingers trace the curves under my— under May's breasts. His collarbone arches under my lips. Hal's arms tighten around me—my arms tighten around May —strong and loving, wanting the warm wetness of her. I hear the soft hum she makes in her throat, and breathe in the smell of her hair. He chuckles in the dark as I wrap my legs around him and pull him closer.

I sit up fast, blinking in the glare of the bedside lamp. I'm breathing hard. This is all my imagination. Hal and May are probably asleep already. Or maybe *I'm* asleep, and dreaming. Hal pushes deeper into me, raising himself on his arms. I shudder, feeling everything start to come loose, like a tired seam giving way. For a moment I want to yell at Hal, something hot and angry—and then I'm deep blue satin rippling in the dark, spreading out toward the stars. May clutches at me, then flings her arms wide, almost whacking me in the ear. I hear her soft moan rising up, and then a long sigh, and I know her face is settling into that loose, easy smile. I move faster, building and building the pleasure until I can't stand it, until it takes over and busts loose— "Oh," I whisper into the dark, "Oh, honey…"

I wake up late in the night, sprawled on top of the quilt, my nightgown twisted up around my waist. The bedside lamp's still on. I get up and smooth my sweat-damp gown, looking around as if someone might be there. No-one is.

I don't know what that was. But I feel good, cool and satisfied inside. I pull back the quilt and lie down under the sheet, then turn off the light and fall asleep without trying.

54

May

Grace stared at me as I settled into the Buick's passenger seat. "I don't believe it."

"What? Oh, my hair." I'd tied a scarf over it—Vera had said otherwise the wind would have it all on one side by the time we got to the funeral home. "I had a run-in with some flypaper."

Grace laughed. "I wondered what it'd take!" She adjusted her own scarf, then pulled out of the driveway. I waved at Mrs. Hooks in her garden, wondering when Grace would start pumping me about Vera.

Not right away, evidently. Grace had talked to a friend of Wilma's on the telephone, and she filled me in on how Wilma was bearing up. When she mentioned Wilma's husband Paul again, I got to thinking about prosthetic legs. How did they make a knee that would bend, but only at the right time? I pictured designs in my head. A ratchet would be too noisy. Maybe the pivot could lock into a slot when weight was on it... Would aluminum be strong enough?

Grace swung right as we met a tractor on the narrow road, startling me. We were almost to 56—I'd been tinkering in my head for miles. Grace wasn't saying anything now. That wasn't like her. I adjusted my sun-visor, trying not to look nervous.

Grace smiled at me. I held my breath. "Well," she said, "It looks like we're having another baby."

I blinked at her in surprise—then smiled back. "Really? That's wonderful!" Grace had wanted another baby almost since Carol was born.

"Yes, it is," she agreed. "Carol's getting too used to being the baby herself."

"When are you due?" In my mind I heard myself asking Vera that, just a few days ago.

"End of January, beginning of February." Grace checked for traffic and pulled onto 56, speeding up on the blacktop.

I counted back in my head, then gave her a curious glance. Grace was plump enough that it didn't show, but she must've known for a while now.

She shrugged, and talked loud over the wind. "You know I miscarried, after Carol."

I nodded. Iva had said it came of getting pregnant again so quick. Not that that was Grace's fault.

"Well, I've had two more, since then," Grace said, looking straight ahead. "So I didn't like to say anything too soon. But the doctor says I'm out of the woods now."

I stared at her with my mouth open. "Two— Grace! That must've been…" *Terrible* didn't seem like a big enough word. Why hadn't she told me?

Grace's mouth looked tired. She checked her mirror, then speeded up to pass a station wagon. "Yes, it was. But you just have to put it behind you."

I tried to relax as we flew past the other car. Grace's driving always made me nervous. She pulled back into the right lane and slowed down to seventy-five, then gave me a crooked smile. "James says if it's another boy, he gets to name it Tubby."

I rolled my eyes. "He's not tired of that joke yet?" Jamie used to tell people we had a cousin named Tubby N. Stout. Did Jamie know about the miscarriages? I didn't know how hard they were to hide.

"You ought to have you another one, May," Grace said. "They'll be almost the same age, if you and Hal get cracking."

"Grace!" I blushed, and swatted at her with my hand. It was true, though—it'd be a wonder if I didn't turn up pregnant soon.

"It'd be cute—two little cousins! We could dress them up to match." Grace edged the car to the left, peering around the delivery truck in front of us.

Vera's baby would be a cousin, too. It'd all be out in the open by then, of course—if nothing else, Vera would surely be showing before Christmas. What would Grace think? She wouldn't take it as calmly as Iva had, that was for sure. I thought of Rye's angry face at Sunday dinner, and looked out the side window. A woman was throwing corn to her chickens. Her red polka-dot dress hung limp in the thick air, while the road-wind gusted around my ears.

Girls did get in trouble sometimes, and go away to avoid a scandal. Of course, Vera was wearing a wedding ring. But there were other reasons she might have left Cartersboro. Her husband could've gone crazy, like that man Altha told me about. Or he could be going overseas. Or if he beat her, and—

I shook my head, disgusted with myself. I wasn't going to lie. Especially not to Grace.

"So," Grace said, "Tell me about Vera."

My thoughts scattered like chickens under a hawk's shadow. I stared at the blue Ford coupe we were slowly gaining on. We were doing well over eighty. "Well," I said, "She's the sister of a fellow Hal knew at the box plant."

I saw Grace's nod from the corner of my eye. "You said that."

There was a silence. I could feel Grace waiting. She'd think I was figuring out the best way to tell Vera's story, to make it interesting and not leave anything out. But I was just watching the coupe pass a farm truck, and wishing I were somewhere else. Wishing I had come up with a better plan.

"Well? You going to tell me any more?" Grace finally asked, teasing.

My stomach felt like it was jammed up sideways into my chest. I cleared my throat. "No, I'm not."

Grace's glasses flashed as her head snapped around toward me. I kept my eyes on the road, knotting my fingers together in my lap. *Trust me, Grace. You've known me all my life. You know I must have a good reason.*

Grace looked at me way too long. Then she speeded up and passed the farm truck and the coupe both, before the curvy stretch north of Vevay. She didn't say a word, through Vevay and all the way down the river road to Madison. Neither did I. I couldn't think what to say. *I'm sorry* felt too puny to lift the weight of Grace's silence. I stared out at the low sun glaring off the river. The dark hills on the far bank looked like hunched shoulders.

At the funeral home in Madison, we gave Wilma our condolences. Wilma's aunts still called us "kids." I felt like I was acting in a play.

We drove back upriver through the twilight. Grace took the curves fast. I folded my arms across the ache where my stomach belonged, and shivered in the warm wind.

When Grace stopped the car in our driveway, my ears rang in the stillness. I got out, and turned to look at her. She was staring out across the garden.

"Grace," I said.

She raised her eyebrows without looking at me. I felt like running behind the rose arbor to throw up. Instead I said, "That's good news, about the baby."

Grace shrugged a little, like she didn't know what I was talking about. Or like it was none of my business.

"Tell Jamie hi."

She waited.

"Bye." I shut the door, and added through the open window, "Thanks for the ride."

Grace nodded once, then drove off, raising a cloud of dust in her hurry. By the time the dust had settled onto the trees by the road, my teeth were gritty with it. It coated the inside of my throat, dry and bitter, like words I couldn't say.

55

Vera

Saturday morning, May and I drove in to Whelan to do the shopping. Katy sat between us in the truck, playing sleepily with the handkerchief doll I'd folded for her. May drove mostly in silence, telling me a road name now and then—Salt Branch to Bates Road, left on 250. The shadows under her eyes were darker this morning. She'd come back from Madison yesterday evening with a tightness around her eyes and mouth, as if she had a headache. She hadn't said how it had gone, except to tell us Grace was pregnant. It'd be nice to know more than that, before Sunday dinner tomorrow—but I could see May didn't want to talk now.

May parked in front of Chase's Finer Hardware, and led the way through the jingling screen door.

"Well, if it ain't Miz Bell and Little Bit!" A tall, wide, beaming man limped out from behind the cluttered counter and clapped May on the back. He was as bald as an egg, with a yellow pencil stuck behind each ear. "Where you been hiding yourself?"

"Nowhere much," May said. "This is Vera—she's living at our place."

"Peck Chase." A big, doughy hand engulfed mine. "Any friend of Miz Bell is a friend of mine!" He turned back to May. "What you needing today? Spare parts for your cyclotron?"

"More like rat traps and paraffin." May almost smiled. Her eyes had lost their pinched look.

Peck chuckled, and winked at me. "One of these days, Tinker Bell here's going to split the atom on her kitchen stove."

May gave Peck a patient look, set Katy down at my feet, and went off between two rows of shelves. Peck sat down on a stool behind the counter. "You known Tinker Bell long?" he asked me. When I said no, he pointed at Katy. "I knew her when she wasn't *that* big. That gal's something else. If she was a boy, she'd be off making bombs in some secret laboratory by now."

"I saw the ladder she made," I said, though a ladder didn't seem much like a bomb.

Peck nodded. "Should've seen her when she was a kid. Making things, inventing things, fixing things... Course, with a family, she doesn't have as much time for tinkering—but she's always got something going. Ain't that right, Miz Bell?"

"Hm?" May put three rat traps and a block of paraffin on the counter. "I need a gallon of white paint, too."

"What you got going?" Peck asked her.

"Nothing special," May said. "Thought I'd get the wash house painted before the weather turns."

"Ah, phooey!" Peck said. "You know what I mean, Tinker Bell. What're you cooking up?"

"Lima beans and fried chicken, as soon as we get home," May said, her mouth twitching. "You want me to get the paint?"

"Don't you tease me, young lady," Peck said sternly. "You can have your paint after you answer my question."

"Well." May let herself smile. "I might need a spring."

Peck chortled. "You see?" he said to me. "Always something going on. —What kind of spring?"

"Like a screen-door spring, but shorter." May said. "I've got this lever, on the chickenhouse door..." Peck handed her the pencil from behind his left ear, and May drew on the side of a cardboard box, still talking.

Katy was trying to climb a shelf. I picked her up, and held her where she could look but not grab. I knew the lever May meant. It let you open the door with your foot—a lifesaver, if you had Katy on one arm and the egg basket in your other hand.

"…but then it turns out you have to kick the lever *back* to get the door latched again," May was saying. "And it seems like—"

"Same old problem, ain't it, Tinker Bell?" Peck chuckled.

May sighed. "I know. I thought I'd put a spring here…" Her pencil scratched on the cardboard.

Peck grinned at me. "Only thing about Tinker Bell," he said, "She can fix about anything, but then she can't get it *un*-fixed."

"Now, most of the time—" May started to protest.

"When she was a kid, she put a ratchet on the well-crank," Peck said. "Easier to haul the bucket up—but it wouldn't go back down!"

"It worked fine once I put in a clutch," May defended herself. "And I fixed that cradle-rocker, too."

"Wouldn't *quit* rocking, the way she had it first," Peck explained to me. He winked at May. "They say every genius has his blind spot."

May rolled her eyes at him. "Well, I know how to fix this one. I just need to see your springs."

Peck shook his head, grinning. "You don't need any spring, Tinker Bell."

May frowned at him. "Well, not if I want to be kicking that lever back for the rest of my life."

"Nope." Peck plucked the pencil from behind his other ear, and drew new lines on May's sketch. "Put your stick *this* side of the doorknob. It'll fall back of its own weight."

"Oh, for Pete's sake," May said, looking at the drawing. "You're right."

Peck looked surprised. "Ain't I always right?"

"Hmm," May said.

"I *thought* I was wrong once…" Peck scratched his chin. "But I was mistaken." He grinned at me, and I grinned back. May shook her head, and went off to get the paint.

"Course, *I* never would've thought to put that lever on the door in the first place," Peck said, smiling after May. "That's Tinker Bell for you. Never one to settle for how it's always been done."

He opened the cash drawer as May came back to the counter. "I don't know what I was thinking, talking you out of that spring," he told her. "I'm liable to run myself out of business. That's two forty-two… And here's two-fifty, three, and five."

May put the change in her purse. "You could start charging for advice," she suggested.

"Now there's a thought," Peck said. "Oh, and I think one of these got broken—" He took a peppermint stick from the jar behind him and broke it in half, looking up at the ceiling. "Here you go, Little Bit." He handed Katy both pieces. She clutched one in each fist, grinning.

May smiled at Peck, shaking her head. "Thanks, Peck. You have a good day, now."

"You too, Miz Bell. Let me know when you get that atom split, hear?"

"I'll do that."

Outside, May put the things in the truck. I traded her Katy for the shopping basket, and we crossed the street. "So Peck's known you since you were Katy's age?" I asked.

"Longer than that." May fended off a peppermint stick as Katy twisted to look at a dog.

"He sure thinks a lot of you," I said.

"I used to come in with Daddy." May turned up the sidewalk toward Bennett's Dry Goods. "Peck would show me how to make things. He was an army engineer, in World War One."

"Is that where he got the limp?"

May nodded, frowning a little. "Shrapnel in his knee. He mostly stays behind the counter, anymore."

Beneath the frown, I could still see the easy lines of a smile in May's face. Her trip with Grace might have given her a headache, but Peck Chase had taken it away.

I found a pink pinstripe for my curtains at the dry-goods store, and then we got our groceries. Whelan wasn't a big place, but half the county seemed to have come in town to do their Saturday shopping. Wherever we went, people were happy to see May. A few men asked after Hal, and women shared bits of news. May must have introduced me a dozen times just in the grocery store. Nearly everybody complimented May on her haircut—which, I realized, Peck Chase hadn't seemed to notice.

We didn't buy much—cheese, coffee, lard, Jell-O, jar rubbers. I added a box of Shredded Wheat. The town wives were buying meat and vegetables and bread, but May had all that at home.

When we came out onto the street again, I saw a soda fountain on the next corner. I thought of offering to treat May and Katy to a malt—the day was warming up fast. But May was looking tired and tense again. She'd probably rather head home.

"You want me to drive?" I asked, putting the groceries in the back of the truck. "I don't have much practice, but I'm okay on the country roads."

"All right," May said, rubbing her forehead.

"You might have to tell me where to turn," I said. She just nodded.

Katy had been quiet among all the people, but she got lively on the way home. I sang "Old MacDonald" with her as I steered the truck along the winding roads. May looked out across the fields, turning her head now and then to follow a house or a garden. I wondered if she was thinking about whatever had happened with Grace. Or about Peck, with his teasing and his bum knee. Or about the lever on the chicken-house door. Maybe she was just resting. I doubted it, though. I had a feeling Peck was right—May always had something going on.

56

Hal

I fish a strand of barbwire out of the honeysuckle, pull it taut to the post. Rye crowds up close to drive the staple. The sassafrass twig in his mouth bobs like a wren's tail. I can tell he's busting to say something. I kept out of his way all week—but mending fence is a two-man job, if you want it to look halfway decent.

I get hold of the next wire with my crowbar. Rye hammers the staple in halfway, then says, "Well, son. Marriage ain't always easy."

He waits. I keep my eyes on the wire. I should've left the tractor running, after I dragged the limb off the fence. Would've drowned him out.

"Thing is," Rye says, waving the hammer at me, "Once you're married, you can't be tom-catting around anymore."

Might as well tell me to shut the barn door after the cows are out. What's done is done. Anyway, I wasn't tom-catting around. "You going to drive that staple?" I ask.

Rye smacks the staple home, hard. He hates when I won't answer him. But talking back just makes him go on longer. "Ivie said I ought to let you-all figure it out yourselves," he says.

"But it's eating a hole in me, son. How can you do that to May?"

I shrug.

"What's that supposed to mean?" Rye says, louder. His face is red, and it's not from the heat. "You don't know and you don't care?"

I keep my back teeth together, and pull the next wire. My fist is tighter on the crowbar than it needs to be. But Rye'll run down after a while. Run down, shut up, drive the damn staple.

Rye glares at me, biting down on his sassafrass twig so hard it about hits him in the nose. Then he says, low and sly, "Think you're real smart, don't you? Got your cake, and eating it too. Like a hound dog with two bitches in heat—bet you can't decide which one to hump first! You—"

"Now that's enough!" I burst out. "You got no call to be talking like that!"

Rye's grin is ugly. "All right for you to do it, but not for me to say it?"

"Jesus, Rye, shut your foul mouth!" I fling my crowbar down —I've lost hold of the wire anyway.

"You don't like *me* talking," Rye says, his grin gone. "What do you think other people'll say? Down at the hardware store and the filling station, and God forbid, the Baptist Church? Talking about May?"

I look away, breathing hard. Damn Rye. It's not my fault. "It was May's idea in the first place," I tell him.

There's a second of silence. Then Rye hoots a laugh. "May told you to go find you another girl?"

"Rye—"

"'Rye!'" Rye puckers up and spits in the grass at my feet. His sassafrass twig bounces off my pants-leg. "To hell with your 'Rye,' boy! You were thinking with your pecker, and you ain't going to fix it by thinking with your pecker some more!"

I bite my tongue. Turn around, go get the scrap wire off the tractor. Nothing I can say'll do any good.

Rye follows me to the tractor and back, talking. "I didn't raise you to be a jackass, son. May's pure gold. Pure *gold!* And here you are throwing her on the manure pile."

So you want me to throw Vera *on the manure pile?* I grind my teeth together. *Maybe you don't know a damn thing about it, Rye. Nobody's on any manure pile.* I throw the scrap wire on the ground and pick up my crowbar. "You going to help me with this, or not?"

Rye holds up his hammer like he was just waiting for me to ask. I shake my head, pull the top wire taut again. He staples it down. I splice the new wires in and pull them to the next post, one by one. Rye drives the staples.

When we're done, Rye ducks through the fence to the road. Stands working his mouth like he misses his sassafrass twig. Sighs. "Well, son. I guess I've said my piece. I hope you'll think on it, good and hard."

I don't answer. Rye walks off toward his house. I spit in the weeds, and gather up my tools.

57

Vera

Making curtains takes more measuring and ironing than sewing. My iron hisses over the pink-and-white fabric, raising sweet steam. It feels strange to be working on a Sunday morning. Last Sunday I hardly noticed, everything was so strange anyway, but this morning I asked Hal about church. He said they don't go, but if I want to I could ride to the Baptist church with Grace's bunch and Iva. Maybe later.

Upstairs, Katy's voice chatters along, following May from room to room. May's still being quiet this morning, and she holds her shoulders like she's carrying something heavy. I guess she's having her monthlies—Hal's pajamas have been on my bed three nights running now. Hal was even broodier than May yesterday evening, when he came in from working with Rye. But he cheered up all right once we were in bed, and this morning he was whistling again.

I stand the iron on its heel and stretch my shoulders, making my neck pop and crackle. Extra loving from Hal is nice, but after sleeping crowded three nights in a row, I feel like an old woman. Single beds are called "single" for a reason.

I've got enough savings, I could buy us a double bed. But I don't know where the nearest department store is—and I'd probably back the truck into a lamppost if I went by myself. I'll ask Hal about it.

I hear May and Katy coming downstairs. Katy's telling some kind of story about a cow. May's broom swishes across the living-room floor as I wind a bobbin for my last couple of seams. Just the casings for the curtain rods to sew, and I'll be done.

"Leave my dirt alone, hon," May says. I shake my head in sympathy. Why are dust piles so irresistible to kids?

"*No*, Katy! Stay *out* of it!" May's voice is sharp. There's a pause the length of a deep breath, before she says more calmly, "Katy, Mommy needs to finish sweeping. You play."

"What's that?" Katy asks. I can picture her, twisting around as May holds her by the shoulders.

"No more dirt, Katy," May says.

"Okay, Mommy."

"You *promise?* No dirt?"

"No dirt," Katy agrees. I hear her trotting across the floor, then a metallic rumbling sound. "Funder!" she says, and makes the sound again. I wonder what she's doing.

"Oh, my," I call through the doorway, as I finish the second seam and clip the threads. "Is it going to storm?"

"*Funder*-storm!" Katy runs into my room, and scratches at the windowscreen with her fingernails. Rumble, rumble. "Funder!"

"Is it going to rain, too?" I climb up on my chair to hang the curtains.

"Yeah." Katy's found the old curtains in a heap by the door. She picks one up, and sneezes at the dust.

"We'll have to put those in the wash," I tell her, standing back to inspect my work. The curtains look good.

"Wash, wash!" Katy shoves the old curtains back and forth on the floor. Then she runs off, dragging a curtain behind her.

I hear giggles in the living room, then May again, angry —"Katy, *no!*" I put my chair back, and go to see if I can help.

Katy's rolling on the floor at May's feet, scattering dust bunnies with the flapping curtain. So much for May's dirt-pile. "Wash, wash, wash!" Katy sings.

"Katy…" May sounds strangled. Her knuckles are white on her broom handle, and the black steel dustpan in her other hand is trembling. I take a breath.

"*Katy!*" May yells, her voice cracking. "*You promised!*"

Katy stops rolling and looks up curiously, a clump of dust stuck in her bangs. Then she laughs. The dustpan in May's hand draws back.

"May?" I say. May jerks her head up to glare at me, her nostrils flaring. I take half a step backward, then hold still. "You want me to take her outside?"

For a second, May looks like she might spit at me. Then she looks down—at Katy, at the dustpan. "Oh, for—I don't—" Her voice is thick. The dustpan clatters to the floor. Katy rolls over, kicking at it with one foot.

May blows out a hard breath. "Just watch her," she mutters, shoving the broom into a corner. She walks out, and I hear the screen door slam.

Katy starts to follow, but I scoop her up. "Mommy needs to be by herself awhile, sweetie. Let's find something to do."

Katy struggles in my arms, then falls apart, sobbing and screaming until my ears ring. I pace the floor with her, crooning nonsense I can't hear, for what seems like an hour. What is it about a crying baby? By the time she's wound down to sniffling against my shoulder, I feel like my brain's turned to Jell-O.

Just when I think she might be asleep, she sits up in my arms. "Go see Mommy."

I look out the kitchen window, but I don't see May. I can hear Hal splitting firewood, out behind the woodshed—unless that's May… Still, not a good place for Katy. "Mommy went for a walk," I tell her.

"No dirt!" Katy yells, startling me. She grins, and adds, "Go see Mommy!"

I sigh. Kids change gears fast. "Let's see, sweetie..." I say, trying to think. There's a half-bushel basket by the porch door. "You want to play basketball?"

"Basketball" is a big hit. Katy runs around the living room, throwing rolled-up socks in the basket and taking them out again, while I cheer her on from the couch.

I feel worn out, and worried. I keep seeing the desperate look on May's face, as her hand raised that dustpan. It wasn't like May. She has more patience with Katy than that. Of course, if she's having her monthlies... Wanda was always a holy terror at that time of month, and Sue usually had a crying jag.

I wish I could talk to Sue. Or somebody. Sybil. Of course, by the time I'd explained it all, whoever I was talking to would think I was a lunatic. *And you're wondering why May's upset?*

But May's the one who thought this whole thing up. If she hadn't had her idea, I'd still be making wedding dresses in Wanda's spare room—or in some boardinghouse on Adams Street. And I get goose-bumps every time I remember that prayer at our wedding. May wants this to work. It'd be an insult not to take her at her word.

Besides, I've been here a week and a half. Now and then it's awkward, but mostly May seems to like me well enough. It's just since Friday that she hasn't been herself. Since she went to Madison with Grace.

Woops—Katy's tripped on the rug. She frowns, considering whether to cry. I get up and set her on her feet. "Wow," I say, "You sure have made a lot of baskets! Can you make another one?"

"Yeah! *Big* basket!" Katy pulls away from me, grabs a sock-ball, and flings it straight down into the basket. I clap and whoop, and she giggles.

If only everybody were so easy to cheer up.

58

May

Smack. The log fell in two halves. I set them on end and split them again, bringing the ax around and down. *Smack. Smack.*

Splitting firewood wasn't what I'd planned on, when I left Katy with Vera and stormed out of the house. I hadn't planned on anything. Half-blind with tears, I'd almost fallen over the pile of logs Hal had dumped behind the woodshed, and it had seemed like as good an idea as any.

I hadn't split wood much since I got married, but it was coming back fast. I lined up three logs in a row, and split them without bending down again. *Smack, smack, smack.* Most of the wood was the oak Hal and Rye had cut off the fence yesterday. It smelled sour inside, like whiskey or vomit.

I'd almost hit Katy. With a steel dustpan. *You promised,* I'd been yelling. I made a face as I picked up another log. Katy probably didn't even know what a promise was. *Smack.* The smooth weight of the ax handle was familiar, and the twist of my wrists as the blade met the wood. And the burning in my chest, and the ache in my belly. Mad and miserable. The way Mom had made me feel. The way I'd felt when Daddy was sick and Mom was cutting me down with her worn-out voice. *Smack. Smack.* Mad and miserable, miserable and mad.

I'd split plenty of firewood back then, with Jamie off to war and Daddy sick. It had to be done, and some days it was the only way I could get ahold of myself. Some days, I'd be out there pretending it was Mom I was splitting with my ax. Mom's meanness, anyway. Mom's meanness, and Dad's sickness, and Grandma Stout being dead... Sometimes I'd swing my ax at the whole war—Hitler, Mussolini, Hirohito, *smack*, *smack*, *smack*. It was a wonder I didn't cut my leg off. But Daddy had taught me right. And Daddy and Sissy, and Mom, were counting on me. So I swung straight and careful, no matter how mad I was.

I swung straight and careful today, too, as sweat dripped into my eyes and I breathed hard. I could feel myself calming down. It wasn't Katy I was mad at, anyway—she was just a baby. Grace's angry silence had been ringing in my ears ever since Friday evening. Angry, and hurt. I'd never wanted to hurt Grace. *Smack*.

I put down my ax, and stacked the split logs in the woodshed. I couldn't hear Katy crying anymore. A little more splitting, and then I ought to go back in, get ready to go to Grace's for Sunday dinner. Maybe Grace had settled down by now. I'd made her favorite Jell-O salad, with canned mandarin oranges and marshmallows. Hopefully she'd recognize the apology.

Grace looked up as Vera and I came into her kitchen. "Hi."

I smiled—she sounded ordinary, even friendly. Then I saw that she was only looking at Vera. The smile turned stiff on my face. "Hi, Grace," I said.

She turned away and opened the refrigerator.

The screen door creaked behind me. "Excuse me, May," Iva said. She did a double-take as I let her past me. "Why, you've cut your hair! Looks nice. —Where do you want the cake, Grace?"

"Over there." Grace waved towards the corner cabinet, her head still in the refrigerator. "I swear I had an open jar of beets in here... Oh, there it is. If it was a snake, it would've bit me."

She shut the refrigerator door. "Vera, you want to go see what the men want to drink?"

"I'll go," I said. "Ice tea, water, and milk?"

Grace handed the jar of beets to Iva. "You can put these out in that two-part dish, with the bread-and-butter pickles."

Iva raised an eyebrow. Grace ignored it. Then Iva and Vera both looked at me. I didn't know what to say. The kitchen felt too small to breathe in. I backed out through the porch, biting my lips hard.

The men were out by the woodshed, with the kids and the puppies. Rye was holding up a stick for Ronny's pup to jump over. He whistled when he saw my haircut—he must be in a better mood, after whatever he'd said to Hal yesterday.

Jamie had seen my haircut, and pretended not to recognize me, when he'd brought Hal home on Friday. Now he glanced at me, and went back to poking at a woodshed rafter with his pocketknife. "How far in do you think these go?" he said.

The rafter-end was full of neat, round holes the size of my little finger. "Carpenter bees?" I asked.

Jamie nodded. "You think they'll eat through the whole ten feet?"

I looked up the slope of the rafters to the far side of the shed. "I never heard of that happening."

Jamie shrugged. "Maybe nobody lived to tell about it. Their woodsheds all fell in on them."

"Good grief, Jamie." I rapped a rafter with my knuckles. It didn't sound hollow. A carpenter bee swooped past Carol, who squealed. It hovered between me and Jamie, then landed on the rafter and crawled into a hole. "Why don't you just spray?"

"I don't know," Jamie said, peering into the hole after the bee. "It'd be something to see, if they did come out the other end."

"I guess so." I remembered what I was supposed to be doing. "What do you all want to drink?"

"Hmm..." Jamie rubbed his chin. "I'll have a whiskey, straight up."

Hal looked up from petting Katy, who was in his lap making puppy sounds. "How about a beer?"

"Buttermilk for me," Rye said.

I rolled my eyes, but I didn't really feel like fooling around. "There's tea, milk, or water. Or Hawaiian punch."

"Here, let me help you," Grace said, splitting open a biscuit for Carol. "James, would you pass the butter?"

"May's closer!" Jamie whined, sticking out his lower lip. "Make May do it!"

I picked up the butter dish from in front of my plate, and handed it past Carol. Grace didn't take it. I set it on the table without looking at Jamie. She hadn't taken any of my Jell-O salad, either.

"So, Grace," Vera said, dishing applesauce for Ronny, "May tells me you were the champion speller, in school."

Grace's eyes barely flickered towards me. "I was pretty good," she said, to Vera. "Too bad Ronny takes after his daddy that way. Seems like girls are better spellers."

"Now, I gave you a run for your money, a couple of years," Hal objected.

"That's true," Grace admitted, and told Vera, "One year it was just Hal and me at the end of the spelling bee, forever."

"What was it you beat him with, 'acquaintance'?" I asked Grace, forgetting myself.

Grace smiled smugly at Hal. "I finally beat you on 'acquaintance,'" she said.

"That's what Aunt May said," Carol piped up.

"He left out the C," Grace told Vera.

"I don't know if I could spell that now," Vera said, and smiled at me.

I cut up Katy's beets a little more, and told her how yummy the chicken was. All the food tasted like stale crackers to me. Iva caught my eye, then frowned at Grace. I looked down at my plate and yawned.

"You tired, May?" Iva asked.

I shrugged. "Didn't sleep too well." I'd had the rat dream again. At least I hadn't woken Hal up—he was sleeping with Vera while I had my woman's time.

"You been snoring, Hal?" Rye asked, pouring gravy over a second helping of potatoes. "Ivie keeps threatening to put me out in the barn at night."

Hal grinned. "I never snore. And anyway—" He shut his mouth suddenly and glanced at me, his face red under his tan. Had he been going to say he wasn't in my bed? Good grief.

"Well, Maydie," Jamie said, "Whatever it is, we can't be having that. You need your beauty sleep."

"Thanks," I said drily. I didn't need a mirror to see the dark circles under my eyes. Grace never seemed to get those.

"You're welcome," Jamie said. "You want some more chicken?"

"No, I'm still—"

"Did you decide about that tobacco, James?" Grace asked.

"What?" Jamie looked at Grace, then back at me. When I shrugged, he answered Grace. "Tobacco? Oh, that's right—can you all come cut next Saturday?"

"Mighty late, aren't you?" Rye asked.

Jamie shrugged. "Got in late, in the spring."

The men started planning their Saturday, while Ronny and Carol got into another argument over whose puppy was cuter. I tried to eat some more of my dinner. Starving myself wouldn't help, and neither would wasting good food. Grace would get over it eventually, I told myself. She'd been mad at me before. For an hour, or an afternoon...

My stomach hurt. Mad and miserable—more just miserable, now. I pictured my ax splitting a log, breaking open Grace's coldness. *Smack.*

At least it wasn't like when Daddy was sick. Nobody was sick now. Nobody was dying. Nobody was slapping me around, telling me I was full of the Devil. It was just Grace, being hurt. Being mean... I blinked hard, and took another bite of something I couldn't taste.

59

Hal

Vera's washing up before bed. I lean back on my pillow to watch. Her nipples stand up from the cold water till you can see them in her shadow on the wall. She cocks one hip, runs the blue feed-sack washrag between her legs. Her hipbones don't show like they did—she's putting on some weight, with good farm food. Unless... Nah. She'd have told me, if she had news like that.

Vera hangs up her washrag. I grab her around the waist before she can get her nightgown on. She giggles, tries to get away—not very hard.

We're wrapped around each other good and tight, when Katy starts crying upstairs. I stop moving, lean on my elbows so I won't squish Vera. May's footsteps creak overhead.

Vera trails her fingers down my spine. I shiver, but hold still. I don't know why I'm acting like a kid playing hide-and-seek. It's not like we were making a lot of noise. Or like May doesn't know what a man and a woman might be doing together after dark. Last time I slept with May—Thursday night?—she sure seemed to know all about it.

Hoo boy—lying on top of Vera and remembering May at the same time, that's maybe more than a fellow ought to try. About to make me dizzy.

Hound dog with two bitches in heat... Rye's voice jabs in like a handful of rusty barbwire.

"You all right?" Vera whispers. I guess she felt me flinch.

"I'm just about perfect." I nuzzle her hair. Put Rye out of my mind.

But after we're finished, and Vera's asleep, I'm still lying awake. Sweating—this bed's too small for two people, in the summer anyway. But it's Rye that's bugging me. Sticking his nose in. Talking like this is some smutty story in a pulp magazine. *Can't decide which one to hump first.* Like that's the only thing on my mind. Like I don't care if May and Vera are happy.

They *are* happy. Vera was singing like a whole church choir this morning. And May... Well, May doesn't sing much. But you can't tell me she wasn't happy Thursday night. Grinning so hard she got a cramp in her cheek. I like when she leaves the light on. May's face is so sober in the daytime, you'd never guess how she looks at night.

May has been a little testy this weekend. Her woman's curse does her like that, sometimes. Well, and Grace acted downright odd today at dinner. Come to think of it, May's been a little off ever since she and Grace went to that visitation. She never said how that went. If Grace got a whiff of what's up, I imagine she had something to say.

What do you think other people'll say? Talking about May.

Dammit, Rye—you think I care what some knucklehead down at the filling station says? None of their god-damn business. Or Grace's, either. All I care about is May and Vera and Katy. Everybody else can go to hell.

60

May

Iva was pouring the paraffin onto a batch of jelly, and her kitchen smelled like grapes. "Hi, girl!" she said, as I carried Katy in. "Wash day again already?"

"I fall down," Katy told her.

"Oh, bless your heart." Iva finished her job, then kissed the scraped hand Katy held out. "You had your breakfast?"

"She has," I said. "Ready and raring to go."

I straightened the shoulder strap of Katy's sunsuit and gave her a squeeze, then let her slide to the floor. She ran off into the living room, yelling "Pappaw!"

"He's in the bedroom, sweetie," Iva called after her. Then she cocked her head and studied my face. "And how are you, May?"

"I'm fine." I knew she could see the hours I'd spent awake last night, thinking about Grace—and probably the crying I'd done too. I looked at the jars of jelly on the table. "I guess I need to get out and pick *my* grapes."

Iva's eyes stayed on me a moment longer. Then she sighed, and started putting things away. "How'd your vines do this year?"

"Not bad," I said. "What the goat left us, anyway."

"What, the Hooks's goat?"

"I didn't tell you about that?" At least it was a change of subject. "A couple of months ago. I was pushing a wheelbarrow-load of weeds up that rise to the chickenhouse, with Katy on top of the load—and she'd squirmed around sideways till it was about to go over…" Iva chuckled as I acted out my pushing and wobbling.

"Oh, and I had my sickle stuck down the side of the load, so I was worried about that too…" I shook my head. I'd been a fool to let Katy ride on there in the first place. "And then I saw that goat—up on his hind legs, eating my grapes! There wasn't a thing I could do about it—I just had to keep going—" My voice went hoarse all of a sudden, and I cleared my throat. I was sweating, my fists clenched around wheelbarrow handles that weren't there. I opened my hands and wiped them on my skirt. "But it worked out," I finished, not looking at Iva. "Mrs. Hooks heard me yelling, and came after him. She gave me three quarts of cherry pie filling, to make up for it."

"Mammaw!" Katy yelled, running in and flinging her arms around Iva's legs.

Iva patted the back of Katy's head. "What do you think, young'un? Should we gather the eggs first, or water the flowers?"

"Flowers!" Katy grabbed Iva's skirt and pulled her towards the door. "Mammaw, come!"

Iva followed her, and held the door for me. "Only so much one woman can do," she said, as I came down the steps.

"I guess," I answered. I couldn't tell if she meant the goat, or not.

Vera was sorting clothes on the washhouse floor, and singing. She had a pretty voice, but the song sounded like something from Mom's church.

"Put my yellow dress to the side," I interrupted, dumping my water buckets into a rinse tub. "I got grease on it, messing with the porch pump."

Vera nodded, and started singing again as I went after more water. "'Ere we reach the shining river, lay we every burden down...'" I tried not to be irritated. Plenty of people went to church, and sang hymns, without being like Mom. Iva, for instance. Jamie and Grace. I wished I could stop thinking about Grace. I pumped the buckets full, and picked them up with a grunt. My shoulders were sore from splitting wood, and the bucket handle pinched a blister on my right palm.

I had to step around one of Vera's piles of clothes, to fill the second rinse tub. The wash wasn't really a two-person job, but she'd wanted to help. She broke off the song she was singing now—something about "he never drank water, he only drank wine"—and asked, "What do we need to do this week?"

I had to think a minute. I was used to keeping my plans in my own head. I was used to keeping everything in my own head, and doing the wash by myself—but there was no point getting worked up about it. "Well, the grapes are ready, so we can make jelly. And we ought to can some more mustard greens." I dipped my yellow dress in the hot water where the sheets were churning, and sprinkled soap flakes on the grease stain. "Probably get the rest of the horticulture beans in, maybe make some ketchup. And the regular stuff. Why, did you have something in mind?"

Vera was checking the pockets in a pair of Hal's pants. "Well, I wondered if you wanted new curtains anywhere else. Or I could run you up a dress, if you want."

I waved a soapy hand at her. "You don't need to do that." Oh, and I wanted to get the wash-house painted, too.

Vera smiled. "It's not any trouble." I could feel the doubtful look on my face at that. "Don't you like to sew?" she asked.

I scrubbed at the dress with my knuckles. The stain wasn't coming out. "Somebody's got to. I'm not much good at it."

"Did you make the dress you're wearing? It looks nice."

I looked down at the blue-and-white feed-sack fabric. I'd had to redo that button placket three times. "It about killed me."

Vera laughed. "Well, it's easy for me—really. I do it all the time."

"Well," I said, "I imagine our curtains will do us for a while. But it looks like I could use a work dress—this one's about seen its day." I tossed the yellow dress onto a pile, stopped the washer, and started running sheets through the wringer.

Vera squinted at me, like she was seeing the new dress already. "You might like some of the colors they've got now. When will we be going in town again?"

"Why, you need something?"

"If I had the fabric, I could go ahead and get started." She plunged her arms into the rinse water, swishing the sheets. "Mmm, that's cold."

I swung the wringer over and locked it between the rinse tubs, then piled clothes into the washer, pushing them down under the suds. I hated to make an extra trip to town, but I wouldn't need anything for at least a week. I slapped the knob to start the washer. "We'll have the truck Friday, we could go then."

Vera fed the corner of a sheet into the wringer, her fingers dancing back from the heavy rollers. She seemed to know what she was doing. "What about Hal?" she asked.

Hal? "He'll ride with Jamie on Friday."

"No, I mean, does he need any shirts?"

"Oh. I usually just order his."

"I could make him up a couple." Vera fished a pillowcase out of the water. "And does Katy need anything, for this winter?"

"No," I said, wishing she'd let it drop—I'd said yes to the dress. "She's got hand-me-downs from Carol." I tossed a stray sock into the washer. Grace's new baby would be next in line for hand-me-downs. Surely by then Grace would be speaking to me. And then there'd be Vera's baby... I sighed.

"What?" Vera asked, stirring the sheets in the second rinse.

I shrugged my shoulders, feeling the pull of tired muscles. "Nothing," I said, and reached for the clothespin bag.

61

May

My tired yellow dress picked up another stain Wednesday morning, when I slopped a jelly bag full of cooked grapes against my front. Katy kept peeking under my apron to see where the purple had soaked through. She was interested in the jelly bag, too, but I took it out to the chickens before she could get into any mischief. The chickens clucked and crooned as they pecked at the sweet grape pulp. I clucked back at them, enjoying the simple conversation. Katy was full of ideas this morning, and Vera was chatty—asking questions, talking about making crabapple jelly with her mom. It was nice to take a break.

Things were getting easier as the week went on, though—chatting with Vera, not thinking about Grace, holding myself together. I just had to keep at it. Maybe I'd get used to it all, like spring blisters turning into summer calluses.

When I got back to the porch, Katy was hopping around the floor making chicken noises. Vera was testing the jelly, watching thick purple juice drip off the spoon. Almost ready. She stuck the spoon in her mouth and sucked at it slowly, her eyes half-closed. Then she saw me, and blushed bright red as she laid the spoon on the table and wiped her mouth. I dropped the jelly bag in a dishpan and pumped water over it, keeping my eyes on the purple-stained linen. I didn't know what she was embarrassed about, and I hoped she wouldn't explain.

In the afternoon we pulled the horticulture bean vines—I'd gotten two pickings off them already. Katy tried to help, and mainly managed to get dirt in her hair. I pushed the wheelbarrow full of green vines to the chairs in the shade of the mulberry tree.

"These are pretty." Vera held up a pod, pale green and streaked with pink. "What kind are they?"

I set a bushel basket between our chairs. "Tongue of Fire."

"I've never heard of that."

"Grace gave me the seed." Saying Grace's name was like jabbing myself with a straight pin. I sighed, and pulled a bundle of vines into my lap.

"Look," Vera said to Katy. "*Now* you can help pick!" She showed Katy a bean, then held tight to the vine as Katy yanked it loose. "Put it in the basket, and we'll shell it later."

"Pick!" Katy yelled, and ripped another bean off the vine. Vera smiled at her and held the vines steady, picking beans off with her free hand. She was good with Katy—I could tell she'd been around kids.

"Woops! In the basket, sweetheart!" Vera bent over to pick up a bean Katy had flung on the grass. She winced as she straightened up, twisting her head with a sound like a ratchet. Katy peered at her curiously.

Vera rubbed her neck, then went back to her beans. After a minute, she said, "I didn't see a department store in Whelan."

"No." I dropped a handful of beans in the basket. There wasn't a department store in Whelan. "Did you need one?"

"Well, I was thinking..." Vera reached to pick a bean leaf out of Katy's hair, but Katy ran away. "That single bed's pretty tight, for two."

What did that have to do with a department store? —Oh. "You want to buy a *bed?*" I'd never bought a bed in my life. Hal and I had the one Sissy and I used to sleep in.

Vera nodded, as if she bought new beds every day. "Unless you have another idea. Hal said you were the one to ask, about furniture."

"Hmm." I picked a few more handfuls of beans. Vera's bed wasn't that tiny. Hal wasn't a big man, and Vera was smaller than I was. Of course, when her belly got big...

"Honestly," Vera said, smiling at me, "I'm about to fall out on the floor."

I sighed. "We can see what they have in the Sears catalog." If we had to spend money, it was a good time to do it—not like in the spring, when everything had to go to the farm.

Vera rubbed at her neck again. "I was thinking, if we went to a store, we could probably take it home the same day."

"You pay for the privilege, too." Spending was one thing— no need to spend more than we had to.

Vera watched Katy dragging a picked-over vine around the yard. "Well," she said, "I've got some savings. A mattress shouldn't be more than twenty-five dollars. And for a bedstead —is there a used-furniture store?"

I nodded. "In Aurora. They've got a department store, too." Carson's, or Peterses, or something. I'd never had occasion to go there. "I've heard you can make a mattress," I said. Grace had made one for her and Jamie during the war, with directions from a pamphlet. I remembered her laughing about it. *You should've seen the mess, May—cotton lint all over Creation!*

"I don't think it'll cost too much, to buy one," Vera said.

I shrugged. "I guess we can go to Aurora instead of Whelan, on Friday. You can get your fabric there, too."

Vera nodded, and started picking off beans again. We worked in quiet for a little while, except for Katy's tractor noises. The basket of pods was getting full.

"You pressure-can these?" Vera asked.

"Yes."

She pried open a pod, and smiled. "Oh, look, the beans are striped too! We always just dried our beans, and threshed them out with an axe handle."

I nodded. "I've got some for soup beans, too." They'd be ready in a few weeks. Dry beans were easier, but they never cooked up as creamy.

Vera picked a few more beans, then cleared her throat. "I didn't mean to sound..." She paused, biting her lip. "I was thinking..."

I stifled another sigh. Vera seemed to be thinking an awful lot today.

"About my savings," she went on. "I ought to put that in with your money. Do you use a bank?"

I frowned. Was she going to want to go to the bank tomorrow, too? "Farmer's, in at Whelan."

"I just meant..." Vera said, "I mean, I'm living here, and eating here, and all, so it seems like..." She trailed off uncertainly as I stared at her.

Living here? Eating here? Was that what Vera thought she was doing? Was that what I was holding myself together for, losing Grace for? For Vera to have room and board? "Nonsense," I said.

Vera blinked. "What?"

I tried to smooth the scowl off my face. "You're not living here and eating here."

She squinted at me like I was blurry.

"For Pete's sake, Vera," I said, "You're part of the *family!*" I flung a handful of beans into the basket.

"Oh," Vera said, sounding relieved and confused both. "Well, yes. I mean, I know." She raised her hands a little, like a shrug. "But I didn't want to..."

"Presume?"

The word came out bitter and hard, like a slap. There was a silence. I kept my eyes on the beans in my lap, feeling my face go red. I hadn't meant it to sound like that. Vera was just trying to...whatever she was trying to do. And it made sense, about the money. But I didn't trust myself to say so.

Out of the corner of my eye, I saw Vera sitting with her mouth open, like she was tasting the word on her tongue. After a minute, she said, "Yes." Then she put her last stripped vine on the pile and stood up, brushing off her dress. "I think I'll go get a drink."

I nodded, and didn't look up.

62

Vera

On the way home from Aurora, Katy kept wanting to stand up on the truck seat to see the mattress in the back. I let her look a little, then got her to sit down and sing with me. We sang "Happy Trails" and "Skip to My Lou." May just drove.

May had insisted on paying for half of the mattress and bedstead. Did that mean she didn't want my money to go in the bank with theirs? I didn't feel inclined to bring it up again. I'd thought May was quiet before, but...well, she wasn't being *quiet* now, exactly. I tried to think of the word for how she'd been these couple of days, since that stomach-churning conversation over the beans, but I couldn't.

When we got home, May went straight to work stripping my old bed and taking it apart. We carried it up to Katy's room, then brought the new bedstead and double mattress in from the truck. Katy mostly got in our way. As soon as the new bed was put together, she climbed up on it and rolled around.

May and I were folding the quilt I'd been using, bringing the corners together and shaking it smooth, when something struck my shoulder—hard. "Ow!" I turned to see Katy standing on the bed, waving my hairbrush. "Did you hit me, Katy?"

Katy nodded cheerfully.

"That hurt! Don't hit me!" I made a sad face.

"No hitting!" May agreed.

"Ow!" Katy said, grinning. She raised the hairbrush again.

"*No hitting,* Katy!" May's voice was sharp. She snatched the hairbrush and put it on my dresser.

Katy frowned, then sat down on the bed and started to cry. May and I doubled the bright fabric of the quilt between us, stepping close and away, while Katy cried louder. Finally May gave me the folded quilt. "That goes in the cedar chest upstairs," she said, picking Katy up. "The Fish Tail quilt's a double, or the Log Cabin. Get you some sheets from my closet."

It was as hot as an oven upstairs. I grabbed the Log Cabin quilt and two sheets, and hurried back down, sweating.

"You look warm," May said, as I dropped the bedding on the mattress. "Let's get some ice tea."

Katy leaned against May's shoulder, sucking on her finger and looking at me sideways. I smiled at her so she'd know I wasn't mad. I smiled at May, too, but she was already headed for the kitchen.

Polite. That was the word. May seemed polite, and considerate, and far away. Just last week we'd been picking apples and joking together, chatting while we washed the dishes... I was starting to get lonely.

May and I were doing the supper dishes when the phone rang. Hal answered it, balancing Katy on his free arm. "Hello?" He listened for a minute. "I can ask her. —May, James is wondering if you can cut tobacco tomorrow."

May frowned at the dishwater. "Isn't that what we're doing?"

Hal held the phone receiver out of Katy's reach. "He's wanting you to *cut.* In the field, with the men."

"Why?" May asked, handing me a plate to rinse.

"Joe Mack ran a nail through his foot," Hal said.

I winced. "Which one's Joe?"

"Older one. —James can't get anybody else," he told May, "And he can't afford to be a man short and not get done—Grace'll kill him if he misses that wedding on Sunday. Sunday'd be pushing it anyway. Bucky Morris says it's fixing to rain Wednesday."

I sorted that out in my head. May and Iva had explained tobacco harvesting to me, when we were cooking for the crew here—was that just a week and a half ago? The cut plants have to dry a few days in the field, before they go in the barn.

May turned her frown on Hal. "Who's Bucky Morris?"

"Fellow at the yard." The phone receiver squawked, and Hal put it back to his ear. "Hold your horses, James, we're working on it."

"Trotty-horse!" Katy said, bouncing on Hal's arm. He jiggled her absent-mindedly, and she kicked her heels.

"What's he got to do with it?" May asked.

"Bucky?" Hal said. "He's always right about the weather."

May snorted, and went back to the dishes. "Nobody's always right."

"Trotty-horse!" Katy yelled. I dried my hands and took her from Hal, sitting down to bounce her on my knees.

"May says nobody's always right," Hal was saying into the phone. "...No, about Bucky. ...Oh." He shrugged at May. "He says Bucky's always right about the weather, and always wrong about everything else."

"Mm-hmm," May said skeptically, scrubbing at the corn plate. Katy slid off my lap and ran into the living room. I went back to rinsing and drying.

"Anyway," Hal said, "You want to help? You're as strong as Henry, anyway. And Grace can probably spare you in the kitchen, with Vera helping."

"I guess," May said, without looking up. "Show me what to do."

"All right," Hal told James. "She'll help out. ...Yeah, that's what I always say. See you tomorrow." He hung up the phone.

"What do you always say?" I asked.

He grinned at me. "May's all wool and a yard wide. Right, May?"

"Mm-hmm." May took the dry corn plate from me, and put it on the top shelf. "I'll want a pair of your pants," she told Hal.

"Have at 'em. I like a woman that wears the pants," Hal said, patting May's behind. May stepped away from him, reaching for a jar. Hal winked at me. "What about you, Vera? You need any pants? Might have to roll some cuffs."

I flicked my dishtowel at him. "I think I'll be fine. Anything I need to take with me?" I asked May.

"I always take my own paring knife—Grace's don't suit me." May scrubbed at the rim of the jar. "You might like them, though."

"I'll take one, just in case."

I swept the kitchen floor while May was putting Katy to bed. When I passed by Hal's chair, he stuck out an arm and pulled me onto his lap. "Need any help breaking in that new bed?"

"Mm-hmm," I said, as he kissed me. Hal's pajamas were folded on top of my new Log Cabin quilt. I started to get up, but he kissed me again, longer, his fingers in my hair. My lips felt like warm candle-wax, melting into his.

Katy called something, upstairs. I pulled away, catching the broom before it could clatter to the floor. Hal grabbed me around the waist as I stood up. My heart was pounding—from Hal nuzzling my breasts, or because May might walk in any minute, I couldn't tell. Hal stood up to kiss me again, and the warm-wax feeling spread all the way to my toes. But I had a cold-dishrag feeling, too, telling me this wasn't right. Hal's lips opened against mine, soft and hot. He had every right to kiss me. To kiss his own wife. I stepped closer, feeling heat pouring off his body. To kiss his own wife, in his own kitchen...our own kitchen...

It was May's kitchen. I pulled away from Hal, breathless. When he reached for me, I put the broom between us, and smiled. His eyebrows crinkled like a puppy's. "No?" he said.

"Later," I told him.

Hal sighed, then went out to the porch to wash. I looked around for the dustpan. My lips felt softer than usual, and bigger. I wondered if May would notice.

May's kitchen—but my bedroom, and my bed. If this bed's not "broke in" now, I don't know what it'll take. It must be almost midnight.

Hal's falling asleep. I walk my fingers across his chest, slipping a little in the sweat. Sometimes being sweaty is all right. My leg is draped over his. I think about moving, stretching out in the breeze from the fan, but I don't seem to have any bones left. I chuckle.

Hal stirs. "Hm?"

"I was just thinking," I whisper, "We've got our double bed, and we're *still* all squashed up against each other."

He smiles without opening his eyes. "Mm-hmm."

It's funny how many things "Mm-hmm" can mean. Maybe it depends on what it's not saying. And tonight, between me and Hal, everything's been said. My neck feels better already.

63

May

"Maydie!" Jamie hollered, slapping me on the back. "Hallelujah! —Hi, Hal."

"How come I don't get a hallelujah?" Hal asked, nodding at Rye and Henry.

Jamie grinned at him. "You're not as good-looking as May. Runs in the family."

Hal laughed, and we all followed Jamie out to the field. Rye was telling Henry how to witch a well. Henry kept glancing at me sidelong in the dawn light. He wasn't used to me having short hair—or wearing pants, for that matter. My legs felt odd and bulky in the heavy fabric. I'd tucked in an old flower-print blouse, and tied a scarf over my hair. Hal had called me Rosie the Riveter again at breakfast.

Hal handed me a tobacco knife, its long handle smooth and black with use. He pointed to the hooked blade. "You want to catch hold of the stalk and pull," he said. "Don't swing at it." I nodded.

"So, Maydie," Jamie said, picking up the nearest tobacco stick, "This here is called a *tobacco stick.*" He pronounced it slow and loud, as if I was deaf and ignorant both. I gave him a look.

"Here's your spike." Rye handed me the shiny steel cone. I turned it over in my fingers. Hal had run one through his hand, years ago—he still had the scar.

"It's not so hard, even for a girl," Jamie said, still teasing me. He jammed his own spike onto the pointy end of the stick. "Just think of the spike as your needle, and the stick's your thread."

I scowled at him. "Nobody told me I was going to have to *sew!*" Jamie laughed, and I felt a smile tug at the corner of my mouth.

Rye held up his knife. "Put the thong around your wrist, so your knife can hang when you go to spike your plants."

"Cut five plants and stack them up neat," Jamie said, "And then you spike those five." He held up his fists and pretended to drive a plant down on his tobacco stick.

"But...but not all five at once," Henry added, turning red. "It don't work." Rye grinned at him.

"Try to keep your spike centered, and don't go too close to the end," Jamie said. "And you want to watch your hands."

I tapped my knife against my leg, trying to look like I wasn't half asleep. I'd been up since two o'clock, after dreams I couldn't quite remember—hanging onto something, fighting my way out of somewhere, arguing with somebody.

Hal glanced at me. "Why don't you just let her try it," he told Jamie. "You didn't give Henry half this much advice."

"Watch me a couple times," Rye told me. He went on talking as he picked a row and bent over the first plant. "If your knife's sharp, it don't take much..."

I got the hang of it fast enough, and Rye went off to another row. I cut and stacked and spiked, over and over. As the day heated up, the sun brought out the sweet-bitter smell of the tobacco, and sap turned my hands black and sticky. The men slowly pulled ahead of me in their rows, bobbing up and disappearing like ducks on a pond. When I bent down, long yellow leaves blocked out the sky.

After a while, Jamie traded rows with Henry, and Hal traded with me, to keep us all even. Hal's blue shirt was dark with sweat. "How you holding up?" he asked.

I wiped my face on my sleeve. "Better than sewing." Hal smiled, and winked at me.

It was better than sewing. And better than lying awake worrying about Grace, or trying not to be grouchy with Vera by mistake. I cut and stacked and spiked, feeling like a body without a mind. Just hands gripping the knife or the stalk, eyes watching out for the spike, back and knees bending, sweat running down inside my pants-legs and sticking my blouse to my back.

About midmorning Vera came out to the field with a couple of earthenware jugs. I expected water, but it was more like watered-down lemonade. My tar-blackened hands stuck to the jug as I passed it to Hal.

Rye handed his jug to Jamie, and wiped his mouth on his collar. "What you got in there, vinegar?" he asked Vera.

She nodded. "And sugar and salt. It's haymaker's switchel—I figured it'd do for tobacco cutters too."

Jamie smacked his lips thoughtfully. "Tastes kind of like sweat," he said. Then he added hastily, "Good sweat, I mean. The finest sweat."

Henry laughed in the middle of taking a drink, and coughed himself red in the face. "It's good," he said shyly to Vera, once he'd recovered.

She smiled at him. "Didn't want you to dry up and blow away."

Vera's face was pink from the heat, and there was a streak of flour on her cheek. I thought of her spending the morning in the hot kitchen with Grace and Iva, cooking our meal while the kids ran in and out. The pies would be cooling by now, and they'd be putting the vegetables on. I'd done it all a hundred times, but it seemed miles away from me, standing among the men with my tarry knife dangling from my wrist. I took the jug from Henry and had another drink.

"How you holding up, Maydie?" Jamie asked.

I shrugged, and felt my back give a twinge. "Fine, if I don't stand around too long."

Rye nodded agreement. "No rest for the wicked."

"Appreciate it," Hal said to Vera, as she took the empty jugs.

"No trouble at all," she said. "See you at dinnertime."

64

Vera

Grace and Iva had pretended to argue over how to serve the meal—everybody sitting down together, or in shifts?—but it was obviously an old debate, and neither of them was surprised when Iva won. We fed the kids first, and chased them back outside. Then Iva set the table again, with five places, while Grace put the biscuits in the oven and I rang the dinner bell on the porch.

The men and May came in dripping from the yard pump, mixing the smell of sweat and tobacco with the hot biscuits and ham. They fell into their chairs, exclaiming over how good the food looked. James tried to smooth his cowlick down, but it stood up stiff with sweat. Rye's forehead was crisscrossed with the print of his straw hat.

As they all dug in, I leaned on the counter and kept an eye on the serving dishes. We had more creamed corn and green beans on the stove, and another quart of applesauce if we needed it.

I kept an eye on Hal, too. I couldn't help it. His shoulders moved loose and strong under his shirt, and he smiled—at May, at Henry, once at me. I watched his tobacco-stained hands splitting a biscuit in half, and thought of those hands sliding over my back in bed last night... I felt my cheeks getting warm, and looked away. Rye was spooning sugar over his tomatoes. I'd never heard of anybody doing that. Rye still wouldn't quite meet my eyes, but he thanked me when I poured him more ice tea.

They all ate more than seemed possible, finishing their seconds and starting on thirds before they slowed down. Somehow they managed to talk most of the time, too—mostly Rye.

I couldn't tell whether Grace was still snubbing May. Maybe she'd gotten it out of her system. She'd been cheerful enough all morning in the kitchen, and hadn't even asked me nosy questions. But then, last Sunday she'd managed to treat me like a guest while giving May as cold a shoulder as I'd ever seen.

James passed Henry the potatoes. "How's Joe's foot?"

"Doing okay—Ma's got it soaking in epsom salts," Henry said, blushing. I could imagine Petey being just like that, at what, fourteen? Embarrassed to be alive.

"You got to watch out for those deep wounds," Rye said with his mouth full. "I remember once we had a coyote come up in the yard—must've been in '23, or...when was it, Ivie?"

"What are you talking about now?" Iva asked.

James eyed the pie Iva was slicing. "Might be time to talk about dessert," he suggested.

"You've had biscuits and jelly," Grace said, cutting into a chocolate layer cake. "What more do you want?"

"Anyway," Rye said, sticking to his story, "Whenever it was— I took a shot at him, and darned if Ol' Blue didn't jump him, right then! Took a bullet in her shoulder." He shook his head. "Boy! I thought, if I've killed Ol'Blue, I'll never forgive myself."

Grace started putting pie and cake on saucers—both, for everybody—and I handed them around, while Iva went to the cellar for more ice.

"She was bleeding like a stuck pig when I carried her in the house," Rye was saying. "Ivie sewed her up. Blue just laid there the whole time, quiet as could be—like she knew Ivie was helping her."

"Huh," Hal said. "That dog was something else. You reckon I ought to eat my pie first, or my cake?"

James looked like he might offer some advice, but Rye held up a hand. "That wasn't the end of it," he said. "Couple days later, I found Ol' Blue under the corncrib. Down on her side in the dirt, just as still as death." Rye nodded slowly, and took a long drink of ice tea to stretch out the moment. Hal sighed, and started in on his pie.

"Well," Rye went on, "Good thing the vet come out anyway that day, for a horse. He took one look at Ol' Blue, and cut those stitches right open with his scissors. And you wouldn't believe—down in under the skin, it was just a squirming mess of maggots."

Henry went pale, and put down his fork. I was glad I wasn't eating.

"Orion Louis Dixon!" Iva said, rattling the bowl of ice she'd just brought in. "*What* are you telling at the dinner table?"

Rye held out his glass for more ice. "Ah, these boys don't mind, Ivie," he said. Then he glanced at May, and cleared his throat.

"I've got a strong stomach," May said, taking a bite of cake, "But maybe you'd best leave it there."

"That's all there was to it, anyway," Rye said. "Vet said a wound that deep, you can't just sew it up, or it'll fester. Said those little—" He cleared his throat again. "Well, anyway, that's what saved her. If they hadn't kept it clean, she'd have died of it." Rye winked at Henry, who blushed again and gave him a sheepish grin. "Another couple months, you'd have never known it. She didn't hold it against me, either, for shooting her." He shook his head slowly. "She sure was a good dog, Ol' Blue was."

"And *that's* the moral of the story!" James said. He finished off his ice tea, and shoved his chair back. "Well, boys, that was so good, let's all go bend over in the field and see if we can't taste it again."

They all thanked us as they got up to leave. James kissed Grace on the cheek. May picked up a napkin somebody had dropped, and handed a glass to me as I started clearing the table.

"That's all right," I said, "We'll get it."

As the men crowded through the door, May glanced out the window at the kids in the yard. "Katy's going to need a nap…"

"You leave that to Mammaw," Iva said, giving May a little push. "Go on. You're one of the men today."

May glanced at Grace, but Grace was busy getting out plates for the three of us. "All right," May said, and followed the men back to work.

65

Hal

"Tired, Maydie?" James links elbows with May, as we head for the house at the end of the day.

"Not so you'd notice," May says, then leans on him all at once so he staggers sideways. He chuckles.

It's good to see May fooling around. She's as stumbling-tired as the rest of us, but she seems easier than she did this morning. I link up with her other elbow and swerve left, tugging her and James with me. James swerves us back to the right, and I pull left again. We used to do that every day leaving school—Grace too, on James's other arm—and laugh our heads off.

"You got done early," Grace says as we come in the kitchen.

James grins at her. "You should've seen how fast Henry got, when May started pulling ahead of him. —Rye's taking him home," he adds, to Ma.

Katy scrambles down from Ma's lap, and runs to grab hold of May's pants-leg. "Daddy!" she hollers. "Up!"

We all laugh, and May smiles down at her. "Nope, hon. It's Mommy."

Katy stares up at May's face, then squeals, "Mommy haves *pants!*" like it's the funniest thing she ever saw. I pick her up and give her a kiss.

Vera comes to join us, taking a stack of tinfoil-covered pie plates from Grace—leftovers, for our supper. "Now remember," Iva says, "The Jell-O goes on *top!*" and the three of them laugh, like it's a punchline.

James pats May on the shoulder. "Better get this gal on home, before she keels over." May gives him a little shove, but she does look dazed. I know that kind of tired, when you can't even think. It's the bending over that gets you—tobacco plants aren't heavy, but you have to pick every damn one of them up off the ground.

"Thanks for dinner—and supper," May tells the other women. "You outdid yourself with that cake, Grace."

Grace starts to smile, and stops halfway. "Bye, Vera," she says. "Bye, Hal. Katy, you be good."

May's shoulders drop down a couple of notches past tired. I stare at Grace for a minute, but nothing I want to say is fit for mixed company.

"Bye, May," Iva says. "Take care."

"Be good," James adds.

May nods, and we head for the truck.

I'm late for evening milking. Bess is sore about it. She crowds Rosie against the doorpost as they come in the barn, and Rosie grunts in her throat. "You quit that," I tell Bess, smacking her on the flank. I give Rosie an extra pat along with her feed, but she doesn't look too worried. Bess settles down, too, once she's got a mouthful of corn.

I wish people were as easy to straighten out as cows. I imagine it'd take more than a smack and a scoop of corn to make Grace quit acting up. Much as I'm tempted to try it. Grace always did have a mean streak. Spit in my eye once, in sixth grade, with her mouth full of cinnamon rock candy. Burned like fire.

May didn't say a word coming home, and she just talked to Katy at supper. I wish she'd tell Grace to go to hell. She probably won't.

66

Vera

Hal sniffed the air as he came in from morning chores. "Mmm
—you baking something?"

"Coffeecake." I put a slice on the plate with his sausage and
eggs. We wouldn't be having the big Sunday dinner, since we'd
all eaten together yesterday and Grace's bunch had a wedding
to go to—but it seemed like Sunday ought to have something
special about it.

Hal sat down and tucked in. I nibbled at my own piece of
coffeecake. It was good—I could taste how fresh the butter
was, and the buttermilk, and the eggs—but my stomach was a
little unsteady. Maybe I should tell Hal about the pregnancy
now, while we had a moment alone. Of course I should. I
swallowed. "What're you up to today?" I asked.

Hal took a slurp of coffee. "Cutting firewood with Rye. Ma
said she'd feed me lunch, so I guess I'll see you for supper."

Then Katy called out, and I had to hurry upstairs before she
could wake May. Katy looked surprised to see me, but she let
me pick her up. I peeked into May's bedroom as we went by.
May was sprawled on her back, with her mouth open. I smiled.
She'd slept through Hal's getting up, and I'd convinced him to
let her sleep. The extra rest would do her good, after yester-

day's work. Not that May didn't work every day—she hardly sat down. But working in the field, doing the same hard thing over and over all day long, you get a whole different kind of tired. Mama and I had worked like that, back home. Some days I'd be so tired I was crying. It didn't seem fair that everything was made too big—plow handles too thick for my grip, post-hole digger too tall, *everything*. Mama said "fair" was just a word somebody made up. But then she'd come help me, and we'd manage it together.

Back in the kitchen, Hal put Katy on his lap. She opened her mouth like a baby bird for a bite of cake, but shut it tight against sausage and eggs. Hal had a second piece of cake, and pressed the back of his fork on his plate to collect the last crumbs. Then he was off to meet Rye.

So much for sharing my news.

May smiled when she tasted the coffeecake. "That's good, Vera. You're spoiling me this morning—I don't know *when* I've slept so late."

I smiled at her. "Everybody needs a little spoiling now and then." She'd come rushing downstairs close to nine, looking alarmed—but the dark circles were gone from under her eyes.

"Hm." May took another bite of eggs. "I thought we'd get the washhouse painted today, since what's-his-name says it's going to rain Wednesday." That must be why she'd put on her stained yellow dress again.

Which reminded me— "Could I take your measurements real quick?" I asked, as she got up from the table. "That way I can work on your dress whenever I get a chance."

"Didn't you buy a pattern?"

"Yes, but I can alter it to fit you better."

May looked skeptical. "If you say so."

May shut the living room curtains and stripped down to her underthings and shoes, while I wrote "May Dixon, Sept. '49" on a fresh page in my sewing notebook.

I dropped the soft yellow tape down May's back, neck to waist. Katy watched me write down the numbers, then tried to grab the tape. "Hang on, sweetie," I told her, wrapping it around May's waist. "You can play with it when I'm done. — Twenty-nine and a quarter, and your shoulder's...nine inches even." I wrote those down. Katy was eyeing my pencil, so I stuck it behind my ear. "Raise your arms, just—there..." Before I could read the bust measurement, Katy yanked on the tape again.

"Katy, let Vera measure," May said.

"I help!" Katy retorted.

"I know what we need," I said, and went to get my old measuring tape. "You can use this one!"

Katy frowned at the tape's frayed edges, then held it up to May's belly. I moved around May, measuring. She held her arms where I put them, stiff as a doll. At least she stood still— some women wiggled and giggled worse than little kids. Katy tried to wrap her tape around May's ankles, then flapped it up and down, making it ripple in the air.

I knelt down to get the hem length, then wrapped the tape around May's hips. My hands turned suddenly warm, as I remembered my dream—or whatever it was—about May and Hal. His callused hand sliding up over her hip, raising her nightgown... I swallowed hard, and concentrated on the tape's black lines and numbers as I slid it down for the yoke measurement. What was next? Inseam. I took a deep breath, and stretched the tape up the inside of May's leg.

"What do you need that for?" May asked. I jumped guiltily —but she just sounded curious.

"Pants," I said. "Twenty-eight." I reached for my notebook.

"I don't wear pants," May said. "Or I borrow Hal's."

I nodded, and stood up. "I wear them in the winter sometimes. They're warm. Here, bend your arm..." I measured from her shoulder to her wrist.

"You're not making a long-sleeved dress, are you?" she asked.

"No, I'm just getting them all while I'm at it. Mama always said, 'Measure 'em while you've got 'em.'"

"If you say so." May shrugged, and I had to reposition the tape. Katy was trying to measure my leg now.

"Mama was big on planning ahead," I said. "She'd have us canning two years' worth of food, when we hadn't eaten all the last year's yet. Drove me crazy." I smiled, remembering how I used to complain about it. "But I guess she knew her business. She got us through the Depression by herself, after Pop left us."

May shook her head as I measured her upper arm. "I guess we all got through it, one way or another."

I wrote down "10 1/2," still thinking of Mama. "There were a few years, Mama didn't even sing. And then one day we were getting in the wash—it must've been around '32—and all of a sudden she let loose with 'Bringing in the Sheets.'"

May cocked her head. "Isn't that 'Bringing in the Sheaves?'"

I grinned. "She rewrote it for wash day. We laughed till we cried." That was the first time Mama had laughed in a while, too. "After that, she sang all the time. Said it made the work go faster." May was still holding her arm out. I hurried to get her elbow measurement. "Just one more... Does your mother sing?"

"*Oh*, no," May said, as if it was a ridiculous question. "Maybe in church. She was too busy praying to sing, at home. Or too mad."

I wrapped the tape around May's wrist, trying to put 'praying' and 'mad' together in my head. "She doesn't sound very happy," I said—then glanced up at May, worried she'd take offense.

May grunted. "Happy? Mom's about as mad and miserable as a person can get." Then her breath caught, and she pressed her lips tight between her teeth, like holding a pocketbook shut with both hands.

"That's too bad," I said. I wanted to ask questions, but I could see May had already said more than she meant to. She frowned hard at the closed window-curtains, as if she was seeing something else. I could hear Katy talking to herself in the kitchen.

Finally, May sighed. "Are you about done?"

"Oh—" I still had the tape around her wrist. Five and seven eighths. "Yes, that's all I need." Usually after I measured a customer, I'd say something like, "Make sure you don't grow, now!" This time I just wrote down the numbers and closed my notebook.

May picked up her yellow dress from the rocking chair and pulled it over her head. "If we get started scraping the wash house now, we can paint this afternoon."

67

Vera

May grunted a little as she climbed the stepladder under the wash house eaves.

"You sore?" I asked. "I'll do that part, if you want."

"I'll be all right." May reached up and scraped loose a shower of old paint. "The best thing for sore muscles is to work them."

I went around the corner to scrape the front wall. Paint flakes sprayed over Katy, who was playing in the flowerbed. "Look, Katy, it's a snowstorm!"

Katy squinted at the sky. "Funder?" She was probably too little to remember winter.

"Just snow—see?" I scraped some more, showering her with white.

She giggled and held out her hands, then said, "I help!"

"Sure." I handed her a stick. "Just go *scrape, scrape...*"

"No!" She scowled, and made a grab for my paint scraper. "Mine!" When I wouldn't hand it over, she hit me on the leg with the stick. I sighed, and took the stick away.

"Ow?" she asked.

"Ow," I agreed. "Don't hit."

"Did she hit you again?" May asked, bringing her ladder around the corner.

"Not very hard," I said. I moved farther along the wall, careful of the mint in the flowerbed.

"I swear, I don't know what's got into her lately." May climbed the ladder again, and shoved her scraper along a rafter.

"Funderstorm!" Katy ran to get under the falling flakes.

"Woops, hon—" I lifted her clear of the mint, and tried to straighten the plants back up.

"Don't worry about it," May said. "Mint's tough."

We finished scraping after lunch, and started painting. Katy was down for her nap, which made things easier. May swept her brush along the flat lengths of siding, while I did the windowframes. The air smelled like fresh paint and bruised mint. A few late locusts were singing along with the whine of Hal and Rye's cordwood saw from the woodlot.

May seemed content to be quiet. I thought through the alterations for her dress pattern as I worked. Extra length in the hem, of course, so she'd have something to let down. And I'd need to lift the shoulder and let it out, both—all her dresses were tight in the shoulders.

Mama taught me to take as much care fitting a work dress as a nice one. "It'll last you longer if it fits you right," she'd say, and have me adjust my pattern again. I didn't mind. I knew it'd look better if it fit me right, too—and if I didn't look nice in my work clothes, I'd never look nice.

May would look nice, in this dress. We'd picked out a dark green fabric, with little medallions in white and brown and lighter green. It put color in her cheeks, and brought out the reddish highlights in her curls. May liked it because it wouldn't show stains. I smiled to myself as I brushed thick white paint along a windowsill. May and Mama would probably get along.

After a while I noticed I was humming, and started to sing. "…That same old train that brought me here, gonna take me home again…" I trailed off to concentrate on the tricky mullions of a window, then picked it up again. "Darlin', you can't love one...Darlin', you can't love two..." My brush hesitated—maybe that wasn't the most tactful choice of a song. It seemed worse to stop in the middle, though. "Darlin', you can't love three or four, and still say my love belongs to you." I sang the chorus again as I moved to the next window, then switched to "Fox Went Out on a Chilly Night." May just kept working, crouching down to paint the bottom of the wall. Maybe she hadn't noticed the words—the locusts were still pretty loud.

As I finished the last window, I yawned.

"Ready for your nap?" May asked.

I shrugged. "I'll help you finish it out."

"No, you go on, while Katy's still down." May dipped her brush and wiped it on the edge of the can. "The rest of this is just slopping it on."

"All right," I said. I was about to keel over anyway.

I woke to a muffled thumping sound. *Whap. Whap. Whap.* It was familiar, but I couldn't place it. It paused, then started again. Then Katy hollered, and I rolled out of bed to go get her.

"Mommy," Katy said firmly as I carried her down the stairs.

"That's right. Hear that sound? What's Mommy doing?"

Katy listened. *Whap. Whap. Whap.* Her eyes lit up. "Mommy haves a big...*hammer!*"

"You think?" I looked out the kitchen window. The big braided rug from the living room was draped over the clothesline, swaying with each *whap.* Several smaller rugs were piled on the grass. "Look, Mommy's beating the rugs!" May stepped into view on the far side of the clothesline, and swung the heavy wire rug-beater again. *Whap.* Clouds of dust billowed out of the rug. May squinted, with her mouth pressed shut. She didn't look like she was enjoying herself. Probably nobody ever enjoyed beating rugs.

Katy watched, sleepy and amazed, as the plume of dust rose on the thick air and sagged off toward the wash house...where dust was stuck all over the fresh white paint.

"Oh! May!" I yelled. "May!" But the locusts were still making a racket. May whacked the rug again. I rushed out onto the porch and through the screen door. "May! Stop! The paint!" *Whap. Whap.*

"Mommy!" Katy shrieked, clinging to my bouncing shoulder. "Stop! Stop!"

"May!" Whap. "May!"

Finally, May heard us. She stepped out of the dust cloud and rested the end of the rug-beater on the ground, looking at us curiously.

"The paint!" I panted, freeing an arm from Katy to point at the wash house.

"Stop!" Katy sounded frantic.

"It's okay, sweetie," I puffed at her—good grief, I'd only run a few yards—"Mommy stopped. Good job. Shh."

Katy still looked worried. She slid down and ran to May. "Mommy, up!"

May was staring at the wash house's clapboard siding, which had gone from smooth white to fuzzy gray. She kept opening her mouth and then shutting it again. I tried to think of something helpful to say, but May found her voice first. "Dammit!" she snapped. She stomped her foot in the grass, and said it again, louder. *"Dammit!"*

"Um," I said. "Maybe it'll…"

"I just try and *try!*" May's voice was loud and shaky. "And every damn thing—Oh, for Pete's *sake,* Katy, let go!" She yanked her hem out of Katy's hands, and stormed over to the wash house to poke the dirty paint with a finger. "We'll have it all to do over again! Why didn't I *think…* " Her voice cracked, and she stopped. Her shoulders were rigid under the yellow plaid of her dress, straining the seams.

"Mommy!" Katy quavered.

May sighed loudly. Then she scrubbed at her face with her apron and went to pick Katy up. "It's okay, hon. Mommy's just made a big mess, is all."

Katy peered into May's face. "Dammit!" she announced.

May's eyes widened, and she glanced at me. I wasn't sure whether to laugh or not. "Don't say that, Katy," she said tiredly. "It's a bad word."

I went around the corner of the wash house, to look at the north wall. "It looks okay over here," I said. "Maybe we'll just have to repaint that one side."

May gave a resigned shrug. "Anyway, me cussing at it won't help any." She set Katy down and picked up the rug-beater. "Might as well finish this up—I can't make it any worse."

I opened my mouth, then decided not to argue.

"I ought to just get rid of all the rugs, and have bare floor," May said, in between smacking the rug with a vengeance. "You can beat a rug all day and not get all the dirt out."

"That's the truth," I said. "Come on, Katy, let's get out of the dust."

"I help!" Katy said. "Help Mommy!"

May gave her an impatient glance, but when she saw Katy bouncing on her toes and staring at the rug-beater, she sighed. "Oh, all right, you can try."

Katy managed half a dozen swings, laughing in delight at the little puffs of dust she raised. I watched May steadying Katy's arms. The anger was gone from her face, but there were smears of grime where she'd wiped tears away, and her mouth had a weary set to it. She didn't look so well-rested anymore.

68

May

Hal came in as I was getting supper on the table. "Long time no see," he said, kissing me. He smelled like gasoline and sawdust. "Get your beauty rest this morning?"

"Mm-hmm." I stacked hot corn on a plate.

"Where's Vera?"

"Getting stuff from the basement. Go ahead and wash up, supper's about ready."

Suddenly Hal skipped sideways like a cat dodging a snake. "What the— Katy! What'd you do that for?"

"Ow!" Katy grinned up at him, waving a wooden spoon.

"Did she hit you?" I asked. She'd whacked Vera with that spoon while we were putting the rugs back down, and I'd had to smack her bottom.

"I guess." Hal chuckled. "Girl's got an arm on her!"

"It's not funny, Hal!" I said impatiently.

"Hear that, Katy?" Hal picked her up. "Not funny."

Katy raised the spoon again.

"No hitting!" I said.

"What you whuppin' me for?" Hal whimpered at Katy, ducking his head. "I ain't done nothin'!" While Katy was giggling, he slipped the spoon out of her hand and laid it on the table. Then he danced off towards the porch with her, singing. "K-K-K-Katy, beautiful Katy!"

"Hal, for Pete's sake…" Katy would never learn, at this rate. But Hal wasn't listening to me.

"You want these in bowls?" Vera asked, setting jars of relish and peaches on the table.

I sighed. "Yes, and you can pour the ice tea."

When Hal came in from the porch, he kissed Vera—then jumped again, when Katy's spoon hit him in the knee.

"Katy—" I started around the table.

Hal laughed. "Why, I believe my girl's jealous!" he said. "Doesn't want to share her daddy!" Katy giggled.

"It's not funny," I said, taking Katy's spoon and swatting her bottom with it. She burst into noisy tears. I handed the spoon to Vera. "Hide this somewhere, would you? Katy, *no hitting!*"

Katy shoved at me. Hal picked her up. I hadn't spanked her hard—I never did—and she quieted as he bounced her up and down. He gave me a worried frown.

"She's hit Vera three times now," I said irritably. "We can't just let her get away with it."

Hal nodded slowly. "I imagine you know best." He gave Katy a squeeze. "I just hate to see my Katydid cry."

Katy sat up on Hal's arm and looked him in the eye. "Dammit!" she said.

Hal's eyebrows went up. "Where you been taking this girl—the saloon?"

I rubbed my forehead. It was gritty with sweat and dust. "Let's eat our supper before it gets cold."

Katy was out of sorts all through supper. She wanted corn, and then she didn't want corn. She put her hands in her applesauce, and then cried because they were sticky. Vera and Hal chatted, while I cut up Katy's food, and wiped her hands, and reminded myself that she was just a baby. It wasn't her fault I was in a bad mood.

I still couldn't believe I'd beaten those rugs without remembering the wet paint. I'd been distracted, thinking about Mom.

She was mad and miserable, I'd said to Vera—and the words had hit me like a kick in the stomach. All day, I'd kept telling myself it wasn't the same—*I* was just mad and miserable about Grace, not about everything all the time. And I wasn't mad anymore. *I am not like Mom,* I'd been telling myself, swinging the rug-beater. *I'm not.*

I called Mom "mad and miserable" to her face, once. I hadn't thought of that in years. It was back in the worst of it, before Daddy got me to quit fighting with her. Mom was pinning up her hair, and I was sulking about having to clean out the chickenhouse. "Quit your bellyaching," she snapped at me. "Moping around won't get the chores done."

I glared at her. "Well, *you* mope around! You're mad and miserable all the time, and you don't even have any reason!"

Mom took a sharp breath, and dropped the braid she was pinning. I braced myself for a slap, but she just looked at me, while her face turned bright red. Finally she rasped out, "We can't all be happy in this life, Missy. This old sinful world would make the Lord Himself miserable!"

"Well, you—" I stammered. Mom's eyes were welling up. I clenched my fists, and made my voice sharp and hard. "I thought being saved and sanctified made everything all fine and dandy!"

Mom pressed her lips hard against her teeth. "You don't know the first thing about it," she hissed. "Now get on and clean out that chickenhouse, and I don't want to hear another word out of you."

And then I said something smart back, and she did slap me, and everything was like it always was.

Even now, I couldn't see why Mom was so mad and miserable—or so mean, for that matter. She'd talked like it was because the rest of us weren't saved, except Sissy when she got old enough. But Mom never laid into Jamie like she did me, and she didn't fight with Daddy at all. What was it about me, that hardened Mom's mouth and made her eyes squint like she was looking at the Devil incarnate?

Vera laughed. "You could have just said yes," she told Hal, as I looked up from my plate.

"Thought I'd better keep my job," Hal said, winking at me. Vera smiled at me, too, as if I'd been in on the joke.

"Down!" Katy demanded.

"Okay, hon, let's get you cleaned up." I reached for the dishrag. Time to quit brooding about Mom. None of that mattered anymore.

Vera won at rummy again. She washed up our glasses while I put the cards away. Hal went off through the living room, but was back in a minute. "Um," he said, "I don't see my jammies anywhere."

"Oh." I brushed a stray crumb off the table. "I was so discombobulated this morning—did you look around behind the bed?"

"No. I'll do that." Hal had a funny look on his face. He shifted his feet, then added, "I was wondering...I didn't know if you would've put them on Vera's bed, or..."

I felt my face go red. Vera peered hard at the glass she was drying. "Yes, Vera's," I said, not looking at Hal.

His chuckle sounded relieved. "Just checking. Didn't want to get the code wrong!" I looked up to see him grinning at Vera. "May's just like her mother. Pearl used to set my hat on the porch post, when she thought it was time I went home. Remember that, May?" Hal looked at me, and his grin faded. "You all right?"

I shook my head, trying to get a breath in through clenched teeth. "Hal, for—" I couldn't get any further than that. I just shook my head hard again, then pushed past Hal into the dark living room, blinking back tears. What was wrong with me?

Hal said something in the kitchen. Vera answered him—too quiet to hear at first, then, "...dirt all over the wet paint. She was pretty upset..."

She was trying to explain why I was so touchy. I wanted to slap her. My head was roaring like a chimney fire. I wrapped my arms around myself, trying to shut down the damper.

"Hmm… Maybe she's tired of getting beat at Rummy." I could hear the shrug in Hal's voice. He came into the doorway, blocking the light from the kitchen. "You want to play Yahtzee next time, hon?"

It was too dark to see the picture on the wall in front of me, but I knew it was the one we'd had made when we got married. Hal in his uniform, me in my sailor-suit dress. I wanted to pull it off the wall and throw it at him. Instead I clenched my fists and stormed out the front door, stumbling down the porch steps in the dark. The screen door banged behind me.

"May?" Hal called. "May, I was just…" He fell silent as Katy started wailing upstairs. I stomped across the front yard, jumped the ditch, and strode off down the road, walking hard and fast and mad.

I *was* mad. Not just miserable. I was so mad I felt like I might choke on it. Mad as hell at that useless man I'd married. Mad at Vera, with her smile and her singing and her cheerful disposition. I walked faster, my shoes skidding on the loose gravel.

There wasn't any moon. The road was a smudge of grey between rough black walls of noise—katydids, crickets, all the other bugs, making a racket that matched the roar in my head. Hal said he loved me. That night he told me about Vera—*I love you, May.* Shaking his head, tears in his eyes. If Hal loved me so all-fired much, what did he go and get with Vera for? Did he just forget he was married? I felt my face snarl in the dark. Here I was bending over backwards to keep Hal, and Hal wasn't worth a spoonful of spit.

I was out on Salt Branch Road now. I ought to just keep walking. Just leave. I stumbled on a round rock, and slowed my pace a little. Leave—and go where? To Aunt Ciceline's, with Mom? I laughed out loud at that, but it didn't sound like a laugh.

I could stay at Jamie's. Sleep on Grace's couch, with her not speaking to me… No. But I couldn't just go out on my own, with Katy. I couldn't sew, or teach school—and now that the war was over, nobody wanted a woman who could use a wrench.

Not even Hal, evidently. I kicked at a dark spot in the road, but it was just a dry leaf. A dog barked from a farmhouse, and I glared into the darkness as I strode past. *I love you, May...* For awhile I didn't even think—just walked hard, gritting my teeth so I wouldn't cry, and crying anyway.

Mom never wanted me to marry Hal, even after the war. By then I was past caring what Mom thought. I'd figured she was just being mean. But now I wondered. Maybe Mom could see that Hal didn't love me the way I loved him. Maybe she knew how hard I was to love, with my mouth and my moods, my man's shoulders and my wild hair. Maybe if I'd been little and cheerful, like Vera...

The grey smudge of the road opened out all of a sudden. I stumbled to a stop, trying to get my bearings. How long had I been walking? How many times had I gone around the same circles in my head? Tears were dripping off my chin. I wiped them on the shoulder of my dress. That was the Evanses' pasture, stretching out pale in front of me—I was miles from home. My feet throbbed in my shoes, and the muscles of my legs felt like old rubber.

I couldn't go back. Not feeling like this. My head had stopped roaring, but there was a heavy, red heat behind my eyes. I knew that feeling. I was mad at Hal and Vera the way I was mad at Mom—the kind of mad that could sit and smolder for a whole lifetime. A lifetime of sitting across the table from Hal and Vera, smoldering... I shook my head. I couldn't do it.

That was nonsense, of course. People did it. Women did it all the time, suffered through worse things than I could imagine—husbands that beat them, children that died. I thought of Iva, pulling through the Depression with a houseful of babies and invalids. What would Iva think, if I told her I couldn't do it? After all my talk. I'd made my bed, and now I didn't want to lie in it.

That's not it, I wanted to say—to Iva? *It's just...I thought, keeping Hal... I wanted to be happy.*

292

I sighed, then turned around and started walking back up Salt Branch. Probably everybody wanted to be happy. Plenty of people weren't. Look at Mom, jabbing bobby pins into her hair like she hated her own head. *We can't all be happy in this life, Missy...*

"I am *not* Mom," I said out loud. Maybe I couldn't be happy. Maybe I had to be mad and miserable. But I'd be damned if I was going to be mean.

By the time I saw the light in our kitchen window, my feet were dragging and my eyes felt like sandpaper. Hal was reading at the kitchen table, in his pajamas. He looked up when I came in, with that worried little frown. "You all right, May?"

I shrugged. I could feel the anger smoldering behind my tired eyes, but I didn't want to fight with Hal. I wanted to go to bed.

Hal closed his book and got up. "You know I love you," he said, putting his arms around me.

I let him hug me. But all I could think was that "you" could mean one person, or it could mean two. When Hal lowered his arms, I walked away and climbed the stairs to my bedroom.

I'd forgotten my washbasin. I stood a minute in the dark, feeling the sweat and dirt all over me. Then I pulled off my clothes and lay down. It didn't seem to matter.

69

May

"Now do your arms like this," Vera said.

I raised my elbows, rustling the paper bodice pinned to my brassiere, and stifled a yawn. I'd hardly slept last night, after my mad walk. Today I didn't feel mad so much as sick, with a hot, heavy headache pressing down above my eyes. I never got headaches. I'd stumbled through the morning, taking Katy to Iva's and doing the wash. At least Vera hadn't bothered me much with conversation.

I held still while Vera tugged at the paper across my back. She'd made long cuts in the bodice, and taped in tissue paper to fill the gaps. Making room for my square shoulders, I supposed. It seemed like a lot of trouble for a work dress.

"You can put your arms down." Vera stepped around to check the front. "They make patterns for the 'average build,' but hardly anybody's average all over," she said, smiling at me.

I almost smiled back, but my headache gave a fierce stab, and I shut my eyes. The pain settled into a steady, angry pounding. *Damn it,* I thought, *I like Vera.* Why couldn't she have been my neighbor, or my cousin—somebody I could be friends with? Why'd she have to fall in love with my husband? And *marry* him… I felt the weight of Vera's Bible in my hands again. *Love is patient and kind…* What was I thinking?

"There you go. I'll help you out of this mess." Vera's voice sounded cheerful enough, but when I opened my eyes, she was biting her lip. As she eased the pattern down my arm, she gave me a worried smile.

Worried? I didn't know whether to spit or cry. I didn't do either, just reached for my dress and pulled it on.

I'd planned to repaint the wash house in the afternoon, but the wind picked up. Katy got dizzy chasing leaves as I walked her back from Iva's, and the clothes on the line flapped themselves dry in no time.

Hal came in after work, holding onto his hat. "Hoo-ee, Katy-girl!" he said, scooping her up. "Ol' Bucky must be right —*some* kind of weather's coming in!"

"Hoo-ee!" Katy agreed.

"Will James's tobacco be okay?" Vera asked, taking the cornbread out of the oven.

Hal shrugged. "If the rain holds off till Wednesday. He wondered if we could help hang tomorrow evening," he added, to me, and I nodded.

Hal kept looking at me during supper. I wanted to snap at him to quit staring, but I held my tongue. I probably looked awful, after the sleep I hadn't had. "You know, May," he finally said, "It's been forever since you and me had a night out."

I frowned at him. We'd *never* had a night out—and never missed it, either. We'd always been happy with each other and Katy. My head throbbed, hard enough to make me flinch.

"Maybe Vera could watch Katy on Saturday, and we could go see a movie in Whelan," Hal went on. "Have us a soda."

I couldn't see how a soda would help anything. "All right, if you want," I said, and got up to cut the pie.

At bedtime I told Hal I wasn't feeling good. He kissed me, and went on to sleep. I was wide awake and dead tired at the same time. At least the darkness eased my headache some.

I'd done all right, today. Not being mean. Maybe it'd get easier with time. Maybe I wouldn't always be so mad and miserable. *We can't all be happy in this life, Missy...* I squeezed my eyes tight shut. Crying wouldn't help my head any.

I listened to the hollow sound of Hal's breathing, and the katydids scratching away outside. Somebody's dog let out a string of barks, and I remembered the Richardsons' old dog. Talk about mad and miserable—we even used to call it the Mad Dog. It was a dingy white mutt with a face like a rat, that lived in a barrel it was chained to. When Jamie and I came flying down Ort Hill on Jamie's bike, the Mad Dog would go wild—barking and growling, lunging at the end of its chain so hard it choked. I'd scream, while Jamie pedaled hard to keep our speed on the flat stretch and yelled at me to sit straight. When we'd made it past the Richardsons' place, we'd both get the nervous giggles. It wasn't really funny. You could see in the Mad Dog's eyes that it wasn't playing—if it ever got loose, it'd tear us to pieces. It'd tear the whole world to pieces.

I turned over, nudging Hal's leg out of the way, and settled my aching head on a cooler part of the pillow. I'd never wondered before what the Mad Dog was mad about. Not that it mattered, of course. What mattered was that it never got loose.

I barely slept that night, again. Tuesday morning my headache came and went in quick jabs of pain. In between, my head felt dull and queasy, and my anger had turned dull and queasy, too. I wanted to turn away from Hal's goodbye kiss after breakfast, but I didn't. I wanted to tell Vera to quit belting some song about rye whiskey while she was ironing, but I didn't. Katy hung on my skirt like a pup dragging from its mother's teat. I tried to be patient—at least she wasn't hitting anybody.

The wind was still blowing. When I went out to mow the yard it pushed and pulled at me, gusting hot under my skirt and in my face, never steady long enough to get used to. My dress clung to me like a damp rag, and my joints felt like they were put together wrong, but I shoved the mower around the yard till the job was done. By the time I went back inside, I was too tired to snap at anybody.

After supper, Hal and I left Katy with Vera and went over to Jamie's to hang tobacco. We loaded the sticks of half-dry plants onto the wagon and drove them into the barn, where the men climbed up and stood spraddle-legged on the beams. I passed the sticks from the wagon up to Jamie, who passed them to Rye and then Hal in the top tier. My head pounded every time I bent over, and when I looked up, the crisscross of the beams seemed to spin a little.

"You okay, Maydie?" Jamie asked, reaching for a stick. "You're looking a little peaked."

I shrugged. "I'll manage." There was nothing Jamie could do, anyway. I breathed in the sweet, leathery smell of the tobacco leaves to steady my head, and kept working.

The field was empty at sunset, and the whole height of the barn was packed full of long yellow-brown leaves. I didn't bother to stop in at the house before we headed home. Grace probably didn't care to see me.

Even with the the sun down, the air kept getting hotter and thicker. In bed alone, I spread my sweaty arms and legs away from my sweaty body. Thunder rumbled, somewhere far off, and I frowned at the darkness. I should have picked peppers today—if it rained hard, the plants would be down in the mud. My cabbages and melons were sure to crack, too, along with all the ripe tomatoes, and the soup beans were liable to spoil before they dried. The sky outside flickered faintly. Why couldn't I have thought of all this in the daylight?

I sighed. No point crying over spilt milk. Maybe the rain would hold off in the morning, and Vera and I could get it all in. And then put it up. If we picked green tomatoes too, we could make piccalilli. No telling whether Grace would want to trade relish this year.

It was Grace's house Jamie and I used to ride to, on his bike. We played ball there, with Hal, and the Trulow boys, and Grace and her brothers. Grace couldn't run worth a fizzle, but

Jamie was the only one who could catch her line drives. We'd ride over any day we could get away in the summer, flying down Ort Hill in the wind. The Mad Dog snarled and choked against its chain, only it wasn't a dog, it was a rat as big as a dog—

I jerked myself awake, my heart hammering in my chest. Just a dream. I wiped the sweat off my neck and tried to think about something else. Piccalilli—cabbage, peppers, green tomatoes...did it take brown sugar, or white? "I hate those whole dill seeds," Grace said, and I woke up again. Thunder rumbled, off to the west. I sighed, and rubbed my forehead. It was going to be a long night.

70

May

The chickens were still on the roost when I went to let them out Wednesday morning. They eyed me nervously, shifting their feet and ruffling their checkered feathers. Had something been after them in the night? Surely I would have heard—heaven knows, I'd been awake. I shooed them off the roost, and they stepped warily down the ramp to the yard, glancing up sideways at the grey sky. Heavy clouds had moved in overnight.

My head still ached, in a tired way. I watched the hens huddling close to the chickenhouse, as King Tut paced back and forth. Maybe a raccoon had tried to get in. I'd better come out after breakfast and make sure everything was tight.

It was midmorning before I got to it, what with getting Katy up and dressed and fixing Hal's lunch. I put a few more nails in the wire over the chickenhouse windows, scaring the chickens half to death with my hammering, then inspected all the corners. There wasn't a hole big enough for a pencil, let alone a raccoon. Or a rat. The floor was invisible under a thick layer of manure and rotting hay. I kicked at it, and sighed. It was too hot to be shoveling manure, but if there was a rat hole somewhere under there...

I changed into my yellow dress, since it was already dirty, and spent the rest of the morning shoveling ammonia-reeking litter, wheelbarrowing it to the garden, and spreading it where I wanted to plant corn next year. Even in the open air I panted for breath—the heavy, dark sky held down the heat like the lid of a Dutch oven.

I looked over every inch of the chickenhouse floor for gnawed holes, and checked the fence outside for good measure. Everything was tight. The chickens were still wild-eyed, startling at every gust of wind. "I don't know what to tell you," I said, scowling at them. Maybe it was the weather.

Bits of feathers were stuck to the sweaty grime on my neck and arms, and I could taste old manure in my teeth. I'd better wash up before lunch. And change my dress—it was well past dirty now, and I'd busted a shoulder seam.

I came to the table damp but clean. Vera had made egg-salad sandwiches. Katy poked her finger into hers, then looked down the hole like something might come out. I just ate mine—I was hungry, and it was good. Vera had put in more mustard than I usually did, and she'd used the sweet relish—

"Piccalilli!" I said, remembering all at once. I shoved my chair back and stood up, still chewing.

Vera cocked her head at me. "Piccalilli?"

"We need to pick the peppers, and the cabbage, and the canteloupes, and the tomatoes," I said, grabbing an apron. "And pull the soup beans. I can't believe I was forgetting about it. Oh, and the green beans—they're liable to wind up flat in the mud if it storms hard. We'd better get to work—no telling when it'll let loose."

Vera took a last bite of her sandwich and got up. "Tell me what to do."

My head pounded dully as I bent over to pick green peppers. Vera was putting canteloupes into a basket of cabbages. We'd piled the soup-bean vines in the barn to dry. Still the green beans to get in, and tomatoes...

"Look, Mommy!" Katy called. "Chotchy a puppy!"

I looked, without straightening up—it seemed better not to move my head too much. Katy was running along beside the zinnias, pulling Chotchy on a string. The doll's floppy body bounced across the dirt clods.

"Hmm," I said. "Your puppy's getting awful dirty." I tried to smile at her, but my face felt like dried mud. I wished I'd had time for a nap.

I carried the basket of peppers to the house, and brought out an empty one for tomatoes. Vera was picking green beans now, her straw hat bobbing up now and then above the bright hedge of the zinnias. The wind was turning cooler, and I heard a grumble of thunder. Best hurry up. I pulled a heavy red tomato off the vine, and set it carefully in the basket.

"Daddy home?" Katy had left Chotchy somewhere, and was gnawing on a green bean.

"Daddy's at work," I said.

"Mommy home?"

"Yes, Mommy's home."

"Vewa home?"

"Yes."

"Mammaw home?"

"Mammaw's at her house." Answering Katy's questions felt like hauling heavy buckets up out of a cistern. She worked her way through the whole family, including Ronny and Carol and the puppies, then wandered off. I sighed in relief.

My headache was getting worse again. "I never get headaches." I realized I'd said that out loud, and looked around for Vera. She was still picking beans, too far away to hear me talking to myself.

Mom was the one who got headaches. I remembered her breaking beans in her rocking chair, one eye half-closed against the light, silent for hours except when she'd snap at us to be quiet. Maybe Aunt Ciceline was right, and Mom pinned her braids too tight. I felt my lips pressing against my teeth, and made them relax.

"Mommy, Mommy, Mommy, Mommy!" Katy was back, whining like a locust.

"What, honey?"

"Mommy, Mommy, Mommy, Mommy!" She didn't want anything, she was just making noise. Past time for her nap. I moved on down the row, dragging my basket across the dry dirt. "Mommy, Mommy, mom-me-mom-me-mom-me-mom!"

A deep growl of thunder seemed to come from everywhere at once. I looked up at the sky, but it was one sheet of cloud from horizon to horizon—there was no telling when or where the rain would start. "Funder!" Katy whispered. I tried to pick faster.

Was there anything else I'd forgotten, that needed doing before the rain? I shut my eyes to think, and almost fell over. I grabbed at a tomato stake to steady myself. Had I lost my balance, or fallen asleep? Either way, better keep my eyes open. I couldn't think anyway—Katy had stopped singing her little tune, but my mind was still going *Mommy, Mommy, Mommy, Mommy...*

Vera called out something I couldn't hear. "What?" I said, straightening up. She was invisible behind the zinnias.

"Mommy!" Katy yelled, flinging her arms around my leg and drowning out Vera's words the second time.

"Wait a minute, Katy," I said impatiently. "What, Vera?"

Pain shot up my leg. "Ow!" I yelled, and twisted around, yanking up my skirt to look for a bumblebee. Katy let go of my leg and peered at the back of my thigh, where two half-circles of toothmarks were turning red. "Katy!" I said, shocked. "You bit me!"

Katy met my eyes and giggled. "Bite Mommy!" she said—and leaned forward, mouth open to do it again. I jerked away, and she giggled harder.

"It's not funny!" I snapped. Vera called a question, but I couldn't hear her words over the pounding in my ears.

Katy grinned up at me. "Ow!" she said, and giggled again. *The little devil*— I watched my arm swing through the air. My hand slapped Katy's laughing face. Katy staggered sideways and fell on a pepper plant. She lay silent for a heartbeat, then let out a panicked wail.

I stood like a post as the anger rushed out of me, leaving me panting and sick. My palm burned. I raised my hand, pulling it back as if I could undo what I'd done. Katy screamed. Her whole face had flushed red as a tomato—but not before I saw the glaring print of my hand on her cheek.

I made myself move, picked Katy up. She screamed louder, and kicked wildly in my arms. Thunder cracked across the sky, and the air turned a shade darker. The storm was going to let loose any minute.

I felt a hand on my shoulder. Vera, leaning close to be heard through Katy's crying. "Want me to take her inside?"

I looked up at the sky. The clouds were seething like water about to boil. Katy twisted around to push at my face. She didn't want me, and no wonder. I nodded at Vera. She plucked Katy out of my arms and carried her off towards the house.

Once they were inside, I couldn't hear Katy's screaming anymore. I pulled my eyes away from the house, looking down at my basket of tomatoes, out along the dark row of tomato plants. I looked at my hand. The palm was still red.

Lightning flickered bright behind the house, and the thunder was so loud it shook my bones. A few warm drops of rain hit my arms and face, and then suddenly it was pouring down. My tomatoes turned glossy in the wet. Vera's green beans would be ruined if I didn't get them in fast. The rain ran down my skin.

I turned and walked out of the garden, dress slapping against my legs, bare feet slipping in the wet grass. On the porch steps, I stopped to listen. The rain roared on the porch roof. I couldn't hear Katy crying. Maybe Vera had calmed her down. Maybe if she saw me, she'd start crying again.

I gripped the metal curve of the screen-door handle so hard it hurt. Katy didn't need me. Maybe she was better off without a mother who was mad, and miserable, and mean. I let go of the door handle and walked out into the rain.

PART THREE

71

May

I leaned forward over the steering wheel, peering through the swipe of clear glass that followed the windshield wiper back and forth. The rain came in sheets, crashing on the roof of the truck cab, almost drowning out the thunder. A car loomed out of the blur, too far over, and I swerved to miss it.

The warm steel of the gas pedal under my foot was slippery with mud. I wasn't wearing shoes. What road was I on? I didn't remember getting in the truck. All I could remember was Katy. I'd hit Katy... My mouth twisted downward so hard it hurt. I pressed harder on the gas.

The truck had stopped. The rain's roar drowned out everything, but I could feel the engine still running. The windshield wipers slapped back and forth. I shook my aching head. How long had I been driving? Where on earth was I?

There was a gate, with a sign I couldn't read through the rain. Cedar trees with odd, tufty branches, like kids with their hair not brushed. Mount Zion Cemetery. I'd stared at those trees during Grandma Stout's funeral, while Brother Willis droned on about eternity. Grandma Stout hadn't cared for Mom's church, but she'd had a horror of being buried in the flood plain. Mount Zion's cemetery was on the bluffs two hundred feet above the Ohio. The river wouldn't bother her up here.

What was I doing here? —I'd hit Katy. I drew in a sharp breath, then turned off the engine and got out of the truck. Warm rain slopped down on my wet hair and wet dress as I opened the gate.

The driveway's gravel and clover were an inch deep in clear water, swishing my feet clean as I walked. I'd left home without my shoes. I'd left home without thinking, driven here without thinking. I didn't want to think now. My head throbbed, and the rain tasted like tears.

There was Grandma Stout's headstone, pale in the stormy light. And there next to it, of course, was Daddy's. The two stones were just alike, except for the names and dates. 1944, 1945. Daddy hadn't even had time to finish grieving. There was an empty space on the far side of Daddy's grave, where Mom had bought a plot for herself.

I went to sit between the two headstones. The grass was so wet, it was like sitting in a puddle. I wiped rain out of my eyes, and wished it was Grandma Stout and Daddy on either side of me, not just names on stones.

The rain had gone from sheets of water to big pelting drops. It pounded on me and the headstones steady and hard, like it wanted to wear all three of us down to gravel. I drew my knees up to my chest, tucking my wet skirt around my legs, and leaned my face on the warm limestone carved with Daddy's name. What was I doing here?

"Daddy?" I whispered. My voice stuck in my throat, and I coughed. "Hi, Daddy. Hi, Grandma Stout." I pressed my forehead against the rough stone until it hurt more than my headache. "Daddy," I said again. "I just hit Katy. I hit her. Hard."

Then I slumped against the stone, and cried. I cried so hard it felt like throwing up, my whole body heaving and hurting with the sobs. My fingers found the hard chiseled shape of Daddy's name and clung there, while I cried like I'd never stop.

The rain trickled through my hair and down my back, and I remembered warm water poured from a cup, Mom washing me in the tin tub by the stove. I shut my eyes—I wanted Daddy, not Mom—but I didn't have the strength to push the memory away. Mom's bony hand scrubbed at my grimy knees with a blue rag, rough and gentle at the same time. She rinsed away the dirt and soap with cup after cup of warm water. I let the water pour over me, and I cried.

After a long time, I stopped—like rain stopping, not on purpose but just because it's over. I sat up, rubbing my aching forehead. The rain had slacked off to a drizzle, and the sky was lighter. A bird chirped in the brush along the edge of the bluff. I wondered what time it was.

I thought of Katy, at home with Vera. Hal might be home by now, too. What were they doing? I couldn't imagine.

A blue jay landed on a headstone two graves away and peered at me sideways. When I didn't move, he hopped down into a puddle for a bath, flicking his wings and squatting down to dunk his belly. Then he perched on another headstone, fluffing his wet feathers and shaking himself. It must feel good, clean water soaking through those dusty feathers, getting down to the skin.

Goosebumps rose up along my arms. It was getting cooler. I looked down at my sopping dress, my bare feet, and thought about going home.

Home seemed a long way off.

72

Vera

A crash of thunder woke me. I left Katy asleep on my bed, and went to the kitchen. May wasn't there—she must be having a nap too. I went out on the porch to watch the rain coming down in grey curtains.

Lightning flashed, and something pale caught my eye, out in the garden. A bushel basket, there by the beans, and another one in the tomato row. I looked around the porch—baskets of cabbages, canteloupes, peppers, May's shoes... No tomatoes, no beans. I squinted at the garden again. Tomatoes didn't mind a little rain, but wet beans would spoil. Why hadn't May brought them in? I threw Hal's jacket over my shoulders and splashed out after them.

I sat on the porch to break the beans—we'd have to can them right away. When the wind picked up, and rain started gusting in through the screens, I took May's shoes inside, then went to wake May up. She wouldn't want to sleep all afternoon.

May wasn't in her room. I frowned at her empty bed, feeling a flutter of worry in my middle. Maybe she'd gone to the outhouse? No, I'd been up longer than that.

Katy woke up, hollering. I took her out on the porch with me, and she squealed happily when the rain blew on her. It looked like she'd have a bruise by her eye, from May's slap. It wasn't like May to hit her like that. Of course, getting bit wouldn't bring out the best in anybody.

Maybe May was out in the barn. The worry in my middle didn't believe it. I bit my lip, and went back to my beans. Anyway, she couldn't have gone far without her shoes.

The jars of beans were cooling on the kitchen counter and supper was on the table when Hal came in from work. He dropped his wet hat on a chair and gave me a kiss. "Where's May off to?"

I frowned. How did he know May was off to anywhere?

"Up, Daddy!" Katy crawled out from under the table and grabbed Hal's leg.

"Did Mommy go to town, Katydid?" Hal picked Katy up, then noticed my frown. "Something wrong?"

"I don't know," I said. My heart was pounding suddenly. "She was gone when I got up from my nap. I figured she was out in the barn, or…" I trailed off.

Hal chuckled. "I don't imagine she'd drive the truck to the barn."

"She took the truck?" I hadn't noticed it was gone.

Hal nodded, then glanced at the food on the table. "Did she want us to wait for her?"

"She didn't say she was going." I tried not to sound alarmed. There must be an explanation.

"Oh, right—you said that," Hal said. "I'm so hungry I can't think straight. I don't imagine she'll mind if we go ahead and get started." He swung Katy into her high chair.

I poured three glasses of ice tea, and milk for Katy, and sat down across from Hal. Katy banged her spoon on her tray as I dished her some beans.

"May probably needed something, and didn't want to wake you up," Hal said.

I watched him buttering his potatoes. I didn't want to seem like a worry-wart, but... "She left the green beans out in the rain," I said. "And she didn't take her shoes."

Hal looked up. "She went off in bare feet?" I nodded at the brown leather shoes by the door. "Huh," he said, looking stumped. "If that don't beat all."

"She was upset." Or she had been, when I'd left her in the garden. I didn't really know when she'd left. Right after I came in, or sometime later? Hours ago, anyway.

"What about?" Hal reached for a chicken thigh with his fork.

I sighed. "Katy bit her."

Hal raised his eyebrows at Katy. "You bit your mommy?"

"No," she answered cheerfully.

"Hmm." Hal peered at her. "Did you bonk your eye?"

Katy fingered the reddened spot by her left eye. "Ow," she said thoughtfully. Then she stuffed a green bean in her mouth, and grinned as she chewed. "Bite, bite!"

"Bite-bite, huh?" Hal said, and shook his head. "No wonder she was upset. Probably needed to blow off some steam." He wouldn't meet my eyes. Blowing off steam didn't sound like May.

She must've been mad, to smack Katy that hard. Katy had been flat on the ground when I'd come around the zinnias. May hadn't looked mad, though, as she stood there staring. She'd looked lost.

I wasn't hungry. I helped Katy with her food, and sipped my ice tea, while Hal ate in silence. "Would she be at James and Grace's?" I finally asked.

"Not the way Grace has been acting," Hal said, salting his tomatoes.

"Maybe we ought to give them a call."

Hal cocked his head at me. "You're really worried?" When I didn't answer, he pursed his lips, then looked at the glass of ice tea beside May's empty plate. "Tell you what—if May's not home by the time the ice melts in her tea, I'll call James." He winked at me. "May hates watered-down tea."

I nodded, and made myself take a bite of potatoes.

The rain was over by the time I got up to clear the table. It was getting dark out. Hal frowned thoughtfully at May's glass. The ice wasn't melted yet. When he saw me watching him, he winked again. "Guess you're stuck doing the dishes," he said. "You'll have to have a talk with May."

I started cleaning Katy up. "Why don't you just call, Hal? It'll make me feel better." I could see it would make him feel better too.

"Oh, all right." Hal got up from the table.

Katy threw a fit when I washed her face, so I missed most of the phone call. "Well, I appreciate it," Hal was saying, when she quieted down. "I'd go, but...All right. I'll let Grace know if she shows up here. Probably just...Yes. Bye." He hung up the receiver, resting his hand on it for a moment.

"She's not there," I said.

"No." Hal put on his hat. "James is going out to look for her. Might've had a flat tire." Which didn't explain anything.

I finished up in the kitchen and shut up the chickens while Hal was doing his chores. Then I strained the evening's milk and got Katy ready for bed. She cried for May, until Hal came upstairs to tell her a story. I left them together and went to sit at the kitchen table, propping my tired feet on Hal's chair. James hadn't called yet. Knowing he was out looking for May ought to make me feel better, but it just made her seem more lost.

I waited for Hal to come down. After a while, I went to the bottom of the stairs and looked up. May's bedroom light was on. The floorboards creaked. And creaked again. And again. Hal was pacing.

I stood with my hand on the banister, wanting to go up. More, wanting Hal to come down. To keep me company. To admit that he was worried too.

Finally I sighed, and went to get the fabric for May's dress from my room. Time would go faster if I was busy.

* * *

So now it's past my bedtime, and I'm cutting out a work dress on the kitchen table. My hand is steady with the scissors. I'm chewing my lip so hard it's liable to bleed.

All I can think is, What if it's me? The reason May's gone?

It doesn't make sense. May didn't have to do any of this. She *married* Hal and me, for pity's sake. And she's seemed happy enough. At first, anyway. Until Grace went cold on her...

But I keep remembering that day with the horticulture beans, when May said *presume?* The bitterness of it. Was that bitterness the truth? Not all the friendliness before, or the politeness since? If it was, then May's miserable. And not because of Grace, or because Katy bit her. Because of me.

I wipe my eyes with the back of my wrist, and blink hard to see the sleeve I'm cutting out. I can't hear whether Hal's still pacing. I wish he'd come downstairs. I wish James would call. I wish May would come home.

Maybe I'm overreacting. But I just can't stand it that May's out there in the dark somewhere, miserable. I can't stand it that maybe it's my fault.

I lay the sleeve piece on top of the others, smoothing the green fabric. I should have this dress done by the end of the week. May can cut that yellow one up for rags.

I glance at the telephone, for the hundredth time. It doesn't ring.

73

May

Light swung across my closed eyelids. I heard a car engine, and gravel popping under tires. Then the engine shut off, but the light stayed on. I shivered. Why were my clothes wet?

I opened my eyes, to the black silhouettes of gravestones against a glare of headlights. I'd fallen asleep in the cemetery. Of all the nutty things to do... I lay as still as I could, trying to be invisible, but I couldn't stop shivering.

A car door opened, with a familiar squeak. Jamie and Grace's Buick. Jamie stepped in front of the light, his shadow lunging towards me across the grass. "Maydie?"

I sat up, trying to look like I knew what I was doing. "Yeah, Jamie."

He came up between Grandma's grave and Daddy's, and squatted down in front of me. "You okay?"

I shrugged. I felt like I'd cried all my words out, along with my tears.

He patted my shoulder. "How about I take you home?"

"No!" I said it before I thought. Not home. "I—I'll drive myself." To where? I shivered harder, my teeth chattering. For Pete's sake—it wasn't even cold out.

Jamie shook his head, his face moving in and out of the light. "No, you just come on home with me. We'll get the truck tomorrow."

I was shivering too hard to argue. I let Jamie pull me to my feet. It had stopped raining, but the wet grass was slick underfoot. Jamie put his arm around me, and I leaned on him as we walked to the car.

The inside of the Buick smelled ordinary, like damp steel and horsehair. Jamie turned the heater on full blast, blowing a summer's worth of dust out from under the seat. He backed out past the truck, and drove slow up Washboard Road.

Jamie didn't ask why I'd run off without my shoes, or why I was sleeping in the cemetery. He just drove. After a while I felt like I ought to say something. "You came looking for me?" I asked. Of course he had. Nobody went to the cemetery at night in the rain for fun.

Jamie nodded. "Hal called on the phone, wondering if you were at our place. I told him I'd try and round you up."

"How'd you know where to look?" The cemetery was miles from home.

"Had a feeling." Jamie's forehead shone with sweat in the light of the dashboard. I was still chilly. After a minute he added, "I didn't tell Hal where I was going. Figured he might think you'd jumped off the bluffs. You know how people are, when they're worried."

I stared at him. Jumped off the bluffs? "Hal was worried?"

Jamie shrugged. "He was trying not to sound like it."

I looked out at the roadside weeds in the narrow glow of the headlights. Everything else was dark—the lightning bugs were done for the year. "It never crossed my mind," I said, after a while. "Jumping off the bluffs."

"No. It wouldn't." Jamie gave me a quick, shadowy smile. "Not unless you got an idea in your head."

I would have laughed, if I didn't ache so much. Jamie always said I had good sense until I got an idea in my head.

74

May

"Well?"

I squinted up at Grace. The overhead fixture lit up her kitchen like high noon, and the red and blue flowers on her housedress seemed to jiggle in the light. She stood with her hands on her hips, waiting.

I yawned. Once I'd finally stopped shivering, all I wanted was to go back to sleep. It was almost midnight. Jamie had called Hal while I was getting into dry clothes, and told him I was spending the night.

Now Jamie put his arm around Grace. "Honey, maybe—" He broke off when Grace shot him a look. Then he sat down to eat the piece of peach pie she'd cut for him. She hadn't given me any.

"Well?" Grace said again.

I sighed. At least she was talking to me. "Well, what?"

Grace's eyes narrowed behind her glasses. "Well, to start with, how come you're sitting here in my kitchen, looking like a drowned chicken in a borrowed dress?"

I rubbed my face. "Go to blazes, Grace." I wanted to sound as tough as she did, but I only sounded tired, even to myself. "You don't know a thing about it."

"Not for want of asking," she said sharply. "Or caring, either."

I'd thought I was all cried out, but tears started running down my face again. "Doggone it, Grace," I said, slumping in my chair. "I can't stand it if you're going to stay mad at me."

Jamie cleared his throat. "How come you're mad at May, anyway?" he asked.

Grace gave a little huff of a laugh. "Oh, no reason," she said. "May just won't say a word to me. This Vera girl comes out of nowhere and moves into their house, and she's in love with Hal, and Hal's so in love back he can't hardly see straight —and what's May do about it? She has Vera make the potato salad! And every time I ask a question, she clams up like she's got state secrets." Grace's nostrils flared. "No, no reason at all!"

I stared at Grace, my mouth hanging open. She wouldn't look at me.

Jamie was staring at her too. "Hal and Vera?" he said, slowly.

Grace nodded once. "Hal and Vera."

Jamie looked sick. "May? Is that true?"

"That's right, *you* ask her," Grace said. "She won't talk to me. She'd rather keep secrets with some woman that's stealing her husband. She'd rather drive around with no shoes on and fall asleep in the rain, than talk to me! Oh, sit down, James— you punching Hal won't do anybody any good."

Jamie dropped back into his chair, his face red.

My head was spinning. "I thought you *liked* Vera," I said.

"Well, I do," Grace said fiercely. "But some of us know where our loyalty lies." Her voice went faint and scratchy as she said it, and she forgot not to look at me. There were tears in her eyes.

I took a deep breath and let it out. "Would you sit down?" I asked, sounding more pleading than I meant to. Grace sat, pushing up her glasses to wipe her eyes.

"Jamie," I said, "I think me and Grace need to talk."

Jamie pulled at his ear, and looked from me to Grace and back. Then he stuffed the last of his pie in his mouth, and mumbled something about the cows on his way out the door.

There was a little silence. Grace glanced up at me, then looked back down at the table. I could see she didn't really want to fight. "I'm sorry, Grace," I said.

She nodded.

"You really knew, about Hal and Vera?" I asked. "It's that obvious?" Jamie hadn't noticed. And if Grace knew, why had she been so nice to Vera?

Grace sighed. "Not right away," she admitted. "I thought maybe she was pregnant. I could see Iva knew. But Saturday at dinner, the way Vera was watching Hal, and then he was watching her..."

"I didn't notice," I said absently. Saturday—by then Grace had been so furious, she'd have been friendly with Hitler to get back at me.

"I don't know," Grace said. "Maybe I could just see it because I used to be in love with Hal myself. Never did me any good," she went on, as I blinked at her. "Hal never looked at me—he was too busy looking at you."

"But—" I started.

"I got over it, about eighth grade." Grace winked at me, and smiled a little. "I was just glad to see you happy, May. And I wouldn't trade James in." Her smile faded. "But now here comes Vera—and I can't for the life of me figure out what you're protecting her for."

I sighed, and shook my head. "I'm sorry," I said again. "I don't know either. I mean, I do, but..." I caught a whiff of peaches and nutmeg from Jamie's plate, and my stomach growled. "Can I have some pie?"

Grace snorted. "I swear, you're as bad as your brother." She got a plate, and cut me a piece of pie twice the size of Jamie's. When she set it in front of me, I grabbed her hand. "Grace..."

Grace squeezed my fingers, then let go and went to the refrigerator for milk. "Eat your pie, May. And then you're going to tell me the whole story."

* * *

Telling Grace took longer than telling Iva. She interrupted every other word, saying "What?!" or "How come you didn't —" until I begged her to just let me finish. Even then she couldn't help a few skeptical snorts. Jamie came in near the end. He glanced at Grace, and went on toward the bedroom without a word.

"And so that's about it," I finally said. I took a drink of milk, and stared tiredly into the glass. The story had sounded crazier and crazier to me as I told it. It hadn't seemed that crazy when it was happening.

Grace was quiet, but when I looked up, I saw she was just waiting for my attention. Her eyebrows were all the way up in her hair. "Good Lord, May," she said, "That's got to be the dumbest thing I ever heard."

I tapped my glass on the table, trying not to be irritated. I'd thought she'd say it was wrong and people would be upset, like Iva had. "It's not dumb," I said. "Just because nobody's done it before..."

Grace rolled her eyes. "Might be a reason for that?"

"Grace..." I sighed, and poked at a crumb of pie crust on the tablecloth. "I just didn't see what else I could do."

Grace gave me a hard look. "Plenty of things you could do." She started counting on her fingers. "You could do like Etta Vaughn, or do like Carrie Harvey—you send him packing, or you leave him. Or else you jerk his chain good and hard and make him behave, like—like Eileen Davis, when Wayne was running after that Jenny Sims over to North Vernon."

I snorted. "Who's he running after now?"

Grace pressed her lips together. "You know what I mean, May. At least Eileen doesn't have to look at Jenny across the breakfast table. And everybody knows who's in the wrong there."

I flung my hands in the air at that. "Dammit, Grace," I said, trying to keep my voice low, "I wasn't trying to be in the right! I just wanted to get things back to normal, and...and be happy!"

Grace widened her eyes and blew like a horse. "You sure got a way of going about it."

I shook my head, and didn't say anything. My throat ached.

Then Grace sighed, and brushed at the tablecloth like she was clearing a space. "Okay," she said. "Let's say you're right. Maybe you *can* make up a whole new kind of being married, and pull it off. I don't believe it, but you always were making up a whole new something-or-other. And I guess the Mormons used to do it…" She paused, and looked straight at me. "But if you've got it all figured out, how come you ran off?"

I got up and took my empty glass to the refrigerator. My legs were stiff from sitting so long. "You want any ice tea?"

"No," Grace said. "You going to answer me?"

"I'm thinking." I poured myself a glass of tea, and shut my eyes. I could feel my hand swinging at Katy's face, hear the slap, see the red print on her cheek. Every time I remembered it, it felt like something inside me broke a little more.

I hadn't told Grace that part of the story. She wouldn't understand. *Good grief, May,* she'd say, *If Carol bit me, I'd smack her down too!* I took a drink of tea as I sat back down, trying to wash the ache out of my throat. "Well," I finally said, "Just because it's the best idea I could think of, doesn't mean it's easy."

Grace didn't look impressed. "So this is just growing pains?"

I wanted to say yes. Maybe then she'd let me be. But I couldn't lie to Grace anymore. My tears started up again. "I don't know, Grace. I'm just all mad and mixed up. I thought I knew what I was doing, but…"

When I trailed off, Grace got up and went to get me a hanky —one of Jamie's, big and red. "Well," she said, as I blew my nose, "*One* thing's new under the sun. I never heard you admit to being stumped before."

I didn't know what to say to that.

"Anyway, it's time for bed," Grace added. "Things always look better in the morning. Finish your tea, and I'll get you a pillow."

She brought me a nightgown, too, and tucked a sheet over the couch while I was putting it on.

I lay in the dark, listening to the katydids. I wondered if anything would look better in the morning.

75

Vera

I woke with my heart pounding. Somebody had yelled. Or had I dreamed it? I blinked at the moonlight, listening. There—a scared moan. A man's voice. Hal. I rolled out of bed and ran upstairs.

Hal was a dark, muttering shape in the bed. "Hal!" I said. "Wake up, you're dreaming." He jerked sideways, with a frantic sob. Was there something in the bed? I slapped the light switch. Hal sat bolt upright in the sudden glare, staring at me. "That's ours!" he barked angrily. "They're fucking firing on—*Shit!*" I jumped, as he ducked his head under his arms. There was nothing there but him.

I leaned into the hall to listen for Katy, then pulled the door shut. Hal was huddled against the headboard. "Oh, shit," he moaned. "Oh, *shit...* " His eyes were open, but I knew he wasn't awake. It was like those awful nightmares Hester used to have—except Hal was a grown man, not a four-year-old. Better not touch him. Hester had bloodied my lip once, when I tried to wake her up. But I couldn't leave Hal, any more than I could ever leave Hester.

"Jesus," he whimpered, kicking at the sheet around his ankle.

My hands were knotted together against my teeth. I unfolded them, and sat down in the chair beside the dresser. "It's okay, Hal," I said, as he flinched and cried. "You're dreaming. You'll wake up pretty soon." He probably couldn't hear me, but I needed to hear myself. I wanted to hold him. I looked at his strong arms, tense and trembling, and stayed where I was.

I'd been so disappointed when Hal went to bed up here. I was scared and full of questions, even after Jamie's call. I'd needed Hal to hold me. I'd needed to tell somebody what I was thinking, about it being my fault. But Hal had just nodded at the phone, and said, "Well, that's all right then," and gone back upstairs.

After what seemed like a long time, Hal drew a harsh, gasping breath and looked around the bedroom. When his eyes found me, he said, "May?" then frowned. "Vera?"

"That's me." I went to sit beside him, putting my arm around his shoulders. "You had a nightmare."

"Did I?" Hal was shivering, and his pajama top was soaked with sweat. He put his head on my shoulder, scrunching down so I could hold him better. "Vera," he whispered into my neck.

"I'm here," I said. "You're okay. It was just a dream." He shuddered. "Shhh."

I sat holding him, rocking a little. Hester had always gone back to sleep right away, if she woke up at all. It took Hal longer, but he finally relaxed and slid down to lie on the bed. I straightened the twisted sheet and tucked it over him. "Stay with me," he mumbled, half asleep. I sat back down on the bed, then curled up next to him. He put his arm over me, and sighed.

As his breathing slowed, I lay with my eyes wide open. I was with Hal now, where I'd wanted to be. But my skin prickled against the worn cotton sheets. Every nerve in my body knew I didn't belong in May's bed. When Hal's arm was as heavy and limp as a sack of corn, I slipped out from under it. I turned out the light, and tiptoed back to my own room.

* * *

Hal isn't whistling this morning. Even his smile looks tired. He looks like he used to in Cartersboro, before we fell in love. I wonder if he was having nightmares then. He hasn't mentioned anything this morning. Maybe he's forgotten all about it, like Hester used to.

I feel foggy too. Neither of us says much at breakfast.

Hal gives me a kiss as his ride pulls in. "Tell Katy good morning for me," he says. "Oh, and when May gets home, tell her I got that new belt for the washer. It's in the wash house."

"All right." I watch him go, then start clearing the table. I wonder if he's right to expect May back today. He sounded a lot surer than I feel.

76

Vera

Katy woke up fretful, wanting May. It took all my ideas to keep her cheered up—singing "Happy Birthday" over her breakfast, talking to the chickens, playing house under the lilac bush. Even at that, every few minutes she'd look around and say, "Go see Mommy!" She'd probably never been apart from May this long.

Around eleven, I heard a car door squeak and slam. I crawled out from under the lilac bush, and saw Grace coming across the yard.

"Morning," I said, brushing twigs out of my hair.

"Morning." Grace's mouth looked like she couldn't decide whether to smile or not. Katy came out of the lilacs and hung on my skirt.

"The rain's cooled things down some," I said.

Grace nodded. "I came for Katy. May's staying with us awhile."

"Oh," I said. I wasn't surprised, but I felt tears rise in my throat. I swallowed. "Hear that, Katy? Time to go see Mommy."

"Mommy?" Katy said, looking around.

Grace picked her up. "Let's get your stuff together, kiddo."

I followed them to the house. "I can—"

"No, I'll get it," Grace said. She obviously didn't want to talk to me. Quite a change from last weekend. I trailed along to Katy's room anyway.

"Go see Mommy!" Katy said, as Grace piled clothes on a pink blanket.

"That's right," Grace told her. "You still wearing diapers at night?"

"No!"

"She does," I corrected from the doorway. "They're in the bottom drawer."

"No diaper," Katy told Grace. "Go see Mommy! Go see Cawol!" She bounced on her toes, getting excited. When Grace made a neat stack of seven diapers, Katy grabbed two and flapped them around, undoing all the folds.

"I'll pack some things for May," I said.

"You don't—" Grace started, but I was already in May's room, pretending not to hear. I had to do something.

I got May's polka-dot work dress out of the closet, and the blue-and-grey print she'd worn to town. Her underthings were in the top drawer of the dresser.

"Now where's your doll?" Grace was saying to Katy. "Mommy said to be sure and bring that."

"Chotchy goed away," Katy said.

"Leave those diapers be! Where'd Chotchy go?"

"Chotchy bite," Katy said matter-of-factly. "Ow!"

Grace sighed. "All right, let's go look." I heard her going back downstairs.

Hal's yellow-and-brown suitcase was under the bed. It had always sat open on his dresser in Cartersboro, ready to go home. The inside smelled like Brylcreem. I packed May's clothes carefully, and added her hairbrush. Would she be gone long enough to need her rag-bag? If I put it in, would she think I wanted her gone that long? Maybe I should write a note— *Dear May, I don't mean anything by anything...* I got the rag-bag from the back of the drawer, and added one more work dress and a nightgown.

What else? Shoes. I took the suitcase down to the kitchen, and set it on the table while I wrapped May's brown shoes in a sheet of newspaper.

Katy came out from under a chair. "Daddy go bye-bye?"

"No, hon, you're taking this to Mommy." Anything else? May didn't like Grace's paring knives. I wrapped her favorite knife in a dishtowel and tucked it in beside the shoes, then closed the suitcase and set it on the floor. "There!"

"I do it," Katy said, and started dragging the suitcase toward the door.

Grace came in, with lilac twigs in her hair. "I don't know *where* you've put that cotton-picking doll, child," she said, not looking at me. She reached for the suitcase. "Here, let me get that."

"No!" Katy clung to the handle. "I do it!"

I watched their tug-of-war, biting my lip. I ought to help Grace look for the doll. I always hated when people ran hot one day and cold the next—but maybe Grace was being nice to May now, at least. And she wasn't really being rude to me. She just didn't seem to know how to act.

Katy had been playing with her doll outside—was that just yesterday? "I think it's in the garden," I told Grace, over Katy's fussing. "I'll get it."

The doll was soaked through, and muddy. I took it inside and wiped it off. Grace had the suitcase now, and Katy was crying sulkily.

"Here, Katy," I called, wrapping the doll in a dry rag. "Better take Chotchy. He's all wet!"

She glared at me, sniffling.

"Look," I said, "Chotchy is sad! He wanted to carry the suitcase!" I made a crying noise. Katy frowned at the doll, then grabbed it and squeezed it against her chest. "Bye, Sweetie," I said, kissing her blond curls. "Tell Mommy hi, okay?"

"Let's go, kiddo," Grace said from the porch.

Katy ran to catch up. "See Mommy!"

Grace had the suitcase in one hand and Katy's blanket bundle in the other. I went to open the door for her. "Bye, Grace."

She followed Katy down the steps. As I eased the door shut, she glanced back at me through the screen. "Say hi to Hal for me," she said.

It's quiet with Katy gone. I made myself a toasted cheese sandwich, and ate it. Now I'm not sure what to do. The house is tidy enough already. I wonder if May will come home and make her piccalilli, before the green tomatoes and peppers spoil. The thought of boiling vinegar turns my stomach. Maybe I could make some of Wanda's mock mincemeat.

Wanda. Something pulls at the edge of my mind, like a snagged thread. Something about… Oh—Wanda's letter! It must be two weeks since it came, and I never even opened it— all that business with the flystrip drove it right out of my mind. Wanda probably didn't say anything important, but still…

It's in my top drawer, under a camisole. *Miss Vera Stinson, in care of Mr. and Mrs. Hal Dixon.* Wanda's loopy handwriting, on her second-best bluebell stationery.

Friday, Sept. 9

Dear Vera,

We got your letter yesterday. Tom was relieved. He says you should have just told us, instead of sneaking off and worrying us half to death.

You aren't fooling me, though. I knew this would happen, with you running around with the men, but you didn't listen.

However, I am not one to bear a grudge. Stop this nonsense and come back to your family, and we'll do what we can for you. We're having some work done on the room you had before, so you'll have to share with Hester. She can learn a lesson from your mistakes.

When your time comes, Tom and I will adopt it, so it'll have a family. You can go somewhere people don't know you, and start again. Maybe you can find a husband after all. We don't often get second chances in this life, but I am prepared to offer you one.

I haven't told Tom. I don't want him to worry. But I'm sure he will agree. Just let us know when to expect you.

Sincerely,
Wanda Stinson

I stifle an urge to crumple the letter up and throw it, and sit on the edge of my bed, rubbing my forehead.

What *is* it about Wanda? She jumps to the most ridiculous conclusions, but it's uncanny how often she's right.

So now Wanda knows—or anyway, she thinks she knows. And May knows. Maybe James and Grace too—May's obviously told Grace something. Did she tell Iva? Before long, everybody'll know—except the one person it matters most to. *Maybe you can find you a husband after all...*

I give myself a shake, and stuff the letter back in the drawer. Wanda doesn't care about me. She wanted my room before, and now she wants my baby, and she pretends it's all for my own good. How on earth did I stand it, living with her for eight years?

Well. I gather up the pieces of May's dress from my sewing table. I might as well get something done. Hal won't be home for hours yet.

77

Hal

James ignored me this morning, on the way in. He glared at me all through lunch break like he wanted to nail my hide to the barn wall. Now he's having Don Parish take us the long way home, by the river road. Wonder what he's up to.

Don's talking politics. James grunts now and then. I don't give a hoot about Russia and the bomb, I just want to get home to May. Maybe she can tell me what happened yesterday— Vera's tale didn't make any sense.

I yawn so hard my jaw cracks. Had one of my nightmares last night. Who knows what it was about.

There's the cemetery where Everett's buried. James points, and Don pulls over. Our truck's parked at the gate. May's here? I wonder why, but I just get out with James. He waves Don off.

May's not anywhere to be seen. James climbs into our truck, waits while I get in on the driver's side.

I crank down my window to let the heat out. "What's my truck doing here?"

James doesn't answer. On the bright side, he doesn't offer to punch my lights out either. I back the truck out onto the road.

Last winter they found a car up here at the cemetery. Kentucky plates, no driver in sight. Folks said he must've jumped off the bluffs.

Hell, people will say anything.

James sits like a statue all the way to his house. I pull into his driveway and he gets out. I start to say See you tomorrow—but nothing comes out of my mouth. May's coming across the yard from Grace's garden, with her apron full of corn.

What's May still doing here? Oh, she didn't have the truck. Well, but Grace could have driven her—unless Grace is still in a huff...

Anyway, it doesn't matter. I'm just glad to see May. I shut off the engine and go to meet her. When she sees me coming, she stops and waits.

I stop a couple of feet away from her, feeling shy all of a sudden. She looks dead tired—but then, she was out late. "Hi," I say.

"Hi, Hal," she says.

"Ready to go?"

She frowns a little. "What?"

I know I said it loud enough. "Ready to head for home?"

May doesn't answer right away. I notice a piece of cornsilk stuck to her arm, but I don't reach out to brush it off. Finally she says, "I'm staying here awhile."

"Staying here?" I hear a familiar screech—there's Katy over by the woodshed, playing with her cousins. How'd Katy get here? I rub my neck, and try to smile at May. "You're not mad at me, are you?"

May doesn't smile. Just stands there like a stone gatepost. Then she says, quiet, "Yes, Hal. I'm mad at you."

"Oh," I say. She doesn't *look* mad. "Well...you're not leaving me or anything, are you?"

Right away I wish I hadn't said that.

"I don't know," May says.

For a second everything sort of swings loose, like a gate left open. I shift my feet in the grass, try to stay calm. "You fixing to throw Vera out?" I ask. This has got to be about Vera.

"I don't know," May says again. Holding up her apron-load of corn.

"You throwing *me* out?" I try a chuckle. It doesn't go very well.

"I don't know."

"Well, May—" I take my hat off and rake my fingers through my hair. I can't make heads or tails of this. "You've got to do *something*. You can't just stand there saying you don't know."

May gives a little shrug. "That's what I'm doing."

Before I can think what to say to that, she says, "Grace needs her corn," and walks off towards the house. No goodbye, no nothing. I start to follow, but there comes Carol running to meet her.

I stand in the yard a minute. Then I go back to the truck and climb in. I feel like I just got kicked—but I can't tell where yet, or how hard.

78

Vera

Hal pulls into the driveway late, and doesn't come in the house. I wait ten minutes, with supper getting cold and the whole lonely afternoon behind me. Then I go looking.

He's sitting on a fruit crate behind the barn, in the shade of the locust trees. He jumps guiltily when I come around the corner, and stubs out a cigarette. "Oh, hi, hon. I was about to head in."

I open my mouth to tell him supper's ready, and say, "I'm pregnant."

Hal stares at me a second. Then his eyes dodge away, and he nods slowly at his boots. "Well, that's...news."

News? I bite my lip hard. "Hal..."

Hal looks up. "Oh, honey," he says, forcing a smile, "Don't mind me, I was just... You're expecting? That's great!"

That's even worse. And if I start crying, he'll pat my shoulder and be sweet. I don't need sympathy. And I don't need Hal hiding behind the barn, pretending he's not worried about May. I need a husband.

Hal grunts in surprise when I sit down on his lap. The fruit crate creaks under the weight. I lean in and kiss him. His mouth softens, and I shut my eyes and kiss him harder, twining my fingers tight in his hair, feeling my disappointment float away on a warm cloud—along with Wanda's ugly letter, and Grace's coldness, and the lonely house, and my worry over May...

Hal's hand is under my dress, and I can feel him getting warmer underneath me. Or maybe I'm the one getting warmer. I twist around to straddle him as he shoves my skirt to my waist. He's looking right at me now, and his grin is real.

May's forsythia bushes block the view from the road, and behind me it's just pasture and woods. I get up and pull off my underwear. Hal tugs at his belt buckle, hurrying like I might go somewhere. I laugh at him, and start unbuttoning his shirt. He clears his throat nervously, but he lets me peel him out of his clothes. I kiss him all over as I go. He watches me, breathing hard.

Naked except for his farmer's tan, Hal looks wild, like he belongs here in the outside air. Leaves make shifting shadows on his pale skin. I strip off my dress, and drop my brassiere and girdle on top of it. Hal stares up at me, and I feel more than beautiful. As if beautiful is beside the point. I lower myself onto him again, growling softly in my throat.

It's awkward, with the crate and all. Hal tries to move, and almost tips us both over. I set my palms against the grey boards of the barn wall, brace my feet, and swing my hips. Hal holds perfectly still, his face lit up like springtime.

I ride Hal's body until I'm flying off backwards into the sky. Hal pulls me back, into the sweating grip of his arms, and I drip tears on his chest. His legs go tense under me, his feet skid in the dust, and the crate flips over. I land on top of him, and he lets out a loud "Hoop!"

I giggle. "'Hoop?'"

"Mm-hm," he says into my hair, his arms still tight around me.

After a minute I roll to his side, snuggling against him on the trampled dirt. "You okay?"

He looks up at the sky. "Well...I might have a splinter in an embarrassing place."

We lie there, letting the dust settle on us. There's a rock poking me in the ribs, but I don't want to move.

I sneeze. "Bless you," Hal says. He sits up, and hands me his undershirt. I wipe the sweat and juices and dirt off of me as best I can, while he hops on one foot to get into his shorts and pants.

He touches my forehead, smiling. "You've got a streak of dirt right there." I wipe my face. Then I sigh, and start getting dressed again.

Walking back to the house, Hal holds my hand tight, like I might fly away. My hand rests easy in his grip. I'm not going anywhere.

79

May

"Mommy!" Carol yelled, running into the kitchen with Katy close on her heels. "Katy won't play right!"

Katy grabbed my skirt, sobbing something about Chotchy.

I dried my hands on my apron and picked her up. "What's
—"

"Chotchy can't be a airplane," Carol hissed at Katy. "He's a baby-doll!"

"I swear, child…" Grace pointed a sticky wooden spoon at Carol. "You—"

"*Airplane!*" Katy screamed, drowning Grace out.

"Fine!" Carol said, and stomped away. Katy wailed, and I patted her back.

Yesterday morning, when I'd asked if I could stay awhile, Grace had made Carol a pallet on Ronny's bedroom floor and put clean sheets on Carol's bed for me. Then she'd dragged out the pieces of Carol's old crib, handed me a screwdriver, and driven off to get Katy, ignoring my protests. Katy had been happy to see me. But when I saw the bruise by her eye, just turning from red to blue, I'd felt sick.

"Katy! Want to see the horsie cave?" Carol called from the living room, once Katy stopped crying. Katy ran off to play again, and I went back to peeling potatoes.

Katy should have stayed with Vera. She'd be safer, somewhere I couldn't hit her again. Not that I wanted to hit her, now. I didn't even feel mad anymore, despite what I'd told Hal yesterday evening. There was just a raw emptiness in my chest, like a hole scraped out with a shovel. Holding Katy eased it a little. It felt like a comfort I didn't deserve.

"Did I tell you about Dave and Sheila's wedding?" Grace asked, dumping her bread dough on the table. "They were going to have it at the church, but then—"

A car door slammed outside, and we both looked out the window. "Vera," I said out loud, surprised.

"Oh, for heaven's sake," Grace said at the same time, and went to the door. I cut an eye out of the potato I was working on, and wished my heart would stop pounding.

The screen door creaked behind me, and I turned around.

"Hello," Vera said.

"What brings *you* here?" Grace asked, her voice dry.

"Hello, Vera," I said. I'd had enough of Grace being prickly, even if it wasn't at me.

Vera fiddled with a button on her dress. "I came to see May," she told Grace.

Grace didn't say anything, but her eyebrows were up in her bangs.

Vera turned to me. "I wondered if we could talk—just the two of us?"

Grace looked like she wanted to say "Fine!" and stomp away, like Carol, but she just rolled her eyes and went back to kneading her dough.

"All right," I said. It seemed like a reasonable thing to ask. "Just let me finish this."

Grace snorted. "You go on—I'll peel the potatoes."

"All right," I said again, and left my knife in the sink. "We can take a walk. I'll get my shoes."

* * *

It was a pretty day, with a clear blue sky. The goldenrod was blooming, and some of the sumac in the fencerows was turning red.

I waited for Vera to say something, but she didn't, so we just walked. I waved at Mr. Boyer on his tractor, and Mrs. Scott on her front porch. I noticed Vera panting a little on the hills, and slowed down. I'd been winded like that, when I was expecting Katy. Maybe Vera didn't have enough breath to talk.

Just past the Scotts' watermelon field, we turned off onto a tractor road. I walked in one track, and Vera walked in the other, her fingers plucking at the tall grass. We left the tractor road where it crossed the creek, and I led the way upstream.

The three-trunked sycamore was still there, leaning out to shade its pool with leaves that smelled like green corn. I sat down on a snaky root and stretched my legs, digging my heels into the loose rocks by the water. Vera sat down on another root. In a sunbeam across the creek, swallowtail butterflies were drinking on the damp rocks.

"So, um…" Vera cleared her throat. "Hal says you don't know what you're going to do."

I nodded. I wondered if she was going to give me a hard time about it, like Hal had. It wouldn't do any good. I couldn't know something I didn't know.

Vera picked a chip of bark off the sycamore's trunk and tossed it into the water. "I thought it might help for us to talk."

The bark chip floated on the pool like a little grey boat, spinning slowly downstream. I used to make boats for Sissy here, folding sycamore leaves and pinning them with twigs. "Talk about what?" I asked.

"Well…" Vera turned a brown rock in her fingers. "About what's next. Or…what happened. Or anything."

I shrugged. "I don't know what's next, Vera."

She nodded, and set the rock carefully on the tree root beside her. The silence stretched out. The butterflies' sunbeam clouded over and came back. A chipmunk sat up on the bank and whistled at us.

"I got into this mess by deciding what was next," I said.

Vera cocked her head, watching me.

"I thought it would work," I said, then shut my eyes so I wouldn't start crying again. It ought to have worked. I liked Vera—and the family would've come around... I saw my hand swinging at Katy's face again, and opened my eyes. "But it didn't. And I'm done deciding things."

Vera's little bark boat was just floating out of the pool. I watched it ride over the ripples. Vera sat quiet, breaking a twig into pieces. After a while, she said, "Why did you want me to come live here?"

"Why?" I asked, surprised. She nodded. I poked at a rock with the toe of my shoe. "Well," I said, "I guess I wanted Katy to still have a daddy, come Labor Day."

Vera nodded slowly, then suddenly frowned. "You thought Hal was going to leave you?"

"He might've."

Vera shook her head. "No, he wouldn't."

I stared at her, feeling aggravated. What did she know about it? Finally I shrugged, and looked away.

"Hal wouldn't ever leave you and Katy," Vera insisted. "You're his family."

"Lots of men leave their family," I said, tossing a rock into the creek. Then I remembered that Vera's daddy had run off, and I wished I hadn't said that. Vera was watching the butterflies. I sighed. "Well. Maybe he would and maybe he wouldn't. I guess I'm not that much of a gambler."

Vera turned to me with a startled laugh. "Really?"

I didn't get the joke. I shrugged again, and tossed another rock.

After a while, Vera got up and stretched, easing her hips from side to side. I got up too.

The walk back was as quiet as the walk there had been, until we came around the last curve and could see the house. Then Vera said softly, "What do you think I should do?"

I stopped, and turned to look at her. She was biting her lip, waiting for my answer. Her hazel eyes reflected bits of red from the sumac leaves.

What did I think she should do? I tried to put myself in Vera's place, and imagine what I'd do. It was like trying to imagine living on the moon. And I was done deciding things. I started walking again. "I don't have the slightest idea."

Vera hesitated, then followed me. When we came to the driveway, she turned off towards the truck, and paused. "Bye, May."

"Bye," I said. I wanted to say something else, but I didn't know what. "Take care," I finally added, but by then she was walking away.

80

Vera

It's hot. I'm kneeling in the hot dust of the road, looking at footprints. I must be dreaming. It really happened, though, after Pop left—me out in the road, searching among the tracks for something I could follow. This time, in the dream, I find them. Not Pop's—these footprints are just like mine, high narrow arches and long ovals of toes. My mouth is sour with dread, and the air above the road ripples in the glare. There's nobody in sight.

I wake up panting and sweating. My room's like an oven from the afternoon sun. Ten after three. I push away the damp pillow and roll onto my back, letting the fan blow hot air on me. So much for a refreshing nap. I wasn't even sleepy when I lay down—I just didn't know what else to do, with the chores all done and the afternoon stretching out ahead. I don't feel like sewing. The house is too quiet, and I can't stop worrying about May.

I think something happened, when Hal and I had our wedding. I think I ended up sort of marrying May too. It feels like I promised her something. It feels like my happiness and hers are bound together, like mine and Hal's. And Hal's and May's. We're all family now.

I love this family. I love my nights in Hal's arms, and my days with May and Katy. I like Iva and Rye, and the rest of them—even Grace, when she's not mad. I like working in the garden and the kitchen, playing cards, laughing over Sunday dinner. I feel more at home than I have since leaving the farm.

But now May and Katy are gone. And Hal's as lonely as I am. We kept the loneliness at bay last night, but this morning he ate half his breakfast and went out early to wait for his ride. And May... When I first saw her, this morning at Grace's, I thought of that song, "You've Got to Walk That Lonesome Valley." May looks like she's in the valley of the shadow of death. Walking it by herself.

I remember in Cartersboro, when I kept telling myself that Hal and I weren't doing any harm. I thought I cared, about not hurting May. But I didn't—I just didn't want to feel guilty. I was as selfish as Wanda, in my way.

And now that I do care, it's too late. It doesn't matter how guilty I feel—May's already hurt.

What was that? —My hand's resting on my belly, and my belly just *poked* me. From inside, like—

Oh! Oh lands, it's the *baby!* I felt the baby move! That's the only— There it is again—like a finger drawing a slow curve across, and gone. Then another poke...

My heart's racing. There's a *baby* in there! Yes, I knew that, but... That couldn't have been a finger. It must have been a foot, or even a head. It felt like a mouse under a blanket. Oh my goodness. It's a *person*—a tiny person, the size of a mouse, inside me!

Okay, Vera, calm down. This happens every day. There must be a million women in the world with a tiny person inside them right now.

But it doesn't feel ordinary. Suddenly nothing feels ordinary. I'm lying here looking up at the ceiling, and even the ceiling looks amazing. Wonderful. Like my eyes have changed.

I want to tell May. I want May to nod and give that little half-smile of hers. I want her to tell me about when she first felt Katy move—did everything look different to her too? Or was she just practical about it? No. Not even May could be just practical about this.

Poke. Poke. I could lie here all day, feeling this. My face won't stop smiling. A baby!

All at once I'm so lonely for Mama my throat aches. I can see her throwing firewood off the wagon, wearing her favorite feed-sack dress with the print like a flower garden, singing "I Don't Work for a Living" at the top of her lungs.

I haven't seen Mama since last Christmas. We don't write. She's only learned to read since she married Mr. Townsend, and it's still not easy for her. If it weren't for the party line, I'd call her on the phone right now. Mama hates for people to call long distance, and she'd hate to hear what I've gotten myself into. But she'd help me if she could. Mama always did her best by us.

And that's what May was doing, wasn't it. This whole idea—it was just her doing her best by Katy. Because she's not a gambler. There I was in Cartersboro, amazed that May had dreamed up such a wild idea, wanting to meet her, wondering why she wanted to meet me—and all the time May was just being practical. Being May. Being a mother.

I don't know why I'm crying about that. I was just feeling so happy.

Half past three. I wish Hal would get home.

81

Hal

I can't get to sleep. The lumberyard was crazy this afternoon.
Ray decided we needed to do inventory—on a Friday, with the
yard open for business. Bucky kept pulling boards off the stack
I was counting, and Bill about ran me over with the forklift.
Yesterday I'd have been too stupid-tired to dodge. But last
night I slept with my arms around Vera, and the nightmares
left me alone.

In the morning, though, May was still gone.

Everything feels cock-eyed without May, like carrying two
buckets in one hand. Breakfast and supper with Vera, it's like
eating with a stranger. Vera probably wants me to say something about the baby she's expecting. I'm still trying to take that
one in. And whenever I think about Vera having a baby, I think
of Katy being a big sister, and that leads me right back to May.

Bedtime's all right. Turn out the light, everything goes away
except Vera and me. I wish it'd go on forever—but a man can
only hold out so long, with a woman he loves laughing under
him. Now I keep dozing off and twitching myself awake,
thinking I'm still counting two-by-tens. Damn Ray and his
inventory. Maybe I can get on the mill crew, when Fred moves

to California. Millworkers don't have to do inventory, and they get eight cents more an hour. I'll see what May thinks.

When May comes home.

Vera snuggles tighter against me, and I give her a squeeze. She sighs. I guess she's awake too.

"So, honey," she says, "About May…" Trails off.

"What about May?"

"I don't know," she says. "What do you think we should do?"

I shrug, her head bumping my collarbone. "I imagine May'll let us know."

"But she—"

"I'm beat, hon," I say. Turn my back, pull the sheet up.

I can feel Vera lying awake behind me. I don't know what she thinks I can do—I'm not going to haul May home in a sack. She'll come when she's ready, and we'll straighten it out.

Unless she doesn't. Don't think about that. I don't want to trade May in for Vera—never did. And I don't want to lose Vera, either. I just want her to let me sleep.

82

Vera

"Come on in," Iva called over her shoulder. She was washing dishes. Her kitchen was dim after the noon sunshine, and smelled like coffee and onions and bacon grease.

"Hi, Iva," I said.

"Hi."

"I wondered if we could talk." I raised my voice over a clatter from the dishpan. "I'd like your advice." Anyway, I needed *somebody's* advice.

I stood waiting while Iva washed, rinsed, and dried three plates. She was wearing her blue apron over a red work dress, with a dishtowel tucked into one side. I'd walked here on the spur of the moment, leaving my own lunch dishes dirty.

"I might not tell you what you want to hear," Iva finally said.

I nodded, though she wasn't looking at me. "I'd still like to hear it."

"Fair enough." She scrubbed at a fork. "Why don't you go out and get started on those peas, while I finish up in here."

I went back out to the shade of the catalpa tree, where a kitchen chair waited next to a pile of uprooted pea vines. The locusts were done singing. I could hear Iva's chickens clucking out back, and the sound of the tractor and saw in the distance.

It was Saturday, and Hal was out cutting firewood with Rye again. I'd been hoping my weekend wouldn't be so lonely, but he'd left right after breakfast. I'd turned on the radio, and worked on May's dress—I hated to finish it without a fitting, but who knew when I'd see May again. If I'd see May again. At lunch, I ate a tomato sandwich, thinking how much better tomato sandwiches taste when you've got somebody to eat them with.

At night, loving, Hal and I were almost one person. But when I tried to talk to him about May, he was like a shut door.

And May had said she was done deciding things.

Which meant it was up to me.

Iva brought out another chair, and started stripping handfuls of pea pods off the vine. I pulled the string slowly down the side of a pod. It opened like a new zipper, spilling green peas into my pie pan.

"Cat got your tongue?" Iva asked, after a minute.

"Well..." I twirled the curlicue pea-string in my fingers.

"That's a deep subject," Iva said. "Don't fall in."

I glanced up at her. She wasn't quite smiling. "You know May's over at James and Grace's?" I asked.

Iva nodded, the almost-smile gone.

"Well." I took a deep breath. "I don't think things are going to work out." I bit my lip, hearing the words out loud. "I mean, not—" I started, and then stopped myself. There wasn't any way to make it sound better. Blunt and ugly as it was, it was true.

I picked up another pea vine and stripped the pods off, watching Iva out of the corner of my eye. She went on shelling peas while she stared out across the road. Her mouth worked thoughtfully, like she was chewing on one of Rye's sassafrass twigs. Finally she said, "Wasn't any other way it could go. You can't build a sound house on a rotten foundation, I don't care *how* smart you are."

I frowned. Did she think I was trying to be smart?

"You and Hal did wrong," Iva went on. "The two of you hurt May something terrible." She looked at me until I nodded. "And instead of throwing a conniption like anybody else would, May's pretended she's not hurt. That ain't going to work."

I looked down at the pan in my lap, stirring the bright green peas with my fingertips. I thought of our wedding, of the three of us playing rummy, of May's dry voice teasing me while we picked apples. It had seemed like it was working. I wanted to tell Iva that. I wanted her to understand. But I didn't think she would, and there were more important things to say.

"So, I guess…" My voice wobbled, but I pushed the words out. "I guess I'm going to have to leave." Iva gave me a sharp look. I swallowed hard, and said the rest of it. "And I'm expecting a baby, come spring."

Iva's breath hissed in, and stayed in. She let it out after a minute, and dropped a handful of pea-pods into her apron like she was giving up on them. "I've been praying and praying—in the spring, you say?" I nodded. "I guess my praying was a day late and a dollar short, then."

Neither of us was shelling any peas now. Iva looked down at her empty hands. I watched a pair of yellowhammers pecking seeds out of the wild sunflowers by the road, flapping their bright wings for balance.

Finally Iva wiped her eyes. "So what are you going to do?"

"I don't know, Iva," I said. "I don't know, but—" Without warning, I started crying. "I'm going to take care of my baby, I know that. Whatever happens, my baby comes first!"

"Hush, now." Iva's voice was brisk, but not mean. She handed me the dishtowel from her apron. "Crying won't help."

I wiped my face with the dishtowel, and got out my handkerchief to blow my nose. Peas were rattling into Iva's pan again. I went back to shelling too. I hadn't told Hal about feeling the baby move. It had seemed too small a thing to mention. Or too big.

After a while, Iva dumped her pan of peas into the mixing bowl by my chair. "You've got people in Cartersboro, don't you, that you were living with before?"

I nodded. "I don't care to go back there, though."

Iva raised an eyebrow at me. "We can't always have our druthers. Would they take you in?" I nodded again, reluctantly. "Well, then. A roof over your head's nothing to sneeze at."

Food on the table, and a roof to keep the rain off it, Mama's voice agreed in my head. I knew she and Iva were right. And Wanda had offered. *When your time comes, Tom and I will adopt it...* No. Not that. My little mouse-baby wasn't going to have Wanda for a mother.

I could still get a boarding-house room. Tom would help out, and surely Sue and Francine would stick by me. But I knew Wanda wouldn't cover for me, if I didn't do it her way. Everybody in town would be looking down their noses at me and my baby.

"What about your parents?" Iva asked.

I blinked at her. "What? Oh—my mama lives in Illinois, with her second husband. They don't have room for me."

"Could you make your own way, there? You sewed before, didn't you?"

"Yes. I might be able to. The town's small, but if nobody else is doing sewing..." Not much wedding business in High Brooks. But rents were cheap.

"And you'd have your mother close. That's something." Iva pursed her lips at the peas in her lap.

"I've got a friend in Kansas City," I said. Until that moment, Sybil hadn't entered my mind. "Maybe I could go there. Start out fresh."

"A woman with a baby never starts out fresh, sweetie," Iva said. She dumped her peas into the bowl again, and stood up. "You finish those last few, and I'll deal with these vines."

I was thinking. "I could tell people my husband had...had died," I said, as Iva gathered up the spent vines. "So they wouldn't wonder about the baby..."

Iva didn't answer, just went to throw the vines over the pasture fence. Had I upset her? Hal was her son. But when she came back, she just looked thoughtful. "So you'd stay with your friend until you found you a place," she said, "And tell folks you're a widow woman, and nobody the wiser..." Her grey eyes turned suddenly sharp. "That the way you want to live your life? Making up stories?"

"No." I didn't have to think before I answered. I'd had enough of lying. "But it's my mistake, and better I should have to carry it than my baby."

Iva nodded. "That's the most sensible thing you've said so far. Not that you're talking nonsense in general," she added. "You've got your head on straight now. Come on in the house and get a drink."

I carried the bowl of peas in, with our pie plates on top. Iva brought in the chairs, and dipped me a glass of water. "One thing's for sure," she said. "Nobody needs to be raising a child all by themselves. I don't care if you're Mrs. Roosevelt—a mother needs help, and she needs company." She filled a glass for herself, and took a long drink. "Sounds like you've got people in Cartersboro, and Illinois, and Kansas City. It's just a question of who you want to depend on."

I thought of May, and Hal, and Katy, and the family we'd just started to make together. I thought of my mouse-baby growing up in that family, with its daddy Hal to swing it around and be silly. I thought of May's kind ways with Katy, and Sunday dinners with Iva and Rye and Grace's family.

But there wasn't any use in telling Iva all that. I took a drink of water. It was cold.

83

Vera

Hal put down the cards he was shuffling for gin rummy, and took a bite of chocolate pudding cake. "Mmm," he said. "Now that's worth eating."

"It's easy to make," I said. I'd made it just for something to do. I'd been nervous as a cat since I got back from Iva's.

"Good." Hal took a bigger bite. "You can make another one tomorrow."

I watched the chocolate topping dribbling down the side of my cake, and tried to gather up my courage. At least Hal wasn't being so distant this evening. During supper he'd told me all about some kind of "grip-vise" pliers Rye had seen an advertisement for. May would have known what he meant.

Cat got your tongue? Iva's voice said in my head. I sighed. "Hal," I said, "I've been thinking."

"Uh-oh." Hal took a slurp of ice tea, and winked at me. "You don't want to overdo that."

"This isn't working out very well, is it?"

Hal's face went blank, and he drew his head back a little. "How so?"

"It's tearing May apart," I said. "It's tearing you and May apart from each other. It's——" It was tearing Hal and me apart, and May and me, and Hal and Katy… "It's a mess."

Hal scraped a smear of chocolate topping into a line with the side of his fork. "I imagine we'll figure it out," he said. He took another bite of cake, not looking at me.

I felt a drop of sweat run down my ribs. "It's not just that. I'm thinking about the baby. People are going to realize, Hal."

"They'll get over it," Hal said, with a shrug.

"But what if they don't?" My voice was getting higher. "Look at Grace—even your own family…"

Hal gave an impatient snort. "Grace? I tell you what, Vera —" He set down his fork, and pointed at me. "Grace can go soak her head. Rye, too." I wondered what Rye had to do with it, but Hal was going on. His pointing finger drew a circle around the table. "*This* is our family, right here—me and you and May and Katy, and yours that's on the way, and any more we have. That's family enough for me. The rest of them can take us or leave us."

I looked around the empty table, seeing the family he was talking about. Hal and May and me, and Katy and the baby. Five of us, set against the whole world. Who would the kids play ball with, if the neighbors were against us? Who'd help Hal cut tobacco, or bring us food when somebody died? "Hal…" I started.

The telephone rang, two longs and a short. Hal glanced at it impatiently. I got up and answered it.

"Hello," Iva said. "Looks like Sunday dinner's at your place tomorrow."

I felt my eyes get wide. "Um—here? Iva, I don't——"

She interrupted me. "Family's family, Vera, in good times and bad. If Hal has any complaints, he can talk to me."

"It's just——" I started.

"I'll bring meatloaf and an apple salad. May's bringing rolls and dessert, so you can just have a chicken and the vegetables."

May? I glanced at Hal. He was squinting at his left thumb. Maybe he had a splinter. "Um," I said to Iva, "Are Grace and —"

Iva snorted. "Grace'll do whatever Grace does. We'll eat about one o'clock."

"I—"

"Let me know if you need anything. Bye, now."

"Bye." I hung up the phone, feeling queasy.

"You got a needle?" Hal asked.

"Um...maybe... Everybody's coming here for Sunday dinner tomorrow."

Hal stared at me. "You're kidding."

"No."

His eyebrows went up. "You thought it'd be fun to invite—"

"Iva invited them," I said, sharper than I meant. "She said you could talk to her about it."

Hal snorted. "Might as well talk to a steam engine."

I gave a little shrug, and sat back down. Then I remembered Hal's splinter. "You wanted a needle?"

"No," Hal said. "I don't want to mess with it."

He scraped up the last of his cake, and sat staring at the ice cubes melting in his glass. I swallowed, opened my mouth, closed it again. It was a bad time to tell him. I didn't think there would be a good time. My chest felt too small to get a breath in. Finally I whispered, "I'm going to leave, Hal."

Hal looked up. "Come again?"

I cleared my throat. "I'm leaving."

Hal jerked like he'd been hit. "Leaving?!"

I nodded. "You make things right with May. I'm sorry." I shut my mouth, biting my lips hard to keep from taking it all back.

Hal slapped his hands down on the table and stood up, knocking his chair over. "You can't just leave!" he half-yelled at me.

My heart was pounding, and I felt tears stinging my eyes. "Don't—" I said, then remembered that Katy was at Grace's, with May. There was nobody for Hal to wake up.

"I'm *telling* you," Hal said, still loud, "It's going to work out! I *love* you, Vera!" His voice cracked, and he turned away, wiping at his face.

"I know," I said. I was crying too. "I love you too. But that's not the whole world, Hal. It's not the only thing!" I knotted my fingers together and stared through my tears at Hal's back, willing him to understand.

Hal looked up at the ceiling for a minute. Then he turned around and met my eyes. His mouth trembled, but his voice was hard. "So you were just fooling around. Playing with me. Have your little wedding, say 'I do'—that didn't mean a thing, did it? Things get tough, you just run on back to town. Find you another fellow to string along."

I felt cold. "No," I said, my voice barely a whisper. "No, that's not true."

Hal made a disgusted noise. Then he kicked the overturned chair out of his way, and slammed out the back door.

I sat at the table a long time. After a while I saw the piece of cake on its saucer in front of me. I untwisted my hands from each other, and put the cake back in the pan, and put the pan in the fridge. I picked up Hal's chair, and washed the saucers and forks and glasses.

Then I went to bed and curled up tight under the quilt. I felt like I'd never be warm again.

The house is quiet, and dark. I lie in bed, hand on my belly, feeling little mouse-sized kicks against my palm. It's after midnight, Mouse-Baby. You ought to be asleep. Me too.

Kick, kick.

So, Mouse-Baby, I guess it's just you and me. Like it was Mama and me, once Tom moved away... We're the ones moving away now, though. Where are we going to go?

High Brooks is a tiny little place. You'd go to my old school when you got big enough, and we'd have Mama to help us out —your Grandma Stinson. I mean, Townsend. And I guess Mr. Townsend will be your Grandpa. Best take all the family we can get, right?

If we went to Cartersboro, you'd have cousins. I always wanted cousins, but all of mine were in Kentucky. Of course, you'd have your Aunt Wanda, too. There's family, and then there's family…

Or Kansas City. Sybil would have to be our family there, I guess. Aunt Sybil and Uncle Bob, and their kids for cousins.

Oh, lands, I can't do it. Figure out what's next. Be cheerful and hopeful for Mouse-Baby's sake, do eeny-meeny-miney-mo about where to live. Kansas City scares me to death. It must make Cartersboro look like High Brooks. And would Sybil and Bob really be our family? Could I count on them, the way I can count on Tom and Wanda? Even if Wanda's ugly about it?

I guess Hal thought he could count on me. In good times and bad times. Till death do us part.

He still hasn't come back in the house. I don't know if he's out in the barn, or what. I don't know if he really thinks those things he said. I don't know how I'm going to stand this.

I don't even know how many people are coming for Sunday dinner. What on earth is Iva thinking?

84

Vera

Hal didn't come back in the house until Sunday morning. He was still in yesterday's clothes, with bits of hay in his hair. He didn't answer my "Good morning," and he wouldn't look at me while he ate his breakfast. I picked at my egg. When he was almost finished, I said, "You know I love you, Hal."

Hal raised his eyebrows just a little. Then he got up, still chewing, and reached for his hat.

"Iva said they'd be over about one." My voice felt like burlap in my throat. Hal went out the door without answering. I thought of Petey, jamming all the pins down in my pincushion after I'd said I was leaving. This hurt a lot worse.

I made myself finish my toast. Then I did the chores, and killed and dressed out two fryers, and got the vegetables ready to cook. I ached all over. Hal didn't come back in.

I found some brown calico in my trunk that would go with May's new work dress, and started making an apron in her size. When my bobbin thread ran out in the middle of a seam, I burst into noisy, racking sobs that wouldn't stop. I crawled onto the bed, wrapping my arms around my body as if to keep something from falling out of me—but it felt like something already had. I held onto myself and wailed, hoping Hal wouldn't come in. And hoping he would. He didn't.

James and May arrived at ten till one, without Grace and the kids. I was frying the chicken.

"Hi, Vera," May said, setting a basket of rolls on the table.

"Hi." I turned a thigh in the sizzling grease.

James held up a covered cake. "Where do you want this?"

May nodded at the counter, then turned back to the door. "I'll be back in to help." When James started to follow her, she said, "I'm just going to the toilet, Jamie. You don't need to come."

"Oh." James let her go, looking sheepish, and stood by the door like a guard. Why didn't he go find Hal? I smiled at him nervously as I spooned green beans into a serving dish.

James cleared his throat. "I don't want to butt in…"

That meant he was about to butt in. I adjusted the heat under my skillet. James took a handkerchief out of his pocket and unfolded it, then folded it up again. The silence stretched out like an empty road.

Then he said abruptly, "May's my sister." I nodded, not trusting my voice, and he went on. "I don't have anything against you, Vera. You seem like a nice girl. But I wish…" He shifted his shoulders awkwardly. "May's got a family—a little girl, and a home…She's got a lot to lose."

"I—" I started, but James wasn't done.

"I've got nothing against you," he said again. His hands folded the handkerchief into a tiny, thick square, while his eyes pleaded with me. "But I sure wish you'd go on back home."

Tears ached behind my cheekbones. *What home?* I wanted to say. And, *Do you think I don't have anything to lose?* And, *I love May too.*

The screen door creaked, and May came in. She looked at me standing with the fork in my hand, then at James refolding his hanky again. She sighed quietly, and went to get out the plates. James studied me behind her back, a worried frown around his eyes. Without his easy smile, he looked more like May.

I heard Rye's Model A in the driveway. "Dinner's about ready," I told James. "You want to go find Hal?" Hal's name hurt like a fresh bruise. May started setting out the silverware. I went back to my chicken.

Nobody told anybody where to sit, but somehow Iva ended up between me and Hal, Rye between Hal and May, and James between May and me—like they were separating squabbling kids. Nobody said much, after Rye asked the blessing. Hal still wouldn't look at me. I could barely eat for nerves. May wasn't eating either, and Iva chewed like it was a chore to be done. The chicken must be good, though—it looked like the men might finish off both birds, even without Grace and the kids.

They were starting on seconds when Iva set her fork down with a dull click. Everybody looked up except Hal, who kept gnawing on an ear of corn. Iva looked over her spectacles at us, like she was about to make a speech. "Well, here we are," she said. "And it's about time we put our heads together and got this mess straightened out."

Hal dropped his corncob on his plate, making his fork clatter. "Hail to the chief," he muttered, reaching for the potatoes. Iva ignored him.

Nobody else said anything. May looked uncomfortable, and I shifted in my seat—I didn't really want our dirty linens aired all over the dinner table. Rye scowled at his green beans.

Iva sighed. "Everybody know Vera's expecting?"

James gave me a startled look, and turned red under his tan. He glanced at May, who nodded. "Guess I do now," he said.

There was another silence. Iva's eyes went from Hal to me to May. When she spoke, her voice was sharp. "So you-all would rather let an innocent child come into the world with its family tore all to pieces, than open your mouths and *say* something?"

May made a helpless gesture with her hands. "I tried, Iva," she said. "I don't have any more ideas."

"How about you, son?" Iva asked Hal.

Hal laid down his fork with a bite of potato still on it, and finally looked at me. I winced at the bitterness in his face. "I reckon it's Vera there you ought to be asking," he said. "Since you're itching to hear all about it."

Iva raised her eyebrow at him. He picked up his fork and ate the potato, staring off past James's shoulder.

Iva turned her eyebrow on me.

"I'm leaving," I told her. Hadn't I told her that yesterday?

"Leaving?" May said. "Where'll you go?" Her forehead had a worried crease in it. I could've kissed her. Here she should have been shouting good riddance… I tried to smile at her, but it was all I could do not to cry.

"I haven't decided yet," I said. Hal's glower felt like a stove's heat on my face. "I've got some people I can go to."

"That's good." Iva nodded at me, then at the rest of the family. "But it's not easy, for an unmarried woman with a baby."

Nobody spoke. Rye bit into a chicken leg like he had a grudge against it, and glared at the side of Hal's head. Hal's ears were red, but he kept chewing.

"Or," Iva went on, "For a baby without a daddy."

Hal's ears got redder. He reached for his ice tea.

"And that's not the only child that'll suffer, if this keeps on," Iva added, and looked from Hal to May. "You two fixing to patch things up?"

Hal set his glass down with a thump. "Dammit, Ma!" he burst out. "You got to put your nose in *everybody's* business?"

"You watch your mouth, son," Rye said, poking his chicken leg at Hal's face. Hal sat back in his chair and rolled his eyes.

"What I'm saying——" Iva started.

Hal interrupted her. "You going to put up with this?" he asked May. "In your own house, you just going to let Ma walk in and take over? This is between you and me, May." He didn't look at me. "Ma's already talked Vera into walking out—now she gets to run *your* life too?"

Heat rushed into my face, and I opened my mouth to protest. May took a breath too, but James got there first. "Hal," he said calmly, "Just because you feel like a jerk, doesn't mean you've got to act like a jerk."

Hal gave James a disbelieving look. "What the—" Then he shoved back his chair and stormed out through the porch, slamming the screen door behind him. Iva shook her head, and took a drink of ice tea.

After a minute, May said, "I don't know what we're going to do, Iva. I thought I knew, but…"

"But you were wrong," Iva said. "It happens. Important thing is what you do next."

May just shrugged.

"Hal wants you to come back," I said. May poked at a piece of apple salad with her fork. I felt tears start down my face. "I'm sorry, May," I told her. "I didn't think—I was just thinking of myself. And then I thought you wanted… I won't ever do this to anybody again."

May met my eyes. Her face was still, without anger or forgiveness either one. I wanted her to believe me. I wanted her to say it was all right. I wanted it to *be* all right.

James cleared his throat loudly beside me. "Would somebody pass the butter?"

Rye blinked at him, then slid the butter dish across the table. We all watched as James split open a roll and buttered it. Then he fished out his handkerchief, blew his nose, and wiped his eyes. "Anybody want to split that last ear of corn?" he asked, wadding the hanky back into his pocket.

May shook her head at him. There was almost a smile in her eyes. Before she could speak, the screen door creaked and Hal came back in. "Sorry, Ma," he muttered as he sat down.

"Dang," James said. "I knew you wouldn't let me get away with it." He broke his ear of corn in half, getting butter all over his hands, and handed the bigger half across the table to Hal. Rye passed Hal the meatloaf, and the men settled back down to eating. I wondered if they'd ever get full.

Iva picked up her fork, nudged her green beans into a row, and put the fork back down. "So that's settled," she said. "Vera's going away, and you two can start putting things back together. You'll do all right, May. A little forgiveness goes a long way." She took a sip of ice tea, and patted the napkin beside her plate. Then she cleared her throat, and went on, "But that's not the only question."

Hal stabbed a bite of meatloaf with his fork.

Iva gave me a quick, nervous smile. I felt the back of my neck prickle. "It's good that Vera's thinking of her baby," she said, to everyone, then turned to Hal. "But that's your baby too, Hal. And it's me and Rye's grandchild."

Suddenly I wanted to get up and walk out. No, not walk—run. I didn't know where Iva was headed, but I didn't want to be there when she arrived.

"What we've got here," Iva said slowly, looking around the table, "Is a family that's going to hang together. And a baby on the way, that'll need a family. And we've got a young lady who's going to find it a big job, raising a child by herself." Iva turned to me and reached out as if to pat my hand, but my hands were knotted together in my lap. "The baby might have a better life here with Hal and May, Vera. You can stay with Rye and me in the meantime. And then you could make a fresh start, knowing your baby has a good family."

Her voice echoed in my ears. Rye nodded at me as he pulled apart a chicken wing. I put my hand on my belly. *I am Mouse-baby's family,* I thought. That sounded like Hal, with his tiny little family set against the world. Was I being selfish? Maybe, for Mouse-baby's sake… But I knew what I'd say, if I opened my mouth. It was ringing like bells in my head. *No, no, no, no, no.*

"Iva," May said, and Iva turned to look at her. "Iva, I know that's a good idea…" She rubbed her face with both hands. "But I don't know that I could do it." Iva started to speak, but May went on. "How could I be a good mother to it, when I keep getting so mad and…" She looked down at her barely-touched plate. "I'm sorry," she whispered. "I want to be better than that."

James put his hand on May's shoulder, and handed her his hanky. "Ah, Maydie," he said, as she blew her nose, "You're being too hard on yourself. You'll feel better after a while.

Mom was mad at Dad for years, but it didn't last forever. And after that one time, he—"

James stopped, his mouth open. May was staring at him over the hanky. "What are you—" she said. Then her eyes widened, and she took in a sharp breath. "What are..."

Everyone was staring at James and May now, even Hal. They all looked as confused as I was.

James looked around the table, his mouth closing slowly into a silent *oh*. Suddenly he stood up. "Gosh, would you look at the time! We'd better hit the road, May—I'm due over at the church. Sorry to eat and run, folks—"

May let James pull her to her feet. As he tugged her toward the door, she glanced from me to Iva. "But..."

"We'll take care of the dishes," I said. "You go on. Thanks for coming."

They went out. Nobody moved as the Buick started up and pulled away. Hal stared at the door like he thought May might come back through it.

Iva sighed, and stood up. "Rye," she said, "You go on and finish up, now—you've had enough for six people. Does anybody want dessert?"

Nobody did.

85

May

Jamie drove in silence, but his voice kept echoing in my mind. *Mom was mad at Dad for years...after that one time, he...* What else could he have meant, besides what it sounded like? I slumped in my seat, my arms folded over the raw ache in my chest.

Jamie waved at Altha Combs, who was out on her porch. We were almost to Barkworks Road, without a word said. I sighed, and tried to straighten my shoulders. "Well, Jamie, I guess you'd better tell me what that was all about."

He nodded. After another mile, he turned off into a tractor road, nosing the Buick up to the gate and shutting off the engine. Half a dozen white cows were grazing in the pasture, among clumps of milkweed and thistles.

Jamie watched the cows, tapping his wedding ring on the steering wheel. "I'm sorry I said anything. I wasn't thinking. And I guess—I always figured you knew about that."

I shook my head.

"Dad told me," he said, "When me and Grace got engaged. Said if I was fixing to get married, there was something I ought to know... You remember Mrs. Beamer?"

I nodded. The Trulow boys' daddy had share-cropped on Mrs. Beamer's land. She was a widow. I couldn't remember ever speaking to her.

Jamie ran his hands to the top of the wheel, and back to the bottom. "Well," he said, "I guess Dad and Mrs. Beamer had a thing going for a couple of years, back before Sissy was born."

A thing going? I leaned my head against the car door, feeling queasy. Jamie went on.

"Dad said he never quit loving Mom. But Mrs. Beamer—well, she was real pretty, but he said it was more how she *was*. Laughing all the time, glad to see him.

"And then he said, 'Pay attention, now!'" Jamie cocked his finger and thumb at me, like Daddy always did. "Of course, I was already paying attention—I was about to die of embarrassment... You sure you want to hear all this, Maydie?"

I wasn't sure at all. "What'd he want you to pay attention about?"

"Well, first, he said it didn't happen all at once. They were just friendly, for years. He'd say hello, when he was over trading work with Sam Trulow."

I nodded. I could picture Mrs. Beamer—tall and thin, with her red hair pinned up, breaking beans on her front porch.

"Well, I guess one day when it was hot out, she offered him a glass of ice water, and they got to talking while he drank it, and the time got away from him. And then when Mom wanted to know why he was late getting home, he made up some story about Sam wanting him to look at a pig. And then, he said, it kept going a little further, and a little further...he didn't think he was doing any harm. But Mom found out eventually, and it about killed her."

Jamie sighed, and wiped his forehead on his shirt sleeve. It was hot, with the car not moving. "He said he never went near Mrs. Beamer again. Didn't even trade work with Sam anymore... He told me all that, and then—I remember exactly what he said." Jamie cocked his finger again. "'You *ever* find yourself lying to Grace, boy—especially about something little, like a drink of water—you stop cold, and straighten up. I don't want you making the same mistake.'"

It could've been Daddy, saying it. Jamie always had looked like Daddy, but I'd never noticed how much their voices were alike. It made my throat hurt.

"Anyway," Jamie said, staring out at the cows, "That's the long way around the barn—but what I was getting at, back there, was that Dad said Mom was mad at him for a long time, but not forever. Things got better."

I didn't know what to say. I felt a drop of sweat sliding down the side of my face. A bluebird landed on the gate and peered at us, then flew off to perch on a milkweed, knocking loose a clump of white fluff.

"All right," I said.

"Sorry I put my foot in it," Jamie said, scrunching his face up a little.

"It's all right," I said. "Let's go home."

I watched the fencerows going by, and wondered why Daddy had never told me. He'd probably left it up to Mom—but Mom never talked about things like that. She talked about chores, and what I was doing wrong, and the Lord. Did she find out about Mrs. Beamer before she got saved, or after? Before Sissy was born...a couple of years... It must've been right around then. My mind felt dull and heavy, like muscles worked too hard.

We came around the last curve, and there was the house. Except for Grace's nasturtiums spilling orange out of the porch flowerboxes, the place looked just like it always had. I tried to imagine Daddy telling Mom about Mrs. Beamer in that house. Sitting at the scuffed kitchen table and shaking his head, like Hal. Mom being mad for years. How many years?

"Here we are," Jamie said, turning off the engine. He looked over at me like he might apologize again.

I gave his shoulder a shove. "It's all right, Jamie. I'll live."

86

May

"So," Grace said, prying the seed-ball out of a green pepper, "How'd dinner go?"

I shrugged. "It was fine." I poked another chunk of cabbage into the food grinder and cranked the handle. We were making piccalilli, while the girls had their nap and Ronny was off with Jamie.

"You want to tell me about it?"

Not really, I thought. The whole business with Daddy and Mrs. Beamer was between Jamie and me. And then there was the rest of it... I ground some more cabbage, then said, "Iva thinks we ought to straighten things out."

Grace snorted. "She does, does she?"

"Yes. And Vera's going away."

"She is?" Grace looked surprised, then doubtful.

I nodded, feeling the same shudder under my ribs that I'd felt when Vera said it—like the first jerk forward when a loaded wagon starts to move. "She said so, and I believe her," I said. The look on Hal's face would've convinced anybody.

Grace stripped the peel off an onion. "Well, I'll be."

I started feeding peppers into the grinder. "And...I guess I didn't tell you, Vera's expecting."

"Oh, she is?" Grace didn't sound surprised at all now. "Since when?"

"She's due in the spring."

Grace paused to count the months in her head, then nodded knowingly.

I took her meaning. "Hal didn't know about it," I said.

"Oh, he didn't?"

"Would you quit saying 'Oh, she did' and 'Oh, he didn't?'" My voice was sharp, and I stopped myself. Grace couldn't help being Grace. But I wanted to be fair. "Hal wanted to be with Vera because he loves her. She didn't tell him about the baby." Not then—not to make him stay. She must have told him since, though. Jamie was the only one who was surprised when Iva brought it up.

And then Iva had told us her idea. Her good, sensible idea, that I'd balked at like a mule. I blinked hard at the bright green chopped peppers piling up under the grinder's spout. Was I really so mad and mean I'd take it out on an innocent baby?

I'd taken it out on Katy.

You'll feel better after a while...Mom was mad at Dad for years... I flattened the peppers down with a spoon before they could spill out of the bowl. "Anyway," I said, "The point is, Iva wants Vera to stay with her and Rye until the baby comes, and then leave the baby with us."

Grace dropped a chunk of onion. "She thinks *you* ought to bring up Vera's baby?"

"It's Hal's baby too." I picked up the onion and put in in the grinder.

Grace snorted. "Oh—so he'll be the one changing diapers and warming up bottles in the middle of the night?"

I had to smile. It felt good to have Grace sticking up for me. "Well, anyway, that's what Iva said."

"You going to do it?"

I looked down at the grinder, feeling my smile disappear. "I don't know, Grace," I said. My eyes stung with onion fumes. "I don't know anything anymore."

* * *

"SORRRRRR-Y!" Ronny yelled, stomping his blue pawn down on one of Carol's red ones. Carol's pawn flew off the table. Her face looked stormy as she went after it. Katy, half-asleep in my lap, grunted at the racket.

"Not so hard, Ronny," I said. I'd agreed to help Carol play Sorry with him before bedtime, but I was starting to regret it.

"And there's no need to holler," Grace added. She and Jamie were playing gin rummy at the other end of the table. "Carol, if you don't like it, you-all could've played Snakes and Ladders, and let Aunt May play with the grownups."

"Snakes and Ladders is dumb," Ronny said.

"Is not," Carol sniffled, putting her pawn back on the board. When Ronny stomped it again two turns later, she burst into tears and shoved the game off the table.

Ronny glared at her. "Cheater!"

"Shh!" I said, as Katy sat up groggily in my lap. "Katy's trying to sleep."

"Come here," Jamie reached out an arm to Carol. "I could use some help—Mommy's skunking me."

"She has to pick up the mess!" Ronny protested, as Carol climbed into Jamie's lap.

"You can do that," Grace said, drawing a card. "It won't kill you."

Ronny grumbled as he looked for the pieces. I yawned and patted Katy. I was used to quiet evenings—Grace's kids stayed up later than Katy did.

"Ronny's mean," Carol said, snuggling against Jamie's chest.

Jamie made a face at his cards. "Oh, I don't know. I imagine he's just being a big brother."

Grace snorted. "You don't know what teasing is, Carol. The way Bobby and Eddie used to do me... Gin," she added, and laid down her hand.

Jamie sighed. "I can't win for losing."

Ronny put the lid on the Sorry box, and looked thoughtfully at me. "Did Daddy tease you, when you were kids?" he asked.

I smiled at him. "Sometimes. I gave as good as I got, though."

"Well, and I wasn't her *big* brother, either," Jamie added. "Aunt May's almost a year older than me—I'd say it went more the other way."

Carol sat up straight, looking offended. "Aunt May's not older than you!" she told Jamie.

"Is too." Jamie grinned at her.

"But you're bigger!" Carol insisted.

Grace laughed as she shuffled the cards. "Not when they were kids," she said. "May was always taller, and heavier too." Carol stared at me, wide-eyed.

Jamie chuckled. "You remember how Grandma Stout went on about that, Maydie? 'It ain't natural, for a girl to be that much bigger than a boy the same age!'"

I shook my head. "The way she talked, you'd have thought we were twins."

"And then she'd blame the goat," Jamie said, grinning.

I put on my best Grandma Stout face. "'If Pearl had fed your brother herself, instead of putting him on that old goat, he'd be a head taller than you by now. A baby ain't a goat kid, Maydie!'" I finished with a little sniff, like Grandma Stout always had.

"You two might as well have been twins," Grace said. "I don't know what I'd do, with two babies eleven months apart."

"Grandma Stout blamed that on the goat, too," I told her.

Carol was squinting at me in confusion. "They put your brother on a *goat?*" she asked.

Ronny snorted. "Not *on* it like a horse! For milk—like we put that orphan calf on Gertie." Then he frowned at whatever he was picturing.

"But…" Carol started.

I shifted Katy to my shoulder and stood up. "I'm going to put this girl to bed," I said, and left Grace and Jamie to straighten it out.

Katy half-woke when I laid her in the crib. I pinned a diaper on her, and stroked her arm as she settled back down. Her pale hair shone in the moonlight from the square window. This had been my bedroom—mine and Sissy's, once she was out of her cradle. I'd watched squares of moonlight cross its floor and walls and ceiling for twenty-two years, with Jamie right across the hall until he went off to war.

Grandma Stout really had blamed that goat for Jamie and me being so close in age. *I nursed all my babies myself,* she'd say, *and never had more than one in diapers at a time.* I smiled to myself.

Then I frowned—that didn't make sense. Mom had nursed me, and the goat hadn't come along until after Jamie was born. Why hadn't I ever noticed that? Had I just been glad to hear anything against Mom, whether it made sense or not? Of course, I wouldn't have argued anyway—nobody argued with Grandma Stout. Even Mom would just set her mouth and pretend not to hear, if she was in the room. Come to think of it, Grandma Stout only ever talked like that when Mom was in the room.

Daddy took me aside once, though, after Grandma Stout had been talking. "Maydie," he said, with his hands on my shoulders, "I want you to know, your mother couldn't help not suckling Jamie—she was real sick after he was born. Jamie couldn't keep down cow's milk, and the doctor had me buy a freshening goat. That 'old goat' saved your brother's life." He put his arm around me and gave me a squeeze. "And don't you worry about being bigger than him, either. Jamie'll get his growth."

Daddy was right. When Jamie was sixteen, Mom and I couldn't let his hems out fast enough, and by the time he got back from the war he was as tall as Daddy. If Daddy could've stood up to measure.

Katy mumbled something and rolled over. I heard Ronny and Carol coming upstairs to bed. Time for me to get to sleep too. I bent down to kiss Katy's head, breathing in the warm smell of her hair. Then I stood leaning on the crib rail, thinking of Daddy. Daddy tall and strong and well. Daddy making sure I knew Grandma Stout was wrong about Mom.

Daddy lying to Mom about Mrs. Beamer.

And Mom, worn thin with her own meanness and worry, sitting by Daddy's bed to wipe his slack face with a cool cloth...

It was true, what I'd told Grace—I didn't know anything anymore.

87

Hal

I used to sleep out here in the barn when I was a kid, when my bedroom got too hot. Loose hay, back then. Still smells the same, but haybales aren't as soft.

Last night I slept out here because I was mad. Woke up around midnight hollering, all in a lather. And again later. So I'm out here again tonight. I'd rather have the barn cats staring at me, than Vera acting like she cares.

I guess my nightmares are about the war. Nothing else ever scared me that shitless. Maybe I dream about when the Trulow boys checked out. I know I was there. Last thing I remember, we'd found a case of wine the Jerries had left behind, and we were taking it back to camp. Howie and Gus carrying it between them. All of us laughing our asses off.

They said it was a grenade mine. The whole countryside was booby-trapped all to hell, and the sappers had missed that one. Howie and Gus were dead when they found us. I was knocked cold, and cut up like I'd picked a fight with a briar bush. Hardly even lost any blood.

The screen door at the house creaks open and thumps shut. Vera, going to the toilet. I saw her walking over to Ma's yesterday, when Rye and I were headed back to the woodlot after

373

lunch. So I know this whole leaving idea is Ma's doing. I just can't believe Vera went along with it. After all that wedding business and everything.

And then Ma comes sticking her oar in again today at dinner—telling everybody what to do. May didn't go along so easy…

May keeps talking about being mad. She still doesn't look mad. God, I wish she'd come home. She could straighten Vera out.

I ought to straighten Vera out myself. Tell her to go on and leave, if she's leaving. But I'm hiding in the barn instead. And the kicker is, if Vera changed her mind this minute, I'd be back in there like a shot, loving her like crazy.

Maybe that grenade knocked my brains out after all, and nobody told me.

88

Vera

I walked over to Iva's as soon as Hal left for work. Iva was hanging out her first load of wash. Monday morning—a week ago, I was doing the wash with May. When I tried to help Iva, she waved me away. "I'm particular," she said, pinning two black socks up by the toes. I stood by the clothesline pole, putting my hands in my pockets and taking them out again.

"How's Hal this morning?" Iva asked.

I just shook my head. I didn't have words for how Hal was. He didn't yell at me, or say mean things. He'd slept in the barn again. His eyes were hollow at breakfast, and his silence choked the words in my throat.

I watched Iva match up another pair of socks. "I've been thinking about your idea," I said. And I had. I'd thought about it all yesterday afternoon, and through Hal's silence at supper, and alone in bed at night. And my heart had kept on hammering its *No, no, no, no.*

Mouse-baby would have a good home, with Hal and May.

No, no, no, no.

This is the family I wanted Mouse-baby to have.

No, no, no, no.

It's not about what's best for me.

No, no, no, no.

Iva glanced at me as she hung up a shirt, and I went on. "I haven't decided what I'm going to do." *No, no, no, no.* "But I thought it might be best if I got on out of the house…"

"We'll make you a bed on the couch," Iva said. "You got the truck today? Good. Call on the telephone when you're ready, and Rye'll come help you load up."

I'd planned on just packing a bag, but Iva's right. It's more honest this way—I'm not coming back.

So here I am again, with my trunk and my crates, my hatboxes and my sewing machine and my electric fan. It's not much, is it. It only took me so long because I kept stopping to cry.

If May had to pack up and leave this house, she wouldn't know where to start. Furniture, dishes, all the canned goods in the basement, her and Hal's wedding picture… Even with May gone, the house is full of her life.

My life is all here in the bedroom, folded up and packed away. It's as if none of this even happened, like now the matinee's over and everybody's going back out into the sunshine. But it was real. It *is* real. Hal can say what he wants about me just fooling around, but I meant it when I said "I do." I meant forever.

And still, it's over. Even though I meant it. Because I didn't mean I wanted May to be miserable. And I didn't mean I wanted it to be us and our kids against the whole world.

How can something start out so full of love, and end up so awful?

I'm all packed. I've called Rye. May's new dress is hanging in her closet, all done but the hemming. But it's not really over, is it? The hard part's still to do, ripping out the seams where I've sewn myself into this family. And I wasn't just basting things together, trying out a pattern. I made those stitches to last.

89

May

I was peeling tomatoes for supper when the telephone rang. Grace went to answer it, still holding a handful of forks. "Hello? ...I'm fine. ...Oh, you are?" She raised her eyebrows at the telephone. "All right, I'll tell her." My stomach did a flip-flop.

Grace hung up and went back to setting the table. "Vera says she's moved out," she said. "She's staying at Iva's for awhile."

I nodded, and sliced the tomato onto a plate. It was a beef-steak, red and meaty. I couldn't think of anything to say.

Ronny skidded into the kitchen and ducked behind the door. "Ready or not, here I come!" Carol yelled from the living room, with Katy chiming in half a beat behind.

Grace got out the serving dishes, while I started on another tomato. Pink-red juice dripped off my knuckles. Vera was gone. Not gone far. Gone for good? Grace had said "moved out." Why did Grace like her tomatoes peeled, anyway? It was a fussy job.

Carol and Katy tiptoed into the kitchen. "Wonny!" Katy called. "Wonnnny!"

"Shhhh!" Carol tried to put her hand over Katy's mouth, but Katy escaped back into the living room, still hollering. Carol sighed in disgust, and looked under the kitchen table.

"You think she'll stay gone?" Grace asked me.

I shrugged impatiently. "I don't know." Then, before I could stop myself, I said in a rush, "All I know is, if they think all they've got to do is move Vera out, and I'll just come back and cook Hal's breakfast in the morning like nothing ever happened, they've got another think coming!"

"Do they?" Grace looked like she was trying not to smile. "Well, I'm with you there. You don't have to pull a knife on me!"

I realized I was holding the paring knife up in my fist, like I was ready for a fight. Carol was staring at me. I sighed and went back to my tomato, trying not to breathe hard.

"You know you can stay here as long as you need to," Grace said. Her voice sounded odd. When I glanced up at her, she was grinning outright.

"What?" I asked, irritated—at Grace for grinning, at myself for getting all worked up.

"Nothing," she said, grinning at the casserole she was putting on the table. "Nice to see you show a little gumption."

I shook my head impatiently. I didn't want to be mad.

Ronny sprang out from behind the door and ran for the living room. Carol shrieked and chased him, bumping into a chair.

"You-all go outside, if you're going to be rowdy!" Grace hollered after them. Then she reached over and wiped a tomato seed off my arm. "Well, May. If you want to leave Hal, you've got every right. And if you want to patch things up, I'm behind you there, too. It's your decision."

I nodded. But I was done making decisions. I put the last slice of tomato on the plate, and went to wash the juice off my hands.

The girl had carroty-orange pigtails, and wore a blue checkered dress with a white apron, like my doll's. She was just my age. Hal took her hand and tugged her closer to me. She smiled shyly, and Daddy said, "Maydie, this is your sister."

Wait—Daddy was dead. I woke up, frowning. Moonlight poured in through the square window, turning the room into a snapshot. Katy's crib rails threw dark stripes across the wall. *Your sister.* I shivered, and pulled the sheet closer. It'd be cool enough for a quilt at night, before long.

The girl in the dream hadn't looked anything like Sissy. Nobody in our family had red hair. And she was too old. I rolled my eyes in the dark—why was I arguing with a dream?

I'd always wanted a sister. Sissy had been a dream come true, until I realized it'd be years before she could play with me. Grandma Stout always said Sissy was spoiled rotten because she was "practically an only child."

"Ready not, here I come!" Katy said, startling me, but she was just talking in her sleep. Dreaming about her cousins. She'd like a sister or brother, one close enough in age to play with.

I'd told them I couldn't do it—I couldn't bring up Vera's baby. But here was Vera, gone to stay at Iva and Rye's. Hadn't anybody heard me? Maybe they thought I'd change my mind.

I pictured a baby, with Hal's dark curls and Vera's hazel eyes. How could I be mad at a child for something that happened before it was born?

You'll feel better after awhile... Jamie had meant well, but that didn't mean he was right. I saw my hand swinging at Katy's face. And then Mom's hand, swinging at mine. *It didn't last forever...* A cold, sick feeling weighed down my stomach. Had Mom really quit being mad at Daddy? Or did she just turn her mad on me?

I kicked away the sheet and sat up. I wasn't going to go back to sleep. If I were at home, I could get up and do something—bake a pie, clean the stove. But I didn't want to wake Grace and Jamie. I leaned my elbows on the windowsill and looked out at the moonlit yard.

I'd said I was done deciding things. But decisions kept piling up anyway, like socks to be mended. I sighed, and rested my forehead on my arms. I could just stay right here, and not do anything. Even that would be a decision.

The windowframe smelled musty, but the breeze had a sweetness of turning leaves. It was October already. Just a week or two till the first frost. I had squash in the garden at home, and sweet potatoes. I wondered if Hal would think to get them in, if I wasn't there to do it.

90

Hal

Damn. I feel like I ought to be bleeding. Like I've got both arms shot off, and I'm still walking around. First May, and now Vera.

I didn't think Vera'd go through with it. But when I got home, there was her note on the kitchen table. Light pink paper. *Gone to Iva and Rye's until I figure out what's next. Goodbye, always love you.* Like something out of a tear-jerker movie. I threw it in the garbage.

She took all her stuff. I looked.

I knew May kept a bottle of whiskey someplace. Took me ten minutes to find it—in the medicine cabinet.

So now what? Do I just sit here on the porch swing drinking Jack Daniels, and wait for May to come back? If she does come back. Her and Katy... I miss Katy as bad as I miss May. I guess that makes two arms and a leg blown off. The medics wouldn't even bother.

The sun's on its way down, lighting up everything from the side. God, it's pretty. Even as bad as I feel, it's pretty. Sassafrass trees all red, oaks that bronzy green they get, hollyhocks still blooming by the porch.

It was about this time of year, when we got into that pretty country east of Paris. I crawled out of my slit trench that first morning, went to take a leak. There was a little creek there, a house by the road, a few trees. Big old oak on the hilltop that needed some cows under it. Nothing special—except there's a place down on Scott's Pike, not five miles from here, that looks just like that. Tacketts' place. Same shape to the ground, same white two-story farmhouse, same oak tree on the hill. I just stood there staring. Seemed like any minute, Mrs. Tackett might come out to break beans on the porch.

Then Howie Trulow came up and slapped me on the back, saying maybe war was hell for everybody else, but the goddamn flies sure were whooping it up. Howie could make anything into a joke—bad food, trenchfoot, screaming meemies. I don't know what he would've said about him and Gus getting blown to Kingdom Come with a whole case of red wine, but it would've been funny.

I couldn't shake it, though, the way that place looked like Knobs County. For days after that, I was seeing home everywhere I looked. Hills like a woman's body, low places full of willows and weeds and fog. Patches of woods starting to turn color here and there. Little fields and pastures.

Except it was ruined. Even that big oak tree was half blown away, and the farmhouse was missing a wall. Trenches and barbwire all over the place. The Germans had driven through the fields with the ground wet, churning good soil up into muddy ruts, and now we were doing it again. I'd been seeing that kind of mess all along, but this was like seeing my own farm tore all to pieces. I couldn't look at a cut fence without thinking of the farmer that'd have to fix it later. If he ever made it home.

And the hollyhocks. Those got to me. Ma always planted hollyhocks around the privy, back home, and May's mom had them by her porch. I guess French women liked hollyhocks too —they were everywhere. Big tall ones, pink and red and white. You'd have a house blown all to hell, and there'd be hollyhocks still blooming along the back fence, and behind that a field that looked just like the Frys' pasture... I was glad when we got into some different country, so I could concentrate on not getting my head blown off. That, and finishing the job, so home wouldn't ever look like that.

There's not enough whiskey to get drunk on. Vera must've used most of it on May's hair. I take the empty bottle around behind the barn and throw it on the burn pile. Stand there looking at the broken glass and black ashes. I don't know what to do about anything.

Damn Vera. *Always love you,* my ass.

No Vera, no May. No Katy. God, if I'd known it'd end up like this... What a god-damn fool.

After a while I hear Bess bawling, and head for the barn. Cows don't care if you're a god-damn fool. They just want to be milked.

PART FOUR

91

May

"Look, Mommy!" Katy pointed excitedly. "A house!"

I picked a sassafrass leaf and crushed it, breathing in the sweet root-beer smell. Katy had been cranky this morning, and I'd decided the two of us needed a break from everybody else. Instead of going grocery-shopping with Grace and Carol, we headed out for a walk. Katy rode piggyback at first, but after we ate our sandwiches by the pasture pond she was ready to explore. Everything was exciting to her—dung beetles, yellow leaves, sun-bleached bones. She followed a late monarch butterfly, and I followed her. When I helped her over the fence into the Frys' pasture, I knew where we'd end up—it was all downhill from there to the creek in our own woodlot.

And here we were, standing under the twisty sassafrass at the edge of the woods, with Katy tugging on my skirt and pointing at the house. It looked like any white frame farmhouse, with curtains blowing at the windows and hollyhocks alongside the front porch. "Yes, hon," I told Katy. "That's our house."

Katy looked up at me and laughed. "My house?"

"That's right." It must seem like we'd been gone a long time, to her.

"Go my house!" Katy set off, wading through the rough pasture grass. "Mommy, come!"

She'd need help getting through the fence. My legs moved on their own, and I followed her.

It was a Thursday, so Hal was gone to work. I felt nervous climbing the porch steps, as if I was sneaking around somebody else's place. I straightened my shoulders, and let the screen door bang a little as it shut. "This is *our* house," I told Katy again. She grabbed Chotchy from my apron pocket and ran on ahead.

I left my shoes on the porch and stepped into the kitchen. The floor felt gritty underfoot. The skillet on the kitchen stove had a streak of egg white down its side, and a greasy spatula lay on the counter beside Hal's breakfast dishes. I shut the lid of the breadbox. The loaf of bread inside had diagonal slashes on top—one of Iva's.

Katy gave the kitchen rocker a push, then ran into the living room. I heard the rumble of the living-room rocker on the uneven floorboards. She loved rocking those chairs. The sound made the house feel emptier.

"Mommy!" Katy called. I found her in the doorway of Vera's room, staring. It looked like a spare bedroom, the bookcase and dresser bare. Vera's sewing machine was gone, and her trunk. Grandma Stout's Log Cabin quilt was tucked neatly over the mattress.

Katy was gone again, clambering up the stairs, before I could think what to tell her. She was overjoyed to discover her room at the top. I left her digging in the toy box, and went across the hall.

Hal's pajamas hung over the footboard of the bed. The top sheet and quilt lay in a tangle on the floor, as if he'd kicked them away. I wondered if he'd been having nightmares. The air was heavy and close. I glanced over my shoulder, feeling like a trespasser again.

That was ridiculous. I sat down hard on my side of the bed, and looked in the dresser mirror. My arms were folded, my mouth in a stubborn line. *This is my bed,* I thought. But I didn't say it. How could I lie down in this bed with Hal again, after what he'd done? How had I ever thought I could? And yet I had. And it was good, and loving, and sweet—even after Vera came. All I could imagine now was Hal holding me in his arms and thinking of Vera. As if I was two women to him, or only half a woman.

Sadness twisted my mouth, and I looked away from the mirror. It was all ruined. The good life we'd had before Hal went off to Cartersboro, the life we'd been ready to go back to —all ruined, and I didn't have the first idea how to fix it. The rawness in my chest throbbed, as I realized I still wanted to. I put my face in my hands.

Back downstairs, I sat in the living-room rocker, while Katy raced her toy baby buggy full-tilt back and forth between the living room and kitchen. My fingers traced the familiar spirals at the ends of the rocker's arms. I'd nursed Katy in this chair, and Iva had nursed Hal in it long before that. It was our wedding present from Iva and Rye. Hal and I had said our vows in this room, there by the stairs.

Iva and Rye's preacher married us, not Mom's. Iva thought that was why Mom wouldn't come to the wedding. I didn't tell her that Mom didn't want me marrying Hal at all. Mom's reasons changed every time we fought about it. I didn't care. I felt bad about leaving Sissy behind—she was only nine—but I was afraid I'd strangle Mom if I didn't get out of that house.

Jamie and Grace did come, with Ronny and baby Carol, and Jamie sweet-talked Mom into letting him bring Sissy. The six of us crowded into the living room with Hal and Rye and Iva. Reverend Seele smiled at Hal and me, showing his crooked teeth, and told us to be patient and kind and love one another. I could feel the weight of the last few years lifting off of my shoulders. Daddy was still gone—but the war was over. Hal was home safe, holding my hands and grinning. Jamie was home safe, with Grace and the kids. And now I was free of Mom's meanness and misery, for good. Hal and I would make our own life, full of kids and work and love. I laughed when I said "I do," and I tasted my own tears when Hal kissed me.

I startled at a sound—but it was just Katy, scooting a chair in the kitchen. I must be dozing off.

Iva had baked us a wedding cake, and Sissy ate three pieces. I hugged Iva, and Rye slapped Hal on the back. Jamie and Hal joked about when we used to play ball—Hal said now he'd got me on his team, Jamie better watch out, and Jamie pretended he'd thought Hal would be on *his* team now.

"Hal's nothing but a spoiled little boy, and he's sure to break your heart." Mom had said that. Just one of her endless arguments. I tried to shake my head, but it was too heavy. Hal was rounding third base, nine years old and running hard. The ball smacked into my glove. I spun around fast and threw it home.

92

May

I woke with a gasp and a kick, sending Katy's baby buggy flying. "Sorry, hon." I got up and set the buggy back on its springy wheels. Chotchy was upside-down in the basket, and I flipped him over. "Is Chotchy okay?"

"No." Katy glowered at me. She was ready for a nap. "Up!" she demanded, grabbing my leg.

It was too hot to carry her around. "How about I rock you and Chotchy in the rocker?" I settled her in, and she flopped back against the cushion, sucking on her fingers.

The chair rumbled steadily under my hand, back and forth. Katy hummed, her tired eyes blinking slower and slower. When she was sound asleep, I moved her to the couch so she could stretch out, and wondered what to do next. If I wanted her to get her nap out, I had an hour or two to kill before we started back. Plenty of time to heat water and wash the dishes. But that didn't feel right. I rolled my eyes—since when did washing dishes have to *feel* right?—but I didn't go into the kitchen.

I heard a scrabbling noise, and looked out the window. A chipmunk sat up on the porch and chirped, then disappeared over the edge. The porch swing moved a little in the breeze. I could go out and get the mail. I wondered if anything had come for me, in—what was it, a week now, since I'd left home? It seemed longer.

A movement caught my eye, up the road towards Iva and Rye's. When I recognized Vera, I jerked back from the window, my heart pounding. Vera was coming this way. She was walking slow, looking out across the fields on the far side of the road, but she'd be here in a few minutes.

She'd lose sight of the house for a minute, when she passed behind the cedars at the fence corner. I could grab Katy then, duck out the back door and slip around the chickenhouse. I pictured myself crouching against the chickenhouse wall, trying to keep Katy quiet. My mouth twisted in disgust. Sneaking around my own yard like a burglar, while Vera went in the house and...what? What did she want? She'd said she was gone.

Vera disappeared behind the cedars. I waited, sweating, until she came into view again. Katy was sleeping hard. I went into the kitchen. The water bucket was empty, and there wasn't any ice tea in the refrigerator. I poured myself a glass of milk, and took a sip. It was cold and rich in my dry mouth, and it settled my stomach. I carried my glass out onto the screen porch, and waited.

Vera was already coming across the yard. I was in plain sight, standing on the porch, but she was looking down at the ground. When she started up the steps, I cleared my throat. She gasped and jumped back like she'd stepped on a snake. Then she just stared at me through the screen.

She'd been crying. No, she was still crying. Her eyes were red and puffy, her shoulders hunched forward as if to protect her chest. She sniffled, and made a face that might have been meant as a smile. "Hi," she said.

"Hi."

"Um..." she said. "I'm sorry, I didn't think anybody'd be here..." She bit her lip, and reached for the door handle. "Can I come in?"

Everything fell silent. I looked at Vera's red face. The milk glass in my hand was cool and damp, and my bare feet pressed against the rough porch floor. I could feel the shape of the porch around me, posts and rafters, and behind me the shape of the whole house, its white plaster walls and the warped boards in its living room floor, the doorframes opening between the rooms and the steep roof strong overhead. I moved my shoulders a little, like a box turtle shifting in its shell.

Vera tipped her head uncertainly. I took a breath. "Why don't we sit in the yard," I said. "Want me to bring you out some milk?"

Vera's hand fell away from the door handle. "All right," she said hoarsely. "Um...yes, please. Milk, I mean." I waited until she walked away before I went back to the kitchen.

Out in the light and without the screen between us, Vera looked worse, not better. The sparkle in her eyes was gone, along with her smile. *I wonder if Hal would fall in love with her now,* I thought—but that was Grace's thought, not mine. Of course Hal would love Vera. Even I wanted to tell her everything was all right. Instead, I drank the rest of my milk, then watched the white film flow down the inside of the glass and settle in the bottom. I couldn't hate Vera. But I didn't have to tell her it was all right, either.

"How's Katy?" Vera finally asked.

"She's doing fine," I said.

"And how are you?"

"I'm fine." I didn't feel like making small talk. What did she want?

"How's Hal?" Her voice cracked on his name.

I shrugged. I hadn't seen Hal since Sunday. Had she? I could feel the heat of anger gathering around my face. Not last week's suffocating roar—more like standing too close to a woodstove. I leaned back a little in my chair, and turned the cool glass in my fingers.

Vera cleared her throat, and looked toward the house. "Your hollyhocks are still so pretty," she said.

I didn't think she'd walked half a mile to tell me that, but it was true. The rain had done them good. I watched a bumblebee crash-land on a pink bloom and disappear inside.

Vera drew a shuddering breath. "Hal told me once—usually he didn't say much, but once when he'd had a few beers at the tavern—" She glanced at me uncertainly. I just nodded. Hal knew when to quit.

Vera looked away again, wiping her face with a soggy hanky. "He said they had hollyhocks in France, all over. And every time he saw them, he'd think about home." She stopped to blow her nose and take a drink of milk. "He said when he started at the factory, all the noise made the war...come back, somehow. He was a nervous wreck when I met him."

I'd worried about Hal, those first few months he was going to Cartersboro. He'd looked so pale and tired. But he'd said he was all right, and he always did look better after his weekend at home.

"He said he felt like old chewing gum scraped off the bottom of a shoe." Vera gave a sort of sideways smile, still looking at the hollyhocks. "And he said when he—when we fell in love —" Her breath caught in a sob, and she put a hand to her face. "It was like all those knocked-down houses in France stood back up, with the hollyhocks blooming and kids playing in the yard. Like everything was all right again."

I looked at the goldenrod along the road. I didn't want to watch Vera cry. There were tears in my eyes too, but I didn't know who they were for.

After a while, Vera blew her nose again. "I'm sorry," she said in a tired voice. "I don't know why I told you all that."

I shrugged.

"I'm just...It's hard sometimes," she said.

I couldn't argue with that.

Vera sighed. "I'm waiting to hear back from some people. As soon as I figure out where I'm headed, I'll be gone."

I frowned. "I thought—" *I thought you were staying until the baby came, and then...* Guilt stabbed at my belly, and I looked away.

Vera stirred in her chair. "No," she said, when I looked at her again. "Iva might be right, but I can't do it. I can't leave my baby." When she said "my baby," something strong came into Vera's blotchy face. She took a deep breath, and gave me a smile that was small, but real. "I came over to get my ring," she said. "I'm planning on saying I'm a widow."

"Oh." I tried to take that in. "It's still here?"

Vera gave an embarrassed shrug. "Probably on the kitchen windowsill. I took it off to do the dishes." She bit her lip, her eyebrows lifting in a tiny question.

"I'll go look," I said.

I took our empty glasses in with me. The ring was there on the windowsill, behind the vegetable brush. I slipped it over my fingertip and went back outside.

"Thanks." Vera got up to take it from me, and slid it back onto her finger. "I should've had Iva come get it for me. I just..." She trailed off. "If I think of anything else, I'll send her for it."

"All right," I said. Vera was standing sideways to me, and for the first time I could see a roundness in the front of her dress. Would she really tell people she was a widow? I remembered her answering Grace, that first Sunday dinner. *My husband was in the Army...he's a farmer.* Vera could do it, if anybody could.

"Well," Vera said, "Bye."

"Bye."

I watched her go until she was well up the road. Then I walked slowly back towards the house. The hollyhocks stood up in their spiky row, pink and red and white and blue. I imagined the house bombed to a shell, like the villages in the newsreels. It wasn't hard.

Hal had never talked to me about the war. What was it he liked to say—*Better to keep your mouth shut and look like a fool, than open it and remove all doubt.* I shook my head as I opened the screen door. Hal was a fool, all right. Trying to make houses stand back up, by lying down with a woman. And wrecking his own home while he was at it. I didn't know if I could stand being married to that much of a fool.

I stopped by the kitchen table, looking down at the floor. "What I can't stand," I said out loud, "Is how dirty this floor is." I rubbed my right foot against my left ankle to scrape off whatever I'd stepped in—toast crumbs, it felt like—and reached for the broom.

The broom's straws whispered across the brown painted boards, gathering up dust and crumbs. I glanced at the clock. Three-thirty. Hal would be home in a couple of hours. I knew I'd still be here then. And I'd be here tomorrow. This was home.

I thought of the sad, stubborn woman I'd seen in the bedroom mirror. I didn't know what to say to her. That everything was all right? The thought of Hal getting home broke me out in a cold sweat. I didn't know what I'd say to him, either.

I bent down to sweep a pile of dirt into the dustpan. Everything wasn't all right. I didn't know how to make it all right.

But this was home.

93

May

"Oh, good," Grace said, when she heard my voice on the telephone. "I was about to send out a posse."

"I'm over home," I told her.

There was a little silence. Then she asked, "You eating supper there?"

"I guess so." I looked around the kitchen, wondering what there was to cook.

"Come eat with us if you want," Grace said. "Hal too, if... Either way." When I hesitated, she went on, "Peck's got a sale on work gloves, twenty percent off." Grace never could stand for people to think over the telephone.

"I guess we'll just eat here." There'd be eggs, anyway, and garden stuff.

"You know you're always welcome," she said.

"I know, Grace. Thanks." *Thanks* didn't seem like enough to say.

Hal sighed as he came in from the porch. He took off his hat— then saw me at the stove, and froze. I hadn't meant to startle him, but I couldn't leave my gravy.

"See, Katy?" I said, ruffling her hair. "Daddy's home."

Hal quit staring at me, and knelt down on the floor. "Katy-did! Come see me!"

He didn't sound like himself, with his voice wobbling that way. Katy frowned at him from behind my skirt. Then her arm shot out, pointing. "*My* buggy!" she said sternly.

"Your buggy?" Hal croaked. Then he coughed, and said in a normal voice, "Well, I'll be!"

Katy marched over to the baby buggy and picked up Chotchy. "Chotchy! Chotchy!" she sang, waving him over her head. "Moooonshine!"

Hal smiled at her. His face was thinner, and the skin around his eyes looked tired. My stomach twisted. I was feeling too many things at once.

"Push Chotchy," Katy told Hal, stuffing the doll back in the buggy.

Hal scrambled to his feet and bent over the buggy's wire handle. He gave me a quick, shy smile, then started gently towards the living room.

"No!" Katy said. "Fast!"

"Fast?" Hal speeded up to a trot.

"Faster!" Katy chased Hal into the living room and back, yelling "Faster! Faster!" until she was giggling too hard to run.

"Hoo-ee!" Hal said, parking the buggy by the table again. "I'm all wore out!"

Katy held up her arms. "Boo-ful Katy!"

My gravy was sticking. I scraped at the pan, and added more milk. Hal sang "K-K-K-Katy, Beautiful Katy," while I set out sliced tomatoes and deviled eggs, got the biscuits out of the oven, and drained the mustard greens. It was a makeshift supper, but it would have to do. Hal finished his song and held Katy tight, his eyes closed. I could see tears hanging on his eyelashes.

Katy squirmed. "Down."

Hal gave her one more squeeze, and set her on her feet. He looked at me over his red hanky as he blew his nose. "Good to see you, May."

I looked back at him. There wasn't any song he could sing to make it all better with me. I took a deep breath and blew it out, puffing my cheeks. "Supper's ready," I said.

All through supper, something kept bothering me, like Katy tugging at my skirt. Something I'd forgotten, or something I needed to do... I swallowed my food with a tight throat. Hal kept glancing at me, with a shaky kind of smile. Katy filled up our silence, crooning to Chotchy through mouthfuls of tomato and gravy.

After supper, Hal took Katy with him to the barn. I washed up the dishes, then took off my apron and stood uncertainly by the table. What was bugging me? I walked slowly through the house, hoping something would remind me. Everything looked familiar and strange both. I noticed the long-dried drips in the paint on a doorframe. I touched the two-button light switches, the square post at the end of the stairway railing. I climbed the stairs, hearing the different creaks of the different treads.

In our bedroom, I folded Hal's pajamas and made the bed. Sheet, quilt, Hal's pillow, mine—I stopped, clutching my pillow. That was what it was. The thing I needed to do.

It was ridiculous. I couldn't do that. Not again.

But could I go to bed with Hal tonight? And not end up so mad I took it out on Katy?

I went across the hall to Katy's room and looked out the window, towards the barn. No sign of Hal and Katy yet. They wouldn't be gone long, though.

"Oh, for Pete's sake," I said aloud. Then I went back in our bedroom, and started taking dresses out of the closet.

94

Hal

Something's wrong with the bedroom.

At first I thought May'd been moving furniture again, but that's not it.

Oh, it's just the picture gone off the wall. And the bed's made up. No—May's pillow's gone, too. I tap my fingers on the dresser top. Maybe she's airing it out? But she wouldn't air out a picture…

I look in Katy's room. No pillow, no picture. God, maybe I've got it all wrong. Did May just come home to get her things?

I was thinking on my way home, how I was getting tired of egg sandwiches, might ought to buy some canned soup or something. Mainly just trying to keep my mind off May and Vera. But when I saw May standing there by the stove, I knew I could eat egg sandwiches the rest of my life and like it, if only she was home to stay.

And Katy. I took her out with me to milk, let her give the foam to the barn cats. My face hurts from grinning.

But now there's this. I go back downstairs, trying not to let on. I want to know what's up, first. May's chasing Katy around with a washrag. Her pillow's not in the living room, or the kitchen. I check the back porch. Nope.

Back to the living room. Katy's rolling on the floor, giggling, while May scrubs her feet. The door to Vera's room is shut.

I can't go look, with May right here. I sit on the couch, try to read the *Farm Journal*. Try to smile at Katy. That shut door's all I can think about.

May finally takes Katy upstairs. I tiptoe over and open Vera's door.

There's May's pillow, sticking out from under the quilt. Right in the middle of the headboard, no place left for another one. There's the picture on the wall, women working in a field —right where it was when this was our room. I open the closet. May's dresses. All of them, and her good shoes. Like this is her bedroom.

And not mine.

Jesus.

What's she going to do if Vera comes back? I mean, Vera says she's gone, but who knows…

I hear May's footsteps upstairs, and hurry back to the couch. Read "The Hoof-and-Mouth Outlook," try to pull myself together. May's home. Katy's home. That's what matters. Everything else can wait.

95

Vera

Woodlawn Courts N-5
Bloomington, Ind.
Weds., Oct. 12

Dear Vera,

I was so glad to hear from you! Francine wrote that you must've eloped, but she didn't know who with. I won't give you any grief about it. People make mistakes.

As you can see, we've moved back to Indiana, so your letter took a while to find us. Bob's doing his graduate work on I.U.'s fancy new cyclotron.

You're welcome to come stay, if you don't mind sleeping on the couch. They ran out of room for all the ex-GIs on campus, so we're in a trailer, next door to 300 other trailers. "Conveniences" four doors down—Bob hauls water for me every morning before class. Lots of mud, lots of kids. I'm expecting again in Jan., don't know where we'll put it—a kitchen drawer? (Not really.)

Bloomington's smaller than Kansas City, but it's so crazy with all these extra families, I doubt anyone would notice a "widow" with a baby. Some of the wives here take in sewing. I don't know about wedding business—everyone in our little ghetto is already married. You'll have to come see for yourself.

Do come. I'd love to see you. We'll squeeze you in, and have a drink and catch up on things. (Or a soda, if you still don't drink—everyone here seems to!)

Love,
Sybil

Sybil sounds so cheerful. Of course, my letter to her probably sounded like I knew what I was doing.

I don't. I feel like I'm at the bottom of a well. I cry at night, curled up on Iva and Rye's couch. I cry in the daytime, peeling hard-boiled eggs. Iva ignores it. Not in a mean way—more like you'd ignore a fever blister on somebody's lip. I get the feeling that she thinks I'll be okay, which is sort of comforting.

Mouse-baby keeps me going. She kicks and pokes at me, lively as a squirrel. I eat for Mouse-baby. I get up in the morning for Mouse-baby. I sing her a lullaby every night, whether I feel like it or not. I tell her it'll be all right, even if she does have the weepiest mother in the world.

I don't know when I started thinking "she" instead of "it." Mouse-baby feels like a girl. A growing girl—my new sailor dress still fits, but the others ride up at the waist. I'll need maternity dresses soon. I'll need somewhere to set up my sewing machine and make them. How long would it take me, to find a room in Bloomington?

And then there's Mama's letter. I've read it a dozen times.

Dear Vera, I dont know what to say. Of crose you can come home. Theys a nice room to rint over Hazltt's store. Myrtel Pate jest had a baby and shes got more sewing than she can do anway sintce Emmy Norbry move to Crossville. I dont know how foaks woud be, you know how they go on. Hows come you dint tell me? I tol Tom to kepe you out of trobl. Im worry about you so com see me and let me look at you. I love you sweety and I pray for

you ever night. You dont have to rite ahed, just come. Love,
Mama.

I miss Mama so bad. Her handwriting's come a long way, but still a letter's nothing like talking to her for real. Mama's smart, and tough, and funny. And she loves me. Like I love Mouse-baby. Here I go, crying again—Mouse-baby's going to start growing fins.

Bloomington sounds perfect. Bigger than Cartersboro, smaller than Kansas City. Young people coming and going, getting married, having fun.

I don't think I can face it. Maybe being weepy would be okay, if I'm supposed to be a widow. But I just can't do it. I want to go home.

96

Hal

It's almost two weeks May and Katy have been home. I'm starting to believe it now. At first I kept checking, like feeling your pocket to see if your lucky penny's still there. We take our ice tea out in the yard, evenings, watch the sun go down while Katy plays.

I haven't seen hide nor hair of Vera. I guess she's really not coming back. I don't even know if she's still at Ma and Rye's—they've showed up to Sunday dinner without her twice, and nobody said anything. It's almost like Vera never existed. Except for this god-awful torn-to-pieces feeling every time I think of her.

I might have been too hard on Vera. Maybe she wasn't playing me for a fool after all. I wish I could ask her.

And there's the baby, unless Vera's mistaken. I remember when Katy was born. I'd come in from the field in the evenings, hold her while May got supper on the table. Some guys don't like to hold babies. They don't know what they're missing.

Now it looks like I'll have another baby, that I won't know anything about. I guess it happens. After we liberated Paris, you could get a roll in the hay for a pack of cigarettes—must be a lot of French kids, now, with American daddies that don't know anything about them.

It doesn't seem right. But I don't know what I was supposed to do.

Anyway, count your blessings. Katy, picking clover flowers. May looking rosy in the sunset light, her hair a little mussed up from the day. That haircut suits her—makes her look older and younger both.

May's not looking at me, so I keep looking at her. Better than brooding about what's done and gone. A lot better. My eyes trace her calves—slow, like licking an ice cream cone, up to the hem of her dress. Whatever happened to short skirts? In my mind I can see all the way up. Her thighs, white as milk, coming together in the prettiest shape you ever saw. A little damp with sweat, smelling like woman. My fingers stir a little, imagining the curve under May's belly, combing through that thicket of dark hair.

May glances over at me, and I look away. I don't want to bother her. I haven't even touched her, but once, since she came home. Kissed her goodbye, that first morning. She let me do it. That was all. I felt lower than a snake's belly.

May's here. She's home. Cooking the meals, keeping the house. My shirts are washed and ironed, I don't have to strain the milk or feed the chickens. We talk, play a little rummy. But she goes to bed in Vera's room every night. I guess it's May's room, now. She's never said a word about it. I wake up wanting her, she's not there. I wake up from nightmares, nobody holds me.

And in the daytime, it's like she's got a glass wall around her. KEEP OUT.

I know it's only been a little while. And Rye was right, May's pure gold. I'd be a fool to run her off.

I don't know how long I can stand it.

97

May

I added an apple to Hal's lunchbox, latched the lid, and sat down to breakfast.

"Got plans for today?" Hal asked, shaking pepper over his eggs.

"I'm taking Altha shopping this afternoon," I said. "Her neighbor, that usually takes her, got put on bed rest."

"Going by Peck's?"

"I could. Why?"

"I need one of those wire doohickeys for the side door of the barn. It's dragging in the dirt."

I could feel Hal's eyes on me as I wrote "door turnbuckle" at the bottom of my shopping list. It seemed like Hal's eyes were always on me. I yawned.

"How'd you sleep?" Hal asked.

I shrugged. I couldn't remember when I'd slept well.

We ate the rest of our breakfast. Hal tried to chat a couple more times, and I tried to be pleasant. When Jamie's car pulled in, Hal got up and put on his jacket. "Bye, hon."

"Bye," I said, handing him his lunchbox.

"Tell Katy I'll see her this evening."

"I will." I started clearing the table. Hal picked up his hat and went out.

I poured hot water into my dishpan, relieved to be alone. It felt mean, pretending not to notice Hal watching me. Wanting me. It was over a month now I'd been sleeping downstairs—we'd never gone this long before. But when I thought of getting close to Hal, even a hug or a kiss, I just felt mad—a smoldering, headachy mad, like live coals under a layer of ashes. *Mom was mad at Daddy for years...*

And after that, she was mad at me. Why me? Was it really the same mad? Maybe she just thought I was wicked, and it didn't have anything to do with Daddy. She'd started being so hard on me after she got saved—but then, I didn't know when she'd found out about Mrs. Beamer. I wished I could ask her. No, I didn't. I wished I could know, without going anywhere near Mom. Then I imagined Katy feeling that way about me someday, and felt sick.

The bruise by Katy's eye had faded in a couple of days, but I knew I'd never forget it. I ran my dishrag around the rim of Hal's coffee cup, thinking of his wanting eyes. He'd just have to go on wanting. I couldn't afford to get that mad again.

On the way to Whelan, Altha fed Katy orange-slice candies and told me all about her neighbor's pregnancy—and about a McCormick, back in Kentucky, who got put on bed rest and lost her mind. "Course, those McCormicks always were kind of odd," she observed, as we headed up 129. "My cousin Essie married a McCormick. They lived in the old Treadwell place—you remember, back Possum Hollow Road?"

I shook my head. Altha gave a start, then cackled. "Course you don't, Maydie! That's clear down in Kentucky. Forgot who I was talking to..." She turned in her seat to study me as I drove. "You're the spitting image of Candice, with your hair like that. It brings out your eyes."

Candice was Grandma Stout. I smiled at Altha, and tucked a stray curl back under my scarf. I'd gotten used to my short hair, and Grace was keeping it trimmed for me.

"I still miss Candice," Altha said. "Growing up in school, we were like *that.*" She held up a hand and tried to cross her fingers, then frowned at her gnarled knuckles. "When I got married and moved up here, I about cried myself to death. I didn't think I could live without my Candy."

"Candy?" Katy asked, eyeing Altha's pocketbook. Her face was sticky with orange sugar.

Altha laughed, and patted Katy's leg. "You be a good girl, and we'll get you some more candy in town."

"Miz Bell!" Peck hollered. "Long time no see!" He limped out from behind the counter, leaning on a cane.

"Hi, Peck," I said, as he pounded my back. "That knee giving you a hard time?"

"Naw," he said, thumping the cane on the floor. "This is just for looks. What you needing? And where's my Little Bit?"

"She's out in the truck, eating jelly beans with Altha Combs," I said. "I just need a rod-and-turnbuckle, to square up a door."

He pointed with his cane. "Down there with the hinges."

When I came back to the counter, Peck was on his stool again, filling out an order sheet in his neat engineer's handwriting. He licked his pencil. "What you got going, Tinker Bell?"

"Oh, this is just for the side door of the barn." I handed him a five-dollar bill. "Sorry I don't have anything smaller."

"It's all money," Peck said. "And you know what I mean."

I had to smile, he was so predictable—but I didn't have anything to tell him today. "To tell the truth, I'm not tinkering on anything."

"Hmm." Peck counted out my change, then held it out of reach. "What're you *thinking* about tinkering on?"

I shrugged. "I'm not even thinking. Guess I ran out of ideas."

Peck's eyes bulged. "Tinker Bell run out of ideas?! Go on, pull the other leg."

"It's true."

"How about a better mousetrap?"

"Yours seem to do the job."

Peck stuck his pencil back behind his ear. "Those were rat traps you bought this summer. Weather's changing—mice'll be coming inside…" He nodded at the box of mousetraps on the counter.

"All right, you sold me." I picked out half a dozen.

Peck put some of my change back in his cash drawer and handed me the rest. "There's persimmons dropping out back, if you want some."

"You don't think it's too soon?" I said. "We've only had that one hard frost."

Peck shook his head. "Ate one this morning. Sweet as sorghum molasses."

"Hmm." Some trees did ripen early. On the other hand, one green persimmon could spoil a whole pudding. "Maybe I'll wait awhile."

"Suit yourself." Peck winked at me as he slid the mousetraps into a paper sack. "Wait too long, possum'll get them all."

"You got a point there." I took the sack, and picked up my rod-and-turnbuckle.

"Hang on," Peck said. "Peppermint for Little Bit…" As he handed it over, he gave me a mock frown. "Don't you give up on tinkering, Miz Bell. There's not a thing in this world so good it couldn't be a little better."

I smiled at him. "I'll keep that in mind."

98

May

Katy fell asleep on the way home, curled up between Altha and me with one sticky hand clutching my skirt. I half-listened to Altha's gossip from the hairdresser's. I'd been thinking, while we ran our errands. Altha knew everything that went on in Knobs County, and she'd been part of the family since they were all still in Kentucky. She'd know when Daddy's affair had been, if anybody did.

Altha sneezed, and dug through her pocketbook for a handkerchief. Before she could start talking again, I said, "Altha, do you—did you know about...about Mom, and Daddy and—" I couldn't quite say Mrs. Beamer's name.

Altha gave me a sharp look as she snapped her pocketbook shut. "What about them, Maydie?"

I shifted my grip on the steering wheel. "Well, Jamie...he didn't mean to say anything, but—"

"Jamie? Little Jamie knew about that?" Altha stared at me a second, then shook her head slowly. "Well I'll be. After all my promising, Candice..." For a second I thought she had me confused with Grandma Stout again. Then she chuckled softly. "Candice made me swear not to tell a soul. Said she'd haunt

411

me from her grave. And here's little Jamie, knowing all about it…I wonder who told him."

"Daddy did," I said.

Altha drew her head back in surprise. "Now why'd he want to go and do that?"

"He didn't want Jamie making the same mistake."

Altha was silent a minute. When I glanced at her, her mouth had turned sour at the corners. "I wouldn't have thought he'd put it that way," she said.

"Well," I said, "I was wondering—" Suddenly all my questions crowded into my throat at once. I swallowed hard, telling myself that Altha wouldn't know why Mom was always mad at me, or how long I'd be mad at Hal, or whether I might hit Katy again. "I mean, I—"

"You're wanting to know all about it, you mean," Altha said. She nodded. "Well, Candice can't fault me now, if the cat's already out of the bag."

I sighed in relief, and slowed the truck a little as we passed a dog on the roadside. If Altha was going to tell the story, all I had to do was listen.

"Pearl always was a pretty little thing," Altha said. "And Everett—well, I'd helped raise him, maybe I was partial, but he was a fine-looking young man. He was all set to marry Judge Richards's girl." She chuckled. "Candice was just about puffed up like a toad over that. But he was her youngest, too, and she kept having him put off the wedding. I told her Everett was liable to find him somebody else—I was down there that Christmas, visiting—but Candice said he was just a baby." Altha snorted. "He was all of sixteen. You could *smell* the lust on that boy!"

I kept my eyes on the road. It was strange enough hearing Mom and Daddy called by their given names, without remarks like that. And sixteen? Altha was starting at the beginning. I hoped we'd have time for it all before we got home.

Altha tapped one toe on the floorboard in a slow rhythm, as if she were in the kitchen rocker back home. "Well," she went on, "Pearl had hired out to the Flicks that year, down the road from Candice and Jack's. She was a good hard worker. Glad to be out of her own house, I imagine—Old Man Doss drank like a fish, and Pearl's mama had a tongue like a razor blade. Five kids scrabbling for whatever there was to eat. The Dosses never had anything."

I hadn't known Mom's daddy drank. I wasn't sure I wanted to know. But Altha liked to tell a story her own way—try to steer her, and she'd clam up.

"Well, one thing led to another," Altha went on. "Pretty soon, Pearl turns up pregnant."

My head swung around towards Altha, but she was staring out at a field of corn stubble. Mom, pregnant? Before they were married? And if Daddy was sixteen, then... That baby wasn't me.

Altha was shaking her head. "Oh, Maydie," she said, "You never heard such a ruckus! Old Man Doss showed up on Candice and Jack's porch Christmas Eve, said he was going to beat the tar out of Everett. Candice about had a conniption. Doss wasn't but five-foot-four, though, and he was drunk. Everett cold-cocked him, and then Everett and Jack had a shouting match. Jack called him a fool and a lot worse, but by the time Doss woke up, Everett was over at the Fitch place asking Pearl to marry him."

I frowned at the feed truck ahead of us, trying to picture my easygoing Daddy "cold-cocking" anybody—or even having a shouting match. I couldn't picture Grandma Stout in a conniption, either. Maybe Altha was thinking of the wrong family.

Altha had paused, waiting for me to say something. I sighed and pursed my lips, trying to come up with a remark that made sense. She nodded. "Yes, it was a mess. But they went to the J.P., and set up in a little shack on Tar Creek Road.

"Candice wouldn't have Pearl in her house, not even for supper. Said Pearl was a Jezebel trying to pull herself up in the world. I went to visit, though, and I didn't see anything like that. Pearl wasn't proud about the Stout name, or wanting fancy things. That girl wanted love. Her eyes never left Everett. And it wasn't a peck on the cheek she was after, either. I was a married woman—I could see what she was thinking about. And Everett was thinking it right back."

I blushed, and tried not to squirm.

Altha sighed. "I imagine Pearl would've loved Everett if he'd been a traveling tinker. Everett...well, he could've loved anybody. I'm sure Pearl wasn't his first. But he didn't love her any the less for it. And they were both just as happy..."

Altha paused, and sighed again. I turned onto 250, trying to imagine Mom happy. What had happened?

I glanced over at Altha. She was fiddling with the clasp on her pocketbook, and her toe had stopped tapping. Finally she went on. "The Spanish flu hit up here that spring. I almost lost Will. And then that summer, they had it bad down home. Candice and Jack didn't either one take it, but Pearl lost both her parents and two little brothers. She'd been nursing them and Everett, not hardly sleeping, and then she got sick herself. Took pneumonia and pretty near died, and she lost the baby. When Candice wrote to me—" Altha stopped. When she went on, her voice was hoarse. "She said now she wished they hadn't let Everett marry Pearl, because it would've turned out all right in the end. Pearl losing her baby—she called that 'turning out all right...'"

Altha stared hard out the windshield, her mouth a sad line. "My sister in Oklahoma had just died of the flu, when I got that letter. She was expecting, too. I didn't write back to Candy for a month." She sighed. "But it was a hard time. People said things they didn't mean."

I put a hand on Katy, to keep her from sliding off the seat as I turned onto 56. I'd never heard Altha get choked up telling a story before. Maybe it wasn't just her promise that had kept her quiet all these years. She took out her handkerchief again, and blew her nose.

"Pearl took it hard," she said, putting the handkerchief away. "Not that she shouldn't have. Not eating, crying, on and on... After a year, Everett was getting afraid she'd kill herself with grieving. He had me find them a place to buy up here, so she wouldn't have everything reminding her."

Altha reached over to straighten Katy's sunsuit. "Candice made me promise not to tell anybody up here. For Everett's sake, she said, but it was her own pride. Candice always was proud of the Stout name. Her people were Gettys—con men and gamblers, every one." Altha gave a little sniff, but she was smiling. "I told her, pride goeth before a fall. But when Jack died and she moved up here, she found the Stout name as good in Indiana as it was back home."

Altha gave a satisfied nod, and I knew that was the end of her tale. I couldn't imagine what I ought to say. I still didn't know when Daddy and Mrs. Beamer's affair had been. Somehow it didn't seem so important now. *Pearl took it hard... That girl wanted love... They were both just as happy...* "Well..." I started, uncertainly.

"Did I ever tell you about Harvey Getty, the one that sold the mill?" Altha asked. I shook my head, relieved. Altha's toe started tapping again. "You talk about a con man..."

99

Vera

Thurs., Nov. 17

Dear Mama,

    I made it safe. I'm at Sybil and Bob's now, and looking for a place to rent. I miss you. But I'm feeling fine, and I'll be O.K. It looks like I'll be able to get sewing work. I probably can't afford to come home at Xmas, but maybe after the baby comes.

                               Love you,
                               Vera

    I fold the pink stationery and slide it into an envelope. I wish I could put something else in with it—flowers, maybe, or a pie. Something to thank Mama for the past month.

    Mama met me at the bus stop in High Brooks. I was expecting her to tell me what a fool I'd been, but I guess she could tell I knew that already—she just hugged me, and took me home for supper.

I rented a room over Hazlitt's grocery, and worked at Myrtle Pate's dress shop weekday mornings. But my life was in Mama's parlor. I spent every afternoon sitting in the sunshine from those tall south windows, making maternity clothes with Mama. Mama ignored my crying, like Iva had—just asked me to hand her that pincushion, or helped me smooth out a skirt panel. She made me sing with her, "Shady Grove" and "Shall We Gather at the River" and "Keep on the Sunny Side." By the beginning of November, I could laugh again.

And by the middle of November, I was packing my things again.

Mama thinks I left because of the gossip. Somebody said it was unusual that I still had my maiden name, and somebody else wondered why no-one had heard anything about this "Mr. Stinson" I'd married until after he died in a car wreck, and so on. When Mama got wind of it, at her Women's Society meeting, she was livid—madder than she'd been when Pop left, or when the lawyers took our farm. But after a week of fuming, she sighed and told me, "Well, Vera, hens cackle and women gossip. You just hold your head up. It'll blow over." Maybe she was right—it wasn't much of a story. Not like the truth would've been. Meanwhile, I had food on the table, and a roof to keep the rain off it.

But that wasn't enough. I wanted more than food and a roof. Money, for one thing—enough to take care of myself and Mouse-baby, with some left over for a movie or new shoes. I'd never have made that much, working for Myrtle. Even without a baby, I had to eat half my meals at Mama and Mr. Townsend's. And, once I quit crying long enough to notice, I was lonely in High Brooks. Mama was good company, but most of the girls I'd known in school had gotten married and moved away, and the young wives in town were leery of me.

And there was Mama. Mama had a good life in High Brooks, going to church and baking pies for the Women's Society Bazaar. Mr. Townsend adored her, in a quiet way—he was always telling her not to wear herself out, as if she hadn't run a farm on her own for eleven years. But Mr. Townsend wasn't easy with me and my growing belly. He looked uncomfortable when Mama mentioned the baby. Mama ignored him. She quit speaking to her gossiping friends, too, and stayed home from the Women's Society. Mama would do anything for me—but I didn't want her to. She'd already done enough, raising me by herself. And now she'd pulled me up out of the dark well of losing Hal, set me on my feet again in the light of day. That was more than enough.

So I left High Brooks, for the second time. This time I cried, and Mama did too.

Sybil and Bob are happy to have me here, but Sybil wasn't kidding about the tight quarters. The trailer's bursting at the seams. Little Russell is into everything, and the twins make enough noise for quadruplets. It's almost as crowded outside, with neighbors a few feet away. A jazz band practices next door twice a week. Nobody takes any notice of me.

Sybil's not the glowing newlywed she was in Cartersboro. Her nails are bitten to the quick, and she mixes bourbon in her Coke in the afternoons. The kids and the mud and the leaky roof and the jazz band all seem about to get the best of her. She talks about the future—when the kids start school, when Bob gets his degree, when they can buy a real house, when we'll have quiet time to sit and chat. Bob's sweet to her, but he's always off at classes or the lab, or studying at the library where it's quiet. I don't think Sybil ever gets any quiet. I hope she and Bob still have good times in bed. She looks so tired and nervous, it's hard to imagine.

I want to tell Sybil she has everything I wanted—a loving husband, a family she doesn't have to lie about, neighbors who borrow coffee and hand down baby clothes. I don't. I help out with the kids and the housework, and drink Coke, plain, to keep her company. I can't make Woodlawn Courts any quieter, or make the future come any sooner. The smell of her bourbon reminds me of May and the flypaper.

I hope I find my own place soon.

100

May

I woke with a start, my heart going a mile a minute. I listened. Just the wind, rattling the dry stalks of the hollyhocks outside. Maybe there wouldn't be anything else. I'd been waking up like this every night lately, even when Hal—

And there was Hal's yell, upstairs. My heart jumped and pounded again. It was loud, even from down here. I didn't see how Katy could sleep through it, but she always did.

Hal said something, his voice thick and hoarse. He'd be curled up and cringing in the bed, or dodging invisible blows. Crying. I'd seen it enough times. I wiped my own tears on the pillowcase. Hal crying upstairs, me crying downstairs. This was the third rough night in a row. He hadn't been this bad since right after the war, before Katy was born.

After awhile it got quiet. Maybe he was awake. I always used to hold him, while he trembled and calmed down. Now my arms ached, gripping my pillow to my chest. I could go up there now. But then what? Me in my flannel nightgown, him in his pajamas, in bed together... How could I tell him I was only there to hold him? He was a man, not a baby.

Hal let out a high cry, like a scared child. I bit my knuckles, staring at the faint rectangle of the window. "Please," I heard myself whisper, and wondered who I was talking to.

Grace cut a peeled apple in quarters. "These are the best apples I've had in I-don't-know-when!"

"They're keeping good, too." I took a dozen more apples out of the basket by my feet and lined them up on the table, to save Grace bending over. Her belly was getting bigger every week.

"Yes—I don't know why I thought I needed to can pie filling. Don't know when to quit, I guess."

"Thanksgiving's next week," I said. "You should make a rule, no more canning after that."

Grace inspected a fresh apple, and cut out a bruise. "You-all doing all right?" she asked.

I nodded. "Pretty good."

"Hal looked kind of rough the other day."

I gave a little shrug. "He's not sleeping too well."

Grace raised her eyebrows at me. "Neither are you."

I shrugged again. I couldn't deny my dark circles. For a minute I watched the red apple peeling curling away from my knife. Then I said, "Does Jamie ever have...trouble sleeping?"

Grace snorted. "Sleeps like a rock, anymore. If rocks could snore."

Anymore. Did Jamie use to wake up screaming, after the war? I couldn't ask. Smiling, easy Jamie... What happened to them over there?

Grace stuck a slice of apple in her mouth. "You-all ought to get you some kind of sleeping pills."

"Maybe we should," I said. Did they have a pill for nightmares?

I heard a yell from outside, and leaned to look out the window. Katy and Carol and two overgrown puppies were playing tug-of-war with a piece of bindertwine. Katy tripped over the rope, and the brown pup ran to lick her face. She shrieked and giggled.

"Just two pups left now," Grace said. "James took one to Bucky Morris yesterday."

"The fellow that tells the weather?"

"Yes. He's saying sunshine for Thanksgiving." Grace looked out at the kids and pups, and chuckled. "Nobody wants that brown one, with the silly ear. Rye says Ol' Blue had an ear like that, but she grew out of it. Of course, you know Rye…"

"You going to keep him?"

"No, we're keeping the white one." Grace took another bite of apple. She was always eating, these days. "The brown one's smarter, though. You can still have it, if you want."

"Smart, huh?" The girls were crawling around after the pups now, with their tongues hanging out. "Jamie used to have a dog that was so dumb, it'd run into trees."

"Which one was that?" Grace asked.

"Whitey. He even died of being dumb—got his head stuck in a crockery jar, and took off running right over a bank. Broke his neck."

"For heaven's sake!" Grace said. "James never told me that. He wanted to keep this one because it looks like Whitey."

"You'd think after all the trees that dog ran into, his neck would've been—" I stopped, surprised at the hardness in my voice. Jamie had cried and cried over that dog, and I'd cried over Jamie's crying. I picked up an apple and took a bite.

"Well," Grace said, getting up to look in a cabinet, "That brown pup's no dummy. He learned not to bite on the kids' fingers, right away. And the way he looks at you and perks up his ears—well, the one's always perked, but… I hope I'm not out of cinnamon."

I took another bite of apple, tart and cidery. Outside, the brown pup was sprawled on the dry grass, with his ear wrong-side-out on top of his head. Katy stuck the end of the binder-twine in his mouth, but he just yawned and rolled over, legs flopping four different directions. My smile felt good on my face.

"I don't know," I said. "Maybe we could use a dog."

101

Hal

I drop James off, and back out of his driveway, cussing as my
sore foot works the clutch. It hurts more now than it did this
morning. I told James that Bess had stepped on it—I couldn't
very well say I damn near broke my foot kicking a bedpost.
Who knows what I thought I was kicking. When I try to remember my dreams, it's just a cold dark hole.

Two more clutch-stomps for second and third—damn. Just
what I need. Bad enough to be jumping out of my skin half
the day.

This afternoon I yelled at Bucky when he walked in front of
my forklift. He looked at me like a whipped dog. At quitting
time I took him aside and painted red dots on the inside edges
of his shoe soles, showed him how to match them up. No point
in him going around with his shoes on wrong, just because he
can't think straight. Bucky was so tickled, it cheered me up a
little too. On the way home, when James whistled at the sight
of Rhoda Sims, bent over in her garden picking collard greens,
I could see his point. This morning I wouldn't have cared if
Rhoda was dancing naked in the yard.

May still sleeps downstairs. I'm about crazy with wanting
her. It's like a radio in my head, and the longer it's been, the

louder it gets. Until a nightmare pulls the plug for awhile...
This morning, looking at May, I wasn't even thinking that way.
I just wanted her to hold me. Wrap her arms around me and
tell me I was all right. She poured me another cup of coffee,
put a stick of wood in the stove. She didn't ask why I was
limping. Maybe she heard me kicking the bedpost.

I wave at Altha on her porch, make the turn onto Chambers
Pike without slowing down. Altha'll tell everybody I'm a reck-
less driver, but I'm not using that clutch again until I have to.

I guess May's still mad at me. I don't know what she wants
me to do. Vera's gone—Ma told us she'd moved out, a month
ago. I didn't even ask where to. I hope May can see I'm bound
and determined not to do it again. That night when Jamie was
out looking for May...and then later, when I thought she'd left
me...talk about a cold dark hole.

102

May

Hal cocked his head, then looked up at the sky through the bare sassafrass branches. "You hear cranes?"

I listened. Sure enough, there was that sweet, high trill. Hal always loved to see the cranes—in the spring, he'd stop his tractor to watch them heading north.

"Horsie!" Katy demanded, kicking her heels at the branch she was perched on. She'd started calling the twisty sassafrass at the edge of the woodlot her "horsie tree." I gave the branch another bounce, and she giggled, clutching at the rusty bark.

Hal's arm went up, pointing at a long vee of birds straggling across the western sky. "Look at the cranes, Katy!" Katy stared up at the tree, until he plucked her off her branch and carried her into the open. He crouched beside her and pointed again. "See the birds? They're headed south for the winter."

I joined them, squinting at the sky. The pale, slender cranes were hard to see in all that blue, but once my eyes found them they were unmistakable. Three, four...six flocks, some so high up they were tiny specks.

Katy couldn't find them. She tried, tipping her head back until she fell over backwards—then she rolled around in the dry grass, grinning.

"Good idea," Hal said. "Easier on the neck." He lay down beside her, taking off his hat, and pointed at the biggest flock again. "See, right there—way up high…"

Katy put her feet in the air. "Up high!" she sang. Hal chuckled, and tickled her shoes with a grass stem.

I sat down in the grass, glad chigger season was over. It was nice to see Hal having fun. Lately he'd looked so tired. Beyond tired. Some evenings he fell asleep at the supper table. Maybe Grace was right, and we should talk to the doctor. But I hadn't mentioned Hal's nightmares all these weeks, and now I wasn't sure how to bring it up. At least he was taking it easy today, coming for a walk with us. The firewood was all in, so he could afford a Saturday's rest.

There was a scurry and swish in the tall grass, then a short bark. Katy sat up. "Toopy!" she called. Our new pup trotted out of the weeds, his tail waving like a flag. Katy had insisted his name was "Toopy," the day we brought him home from Grace's. A silly name, but it matched his silly ear.

"Come play, Toopy!" Katy scrambled to her feet and led the way back under the sassafrass.

Hal was looking up at the cranes again, smiling a little. I leaned back on my elbows. Two flocks were meeting just overhead. I watched them circle and mingle, their voices ringing like bells. They were right to be heading south—this warm spell wouldn't last. My eyes wandered to the sassafrass tree, tracing its snaky branches to the gnarled trunk. Another tree must have fallen on it when it was little, to make it grow that way. It was perfect for playing "horsie" now, but it must have had a tough time.

Daddy told me once that trees were bigger underground than up top. That was in one of the drought years, when the tulip tree in our yard was dropping its leaves early. I was afraid it would die, but Daddy told me not to fret. "It's just doing what it has to, to get through," he said, patting the tree's strong trunk. "It's got roots going way, way down in the ground. There's water down there that's never seen the light of day. You wait, Maydie—come spring, it'll be good as new."

He was right, at least about that tree—it still shaded Jamie and Grace's yard. A lot of other trees didn't make it through that drought. Maybe their roots didn't go down far enough.

Hal was asleep now, his mouth open to the sky. One hand lay on his chest, his sleeve pushed up past the soft, dark hair on his wrist. I shivered and put my hands in my jacket pockets, remembering the summer I was fifteen. I hadn't seen as much of Hal, in the year since we'd graduated from eighth grade. When he came to cut tobacco with Daddy that next summer, he was taller. His wrists stuck out of his shirtsleeves, covered with new dark curls—or had I just not noticed them before? While Mom and I served dinner to the crew, I kept sneaking glances at Hal, feeling a shiver that was exciting and scary both. Even more exciting and scary, half the time when I sneaked a glance, Hal was sneaking a glance at me.

Katy hollered something at Toopy, and Hal sat up, rubbing his face. He didn't look my way. I hadn't found his eyes on me in days, maybe a week. It had been a relief, at first.

I picked up a twig and fiddled with it, wanting to say something. *It's okay if you look at me, I don't mind.* Or maybe just, *We could play some cards tonight, if you can't sleep...* The words wouldn't come. I poked the twig at the dirt, imagining the sassafrass tree's roots spreading out under me, under Hal, looking for water deep in the ground. Hal yawned.

"Did you know there's more of a tree underground than up top?" I said.

"Huh." Hal looked up at the branches. "Hadn't thought about it. I guess there could be."

"Mommy! Come look!" Katy yelled. We both got up and went to see. Toopy was asleep next to the sassafrass trunk, and Katy was piling dry leaves on him. "Toopy haves a blanket," she explained.

"Looks warm," Hal said. He yawned again, and I heard his jaw pop. He was standing beside me, so close I could smell the Brylcreem in his hair, a whiff of cow manure and old gasoline on his jacket. It ought to have been such an easy distance to cross.

103

Hal

Home. I'm *home*, goddammit. On the floor, backed up against the cold bedroom wall. Smelling my own scared sweat. Just a dream, and I'm not there, I'm home.

Moonlight in the dresser mirror, quilt hanging off the bed. Smell of smoke and— *No*. I'm home, I'm safe. That's woodsmoke from your own chimney, dumbass. Get back in bed, before you freeze to death.

Standing up, every muscle I've got trying to dive for the floor. Breathing like I've run a mile. Under the covers, sitting bolt upright, trying to keep my eyes open. I'm so tired.

I wonder if I'm cracking up. I can't do that. May and Katy are counting on me. I don't know how I get through the days, at work. I don't yell at Bucky anymore—I'm dumber than he is.

Smoke and noise and—I'm *home*, dammit. I wad the quilt against my face, breathe the cotton smell. I always used to bury my nose in May's hair, and then I'd know I was home. Because May was my home. God, May, help me… My heart's hammering louder than the artillery—

No. Get up, do something. Run down the stairs, out into the cold. A shot behind me—I hit the ground and roll—

No, dammit, it was just the screen door. I'm *home.* Lying in May's flowerbed, face-down in the dirt. It smells like dirt. Like home dirt, not that blasted foreign dirt I shoveled and slept in and crawled through. That dirt never smelled like this. I rub my face on the frosted clods, dig my fingers down to the softness underneath. Dirt I've plowed and planted and hoed all my life, bitter and gritty in my teeth. I'm home.

What the— I roll over fast, something big's coming at me in the dark— But it's just the dog. Excited to see me. Wiggling all over, big paws stepping on me, warm tongue slobbering my face. I try to fend him off, but my arms are weak with relief.

I sit up. The dog sits down. Paws at me, whimpers in his throat. I rub his ears, and he flops down across my lap, heavy and warm. I spit out dirt, wipe my face on my pajama sleeve. The dog squirms, getting comfortable. Toopy, that's what Katy calls him. "Good boy," I whisper, and scratch his side. "Good Toopy." He still smells halfway like a puppy. They ought to bottle the smell of puppies, sell it to make people feel good. That, and the smell of a baby's head.

It's past midnight. Half moon overhead. Frost soaking through the butt of my pajamas, a dog in my lap. "Cracking up" doesn't hardly cover it. Better get up, before I get frostbite in a bad place. I give Toopy a last pat, shove him off my lap. My knees creak when I stand up. I feel tireder than I've ever been. At least I know where I am.

I don't want to go back to bed. Fall asleep, start it all over again. I think of May, asleep in the bed that ought to be ours together. God, I wish I could go climb in with her. Smell her hair, hold her close. I guess some fellows would go ahead—take the bed and take their wife too. Say it's their right. I'm not that kind.

Toopy yawns, with a whistly whine at the end of it. Before I think what I'm doing, I bend down and pick him up. He grunts, long legs sticking out every-which-way. "Shh," I tell him. Pull open the screen door with one finger.

I carry him through the kitchen and living room, tiptoe past May's door. May would kill me, bringing a dog in the house.

Up the stairs to my room. Toopy goes around sniffing every-thing, while I straighten up the bed. Then he sits by my feet, thumping his tail on the rug.

I get in bed, pat the quilt beside me. Toopy jumps up. Does his turning-around dog routine, flops down against my belly.

He's heavy. Warm, even through the quilt. I keep my arm outside the covers, wrap it around him. He heaves a big sigh and puts his head down.

I'm so tired. When I blink, it's hard to pry my eyes back open. I slide my head off the pillow, press my face against Toopy's scruffy, doggy back. Shut my eyes, and hang on.

104

Vera

"Okay, here we go." Harriet dropped marshmallows into three cups of hot chocolate, and handed them around. The kitchen smelled wonderful—Harriet's chocolate, Karen's fried onions, cinnamon from the apple pie I'd made. My stomach growled, and Mouse-baby gave me a kick.

Karen stood at the stove, her hair wrapped in a towel. She'd tied a pink polka-dot apron over her housecoat—what she called her Fourth Street Saturday Breakfast Club Ensemble. Saturday breakfasts were already a tradition when I moved in, and my new housemates had been happy to add my pies to the menu. Karen always made an omelet—ham-and-cheese today. "So, what's up in Church Search tomorrow?" she asked me.

I slurped at my hot chocolate. "Assembly of God, I think. The Methodists were a bust—good sermon, bad singing."

"Isn't that what you said about that other one?" Harriet asked, snuggling into the blue velveteen shawl she wore over her pajamas.

"The Baptists? They were the opposite."

Karen handed us each a plateful of omelet, and sat down with hers. "That's six you've tried, without a keeper. You think there's a pattern?"

"Oh, I've got a couple dozen still to go," I said, shaking the ketchup bottle. "And it's fun. You should've heard the Nazarenes' guest preacher, week before last."

"Was that the one with the blond toupee?" Harriet asked, taking the ketchup from me.

I nodded. "And pop eyes. He preached about Modesty."

Karen looked doubtful. "This was fun?"

"Well, it started off slow," I admitted. "Jewelry, makeup. But then he said—" I drew myself up and pointed at the two of them—"'I'll tell you something else. There are women—yea, even here in the body of Christ—women and girls who are burdened by a lust as foul and deceiving as any man's!'"

Harriet giggled as I bugged out my eyes. "Amen to that!"

"What did he want us to do about it?" Karen asked, through a mouthful of omelet. "Wear chastity belts?"

"No," I said. "He was worried about men wearing T-shirts by themselves."

Harriet gave me her best blue-eyed innocent look. "Nazarenes don't wear pants?"

I flipped my napkin at her. "Without a button shirt. 'That thin, stretchy fabric clings to every bulge and curve of your manly body, drawing women's eyes down the path of sin...'"

Karen made a choking sound, and swallowed hastily.

"By the end of it," I said, "He was strutting around and pointing—'Men! I can see your *physical!* I can *see your physical!*'" I only pretended to yell—Rita was on night shifts at the hospital, and her room was right next to the kitchen.

Harriet was laughing silently, her face turning red. Karen raised her eyebrows. "This is how our great nation spends its Sunday mornings?"

"I don't know," I said. "It was educational. I paid attention when we had that spell of warm weather—and it's true, you *can* see their physical!"

"Oh, no!" Harriet giggled, wiping her eyes. "The path of sin!"

"Don't worry." I patted my belly, round as a pumpkin with Mouse-baby. "I think I'm safe at present."

Harriet chuckled, but Karen gave me a thoughtful look. I felt my cheeks warm a little—maybe that story was a bit racy, for a pregnant "widow." But it felt good to laugh, and to make them laugh.

Lots of things feel good, these days. I was lucky to find this house, at Christmas—Bloomington mostly rents on the school calendar. It's been carved up for renters, with my bedroom in the old parlor and Rita's in the dining room, but there's a big front porch, and a living room where I do my fittings. With an ad in the newspaper and cards in a couple of store windows, I've got work lined up through February already, and I'm saving money for when Mouse-baby's born.

Meeting people is slow because I'm busy, but it's not hard. Nobody in Bloomington cares what my maiden name was. People talk about the weather, and football. The married women talk about babies, and the unmarried ones talk about men.

Saturday Breakfast Club with Karen and Harriet is the highlight of my week, and Karen and I go to the movies now and then—Anna Karenina last week. Karen's a third-grade teacher, but she wants to write movie scripts. She writes all the time, notebooks full. I asked her what about, and she said, "Oh, stuff. Marriage, elm trees, the freedom of the individual…" I think she might be a Socialist, but I like her.

I still miss Hal. And May. Mostly Hal. Not so much in a weepy way, now—I guess broken hearts heal, like everything else. More in a crazy way. That preacher was right, about women and lust.

I don't feel foul and deceiving, though. Or fat and ugly either, despite my belly. I feel beautiful—big and round and beautiful, like a Hubbard squash. I feel like a warm smile. I feel like knocking handsome men down in the street and having my way with them. There's a man who walks past my window, cutting through the alley, every afternoon at 4:15. I take my foot off the sewing-machine pedal and watch him go by. Dark brown hair that curls every which way, little almost-smile on his mouth. He walks with his head high—they all do, from the Service—but his eyes are far away, thinking about something. Maybe a girl. Maybe the freedom of the individual. I don't really care. I'm busy imagining how I could hide by the corner of the house, jump out and pull him into the bushes. Kiss that soft mouth, slide my hands under his jacket, pull his hips hard against mine... And then he walks on by, and I fan myself and go back to my sewing.

Anyway, his hips wouldn't get anywhere near mine—they'd bump into my belly first. Bump into Mouse-baby. When I get too worked-up to concentrate on my sewing, I think about Mouse-baby until I cool down. I'm a mother-to-be now, not a wife or a lover. Definitely not a...what would you call it, an ambush kisser? There's a radio show for you: Vera Stinson, Ambush Kisser!

Of course, in my condition, men don't give me a second glance. That's probably for the best. But sometimes I feel like a pressure-cooker with no steam vent. Where's it all going to go?

105

May

Hal still kept his pillow on his own side of the bed, like he was saving a place for me. I pulled the sheet and quilts up over it and tugged them square with the headboard. His bed was easier to make lately—he'd been sleeping better, not kicking the covers all over the place. That night when he'd run outside, and I'd been arguing with myself over whether to go after him, had been the last bad one. He still read until late, and I'd hear him go out to pee after my light was off, but then he'd be quiet until morning. I was almost afraid to notice, as if that would make it all start up again. But the couple of times he'd cried out, he'd settled down right away.

I dusted the dresser-top with a dirty t-shirt, and picked up Hal's pajamas from the floor. Hal had almost seemed like his old self this morning, half-smiling at me like he hoped I'd smile back. I'd tried, but I couldn't quite do it.

There was that smell again. I'd noticed it in here before. It was familiar, but I couldn't put a name to it—a little smoky, a little musty-soured. Maybe I'd missed some dirty socks? I looked under the bed. Nothing but dust. I ought to sweep.

The smell was stronger as I straightened up. I leaned to-wards the bed and sniffed, and something about the top quilt caught my eye. It was one of Grandma Stout's plain quilts, made out of old coats, but it looked...fuzzy? I frowned. Hair. Dark hair, longer than Hal's, clinging to the rough wool. I pinched some up and took it to the window. Curly, coarse, black and brown...Oh. I sniffed again, and this time I knew what I was smelling.

"Well, I'll be——" I said out loud, staring at the quilt. The dog. A dog, in the house, on the *bed*—I jerked back the covers, looking between the white sheets for the black jumping specks of fleas. I didn't see any.

I glared at the sheets a minute more, breathing hard. Then I yanked the hairy quilt off the bed, wadded it into a bundle with Hal's dirty clothes, and carried it out, shutting the door hard behind me. Dog or no dog, I had wash to do.

All the time I was hauling water and shoving clothes down in the washer, stirring the rinse tubs and pinning work pants to the line with half-frozen fingers, my head pounded with disbelief. A dog. In my house. A dirty dog, on my clean quilts. I'd told Katy just this morning, *No dogs in the house! Dogs stay outside.* I had to tell her that almost every day—she was sure Toopy must be cold in his doghouse. But Hal? What was he *thinking?*

When the rest of the wash was done, I stuffed the hairy quilt into the first rinse tub and churned at it with the laundry paddle. Hair floated on top of the cold, soapy water—a lot of hair. Toopy must have been sleeping on it for a while. I heaved the quilt over into the second rinse, gasping as cold water slopped the front of my dress, and stirred at it again. I thought of Hal's footsteps every night, coming downstairs and going out the back door, tiptoeing back up to his room. I'd thought he was just going to pee. He was sneaking out to get the dog.

There was no wringing the quilt. I heaved the soggy weight of it over a clothesline pole, and spread it out as best I could. I'd have to mend it in a couple of places, where Toopy's claws had pulled apart Grandma Stout's tight stitches. It'd never last, treated like that. I shook my head, and went in to change my dress.

My mind kept churning as I ate my toasted cheese sandwich. *Dogs stay outside...* My chest felt tight. *What's next, Hal —the pigs? Bess?* I thought of Altha's house, the piles of old papers and thick dust, all heavy with the greasy smell of dog. Mom, shaking her head—*Keeping those filthy animals in the house*— her mouth set in a hard line of disgust.

I stopped chewing. I could feel that same hard line in my own mouth. Mad and miserable... I rubbed at my lips as if I could scrub the expression away.

She doesn't sound very happy, Vera had said, frowning up at me with her measuring tape around my wrist. After she'd asked me if Mom ever sang. *She doesn't sound very happy.* And then, *That's too bad.* She'd said it like she meant it. Like she cared whether Mom was happy, even though they'd never met.

For a moment, I imagined telling Vera the story Altha had told me, about Mom—about Pearl. How Vera's face would pucker with sympathy as she listened. Tears ached behind my eyes. No, Mom wasn't happy. And not just since I started being mouthy, either, or after Daddy got with Mrs. Beamer. Mom hadn't been happy since she was fifteen years old.

The last bite of toasted cheese was still in my mouth. I washed it down with the rest of my ice tea, feeling tired. Best stick to problems I could solve. That wet quilt wouldn't be dry anytime soon—Hal would need another one.

There was just the Monkey Wrench single quilt left in the cedar chest. It was big enough to cover Hal's side of the bed. I smoothed it over his pillow, tracing a yellow triangle with one finger. Then my face crumpled like a wet hanky, and I sank to my knees by the bed and cried.

Even as I sobbed, I wondered what I was crying about. Toopy in the bed? Vera and Hal? Hal and me? It all felt mixed together, churning me around like a washing machine. Pearl and Everett's lost baby, and Mom's meanness. Vera, caring about someone she'd never met, and going to bed with Hal. Me hitting Katy. Hal's nightmares, and the two of us in sepa- rate beds, and me not knowing how to smile at him anymore... It felt like I was crying for all the misery in the world.

When I was done, I leaned my wet face against the bed for another minute. Then I got up and found a red hanky in Hal's drawer. I blew my nose, and wiped the quilt where I'd dripped on it. My face looked blotchy in the dresser mirror, and my scarf was crooked. But my mouth wasn't in a hard line anymore.

Compared to all the misery in the world, maybe a dog in Hal's bed wasn't that big a deal. And if Toopy helped his nightmares...

Picturing Toopy's brown, shaggy face looking up at me with his ear all sideways, I surprised myself with a laugh. I sighed, and stuffed Hal's hanky into my dress pocket. There was an old tablecloth around somewhere—stained, but good sturdy fabric. I could throw that over the bed, and Toopy could shed on it all he wanted. I didn't know what to do about fleas. Maybe Toopy didn't have any.

106

May

"How are you and Hal getting along?" Iva asked, laying out a pair of Rye's pants on her ironing board.

"Oh, we're doing better," I said. I took a bite of persimmon pudding and let the dark sweetness dissolve on my tongue. Katy and Rye were in the living room, barking like dogs and laughing.

Iva shoved her iron along an inseam. "You sleeping together?"

What? I stared at her. She turned the pants and sprinkled water over them, then looked at me expectantly.

I pointed at her iron, flat on the ironing board. "You're going to scorch that."

"Oh, mercy—" Iva jerked the iron up.

"Grace says apple cider vinegar'll take out a scorch mark," I offered.

Iva rubbed at the ironing-board cover with her fingers. "It's not scorched. I'll save my vinegar for pickles."

"She rinses her hair with it, too, and I don't know what-all," I said. "She's got a pamphlet about it."

Iva snorted, and nosed the iron around the pants zipper. After a minute, she said, "You didn't answer my question."

"No, I guess I didn't." I took another bite of persimmon pudding. Iva raised her eyebrow at me, then stood the iron on its heel and folded the pants.

I drank my coffee for a while. Iva's iron hissed, and the stove crackled. Rye and Katy were singing "Old MacDonald" now. I remembered waking up this morning, stretching my arms out across the bed. Sleeping alone, waking up alone…it was familiar and strange both. Hal had started looking at me again lately. I didn't mind—except I knew he was hoping, too, and I didn't know what to do about that.

It wasn't as if I wanted to leave. Being back home felt right. Everything I loved was there—the smell of Katy's hair, bare trees against the white winter sky, the whisper of my broom on the painted floor.

And Hal. Did I love Hal? I wondered what shape love was, how I'd know it if I saw it. *Love bears all things, believes all things…*

"Talk *too* much, you might get a sore throat," Iva said, with a wink.

I smiled a little. She wasn't mad. "Oh, I'm just thinking."

"Want to tell me about it?"

I poked at my persimmon pudding with my fork. "Well, you know how it says, 'Love is patient and kind,' and bears all things, and believes all things?"

Iva cocked her head. "I thought that was Charity."

I blinked at her, still trying to follow my own thought. "Oh —I guess there's a new translation now. Vera had one." It was the first time I'd said Vera's name since she'd left. I didn't stumble on it.

Iva nodded. "All right. What about it?"

I watched her work the iron around the buttons of a blue work shirt. "Well…" I finally said, feeling for the words, "I was thinking, it doesn't say *you're* patient and kind."

Iva's eyes twinkled. "I do my best."

I waved my fork at her. "I mean, it doesn't say a *person* is. It says *love* is."

"Never thought of it that way." Iva put the shirt on a hanger, then added, "Isn't it six of one, half-dozen of the other?"

"I don't know," I said. "What if love keeps on being patient and kind, and all that, when you...can't? Maybe love's still there, even if..." I stopped. Maybe I was telling Iva more than I meant to.

She pursed her lips at me. "You missed your calling, May. Should've been a preacher."

I snorted. I'd gotten my fill of that, marrying Hal and Vera.

"There are women preachers." Iva ran the iron sideways down a skirt. "That McPherson woman, for one." Then she made a face. "That didn't turn out so good, though."

"Hm. I don't think preaching's for me."

"Well, no," Iva agreed. I wondered how much she knew, about Mom and me. We'd never talked about it.

After a minute, she said, "I guess I'd've said love's more what you do, than how you feel. ...But then, there've been times I couldn't even manage to do. Felt like a creek run dry." She frowned at her iron. "So you're saying there was still a spring running, down underground?"

I thought of Daddy's tree roots, reaching way down to the water. Goosebumps prickled on my arms. "Something like that," I said.

Iva nodded. "I imagine you're right."

I finished my persimmon pudding, washing the sweet stickiness down with a last swallow of black coffee. "I guess I ought to be heading home."

Iva smiled at me. "Come back soon."

I nodded. "I'll do that."

107

Vera

The outside world's bright and quiet with snow, but it's warm here under the blankets. Mouse-baby's doing her morning jumping jacks in my belly. It's so good to wake up rested.

A week ago I felt like I'd never sleep sound again, between Mouse-baby's restlessness and my own. My wanting kept getting worse. Every night I'd lie awake and drive myself crazy, thinking of Hal. Wishing, wanting. I couldn't stop.

And then one night, when I was remembering Hal's hands —warm on my skin, sliding down my hips, reaching fingers under me and into me—I thought: *I have hands.*

It turned out that my hands were as good as Hal's. Better, maybe. And no wonder Hal loved to touch me down there. I never knew I was so warm and wet and open. My hands couldn't get enough. I thought of Hal. Then I didn't think of Hal, just let the wonderful wash over me. That wide-open-endless feeling—as big as loneliness, but warm... Afterwards I cried, maybe out of loneliness, maybe not. Then I fell asleep, and slept hard till morning.

I suppose some would say it's a sin. But just about everything's a sin according to somebody. And it keeps me from getting worked up over handsome strangers. It helps me sleep.

It's not the same, of course. I miss arms around me, eyes to look into. I miss laughing and flirting, being looked at and loved. But I think I'm going to be all right, now. Not just all right enough to pay my bills and get dressed in the morning, but really all right. Mouse-baby and I, we'll be all right together—our own tiny family.

But not us against the world, like Hal was telling it. We'll have Sybil and Bob and their kids, and Karen and Harriet and Rita. I'll find us a church, I hope, with good singing and a good preacher and kind people. Mouse-baby will have her Grandma and Grandpa Townsend, in High Brooks. One of these days I'll tell Tom where I am, and then she'll have cousins.

And Mouse-baby doesn't know it, but she has her daddy, too, with his curly hair and his strong arms. She has May, and Katy. Even Grace's bunch, and Iva and Rye—they're all part of Mouse-baby's family, even if she never meets them. Because they're part of mine. They're part of me.

108

May

Dear Sissy,

How did this week go? I hope you got your math sorted out. I hated long division too, but I beat it in the end.

We're having Sunday dinner here this afternoon. Grace's feet have been swelling, so I made her let me host. I put dried pears in my apple pies—I hope they're good!

Hal got on the sawmill crew at the yard last week. Jamie put in a word for him. It pays better than yard man.

Grandma Stout's cousin, Altha Combs, died this past Monday—slipped on the ice and hit her head. She'd had a hard winter, with her arthritis and then a bad cough. I'll miss her when I put up peaches this summer.

I stopped writing and smiled crookedly at the envelope I'd propped on the kitchen windowsill. "FOR MAYDIE DIXON WHEN I'M GONE," it said, in a pencilled scrawl. It had come in the mail yesterday. Inside was a stained recipe card, with Altha's tiny, graceful script from before the arthritis: *Grandma Combs' Peach Custard Pie.*

A pop and crackle from the woodstove brought me back to the present. I'd better finish up my letter—I'd promised Katy I'd mend her favorite bib overalls before dinner.

> *Have you had any snow? We've just had a dusting since Christmas, but it's plenty cold.*

I wrote a page about Katy playing in the snow with Toopy, and some about Jamie's family. Then I put down my pen, and picked up Sissy's last letter again. School, weather, piano lessons… And the part I didn't know how to answer.

I was talking to Mort Ackerman after church on Sunday, Sissy had written, in her careful seventh-grade script.

> *It wasn't anything. We were just laughing, but Mom jerked me away so hard she like to broke my arm. When we got home she laid into me something awful. Mom's after me all the time lately, at least since Christmas. I've prayed and prayed about it. I know I ought to mind her, but she won't tell me what I did, she just says I'm wicked. What should I do?*

My sigh rattled the blue-lined notebook paper. Sissy never asked for advice in her letters. I didn't know what to tell her. Especially since Mom might read whatever I wrote.

I got up to check on the ham and the vegetables, and looked out the window. Toopy was sitting by the barn door, waiting for Hal and Katy. He didn't seem to mind the cold—he just kept getting shaggier. There'd be a lot of shedding, come spring.

It had been two weeks now since I'd put that old tablecloth on Hal's bed. Neither of us had mentioned it. There hadn't been any more bad nights.

Toopy lay down with his head on his paws. I made myself go back to the table. *What should I do?* I rubbed my face. I didn't know what Sissy should do. What should *I* have done?

I picked up my pen.

* * *

*Ask Mom when would be a good time to come visit. I'll drive
down for lunch. I miss you, and it's time you met Katy.*

I read the words over, wondering if I was going to regret
them. It was Sissy I wanted to visit, but there was no getting
around the fact that Sissy lived with Mom. Still, it wouldn't kill
me. I signed the letter, and stuffed it into an envelope before I
could change my mind.

I took my mending into the living room—the kitchen was
getting warm, with the woodstove and the oven both going. I
was pinning a patch to Katy's blue-checked overalls when I
heard the back door open and shut. Katy ran in and tried to
scramble onto my lap.

"Watch out, hon!" I held the pincushion out of reach.
"Mommy's sewing. You can't get in my lap right now."

"Toopy bibs!" Katy shouted happily, grabbing at the red
embroidered puppy on the front of the overalls.

"That's right. I'm fixing them so you can wear them. You
want to play with your horse?"

Katy hugged my knees for a minute, then let go and
grabbed her wooden horse from the coffee table. When Hal
came in with a cup of leftover coffee, she waved the horse at
him. "Daddy, pet Toopy!"

Hal patted the horse on the head as he sat down on the
couch. "Toopy's one long-legged dog."

I stitched along the edge of my patch while the two of them
chatted. These bib overalls were hand-me-downs from Ronny
and Carol—they were wearing thin, but Katy loved them. Sissy
had been like that about the pink apron I'd made for her, back
when I first learned to sew. *I've prayed and prayed about it...What
should I do?* I sighed.

"Something up?" Hal asked.

I shook my head. "Just thinking."

"Come play, Toopy!" Katy ran to her baby buggy and
stuffed the horse inside, then pushed it full tilt toward the

kitchen. I tied a knot and cut another piece of blue thread, from a spool Vera had left on the bedroom windowsill. It didn't quite match the overalls, or the patch, but it was close enough.

Katy ran back in, turned the buggy around by the stairs, and tore off again. Hal set his coffee cup on the end table and cleared his throat. "May?"

"Hmm?" I squinted, threading my needle.

"Reckon you'll ever forgive me for being such a fool?"

I kept my eyes on the needle, but I could feel a flush in my cheeks. I didn't need any more hard questions. But I couldn't help feeling around in my head, wondering how mad I still was. It made me a little nervous, like playing hide-and-seek in an empty house. My mad had never been hard to find, before. Was it gone?

I took half a dozen stitches. Then I said, "I think maybe I already forgave you."

"Oh." Hal sounded surprised.

I sewed along the third edge of the patch, thinking what a fool I'd look if all the mad came back tomorrow. Katy started making train noises in the kitchen.

"Do you..." Hal said. "Do you think we'll ever make it like it was?"

My thread twisted itself into a loop—I'd have a knot if I wasn't careful. I straightened it out with my needle and pulled it through. Hal shifted on the couch, and I shrugged a little. "Nothing's ever like it was, Hal." I wasn't even sure I could remember how it was.

Katy and the buggy clattered into the room again. She yelled, "Look, Mommy! Toopy is a horse!" and raced back to the kitchen without waiting for an answer.

Hal rubbed his hands on his knees. "Well," he said, "Do you think we can make it like...something?"

I glanced up, but he wasn't teasing me. He was looking at me hard, like he wanted to see into my head. I took another stitch, holding the thread so it wouldn't twist. "I imagine we'll manage."

I saw Hal nod, out of the corner of my eye. His hands rested on the dark fabric of his work pants. I didn't know what else to say.

I finished sewing the patch, while Katy made another round and Hal shifted his feet on the rug. I could feel the space between Hal and me like something solid—curving along the side of my face, following the folds in Hal's rumpled sleeve. I tucked my needle into the spool of thread, and tapped the spool twice on the arm of my chair. Then I looked at Hal, my heartbeat suddenly loud. "I'll tell you one thing, though," I said. "You're not bringing any dog in *my* bed."

Hal sat perfectly still, his eyes on mine. Outside, a car door squealed open. Hal's mouth trembled a little, then pulled itself up into a shy grin.

More car doors slammed. I stood up, folding the bib overalls. "Sounds like they're here," I said. My voice was a little shaky.

"Sounds like it," Hal agreed, still smiling.

I swallowed hard, and ducked away into the kitchen.

109

May

"See?" Carol put two beans on Katy's highchair tray. "One, two!"

"Two," Katy agreed. "Toopy!"

"No, not—" Carol started.

"Pay attention to your own food, Carol," Grace said, then turned to me. "Speaking of Toopy, how's he working out?"

"Well, his ear's not as sideways as it was." I passed the salt to Iva. "And he seems smart enough."

Hal glanced sidelong at Rye and said, "Might be better than Ol' Blue, by the time he's grown."

"Now, don't get carried away." Rye put down his fork. "Did you know Ol' Blue could count to five? One time when the cows had got out..."

As Rye went on, Hal caught my eye and winked. I looked away, blushing. I wished he'd settle down some. People would notice, the way he kept grinning like a fool. I tried to act normal, but my stomach was fluttering like I was a teenager.

Ronny and Carol were wide-eyed at Rye's tale. "I'm going to teach Princess to count!" Carol declared.

"I already taught her to roll over," Ronny said.

Jamie speared a deviled egg with his fork. "Between the two of you, I bet you can get her to roll over five times."

"This potato salad's good, May!" Iva said, dishing herself a little more. "Tastes like summer."

I smiled at her. I'd done Vera's trick with the relish.

Grace fanned herself with one hand. "It's about as *hot* as summer in here."

"Why don't you open the door a minute," I told Hal. "That hickory burns hot."

The rush of icy air felt good. Hal fanned the door back and forth, then shut it and sat down again. "Bucky says February's coming in cold."

Grace shook her head. "I hope we don't get any more ice. It scares me to death. Look at Altha—" she shuddered. "One slip, and you're gone."

"Oh, I don't know," Jamie said. "Seems like that'd be the way to go—all at once." He kept talking as he chewed a bite of meatloaf. "If I ever get where I can't tie my own shoes and feed my own hogs, you-all just knock me in the head and throw me in the holler."

"That's not funny, James!" Grace glanced at the kids—but Carol was making faces at Katy, and Ronny was chasing his peas with his fork.

"Sorry," Jamie said lightly. But he glanced at me as he helped Ronny corral the peas, and I could see he hadn't been kidding. Those last, long weeks of Daddy's, Jamie had come over almost every day. One afternoon I'd walked into the kitchen to find Mom wrapped in Jamie's arms, crying with loud, harsh sobs. I'd never seen Mom cry like that. I backed away fast, before they saw me, and tried to forget about it—it seemed like just one more way Mom favored Jamie. But now, remembering Mom's thin shoulders shaking, I heard Vera's voice: *That's too bad...*

I pushed back my chair. "Does anybody need more ice tea?"

I went around the table, filling glasses. When Hal looked up at me, the flutter in my stomach got worse—or maybe better.

"Thanks, hon," he said as I handed his glass back. I laid my hand on his shoulder for a moment. It was the first time in months I'd touched him on purpose. My fingers could feel every thread in the blue cotton of his shirt, and the warm curve of the muscle underneath.

Rye sat back with a sigh. "My, that was good." He glanced at Iva. "Time for dessert?"

"May's in charge," Iva said, handing me her glass. "Ask her."

"As soon as everybody's done, we've got apple pie," I told Rye. "Well, sort-of apple pie. It's got dried pears in it too."

Grace gave me a skeptical look as I sat back down. "You're tinkering with *pie* now?"

I shrugged, and scraped up the last of Katy's food with my fork. "Just trying something new. It might not be any good."

"Pie!" Katy said, catching up with the conversation. She dodged the forkful of potato salad I was trying to feed her. "Apple pie, pumpkin pie, cherry pie!"

"That's the spirit!" Hal said. Then he frowned playfully at me. "What do you mean, it might not be good? It's pie, isn't it?"

I pursed my lips and rubbed at my chin, then nodded slowly. "Yes," I said, "I guess you'd have to say it's pie."

Hal grinned. I looked down at my plate. Under the table, I put a hand on my nervous stomach and patted it, like settling a restless baby.

Then I looked up at Hal, and smiled back.

Gratitude

To Sean Breeden-Ost: Falling in love with you first inspired me to write dialogue. Thank you for sharing family, farming, and the garden; for your deep respect for my creative life; for showing me what it means to belong to a place; and for your extraordinary love.

To Glen Breeden-Ost, who provided the joyful and exhausting details of early parenting: Thank you for making me a mother, and for showing me how large love can be.

Thanks to Mom and Dad for almost half a century (so far) of enthusiastic fandom. And to Dietrich Breeden, for the loyalty, the strength, and the playfulness of brother love.

Some of the sweetest sounds in my memory are Baker voices talking in the kitchen before breakfast, and Breeden voices singing in harmony. Many thanks to my extended families, for love that makes room and makes do.

Jack, Nina, Eric, and Karl Ost supported this project in many ways, from financial generosity, to tech empowerment, to house and home. (And thanks especially for Sean.)

Deepest gratitude to Mary Ann Macklin—first reader, gifted coach, and novel-writing Buddhy. This is the book I wrote; your steadfast company made it possible.

Thank you to Shana Ritter, Sue Swartz, Kayte Young, and Rebekah Spivey for conversation, feedback, and well-timed reminders that I'm not the only one; to Marti Crouch for the Marti's House Writing Residency, Altha's peach pie recipe, and Practical Dress Design; and to Stacey Decker for applesauce—complete with laughter, cow-bees, and kids.

At Women Writing for (a) Change Bloomington, dozens of writers listened this story into being and helped me learn what I needed to know, while Beth Lodge-Rigal held the space with grace. Carol Marks's "Alice Chalmers" poem incited the story. Molly Mendota said "That sounds like a novel." Jim Thom provided encouragement, both early and late. Licia Weber made the cover beautiful. Thank you all.

Thanks to Beta readers Beth Lodge-Rigal, Bill Breeden, Glenda Breeden, Alessandra Ogren, Jim Thom, Shana Ritter, Sean Breeden-Ost, Molly Mendota, Tony Baker, Kayte Young, Bev Hartford, Rebekah Spivey, and Licia Weber. This book is much better for your feedback.

I am grateful to Darrell Breeden, Gabe Langdon, Harriet Pfister, Jeff Padgett, Guy Loftman, and anonymous or already-mentioned others, for generous answers to odd questions. Research gratitude to the fine librarians of the Monroe County (Indiana) Public Library; to IU's Herman B. Wells Library and Office of University Archives and Records Management; and to the good people of the internet commons, who shared their knowledge of bike sabotage, feedsack dresses, crate manufacture, and other riveting details.

To Ursula K. Le Guin, Alice Walker, Zora Neale Hurston, Wendell Berry, and all the other storytellers: thank you for lighting my way.

The Earth has supported the writing of this book—literally, and in all other ways. Daily gratitude for life, seasons, plants, and creatures; for sustenance, beauty, and home; and for all of these wonderful people.

About the Author

Judging from her baby pictures, Denise Breeden-Ost has been listening intently all her life. She has also edited and proofread books, built her own house from scratch, raised a child, co-run a market farm, and facilitated writing circles for women and children. When she isn't writing, she can often be found making cornbread. Denise lives on a ridgetop in south-central Indiana, with a small family, a large garden, and innumerable trees.

Made in the USA
Monee, IL
10 November 2021